The Maestro,
the Magistrate &
the Mathematician

MODERN
African Writing
from Ohio University Press
Ghirmai Negash, General Editor
Laura Murphy, Series Editor

This series brings the best African writing to an international audience. These groundbreaking novels, memoirs, and other literary works showcase the most talented writers of the African continent. The series also features works of significant historical and literary value translated into English for the first time. Moderately priced, the books chosen for the series are well crafted, original, and ideally suited for African studies classes, world literature classes, or any reader looking for compelling voices of diverse African perspectives.

Books in the series are published with support from the Ohio University National Resource Center for African Studies.

Welcome to Our Hillbrow
  A Novel of Postapartheid South Africa
Phaswane Mpe
ISBN: 978-0-8214-1962-5

Dog Eat Dog: A Novel
Niq Mhlongo
ISBN: 978-0-8214-1994-6

After Tears: A Novel
Niq Mhlongo
ISBN: 978-0-8214-1984-7

From Sleep Unbound
Andrée Chedid
ISBN: 978-0-8040-0837-2

On Black Sisters Street: A Novel
Chika Unigwe
ISBN: 978-0-8214-1992-2

Paper Sons and Daughters
  Growing Up Chinese in South Africa
Ufrieda Ho
ISBN: 978-0-8214-2020-1

The Conscript
  A Novel of Libya's Anticolonial War
Gebreyesus Hailu
ISBN: 978-0-8214-2023-2

Thirteen Cents: A Novel
K. Sello Duiker
ISBN: 978-0-8214-2036-2

Sacred River: A Novel
Syl Cheney-Coker
ISBN: 978-0-8214-2056-0 (hardcover)
    978-0-8214-2137-6 (paperback

491 Days: Prisoner Number 1323/69
Winnie Madikizela-Mandela
ISBN: 978-0-8214-2102-4 (hardcover)
    978-0-8214-2101-7 (paperback)

The Hairdresser of Harare
Tendai Huchu
ISBN: 978-0-8214-2162-8 (hardcover)
    978-0-8214-2163-5 (paperback)

Mrs. Shaw: A Novel
Mukoma Wa Ngugi
ISBN: 978-0-8214-2143-7

The Maestro, the Magistrate &
  the Mathematician
Tendai Huchu
ISBN: 978-0-8214-2205-2 (hardcover)
    978-0-8214-2206-9 (paperback)

TENDAI HUCHU

The Maestro,
the Magistrate &
the Mathematician

A NOVEL

OHIO UNIVERSITY PRESS   ATHENS

Ohio University Press, Athens, Ohio 45701
ohioswallow.com

© Tendai Huchu, 2014

Printed in the United States of America
Ohio University Press books are printed on acid-free paper ⊚ ™

First published in 2014 by 'amaBooks
P.O. Box AC1066, Ascot, Bulawayo

Cover design by Sebastian Biot

Acknowledgement is made to Carcanet Press Ltd for the use of the extract
from Hugh MacDiarmid's 'Scotland', from *Complete Poems,* edited by
Michael Grieve and W.R. Aitken (1993-4).

26 25 24 23 22 21 20 19 18 17 16   5 4 3 2 1

ISBNS:
978-0-8214-2205-2 (hardcover)
978-0-8214-2206-9 (paperback)

TENDAI HUCHU is the author of *The Hairdresser of Harare*. His short fiction and nonfiction have appeared in *The Manchester Review, Ellery Queen's Mystery Magazine, Gutter, AfroSF, Wasafiri, The Africa Report, Kwani?* and numerous other publications. In 2013 he received a Hawthornden Fellowship and a Sacatar Fellowship. He was shortlisted for the 2014 Caine Prize for African Writing.

So I have gathered unto myself
All the loose ends of Scotland,
And by naming them and accepting them,
Loving them and identifying myself with them,
Attempt to express the whole.

from 'Scotland', by Hugh MacDiarmid

EDINBURGH

There was a knock on the door of the last house on Craigmillar Castle Road. The tat came before the rat, though the a-tat remained in pretty much the same place, producing a distorted, yet familiar sound, but then Alfonso Pfukuto, the knocker, was an ambiguous man. Nothing was quite what it seemed.

Alfonso waited a moment, whistling *Fishers of Men*, his favourite ditty, and then pressed his ear against the door before bending down and pushing the flap on the letter box open and shouting, "I know you're in there. It's me." He fidgeted, sighed, paced, knocked again and waited. Once, he'd been a welcome visitor. If they didn't want to see him now, let them tell him to his face. He was a shameless man.

The sky overhead was a brilliant blue. The weather held the muddle of spring: one day, dark clouds and summer warmth, the next bright and bitterly cold. His fingers turned white. He hopped about to keep warm, blowing on his hands.

Finally, picking up his white plastic bag, he walked round the back to the kitchen, stepping over a rake that lay buried in the overgrown grass. The Magistrate was at the sink, washing dishes. Alfonso knocked on the window, startling the older man who pointed to the back door.

"I thought no one was going to let me in," he said, trying not to sound resentful. He leapt in quickly. "It's freezing out there and I have come up with a new theory. You know why these people colonised us, right? It's the cold, it drives a man mad, so, when they came to Africa and saw us lounging in the sun, it drove them absolutely berserk."

"As always, your theories continue to astonish." The Magistrate let out a sigh.

"Big game today, Magistrate. I told you those two would be in the Cup Final."

"I don't recall you saying so."

1

"I'm sure I did. Remember, last time I was here. I really did, honest."

The Magistrate turned back to his dishes. Alfonso looked at him, desperate to make conversation. Fussing about, he switched the kettle on, fiddled with the toaster and then walked over to the sink. A short man, he stood just shy of the Magistrate's shoulder.

"Is there something you want to tell me?" the Magistrate asked, feeling his space invaded.

"Who me? Oh, no. What would a man like me have to tell a man like you?" Alfonso spoke in rapid bursts. "I was just thinking how nice it is for us to hang out like this. I feel right at home." He looked up at the Magistrate like a small child.

The Magistrate grunted and looked down at Alfonso's expectant face, and what a face it was, like a meerkat, complete with whiskers.

Alfonso reached into his plastic bag and brought out a bottle of own brand whisky.

"Only the best for you, Magistrate." He handed the bottle over. "Some of us can't handle this strong stuff. Too rich, too distilled. Back home we used to drink Seven Days, home brew chaiyo."

Deserting the drying up, the Magistrate poured himself a double on the rocks while Alfonso opened a can of Stella. "To the motherland." He raised his glass and, in that gesture, the Magistrate instantly recalled his days at college, the burning rhetoric, fiery speeches, pan-African sentimentality. Then, everything was possible. What had happened to those young men, his peers? The grand ideas debated on campuses and in bars had vanished. Nothing remained but shadows, distant memories echoing in the dark crevices of the mind, conjured up now and again by a simple toast or some grand gesture. The age of possibility was over.

"Was it something I said?" Alfonso asked, looking at his sad face.

"No, nothing, nothing at all. Shall we go in the living room?"

Chenai was lying on the sofa, absorbed by gyrating, near naked babes performing around a hunk lounging on a deckchair. They wiggled their bottoms and flashed their big breasts at the man who sang so fast the Magistrate couldn't understand the content of his lyrics, save for the word 'bitches', which he repeated at intervals with great vehemence.

"So, this is what the kids are listening to these days." Alfonso reached into his coat pocket.

"I'm not a kid anymore. I'm fifteen." Chenai rolled her eyes.

Music forms memories. The Magistrate, who was often transported back to some point in the past when he heard a familiar tune, shuddered to think that Chenai's memories would be formed by this soulless, commercial music. Alfonso picked up the remote and changed the channel.

"Hey, I was watching that," Chenai said, sitting up.

Alfonso tossed a Kit Kat to her. "It's time for football."

"But I'm watching my music, pal."

"Show some courtesy, he is our guest. And, don't call him 'pal', call him Babamudiki Alfonso. Okay?" The Magistrate felt his daughter had been here too long. Already her speech had a slight Scottish inflexion, those rolling Rs, the coarse tongue, guttural Gs.

"Uncle Alfonso," Chenai compromised. Babamudiki – uncle. Equivalent? Baba – Father. Baba-mudiki – Little-father. Baba-mukuru – Older-father. That was on the paternal side. The uncles on the maternal side all held the title Sekuru, equivalent to grandfather, indicating an elevated status. So many fine intricacies woven in these blood ties that the young did not care to learn. In Shona culture, relationships were everything. The Magistrate held a register of relations, far and near, in his mind. He stayed abreast of births and deaths in the family, each one representing a slight shifting of his position within it.

Chenai bit a chunk off her chocolate bar. She picked up *Harare North*, which lay on the glass- topped coffee table and opened the first page. The prematch commentary had begun. Andy Gray and Richard Keys were debating the relative merits of the Liverpool and Chelsea formations.

"Chelsea have a problem on the left," said Alfonso.

"I know. I can hear them too." Alfonso annoyed the Magistrate when he regurgitated the commentary or lines from the *Sun* as if they were his original thoughts.

"Who are you supporting today?"

"Liverpool, the same team I support every week. I've been with them since Bruce Grobbelaar, the days of Rush and Barnes. I could never switch."

"You see, that's where you and I differ. I support the winning team. Last year I was with Arsenal all the way. Before that it was Man U. This way I'm never disappointed. I don't understand this business of heartbreak and anguish over a couple of men kicking a ball."

"Then why do you come here every week?" The Magistrate felt his blood pressure rising.

"Because you have Sky. I'm building a mansion back home, in Kuwadzana. Did I tell you that? Of course I did. Window level, that's where I am now. These things take money. I can't afford the sports channels like you. I don't even pay my TV licence."

The Magistrate shook his head at the honest skinflint who so openly admitted leeching on him.

"Dad, if this guy cannae be bovvered to learn proper English, why did he write a novel?" Chenai slapped *Harare North* back on the table. The Magistrate didn't have an answer. He'd seen the book in Waterstone's in Cameron Toll, whilst perusing legal texts, and had bought it on a whim. He couldn't get into it either. It appeared to have been written to deliberately turn the English language inside out. He wondered how the book had ever got published. He wasn't one for fiction anyway. A serious man concerned himself with facts, newspapers, journals, textbooks and the occasional biography, especially if the subject was an influential figure in law or politics.

A sharp whistle sounded from the kitchen as the kettle boiled.

"Would you like a cup of tea?" the Magistrate asked Alfonso.

"Oh no, I'm drinking my beer." Why, then, did you switch the kettle on, the Magistrate felt like asking, irritated. The referee's whistle blew and the crowd roared. Alfonso kept pointing out the obvious, yelling, "Did you see that?" like an excited teenager whenever there was a near miss, and always queried offside decisions, even against slow-motion camera replays with computer generated lines showing the positioning of the defence against the straying attacker.

How could a man be so capable of challenging incontrovertible evidence put right in front of his eyes, the Magistrate wondered. The referees could be forgiven, they made decisions in real time against a fast-flowing game, but Alfonso refuted the replays from multiple angles. Worse still, from time to time he would look at the Magistrate, with his little eyes, seeking affirmation. He'd seen this in his courtroom. The defendant, usually a thief, overwhelmed by the evidence against him, still refused to plead guilty, only to catch a heavier term because of his specious mindset. The defendant would square his shoulders, look into the distance beyond the Magistrate with the self-righteous air of a martyr, occasionally shaking his head reproachfully at the irresistible testimony; and when the judgment was returned against him, he, with a shocked air, would turn to the gallery as if appealing to the public against some grave injustice.

"I'll be in the kitchen, cooking." The Magistrate excused himself.

"But the game's still on," Alfonso said. "Tell the girl to do it."

"I go to school. Mum goes to work. Dad disnae do anything. That's why he has to do the housework." Chenai gave Alfonso a wicked stare.

Just as the Magistrate rose to leave, a goal was scored. Liverpool was down. He went to the kitchen without waiting for the replay. Alfonso's voice followed him. "Did you see that, did you see that?"

It was strange that of all the things the Magistrate missed, his golfing buddies, his family, the sunshine, wide-open spaces, it was the maid he missed most of all. That quiet woman in her starched uniform, humming as she worked in the background, almost invisible to them. Mai Chenai had never been satisfied with her. The food was never cooked well enough. The house was never clean enough. The maid had a thankless job but she never grumbled. Looking back he'd never given it a moment's thought. The house was a woman's domain. Now he found himself questioning the conditions under which the maid had worked for him. The first time this had occurred was when he was bent over, brush in hand, cleaning the toilet bowl. In his entire life, he'd never imagined himself carrying out such a humiliating task. The maid, though, never complained. She did the laundry, walked Chenai to school, worked all day, and only got one day off in seven (a day off which could be revoked on a whim). Why did I never question this before – an injustice in my own house, yet there I was dispensing justice every day while I kept a virtual slave in my own house? How could this have seemed normal?

He sliced the greens. The can opener was broken so he had to use a knife to open the tinned tomatoes. He had bought hupfu from the Zimbabwean shop in Gorgie that sold exotic meats, Mazoe and little portions of heaven that reminded him of home. Thank goodness for hupfu. He put all these ingredients on the faux granite countertop and studied them as if they were the roots of some complex legal conundrum.

Cooking was a complicated business. Sometimes he watched the wrinkled chef on TV, shouting and swearing, all the while making the preparations look effortless. How could the simple maid have done this with such ease? Worse, the Magistrate somehow had to extract taste out

5

of bland British ingredients. He prepared the sadza. Ravakukwata, the boiling mix, leapt out of the pot, stinging his arms. It looked like a white volcano, active and dangerous. Rising steam filled the room, painting itself a thin film on the window. He worked on the beef, which he mixed with veg in the wok, adding a light mix of spices, stirring, smelling the rich aroma as it wafted around the kitchen.

"Zviri kunhuwirira," Alfonso called out from the living room.

He heard the sound of footsteps on laminated flooring upstairs. His wife was up. He imagined her reaching down and picking up her gown from the floor. After all these years, she still slept naked. The thought made him smile. He opened the sadza pot, added more hupfu, and stirred. The trick lay in squashing any lumps against the side of the pot. Heaven forbid he should end up with mbodza. He added more hupfu until it thickened and became sadza gobvu. Nhete was not for connoisseurs like him. He let the mixture simmer, listening to the hiss of escaping steam. One should never rush sadza. At this stage, the TV chef would call for a commercial break.

He could hear the faint splash of bath water upstairs. He arranged four plates and prepared to dish up his meal. The wrinkly chef was tough on presentation. Half the taste lies in the presentation, in how enticing the food looks. In the cartoon, something else he'd never have dreamt of watching back in the day, the rat wins the critic over by giving him ratatouille, a little taste of home. The Magistrate had become the anthropomorphic rat conjuring a minor miracle with each portion he put on the plate. The sadza lay on the top half of the plate, plain white and a sharp contrast to the red, green and brown of the stew and veg. Soup ran along the plate, meeting the base of the sadza.

"Goooaaal," shouted Alfonso. "Two – nil! Your team's as good as finished. It's over, I'm telling you. The fat lady is singing."

The Magistrate picked up two plates and returned to the living room. Alfonso clapped his hands. Chenai took hers with a quick, "Cheers, Dad." He collected his own plate and joined them.

"You're a fantastic cook, Magistrate," said Alfonso.

"We should call you Jamie," Chenai said.

"I think it's all due to your profession. This is my theory, you were supposed to weigh facts, sieve out the kernels of truth through the rubble of falsehood. What better training is there for cooking? None. They call these 'transferable skills'." Alfonso smiled importantly. He loved postulating his little theories and, at the drop of a hat, would expound the improbable and claim it was biblical truth. The Magistrate felt torn between accepting the compliment and pointing out its ridiculousness. He reserved judgment.

The sound of stairs creaking and sighing as one foot followed the other preceded Mai Chenai, who walked into the room graceful, in spite of her blue tunic.

"Aika, Alfonso, you are here." Her familiar tone bothered the Magistrate. Back home he would have been Babamudiki or VaPfukuto at the very least. This western business of calling people by their first names riled him. He reasoned it was the consequence of an individualistic culture, as though everyone had simply sprung up from nowhere. Some utopian ideal of equality – calling Her Majesty, Liz! The Shona way, the right way, stressed the nature of the relationship. The individual was the product of a community and had to be placed in relation to the next man. It was the glue that held them together, giving each value.

She sat next to her daughter, away from the two men. The Magistrate went to the kitchen and brought her supper – or was it breakfast? He watched as she took a small portion of sadza, rolled it gently in the palm of her hand and dipped it in the stew. Her lips parted. He watched her chew, admiring the soft line of her jaw, the tenderness of her face. He observed the fleeting bulge on her long neck as she swallowed, then she turned to him with a smile.

"Baba Chenai, murume mukuru anobika mbodza so. I'll have to get a takeaway to eat at work." She rose, kissed Chenai on the forehead, and left the room. The Magistrate realised that those were the only words she'd said to him all week.

The bedroom was a misty blue from the morning light. The Magistrate yawned as he stretched his back. He checked the time on the radio clock. He was only vaguely aware that it was a weekday. Days rolled by in purposeless succession. He rose, felt the cool floor under his feet and shuffled to the toilet. His face was wrinkled from too much sleep, eyes puffy and red. He washed his face, shaved and combed his moustache. A face he seemed only vaguely to remember stared back at him from the mirror. He took his medication with water straight from the tap.

"Dad, hurry." Chenai pounded on the door. "I cannae hold it in, Dad."

"Good morning to you too," he said. She pushed past him. "I feel so loved."

"I love you, Dad," she replied mechanically from behind the closed door.

The Magistrate returned to the bedroom and began making the bed. First, he smoothed the bottom sheet. Mai Chenai loved to complain if it wasn't straight when she came in. This was their routine. He would make the bed for her in the morning and in the evening he would find it perfectly made as if it hadn't been slept in, as if they were trying to erase each other's presence. They were becoming strangers who, except for the subtle scent of sleep that clung to the sheets and hid in the pillows, never shared a bed. On Mai Chenai's days off the Magistrate watched television until the early hours and slept on the couch downstairs. If he used the small, third bedroom, Chenai would know something was wrong, though he wondered if she hadn't already noticed.

"Dad, we've run out of sugar, again," Chenai called from downstairs.

"Tell your mum later."

What could he say? That he'd get it? He hardly had a penny to his name. When the gas beeped, or, God forbid, the electric ran out, he had to wait for Mai Chenai to sort it out. It was not meant to be like this. The shame sat somewhere in his gut, looping round his intestines, a dull ache that was with him every minute of every day. In the time of his father, whom he'd never known, a man's role was clearly defined. He was the provider. Nothing else was required of him. He had no duty towards his kids, save for the occasional moral correction – by the belt. The Magistrate imagined the past a simpler time, free from the overwhelming complexity of modern life.

He left the house and walked down the road, past the robots and the light early-morning traffic. He went past the police station into the residential area. Through one window he saw a family sat at the breakfast table. Further along, a commuter anxiously watched an AA man in a fluorescent jacket fiddle with his engine. The morning air was cool and fresh. The Magistrate filled his lungs as he walked slowly down the road, round the bend, then along the fence through which he could see his daughter's school. He could not remember when he had begun taking these morning walks. They had become a timeless, comforting ritual.

He found he could clear his mind when walking. It was as though the act of perambulation was complemented by a mental wandering, so he could be in two, or more, places at the same time. His physical being tied to geography and the rules of physics, his mental side free to wander far and wide, to traverse through the past, present and future, free from limits, except the scope of his own imagination.

He turned into Duddingston Village, walking along the pavement beside a narrow cobblestoned road. The cars parked on the side of the road meant only a single lane was free for traffic to pass through. To his left was the old stone wall, a little taller than a man. Quaint Georgian cottages stood to his right. The houses in Craigmillar were modern, brightly coloured yellow, blue or lime green. They did not possess the weathered, timeworn look of the village. They did not have its charm or the same sense of being rooted in the city, eternal, indelible. He walked past the Kirk, built of the same grey stone as the cottages and the wall, the past stealing its way into the present.

He crossed the road and walked onto the gravel and grass that led to the loch. A woman with a shawl wrapped round her shoulders was feeding the ducks and swans with bread. They swarmed round her, quacking and scurrying about. The water was a broken mirror of undulating waves lapping the shore. The conifers and heathers caught the morning rays as dew melted off their leaves. The woman's face was serene. She gave the Magistrate a light nod. They often met here, sharing the space, never once speaking as though voices would have shattered the morning's peace.

On the horizon, the sun was an icy orb hidden behind a thin veil of wispy white clouds. The Magistrate looked straight at it for a few seconds, its power lost in the stratosphere. With a bit of glue and feathers, he could touch it. He'd never have dared look the Bindura sun straight in the face like that. It came to him that each place had its own little sun, different from anywhere else. In Edinburgh the sun was this cold disc, distant, vague, powerless. For much of the year it was hidden behind grey clouds and, when it did come out in its brilliance, it felt awkward, alien. Here the North Wind reigned. In Bindura, the sun was all-powerful and magnificent. The air shimmered there, tar melted and buckled. People walked with beads of sweat rolling down their backs. Yet, even in this small town, there were two suns. In the low density suburbs the sun was wondrous, a joyful gift of warmth and light, but one had only to cross Chipindura Road from the east or Chipadze Road from the north into the high density suburbs to find the sun fierce and angry. There it assailed the residents, wilted the few patches of grass, stripped everything bare, revealing brown, cracked earth. If the sun infused life's essence into the low density suburbs, in the townships it drained this very same essence away.

When he thought about home, the Magistrate often looked to Arthur's Seat. He left the loch, tracking back up the road. The gorse gripping the sides of the hill was the bright yellow of the Bindura sun. The plants were strong, aggressive, making a niche on the bare sides of the hill. There was a hill in Bindura too, right in the middle of the town. It was made of granite that had formed deep in the bowels of the earth, patiently waiting until wind and rain had, slowly, over many millennia, stripped the soil off and left the hill high above everything else. Arthur's Seat was a volcanic creation. Magma had pushed violently up from the belly of the earth, sculpting itself by sheer will.

Funny, the Magistrate thought, how old geography lessons hidden in the grey lesions of the mind crawled back to the surface after so long. He thought of the hours spent cramming useless information about the limestone regions of England. Stalagmites and stalactites. Igneous, metamorphic and sedimentary rocks. The rock cycle. Weathering. Different types of rain formation – the latter, he supposed, was always useful in Scotland. Crammed notes forced in by the master's cane came flooding back. What was Chenai learning? Computers? Media Studies? Things were much more straightforward back then.

The traffic grew heavier. He could hear the drone of engines creeping along the road. He descended the slope to the other face of the hill. A man on a bicycle was holding up the traffic and a long tailback formed behind him. The white dome of Dynamic Earth appeared behind the foliage. No wonder I've been thinking about geography, he thought. He put his hands in his pockets to keep warm.

The Magistrate's daily circumambulation of Arthur's Seat meant that he would not see Mai Chenai. Morning encounters when she was tired from the night shift were best avoided. High above, on Radical Road, early walkers scaled the summit. For all his love of the park, the Magistrate disliked its roads. He was happy with the footpaths, worn over the centuries. But the tarred road, the brute imposition of man's will on nature, was not something he found pleasing. A thing of beauty like this should not have been tamed thus.

The parliament appeared to his left and opposite it stood Holyroodhouse, another of Her Majesty's palaces. The restored parliament with nationalistic leanings right next to the English monarch's residence. And along from it, blocks of low rent council flats. A tumultuous history and the contradictions of modern Scotland side by side. Yet, somehow, it all worked.

His eyes were drawn to the green spaces, the lawns ahead. A woman was being dragged along by a black mastiff on a long lead.

"Princess, stop," she said. "Stop right now, Princess."

What a name for a dog! What a choice of pet for a woman who, in all likelihood, lived in one of the flats nearby. He checked his watch. It was only a little after eight. In the early afternoon he liked to watch the *Dog Whisperer*. There were a few daytime programmes that he watched religiously, *Columbo, Murder She Wrote, Countdown, Judge Judy* and *Poirot* formed the rest of his selection, which was only occasionally broken by cookery programmes. Of all the shows he'd watched, none gave him the same insight into the insanity of western society as the *Dog Whisperer*.

The woman pulled on the leash, but the dog was too powerful, forcing her to take giant strides to keep up. Coming in the opposite direction, a man and his whippet walked side by side in perfect harmony. "Calm, submissive state" was what Cesar Millan would have called it. The ideal relationship between man and dog. Before he could begin to appreciate the show, the Magistrate had had to get his head round the fact that 'these people' lived indoors with their dogs. When Cesar went round saying that he rehabilitated dogs, and trained people, it made perfect sense. Anyone who lived indoors with a filthy animal clearly needed help.

The show's format was always the same. A distraught dog owner, usually a woman – occasionally with a partner whose dislike of the dog could never quite be expressed in front of the camera, except, that is, by cold stares, or the resigned shaking of the head – would speak about Fifi, or Bubu, or Coco whom she loved as much as life itself, but who was driving her to distraction.

Cesar Millan, the Third Worlder, the Mexican, would be called in. He was a small man, with perfect white teeth and a ridiculously well groomed beard. He would arrive smiling, always smiling, and sit down with the family. While they explained their problem, Cesar listened patiently, observing the dog and sometimes pushing it off his couch if it tried to sit with him uninvited. His diagnoses were usually simple. The dog was a pack animal that shouldn't be treated as a child, but treated as… well, a dog.

Cesar would then work with the dog, master him, and correct the problem. He would teach the owner correct body postures and subtle ways of understanding their dog's mind. His method was psychological, an attempt to restore balance. The dog, unused to discipline, would revolt. Cesar would poke it in the ribs, or click his fingers, point and say, "tsh." The animal would resist, sulk, go mental, but Cesar would not relent. Some of the battles were of mythic proportions, like Jacob and the angel. No matter how long it took, Cesar pressed on, until finally, as if by magic, the dog succumbed. The tail would go down, the animal would relax into the "calm, submissive state", and only then would Cesar, the stern master, show it affection.

Almost always his prescription involved the need for more exercise. The episode would conclude with smiling, grateful dog owners whose lives had been turned around, and who now kept their animals in a "calm, submissive state". A shot of Cesar walking in the wilderness, holding a shepherd's staff, surrounded by his own happy, peaceful pack of dogs faded with the credits. The same format, week in, week out, and the Magistrate could not get enough of it.

The silver birches, bared of their leaves, stood like skeletons on parade by the pond on the Meadowbank side of the city. The giant struts of the stadium and sports centre loomed over the locale. The Magistrate saw a red kite, which he mistook for an eagle, soaring in the sky. He breathed faster from the exertion of the walk and felt better for it. His calves throbbed a little as he walked up the incline. The ruins of St Anthony's stood below him and, when he looked down onto Holyrood, he could just make out the ruined abbey adjacent to the palace.

The Magistrate's vision skimmed over the roofs of the city. Cranes in the west looked like brontosauri feeding off the rooftops. The houses were tiny, like dolls' houses huddling together from the cold. The Restalrig high-rises brutally punctured the cityscape, and he swept over Leith to Granton, where flats fractured the skyline. In between the extremes, a hundred church spires stood out. From this point he could take in most of the city and, beyond, the Forth, calm and grey. On a day like this he could even see across to Fife. The Magistrate felt like a colossus striding over the narrow world. Everywhere he turned the view was breathtaking. Right then the saudade hit him pretty bad and, for a moment, he could see Bindura, the low prospect, the giant mine chimneys in the distance, but the memory was like a flicker from an old videotape that had been dubbed over. He could only hold the image in his mind for a brief second before it vanished into the mist hovering over the Forth.

Farai opens his eyes, sits up and swings his legs off the bed. The red LCD on his radio clock tells him it's `06:01:23`, meaning he's 1 minute and 23 seconds late. He doesn't use an alarm, his body knows when to rise and right now it's telling him he needs to pee. He rubs his eyes and yawns.

Eminem, Malcolm X, and Adam Smith (no relation to Ian) look down on him from the posters on the wall. He steps on layers of white printed paper with black ink lettering, numbers, symbols and words from his inkjet. Around the bed are various thick textbooks. The papers feel smooth under his bare feet as he walks across the room and opens the curtains. His bladder screams out. He ignores it. He'll go in his own time.

He goes to the living room and says good morning to Mr Majeika, who is hopping around in his hutch. Mr Majeika is one of those unoriginal rabbits trying to imitate dairy cows. Farai opens the hutch and strokes his black and white fur. 'Your bedding needs changing, Mr Majeika. Fancy a bit of lettuce, just to get you started today? It's good for you, coz you're getting fat, *shasha.*'

Mr Majeika wiggles his whiskers in reply and observes Farai lazily.

Farai gets himself a glass of water and a few leaves of lettuce for Mr Majeika. He turns on the TV, switches it, via remote, from the live reality TV feed of housemates in the Big Brother house to Bloomberg. The Nasdaq is ↑, the Dow's ↑, FTSE's ↑, so life is good. He fires up his Vaio FE550G. He thinks about how it'd have been great to buy defense shares before the war. Raytheon's ↑, doing great with all those Tomahawks flying across the desert, lighting up Iraq.

He checks his uni email account, 43 unread messages, and it's only Monday, before the start of the business day. Most of it is junk. He logs off and goes on zse.co.zw. The connection is slow. The screen blinks like he's on dial-up. He taps his fingers on the keyboard, trying to absorb the news on TV, making sense of the red, silver and green data stream running at the bottom of the screen. The ZSE page is down.

'Fuck's sake,' he says, leans back in the chair and picks up the landline. He dials out international – direct, *spare no expense when it's business*. It's the AIMs where the fun stuff happens.

'Hello.'

'Dad, it's Farai, how's Mwana doing?'

'I'm *fine*, your mum's fine too, so is the dog and your little sisters, thanks for asking, Comrade Fatso.'

'Sorry, Dad, I haven't had my coffee yet. I'm still booting up.'

'Mwana's dead, I told you to get out of nickel ages ago.'

'Commodity prices keep going up, China's insatiable, they can't get enough of the stuff. How come Mwana's underperforming?'

'I'm in Zimplats, and we're doing alright. Really positive policies on PGMs, so Hartley or whatever they call it now is looking great, but everyone else in the industry is struggling. Gono's hording all their forex and swapping it with Mickey Mouse money so they can't function. They're gonna sink. Do you want me to get you out?'

'No, I'm in this for the long haul. They've got good proven reserves and their PGMs will be coming online soon. They've got eggs in quite a few baskets.'

'It's your money, little bull, but I say quit while you're slightly behind. No one ever quits while they're ahead.'

'I'll talk to you later, Dad,' he says, hangs up and sighs.

Mr Majeika chews his lettuce, barely making a crunching sound as he watches the news from his hutch. Farai takes a sip of water and flicks over to CNN. Recycled footage: green, night vision clips of videogame-like explosions. It looks beautiful on the Sony widescreen plasma TV. He can almost feel the heat from the blast and taste the chemical smoke pluming in the air. The commentary uses words like, 'surgical strikes', 'collateral damage', 'weapons of mass destruction', and when the footage changes to armor-plated Humvees and Abrams, he knows for sure he should have bought into defense.

He goes to the bathroom, takes a long piss, and showers. He comes back out, towel wrapped around his body and knocks on Brian's bedroom door.

'Wakey, wakey,' he shouts.

Brian replies with a torrent of abuse about his mum's genitalia and wholly unfounded assertions about her sex life.

'I love you too,' Farai says, and goes back to the living room.

Water streams down from his short Afro onto his back. He can't be arsed to use a hair drier. He moisturizes, using L'Oréal for men, because he's worth it. His stomach grumbles; he won't eat till midday though. He wants to have full mastery of his body, of every thought and emotion that comes from it.

'Why the fuck do you have to fucking wake me up so fucking early in the fucking morning when I've fucking told you before to fucking leave me the fuck alone?' says Brian, voice slurring, breath reeking of last night's bender.

'Dude, you have a stiffy,' Farai replies. 'Don't point it my way!'

Brian takes a look at the bulge in his boxers and raises his eyebrows.

'It's *not* aimed at you. It's just a morning glory, perfectly natural, nothing suspicious there.'

'Didn't you get lucky last night?'

'Would I have this affliction if I had?'

'What happened? I set you up with that Filipino chick, and you looked like you knew what you were doing. Please tell me you at least got her number.'

Brian sits beside him and uses a cushion to cover his flagpole. Some Arabic women in black are running across the screen, wailing, raising their hands to the heavens and beating themselves on the head. The voice-over states that laser-guided missiles are accurate to within a few centimeters though the occasional `collateral damage` is inevitable.

'Listen,' says Farai as images of charred Iraqis fill the screen, 'you're walking around with a loaded gun. It's unhealthy for a young, healthy male such as yourself to live like this. A man must allow for a maximum of 4 weeks between sexual intercourse. Look at this. These guys are on 6 month rotations, they're not getting laid and that's why atrocities happen. After 4 weeks of no action, blood flows away from the brain, and there's *way* too much testosterone in the body wreaking havoc in the amygdala. You carry on like this, mate, and you're a danger not only to yourself, but to society at large.'

A loud, very human cry comes from one of the bedrooms. Brian moves quickly to see what's up. Farai shrugs and flips the channel to Al Jazeera where he is met with even more distraught Arabs. He decides it's all too depressing and logs on to hi5 to see if he's got any new messages. As the page is loading, he flicks to a half-finished chess game against his laptop. It bores him, he's playing at level 10, the highest level, and the AI can't keep up with him. Its gigabytes of processing power don't match up to his integrated organic circuitry.

'Farai, can you come and give me a hand here?' Brian calls out.

'I'm busy,' he replies.

'Come on, man, this is serious.'

Farai gets up, tightens the towel round his waist, and walks down the dim corridor to the last bedroom on the right. The pong of stale man-sweat hits him. Brian's standing at the door. A naked, skeletal figure lies on the bed, staring up at the ceiling. At intervals he moans. This is their friend, Scott. Farai opens the window. Fresh air rushes in from outside.

'Dude, what the hell do you think you're doing? We've got neighbors. This is a respectable area, they'll *skeem* we're killing a goat in here or something.'

'She didn't text me back,' Scott groans.

'Would you like something to drink, tea, coffee, water, anything?' asks Brian.

'My life's *over*. She hates me.'

They stand awkwardly around their naked friend, not quite knowing what to do. Brian fetches a glass of orange juice and gives it to Scott. Farai can't begin to understand why someone would go crazy like this over some piece of ass. He paces around the room, picking up dirty clothes and putting them into the laundry bag, an activity that hardly makes a dent on the mess.

'She totally hates me.'

'That's chicks, man. They promise you the moon and all you get is a tiny little star, like this.'' Farai indicates a tiny little gap between his index finger and thumb.

'Everything's fucked.'

'Do you mind putting something on, coz, no offense, but your naked ass and his stiffy are kinda freaking me out here.' Farai laughs at his own joke.

Scott lies there, immobile. His eyes bother Farai, pupils dilated, the whites, red and bloody. He knows the story though, Scott has spent the last week psychotexting his ex, C, trying to win her back with romantic declarations, freaky poems, and not-so-subtle emotional blackmail about how life isn't worth living without her. The chick was hot, no doubt. Farai remembers her – great tits, curvy ass, cliché Coca-Cola bottle body, smart, funny, and quick as a whip. A classy *tsvarakadenga*. He knew it would never last with his mate Scott. The chick had standards, yo.

'You're calling her too often. You're giving her too much power over you, bro. You gotta hang back and wait until she wants you. Guaranteed she's gonna come crawling back. Straight-up homies like us are hard to come by in this city.'

'You think so?'

'Would I be saying it, if I didn't think it?' Farai feigns offense. 'Now get up your rasclut, you've got work this morning, haven't you?'

'I'm calling in sick.'

'You can't. You owe me, like, 2 months' rent already.'

'The wealth of the sinner is stored up for the righteous.'

'What the *fuck* does that mean?'

'Proverbs 13 verse 22,' says Scott, and covers his head with a pillow.

Brian and Farai return to the living room, to the soft monotone sound of traffic picking up on Commercial Street. Through the window, Farai can see the river and a bit of the docks in the distance. He likes living in Sandport, by the water, especially at this point where the Water of Leith empties into the sea. There are great pubs and restaurants a short walking distance away. Everything a student could want.

'We need to find, like, some serious mental help for Scott. I don't dig this vibe he's got going on,' says Brian.

'Well, Florence–'

'I've told you before, don't call me that.' Brian raises his voice.

'Aren't we touchy this morning? See what I told you about all that testosterone in your bloodstream.'

'Look, Farai, this dude's acting all mental and we need to get it sorted, otherwise who knows what he might do?'

'Weren't you telling us just last week that some of the psychiatric models they use have no relevance to African people? Or have you changed your mind now and you want to see our friend's brilliant brain warped by mind altering chemical concoctions your quacks are always so quick to prescribe?'

19

'You're twisting my words like you always do. You saw him. This guy's having some sort of breakdown. He needs professional help.'

'All he needs is a couple of shots of Sambuca to get his head straight. Can you do that for him?'

'That's the last thing he needs.'

'You're the nurse and I'm the doctor, comprende?'

'You're doing a PhD in economics, that doesn't make you a physician.' Brian frowns.

'Just give him the damn Sambuca and give Mr Majeika a hit too. He likes that on a Monday morning, fires him up for the week ahead,' Farai says, turns impatiently and goes to his room to get dressed. He's already wasted too many of his precious morning minutes on this palaver. He wears a pair of Cavallis jeans, a cheap pair of Internationals (Bata) and a white cotton stretch dress shirt (M&S), on top of which he wears his black deconstructed overcoat (Religion). He slips on the Patek Philippe his father bought him when he turned 17. Then, he collects his keys and leaves the flat, but not before grabbing the handmade woollen scarf on the coat hanger, a gift from grandma.

***

Farai's caught up in what passes for congestion in Edinburgh, seat laid back so his arms have to stretch to reach the steering wheel, gangster style, listening to Radio 4 – *Thought for the Day*. His car, a black PT Cruiser, which he bought because it looks like a monster, is fully equipped with a custom Kenwood KDC-X993 complete with subwoofer that gives the voice on the radio extra kick. The 22 cruises by in the bus lane. A woman in the green Corsa in front chats on her cell phone and uses the rear-view mirror to check her lipstick.

'They don't have congestion in Saudi Arabia,' he mutters to himself.

The vicar talks in a flat voice, pondering the mystery of God's will and the war. Using tortuous logic, he explains how war may be the ultimate proof that God wants us to have everlasting peace. The lights turn green and Farai begins to move again, slowly creeping up towards North Bridge.

The Scotsman, a red sandstone Edwardian building, looms up ahead. His wipers squeak against the windscreen because it is raining ever so lightly. The fuel gauge flashes red. He can never seem to remember to top up. The last time he ran out was on the M8 to Glasgow and the RAC hit him a £90 charge.

Traffic is clogged up on Nicolson Street and he has to navigate his way through an obstacle course of orange traffic cones. There aren't any workmen on the closed-up section of the road, that's just the way it is. Black soot covers the grey walls of the old buildings. He turns right after Surgeons' Hall to find parking at the mosque.

'*Asalaam Alaykum*,' the bearded dude/car park attendant says, as Farai lowers his window.

'*Wa 'Alaykum Asalaam*, to you. And no, Salman, I'm not converting this week. I already told you guys that I'll only convert if you guarantee me 1 free meal a day from The Mosque Kitchen.' Salman laughs and waves him through to a free spot.

The mosque, a gift from the Saudis, is a blocky solid building, fusing Islamic architecture with a baronial style that blends in with the stocky, gothic architecture of the rest of the city. Farai walks round it to Potterow where the minaret stands.

He crosses the road and walks through the university buildings, on to Bristo Square, and from there down to George IV Bridge. This takes him past Medina, Doctors, Frankenstein's and a number of other pubs and clubs he's trawled through on wild nights with his boys. A car hoots as he crosses the next street. He doesn't look. It's a reckless stunt and, reaching the other side, he congratulates himself on being the first black man to cross over Candlemaker Row against such odds. He thinks, *It's so easy to make yourself the first black man at anything. The first black man at this university, the first black doctor in such a hospital, the first black person to take a dump in a formerly all-white toilet in Joburg.* To his mind, there's something silly about the cult of 'the first black ___ ' and anyone who calls themself that deserves to be patted on the head and given a biscuit. Perhaps it served a purpose in the colonial era, but for Farai, a child of the revolution who comes from a dominant majority, it's just bullshit.

He walks into the Elephant House where he's the first black man to buy coffee that morning.

'The usual?' the girl at the counter asks. She wears a little apron that turns Farai on.

'Quadruple espresso every time,' he replies with a smile. She lingers, holds his gaze, as if she wants him to say something else.

21

The Mathematician

Every Monday morning he frequents this rather quaint café – of which there are many in Edinburgh – which became famous when some woman wrote a children's book about wizards and inexplicably became a billionaire. In reality, there is nothing particularly special about the venue except for its bizarre collection of elephant statuettes. It's not particularly clean and has rather dreary terracotta walls.

He avoids the empty tables and goes to the one by the window, where an old man wearing a trilby is sitting alone, sipping green tea, a copy of the *Telegraph* on the table.

'It seems rather busy today. I hope you don't mind if I sit with you?' Farai pulls up a chair.

The old man offers a brief incredulous look. A 'humph' that escapes from his throat is his only sound of protest. Eyeing Farai warily, he takes a sip of tea.

He has a sharp, beak-like nose and bright eyes behind a pair of spectacles. He maintains an aggrieved air under Farai's glare. The waitron serves Farai's espresso in a medium sized mug, placing it carefully on the table.

'Will that be all? The muffins are great today,' she says.

'Thank you, but I have to watch my figure,' Farai replies, his eyes never leaving the old man.

He smells the bitter aroma coming from his black brew. It almost knocks him back, the true sign of a good, strong coffee. 2 middle-aged professional women sit at a nearby table. A bony woman, with a pale face and dark rings around her eyes, stares into space, looking down periodically to jot something in a ring binder notebook. A man with a backpack on the table listens to his iPod. Farai's attention remains intensely focused on the old man.

At last the old man breaks.

'Miserable weather we're having, don't you think?' the old man remarks in a thin voice.

Farai shrugs. He could have given a few stock responses; it's not as if he doesn't know the ritual exchanges about the weather.

'When you reach a certain age,' the old man sips his tea and continues, 'and you have a bit of arthritis in the joints, and you wake up in the middle of the night, 10 maybe 20 times just to spend a penny, then yes, the rain can make you a little miserable.'

'I think you should stop drinking so much tea. It's a diuretic. The upside is the anti-oxidants will get rid of those pesky free radicals, which are eating you up as we speak. But, no, honestly, I don't have to worry about old age. There's a short life expectancy where I'm from.'

'Then I feel sorry for you. There's nothing better than hearing the sound of your grandchildren playing in the garden. What's your name by the way?'

'Rumplestilskin,' Farai says, and the old man laughs. They are two strangers and meet here every Monday morning, following the same ritual, staring each other down until one of them speaks. Last winter, they had an epic encounter lasting 2 hours. Finally it was Farai who broke. It's a pointless exercise, but 1 they enjoy. And they still don't know each other's names.

Farai takes a sip of his coffee, which tastes like tar and is therefore exquisite. He sighs and feels sleepy.

'Are you teaching today?'

'The uni uses its postgrads like slave labor. The first-years are spoilt, clueless little twats. How on earth did they pass their Highers if they haven't mastered basic stats? And so, I wind up with them, on zero pay.'

'In my day you just went to work and made your way up the ranks. Today, graduates who don't know anything are given all the top jobs. Nothing beats experience, if you ask me.'

Farai begins to enjoy himself. They are moaning now. Moaning is an essential ritual here, and a learnt art. One must find at least half a dozen things to complain about before breakfast.

He takes in the view of the castle and the rooftops over the Grassmarket through the smudged windows of the café. 2 blonde girls wearing identical pink jumpers walk in, giggling. Their loud voices pierce the tranquillity of the room. The statues of the elephants that line the café, in the corners and on the banisters, give them frozen, reproving stares. The younger of the 2 fidgets as if she's on a sugar rush.

'I once saw Alexander McCall Smith here.' Her voice carries across the room.

'Isn't that him over there?' Blondie2 speaks in a staged whisper.

The pale writer in the corner puts down her pad and looks at Farai and his companion. There's a sly smile on the old man's face. He seems amused at being mistaken for a celebrity, even more so when everyone in the room is stealing glances their way. Farai scowls at the blondes whose conversation stops. He leans forward.

'Are you some type of pervert, picking up young girls under the pretense of being someone you are not?' he asks. That'd make sense in a café in which the male toilets are full of graffiti from Harry Potter fans expressing their love for the author.

'What's it to you if I am?'

'Aren't you giving them a raw deal? No offense, but old folks all look the same, and if they're gonna roll with an old guy then they'll want the genuine article.'

'In our heads, we're all celebrities.'

'The way I see it–'

'Have you ever read his novels?'

'I'm a serious man. I don't read novels. They're a waste of time. The last one I tried was Don Quixote, which was forced on me in my lit class in high school. I didn't even bother; I just bought the video and even that was boring. I thought, *sod this for a game of marbles*. In the end, I dropped the subject. Give me numbers, $, £, symbols.'

The old man rises up slowly, deliberately adjusts his tweed jacket, allowing everyone in the room to take a nice long look at him. He places a £2 coin on the table, which Farai pockets.

'Oh, you are a rascal. See you same time next week,' he says as he leaves.

Farai watches a woman near the counter ask if she may have a photograph taken with his erstwhile companion and grins as the old man obliges. He picks up the *Telegraph*, scans the familiar diet of war stories, crime and scandals. He notices an article in the sports pages passionately advocating an international boycott of Zimbabwean cricket. Farai considers making a scene and accusing the waitron of watering down his espresso, but decides he doesn't have the energy, and so takes out his wallet and retrieves a £5 note that he leaves under the mug. He winks at the waitron as he makes his way out to class.

The bin men came on Tuesday mornings. The Magistrate was at the back of the house, forcing an extra black bag into the wheelie bin. He pushed with all his might, but the damn thing kept popping back up – to think that a household of three could generate so much waste. The bags were full of wrapping, plastic bags, containers, food. Everything was disposable. He wheeled the bin to the front and went back inside. There was so much to do. No sooner had he cleaned the house than it needed cleaning again.

He went for his daily walk around Arthur's Seat. When he returned it was time to work. He started on the glass coffee table in the living room stained by cup marks. Then he picked up the junk lying on the carpet, the cups hidden at the foot of the sofa, the random socks – never a pair. Where did it all come from? He'd have gladly traded anything for a maid a few hours each day.

The news played in the background. A twenty-four hour depressing feed of the world's ills. The Magistrate flicked from Sky, to the BBC, to ITV and the American channels, only to find they were all talking about the same thing – spectacular night vision footage, an eerie green, targets lit up in one Middle Eastern country or another. The reporters stressed that all efforts were being made to minimize collateral damage. The Western troops looked heroic, larger than life, liberators, not conquerors. The footage was a hypnotic stream of live action, dazzling explosions, dramatic commentary. But it wasn't what the Magistrate wanted to see. He waited for the story to change, hoping there might be a piece about Zimbabwe, but the country never featured when there was real news. It seemed to him that Zimbabwe was a filler used when something about dystopian Africa was needed for comic relief. Still, he needed to keep abreast of what was happening back home. He longed for a sudden change so men like him might be called upon once more to rebuild the country. He kept this hope alive in his heart, a warm ember cocooned by despair, weighed down with each report that things were in fact getting worse. His country ticked all the boxes for a sensational African story: add one dictator, a dash of starving kids, a dollop of disease, sprinkle a little corruption, stir in a pot of random, incomprehensible violence, and voilà, the stereotypical African dish – all served out daily for the Western reporter, speaking in a low conspiratorial voice in front of the cameras, hoping to make a name for himself, a white saviour in Africa.

He kept his music collection near the TV, a tower of jazz CDs: Miles Davis, Chuck Mangione, Billy Cobham, Louis Armstrong, Aretha Franklin. They reminded him of his days at the country club, listening to music and drinking with friends after a round of golf. Beside the CDs was a smaller collection of tapes, which Alfonso had given him. At first he only listened out of politeness. Sungura wasn't his style, rather something in the background of the culture that could not be avoided, but after a while this peasant music with its whiny guitars and hard drums had grown on him. He picked a cassette labelled *Marshall Munhumumwe and the Four Brothers' Greatest Hits* – a pirate copy from a decade ago, which felt as if it might as well have been a century ago.

He switched the TV off; the static from the blank part of the tape began to play, followed by the lead guitar with a dull twang, monotone and repetitive. It sounded like a mbira being plucked. Then the electric guitars joined in, a vibrant contrast of the old and new. The drums entered the fray, all the instruments looping around the lead guitar, which ignored them and continued its monologue, the sounds slow and melodious, the whole mixing and riffing until Munhumumwe's voice came through, calm and flat.

The Magistrate had long realised that Sungura was the polar opposite of the jazz he so loved. The music was seldom abstract and the lyrics were central, the artist spoke directly to the listener. The song, *Ndibvumbamireiwo,* was slow, music as prayer, something the Magistrate needed. His troubles merged with those of the singer, as though Munhumumwe was sharing the load. He thought it was interesting that Munhumumwe's prayer was not directed at the Christian God, rather it was communing with the ancestors. But Munhumumwe had also sung *Vatendi,* more Christian gospel than Sungura, displaying the easy syncretism of his pre-Pentecostal generation, though *Vatendi* lacked the same heartfelt emotional depth as *Ndibvumbamireiwo*.

The Magistrate remembered seeing Munhumumwe and the Four Brothers perform at the Kimberly Reef in the nineties, on a night out with his workmates. At the time he didn't rate the group, now he'd changed his mind. The lyrics of the song were repetitive, every word enunciated, something essential in an oral culture for the listener not only to hear, but to remember, for only through remembering could the meme pass on from mouth to ear, person to person. And this was aided by a two-minute instrumental section in the middle of the song, which gave the listener time for introspection before the song started up and repeated again.

The first time the Magistrate listened to *Ndibvumbamireiwo*, he knew it was a work of beauty and compassion, something equivalent to St Francis' Prayer. He felt a shiver up his spine as the song drew to a close. He was astonished by how Munhumumwe captured something so essential about the human spirit in such a short song.

The Magistrate was so lost in the moment, drifting in the interstices between the chords, that he did not see Mai Chenai standing in her dressing gown by the doorway.

"Nhai, Baba Chenai," she said, startling him. Her eyes were red. She was tired from her shift.

"I'm sorry, I didn't see you."

"Turn that stupid music off. Some of us have to work, you know." She turned her back on him without waiting for a reply and went back up the stairs. The house fell back into silence. He knew her words would play over in his mind all day. He picked up his keys and left the house, slamming the door on his way out.

The Magistrate walked up and down Niddrie Mains several times. His pulse was racing. He walked right to the Thistle and back again. I don't want to do this, he told himself. He was running out of options, getting desperate. He walked past Londis, going towards the robots.

"I never wanted to come here in the first place," he muttered angrily. A kid wearing a hoodie bumped into him, apologised and walked away. The Magistrate barely noticed.

He stood in front of a white door, next to the newsagent's. This was not how he'd wanted things to pan out. Life was hard enough without resorting to this. He opened the door and walked into a little office. A

29

woman, a telephone receiver tucked between her shoulder and ear, was sitting behind a desk, filing her nails. She pointed to an empty chair.

"Didn't I tell you he's a cheating bastard, you have to leave him." Her voice had an emphatic rasp. A mist of nail dust floated up to the ceiling as she blew on her fingers.

The Magistrate waited, listening to her strident advice, while she did not even look in his direction. He felt small, a gnat, intruding on her space. The office had two desks placed together in an L shape. The other desk was empty. Both were untidy with paperwork chaotically stacked, a scattering of empty mugs with dried lipstick stains around the edges. The Magistrate remembered a time when he walked into places and people rushed to serve him. Mwana wamambo muranda kumwe. The wastepaper basket between the two desks was overflowing. The windows were grimy.

The bench was a lifetime ago. It pained him to think of his past, to recall memories of what once had been. If only he had no memory, no sense of his old successful self, then it would be easier to accept his new circumstances.

"Men like that need to be taught a lesson. If my boyfriend did that I would chop his thing off... Yeah, he knows it." The woman on the phone was explaining her philosophy for a stable relationship. The Magistrate involuntarily crossed his legs. Attempted murder? Grievous bodily harm? A crime of passion? The most popular one with aggrieved women back home was to pour boiling cooking oil over the philanderer's face, though none of those had ever reached his court. He'd dealt with a lot of domestic violence. But then again crime feels common if it's all you deal with day in day out. In his line of work it was natural to assume society was sick. The law was rather mute on couples that actually loved one another, except, that is, for marriage, a ceremony he disliked presiding over.

"Excuse me," he said.

"Can't you see I'm on the phone?" The woman returned to her caller. "Some people are just so rude, ha, they can't wait just a few minutes."

"I've been waiting for twenty minutes!"

The woman continued her conversation as though he was not even there. He could feel rage swelling up within him. He stood up abruptly and his chair fell over. "Calm submissive state, my arse," he thought. The woman gazed admiringly at her nails.

"Have a nice day," he said, making for the door. As he opened it, Alfonso fell in, struggling with several plastic bags.

"Aikaka, Magistrate, you're here?" Alfonso blew air from his mouth.

"I was just about to leave."

"And go where? I've just arrived," Alfonso said, ushering him back in. "I'd just gone to Lidl for my shopping. It's called multitasking. I have a theory–"

"Your receptionist is very unhelpful."

"I'm an administrator," the woman called out.

"No, no, there must be some misunderstanding. Don't worry; I'll take care of you. Here at Busy Bodies Recruitment and Employment Solutions we aim to provide First World service to Scottish businesses, governmental departments, the charitable sector, and other not-for-profit organisations. We are the one stop shop for all your recruitment solutions." Alfonso was really trying to say he was sorry but couldn't do anything about it since she was his small house. "Please, please, sit down. Let me just put these to one side and then we can talk."

The Magistrate was reluctant but Alfonso's imploring face with its comic meerkat-like appearance stayed him. Alfonso rushed round to the other side of the desk and sat down. He straightened his tie. He was a small man and behind the desk he cut a ridiculous figure.

"So, what brings you to our offices?" Alfonso smirked with apparent relish.

"I need a job," the Magistrate replied in a low voice.

"Sorry, I didn't get that." Alfonso cupped his left ear and leant forward.

"I need a job."

"Aha." Alfonso leapt up. "I told you he would come, Spiwe. Didn't I tell you he would come?" He looked intoxicated, gleeful; casting his hands wide open as if embracing the whole world. "I knew it. I just knew it. How long has it been? A year?"

"Not that long."

"Near enough." Alfonso nipped round his desk, grabbed Spiwe's phone and cut her off.

"What do you think you're DOING?"

"I told you he'd come." Alfonso spoke in a frenzy. "This man is like a brother to me. He's smarter than me; he has a degree, a Master's, and many, many certificates. But let me tell you one thing, he doesn't know the UK like I do. I tried to tell Mai Chenai. I said to her, 'Look, tell him to stop applying for those posh jobs in the newspapers. They are not for the likes of us.' This country now uses a system I call voluntary slavery. They used to bring you people in big boats, shackled together – you didn't even need a passport, and then you started refusing, saying you wanted equality. Now you flood their borders looking for work. What do you expect them to do? I've seen it all before, many times: Nigerians, Jamaicans, Polishans, Congoans, Russians, Indians, you name it. There was an electrician from Bulawayo, you know Mdala Phiri... of course you do. Phiri came here with his wife, a nurse, he thought he was going to get an electrician's job. I told him, 'Phiri, this is the Civilised World, forget it,' but he didn't listen, no one listens to Alfonso. So, he went for an interview and do you know what the man said to him? He said, 'Look here, why are you bothering us? Can't you see the electricity we use is different from the electricity in your country?' You don't believe me? I swear it. Phiri himself told us. Spiwe here is my witness."

"Leave me out of your stories, Mr Pfukuto," said Spiwe.

Alfonso strutted around the room with a limp, as though one leg was slightly longer than the other.

"It's even worse with the law, Magistrate. I tried to say it but no one listens to Alfonso. They think we come from the jungle. They think we have kangaroo courts. They will say, 'How can you practice law here when you couldn't even preserve the rule of law in your own country?' I knew your applications would come to nothing. They didn't even reply you, did they?" Alfonso ignored the Magistrate's obvious discomfort. "Only nursing is the same, because no matter where you go in the world, wiping bums is still wiping bums. But don't worry, that's why I'm here. I am going to make sure you get a good job with good rates of pay too. You're not like these tsotsis weaving and ducking without papers. No, you will get a good job, a very good job."

Alfonso threw an application form in front of the Magistrate and gave him a pen. He picked up the phone, flicked through a diary and dialled out.

"Spiwe, help him to fill it out." Spiwe gritted her teeth, but she stood up and went to the Magistrate anyway. She hovered over him as he filled the document in. He was slow, thorough, reading each question carefully before writing. He was used to going through legal documents where he could not risk misinterpreting the contents.

"Hallo, hallo, is this Olu?" Alfonso asked, in a faux Nigerian accent, to someone on the phone. "Oh, my sister-wo, how are you in the name of Christ Jesus our Lord and Saviour... Yes, I am fine... Listen, Olu, there has been a problem with your shift tonight. They have cancelled it... I know it's terrible. I said to them, 'Why did you book it if you knew you were going to cancel it?' Don't worry I will call you as soon as I get something. You are my number one... God bless you, my sister-wo."

He got off the line and smiled at the Magistrate. "I've got you a shift. You start tonight. First we must give you a pair of safety shoes, a tunic and some industrial gloves... Don't worry we'll deduct the cost from your first pay cheque... It's okay, don't thank me. That's what friends are for."

The Maestro took out a pack of fags from his back pocket. He flipped it round so he wouldn't see the pair of black, rotting lungs pictured at the back. Instead the big font, SMOKING KILLS, printed at the front, assailed him. There was something perverse about taking a product that promised death; then again, salt might kill you, crossing the street might kill you, life itself was a set of small, incremental steps leading towards a certain end. He remembered an advert from way back that said: It's not the destination, it's how you get there, or something like that. There were a lot of adverts to remember, all saying different things. It was hard to keep up with the barrage at every corner that told you what to buy, what to eat, what to wear, what to think. He lit the cigarette and inhaled the smoke deep into his lungs, savouring the harsh taste tempered by menthol. He exhaled, watching the blue smoke dissipate in the air. Grey clouds hung heavy in the sky. If he looked closely, he could see they were a patchwork of dark and light, a small bright region indicating where the sun might be. This was his routine, one last fag in the car park before work. All around were cars, new, old, shiny, dirty, the SUVs and people carriers, bright colours, a dozen shades of green, more of blue, then the whites, the reds, and the stunning pink of a Fiat Panda. Shoppers went by with their trolleys, prams and brood, swallowed up by the large glass jaws of the doors. It looked Dr Whoey, for every three that went in, only one came out. Like, where do the rest go? Shit, I'm stoned. Hey, Maestro! A woman waved from across the road. It was Tina from the deli. He smiled, waved and pushed his hair back in a nonchalant gesture. The Maestro stood just shy of six feet, had emerald green eyes and freckles that ran across the bridge of his nose. Aren't you coming in yet, or you're waiting till the last minute? Can't blame you, I hate this place, Tina said as she walked past. He watched her, a round blob, self-conscious under his gaze, going until the glass doors swallowed her up. Everyone moaned about the place, but they kept coming back. Every little helps. This place, his work, was the greatest show on earth. Twenty-four hours of reality TV with a cast and an audience that didn't even know they were taking part in an act in the ultimate playhouse, a performance replicated in every city and town. He looked at the spandrels and the steel girders that supported the glass front of the building, open and inviting, free entry, bring a friend. The sheer size of it, the huge, bold letters spelling T.E.S.C.O. high in the air, a beacon for all to see, making this place a cathedral, an awesome sight. I feel high, he thought, really shouldn't have had that last joint this morning. Next I'll be talking to myself, Tim Marlow at Tesco. He finished his fag, threw it on the ground and crushed it under the heel of his boot. The last cloud of smoke hung in the air just above him. He walked down to the shop, past the cash machines, the railing with shopping trolleys stacked one behind the other, and through the glass doors. Hey, Maestro, turn that smile upside down, you're here to work. That was Peter Aaron, the security guard, standing behind a construct that looked like a pulpit with screens that allowed him to watch what was happening in every corner of the store from the CCTV cameras dangling from the ceiling, feeding in from every aisle. The Maestro saluted him and went by. He felt like Superman as he removed his jacket, revealing a chequered blue shirt with his name-tag in clear lettering. The symphony of the checkouts bleeping filled the air. It was mechanical, hypnotic, a ceaseless intonation; the soundtrack of commerce so familiar to him after four years working in the store. Had it been that long? Time was warped in this place, bent, buckled, packaged into little packets called clocking in and clocking out. Everything had a price tag, a value assigned to it by some unseen authority. An old woman stopped him. Can you tell me where I can find the antipasto? He didn't miss a beat. Aisle twenty to the left of the cooking oil, you'll find it on the third shelf from the top beside the artichokes. She thanked him and tottered along with her basket. He had to clock in. There was nothing worse than being deemed late when you'd actually come in on time. He made his way through the familiar aisles. Above him were the steel struts of the roof, crisscrossing one another, the fluorescent lights suspended there made the building feel like a spaceship. Everything about it felt as though it could just take off at any moment, nothing was permanent, nothing was fixed; it was just a space, a form that could be taken apart and reassembled anywhere else – transient, with no pretence of an eye on eternity. He went back stage, staff only, gloomy and functional without the polish of the shop floor. I see you finally made it, said Tina's disembodied voice from somewhere. I always make it, he replied. They've stuck you back on frozen foods, I'm afraid. She emerged in her coat, with silly netting round her hair. The look suited her. That's the way aha, aha I like it. He serenaded her and grabbed a trolley. Barry came up behind him and slapped him on the back of the head. That's for being too damn cheerful, he said, and went on his way. Aye, grandpa, I'll have a bullying lawsuit on ya. You wait and see. Laughter erupted from unseen corners of the warehouse. He pushed his trolley out. It was time for work. He got to the freezers, feeling the chill within. A man and a woman walked past. The woman, his partner perhaps, was in the lead. The man followed dull-eyed and dazed, his primitive brain forged in the hot, sparse savannah was overwhelmed by the bright lights, bright colours, the incredible range of choice on display, so that an elementary defence mechanism kicked in, a fuse breaking the circuit, shutting it down. He was zombified, mute, out of his depth. His partner led confidently, navigating the aisles by instinct, using her superior evolutionary gifts to sniff out the frozen parsnips, somehow knowing to choose Aunt Bessie's, because somehow, just somehow, maybe x-ray vision piercing through the multi-coloured plastic packaging, perhaps genetic memory passed down through the matrilineal DNA, she knew they were better than the rest. The poor man was relegated to the role of trolley pusher. The Maestro arranged the merchandise, first checking the chicken thighs in the fridge were not past their sell-by date and loading the latest batch underneath. His fingers were frozen and numb. A pair of gloves was stashed in his back pocket, unused. A nasal voice came on the tannoy asking the in-store cleaner to report to Beers, Wines and Spirits. He checked his watch, the hands barely moved. That's what this place did to the fourth dimension; outside of it time rushed by too quickly, but inside it was dilated by some sort of Tardis effect, which also made the store feel bigger on the inside. I have to stop smoking pot, he told himself. He met Carrie at the dairy section, offloading some Yakult. Hey, Carrie, he said. She handed him a pack. Have you tried this stuff? she asked. He shook his head. It's got Lactobacillus casei, it will improve your digestive system. Do you know you've got good and bad bacteria in your gut? Of course not. Well, Lactobacillus casei is good bacteria. Each small bottle of Yakult contains over six billion bacteria in it. Impressive, hey? He shook his head; he didn't want six billion more bacteria in his gut, he was happy with what he already had. John came by, looking all-serious, face pockmarked with acne. You guys should be working, said John, who was one of those supervisors drunk on an ounce of power. Carrie replied, I was just informing Maestro about the benefits of having a probiotic drink once a day to boost your immune system. John frowned, the Maestro backed off, worried that he might burst a whitehead. It's true, he said, I have to know stuff like that in case a customer comes by and asks, you know, like, how many bacteria are in a bottle, that kind of thing. John looked him in the eye, De Niro style, and told him to go outside and stack trolleys in the car park. How come he gets to go out and I stay in the freezers? asked Carrie as he walked away. The Maestro turned round and winked. He always found himself shunted between one department and the other, ping ponged round when there was heavy grafting to be done. It was better like this when there was stuff to do outdoors, he'd have hated doing personal shopping for online orders. He took his jacket from the warehouse. It was nippy outside, but he knew, after a couple of minutes running about, he'd have to take it off again. Peter stopped him at the door. I know you've got a piece of frozen chicken in your left pocket, it's all here on CCTV, pal. The Maestro shook his head; Peter was going on loud enough for anyone in the vicinity to hear. The ladies at the cigarette kiosk laughed. Betty called out, Leave him be, Peter, he's only skinny, he needs the nutrition. He felt himself turn crimson, couldn't find a comeback line. The brain's too slow after a stint in frozen foods. The ladies at the kiosk were little oldies with honest faces, the kind that made you think it was a good idea to buy a lottery ticket. He walked out into the open, surveyed the car park all the way up to the green building, Corstorphine Police Station, sweeping round to the lane between PC World and McDonald's. Empty trolleys lay between the parked cars, used and discarded. No one thought about the poor sod who had to clear up after them. He watched a toff push a trolley into the middle of the road and leave it there before he drove off in his brand new Prius. Wanker, he thought. The cold made him crave a fag. He pushed those trolleys. For each one he parked in the rack, two more popped up. Hercules' Hydra. The Maestro felt the sweat drip from his armpits. Should have pinched a puff of Sure from Health and Beauty. He loved it outdoors, watching the cars negotiate the roundabout by the McDonald's, the American

Golf store beside the police station, the pet shop, daily life, commerce, people going by, the senseless muddle of it all. He stacked up more trolleys, creating a metallic millipede, bent his back and pushed them, straining the muscles in his arms to keep them on course. The last thing he needed was for them to crash into someone's car, ruining the bodywork, like Gary had done a few weeks back. It wasn't worth the hassle of the disciplinary: the inquiry, the formal letters, the health and safety training. Though Gary had come out of it all alright and got redeployed to the checkouts where the only risk that remained was of him dropping a can of baked beans on a customer's toe. He tried to drive his stack into the other trolleys by the railings, but he hit into the side of the last one. The impact jolted his shoulder making him wince. He pulled them back and tried his approach again, a complicated manoeuvre like a Harrier landing on a carrier. A cab pulled up. The cabbie got out and helped a mum with two tots load her shopping. He watched them drive away, out of the car park and then get caught at the traffic lights. You're daydreaming, Maestro, we don't pay you for that. It was Colin, coming to relieve him. Time for the Maestro's break. He went round the back, to the bins and the loading bays where the deliveries came through. A lorry was backing up. He smoked, watching it reverse, a robotic voice announcing: Attention, this vehicle is reversing. Attention, this vehicle is reversing. It bored through his skull and he could still hear it long after the lorry had stopped, its engine switched off. He watched piles of expired food being tipped into the skips outside, perfectly good food going to waste just because a label said otherwise. He was thinking. He had to stop himself from thinking. There were processes and procedures, a rule for everything, thought out and planned by head office. Once you started thinking for yourself, you were lost. At least that's what he thought about his job, and so far the idea of putting his brain in neutral at work had served him well. He'd seen blokes come in, get tired of the BS and leave in a matter of days – blokes who thought too much. He finished his fag, watched the lads offloading the lorry for a bit, and then went back to work. There was nothing else for the Maestro to do but to push and pull the trolleys back and forth across the car park like a robot, until the lights dimmed, the sun set and then it was time to go home. When he left, the lights in the store were still on, customers dribbled in and out. It was a twenty-four hour store, tills always ringing, never resting. He took the 12 on Meadow Place Road and watched cherry blossom swaying in the wind, carpeting the pavements with rich pink petals. It took him on to Bankhead Drive, where he dropped off just opposite Powerleague. He walked through Sighthill, with the towering block of Stevenson College to his left. It was empty, the lights left on. He went past the Lloyds offices and the sprawling buildings of HMRC, where he imagined goblins totting up cash destined for secret vaults. I've been watching too much Harry Potter, he thought. There was a spring in his step, the post-work endorphin surge working its way through his body. A few minutes later he was in the lift in Medwin South, one of the three high rises that brutalised the skyline in this part of the city. The doors opened and he walked through the screen door, which was broken, unlocked his front door, got in and closed it. The chirpy expression on his face dropped off like a mask falling from an actor's face. His shoulders slumped. He was offstage now. The strain of the heavy work caught up with him inside with a ferocious vengeance. He took off his shoes and stretched out his toes to sooth his aching feet. The Maestro moved to the bathroom and ran himself a warm bath, sprinkling Radox in it, churning it until it had a layer of bubbles. The foam clinging on to his arm crackled and popped. He stripped off and lowered himself, sinking down until the water touched his chin. It smelled divine, of sage and other herbs. Immersed in the water, there was nothing else for it but to close his eyes and relax, feeling like he was floating in the sea, somewhere warm, beyond the confines of his cramped flat. The day dissolved into the water, sinking away until nothing was left except the sound of his breath. He let more hot water in, not wanting to get out, lost in the wonderful, fragrant feeling in which he was cocooned. From outside he could hear two dogs barking, the sound travelling eight floors up to his flat. He let himself sink lower, raising his knees to create more space in the bath for his head to slip below the waterline, holding his breath as he drowned, the water entering his nostrils and ears. Everything was silent down below except the subtle noise of shifting water whenever he moved. He held on for as long as he could, emerged and took a deep breath of air. Afterwards, the Maestro dried himself and wrapped the towel round his waist. A few minutes later he was in the kitchen where he made himself a ham and cheese sandwich for tea. There seemed to be no incentive to bring out his pots and pans to cook just for one. The labour required, for today at least, was something he could not muster. Outside his window, he could see Dunsyre and Cobbinshaw, the two other twelve-storey blocks identical to his own, the only difference being the red and blue strips at the top of the respective buildings. Medwin had a yellow strip. He ate standing up, looking out into the night, his reflection in the double glazed window mirroring him. It was his lonely companion. A crescent moon hung somewhere in the sky, above the airport, in the distant west. The clouds had lifted and he could see it, an orange C sat above the horizon. There were no stars in the sky. He seldom saw them, blocked out as they were by the brilliance of the street lights. The city never knew night. He missed seeing the Milky Way stretching out, millions of stars, the vastness of creation. He finished his sandwich and washed it down with tap water. There was a brown envelope on the mantelpiece above an electric heater fashioned into something like a fireplace, a cheap imitation that was broken and which he had not bothered to replace. He took the envelope, ran his finger along the edge and replaced it. Books lay piled on the floor, against all four walls of the room, rising up to window level. The walls were white, bumpy where old bits of wallpaper had been painted over. Two unopened Amazon packages sat at the bottom of the fireplace, more books to add to the collection. He reached out for the Consolation of Philosophy, which he was reading, and had been, slowly, contemplatively for a week. This book, Boethius' masterpiece written when he was in prison, was one of those favourite texts he returned to time and again, hoping with each reading to unlearn the last and discover it anew. Each time he read the poetry of the words, he felt a kinship, as though he too was in bondage, searching for a higher meaning to life through reason. The pages were dog-eared from when he'd lent the book to Tatyana. While he was careful and used a bookmark, she folded the pages as though forcing her presence onto them. He opened the window, swinging it wide, placed the book on the ledge, pulled himself up and twisted round so he sat on it, looking into his flat, his back to the world. He could read easily with all the light coming from the streetlights below. Pg 38: Love governs lands and seas alike/ Love orders too the heavens above. Boethius thoughts captured, sealed in this vessel, the book, transmitted over the centuries to him. That was a mystical thing, he thought, as he read on. He arched his back, slowly controlling his movements like a ballerina until he found the exact point where his lower body and upper body were balanced, with the ledge acting as a pivot. He relaxed his muscles, feeling the cool breeze rush by. It was a precarious position; one that he found improved his concentration. After midnight there was stillness in the air, as if the city sighed and held its breath. There was no sound to be heard anywhere. It was the briefest of moments; so fleeting, so fragile that if you breathed you missed it. The Maestro had discovered this magical moment while reading a book by Jon McGregor. McGregor, that chronicler of ordinary life, finding little snapshots of beauty in the mundane and capturing them in amber, poetic prose. Every night, especially on nights he couldn't sleep, the Maestro looked for this one moment, and took pleasure in finding it, in the thought that he might be the only one experiencing it in the entire city. He flicked to the next page; the sound of the paper turning shattered the moment and the city started up again. In the distance he could hear a big lorry going along the bypass, the sound of a loud television coming from one of the flats, his own breath, the whole world turning in that familiar way, a confluence of old and new events, organisms that lived for a few minutes died next to those that lived for hundreds of years, instants piled upon moments becoming the fletching in the unidirectional arrow of time. He felt the familiar craving for a fag. He could hear the cranking of the cogs in his mind, a thought forming. Let there be light! Did this moment exist before he'd read McGregor, or had it always been there? And if it had, then why hadn't he noticed it before? Perhaps, he thought, it did not exist and only came to be after I read the book. If that was the case then he had to accept the terrifying notion that fiction had created a real moment in the real world from nothing but word. He recalled a trick by a writer who embedded the word – yawn – in his text and the readers who read this word found themselves yawning automatically once they had passed over it. A cheap trick or a small indication of the power of the word? Pg41: Mortal creatures have one overall concern. This they work at by toiling over a whole range of pursuits, advancing on different paths, but striving to attain the one goal of happiness. The Maestro felt lightheaded, the effect of blood rushing to his brain. In that moment he pondered if he were to let go, to cast himself down from this ledge (it was another of those intrusive thoughts, one so familiarly woven into the fabric of his mind that not a day went by without him thinking it), if he let go, would He send one of His angels so that not a hair on his body would be harmed. It was an appealing concept, the idea that once every so often the Divine intervenes in the workings of the cosmos, Joshua stops the Sun, Moses parts the Red Sea, so as to make His presence known, yet, in all likelihood, and the Maestro always came to the same conclusion, he would hurtle into the void, accelerating at nine point eight metres per second squared, simple physics, the predictable effects of gravity on an eleven stone, twenty-seven year old male body falling through the atmosphere, leaving only the hope that through the panicking, firing neurons there would be a moment of clarity in which everything is illuminated, a split second in which life itself was explained, the meaning of it all, past, present and future laid out, all making sense so that when, when he hit the ground, then at least it would have been worth something more than the aching emptiness he felt every day with each sunrise and sunset. The image of the falling man from 9/11 flashed into his mind. What had the man thought on the way down, was he just thinking, oh fuck, oh fuck, or was there some fundamental insight on the journey, plummeting to earth, the concrete-scarred ground rising to meet him? The scary thing, the Maestro realised, was not the falling, but what happened after the fall, Nothing, not even the nothing of the darkness of night or the nothing of emptiness; those were something at least, those were nothings that could be measured by the absence of a particular thing, and so they had an essence to them, a core beyond the event horizon. Not this, this was an incomprehensible Nothing, the nothingness of non-existence, beyond consciousness, a Nothingness that was not something, and so far beyond intellect that entire religions had to be formed to cover it up, to speculate its very being, a function of the causality-seeking neurons in the brain. So religion said the end was not The End, there was something larger, another chance, the weighing of scales so that there was a final justice, immortality, punishment, God, anything at all except the Nothing beyond proof that was waiting for the Maestro if he fell. This for the Maestro was the reason he read these books, to try to make sense of life, the side of the equation that was at least known. And so he hopped and hoped from one to the next, searching, trying to unlock the secrets of Kafka, Sartre, Dostoevsky, Nietzsche, hoping that one of them had peered behind the veil, into the unknown, so that a sliver of the unknowable was captured and contained in the words on a page. His mobile rang, startling him, and he let go of the book. It fell, hitting him on the chin, tumbling, flapping in the air like an owl trying to gain flight as it continued on its death spiral, round, round, round it went until it landed on the pavement with a clap. He hauled himself up and leapt off the windowsill into the flat. He answered his phone. Hello, he said, and it came out sounding more of a challenge than a greeting. The person at the other end was silent. In his haste he'd not checked the number, but he knew who it was. Maestro, why you are breathing so loud? Is this a bad time? It was Tatyana, the only person who would call him at this time, the only person who would call him at all. She mostly worked nights and, once she knew he was an insomniac, took it as a licence to call at any odd hour. I was just reading, he said. You're always reading, every time I telephone. Go out, boogie, it's Friday night, she replied. He waited for her to say something else; there was a silence that had to be filled. When he couldn't take it anymore, he asked, How's work? She thought about her answer. Tatyana was the kind of woman who could stare you down and win. It's busy as usual; nightshift is always busy, so many shelves to stack. You want to come and see me some time? He mumbled a reply about how he was busy and had a lot of reading to catch up on. She coaxed him and made him promise that they'd meet soon. Then she hung up. He closed the window. It was only now he noticed the chill in the night air. He ignored his familiar craving, telling himself he wasn't going to have another fag until morning. Almost without thinking, he ran his finger along the cold spine of a book. Of late, he found himself preferring the company of his books to the companionship of people. Tatyana was virtually his only friend, if he could call her that. Everyone else had forgotten him or given up on him once he'd withdrawn, almost as though he'd quietly sunk into quicksand that no one else could see. At work he was friendly, exuding something resembling warmth, but outside of work he kept to himself. There was something safe in the white pages of a book. A book could be opened and set aside. It could be read and reread, each time a new, deeper meaning deciphered. People, well, people were harder to read. So much was hidden in the twitch of the brow, a sweaty palm, the tenor of the voice, subtle gestures, and things left unsaid. People were moving, dynamic, inconsistent in a million ways. He imagined Tatyana at her shift, wiping shelves, replenishing them. He counted sheep, got to a hundred and stopped. He switched the TV on, flicking through many channels, and failing to find anything worth watching. There was an overwhelming choice, even avoiding the temptation of Playboy, Babestation and the late night adult entertainment channels. On National Geographic, a crocodile waited patiently in a river for a herd of kudu taking tentative steps to the banks. The narrator spoke in a cool, soothing voice, explaining how it had been a long dry season and that this was the only source of water for hundreds of miles. The kudu walked along the muddy banks, reached the river and began to drink. The Maestro watched as the crocodile drifted nearer and nearer, a floating log in the muck, and then in a flash it was all over for a baby kudu. Its mother watched helplessly from the banks as it was dragged into the murky brown waters. He remembered Boethius. He dressed, left his flat, took the lift and walked out of the security doors into the night, where he found the book on the pavement, unscathed.

The Magistrate prepared supper. He made a simple pasta bolognaise with a generous sprinkling of cheese. Another recipe from the TV. Chenai walked in, wearing faded jeans and a Biffy Clyro T-shirt. She kissed the bald patch on his head and rubbed it.

"Careful, one day you're going to be as bald as me," the Magistrate said.

"Eew."

"It's hereditary, remember your tete, Mai Munashe?" he laughed. "I'm going out to work tonight. You're a big girl, I'm sure you can look after yourself. You've got your mum's number and mine in case anything happens. Is that okay?"

"You got a J.O.B. Wicked." She jumped up and down, and hugged him as if she wanted to squeeze the breath out of him.

"It's only temporary, agency work, until something better comes up. Food's ready, help yourself."

He left before Mai Chenai was up, took the 21 on Niddrie Mains and paid for a single. The neighbourhood fell behind, the derelicts to his left and the new-builds that came after. He went past Alfonso's place near the Jack Kane Centre, an angular block of concrete that stood amidst open fields. He felt nervous; his entire life had been dedicated to the law, now he found himself taking the first tentative steps to a new profession.

When he thought about it, he found his life was coming full circle. Falling out of the middle class was harder on him than he could have imagined. The Magistrate grew up in the open spaces of Gutu, at his maternal grandfather's kumusha. His grandfather, a kind, hardworking man, had been a farmer. It was only through chance, the once in a generation aligning of stars, that the Magistrate had broken free from

47

the soil. He came of age at a time when the right education meant open doors and limitless opportunities.

The 21 rolled on, stopping at many stops, people getting off and others getting on. A man fumbled through his pockets, looking for the correct change. He threw his money down the fares box and off they went. They passed through Portobello, past the shops, the police station and the dog salon, the smell of salt in the air, over the robots and on to Seafield Road.

Travelling on the bus, he did not feel quite the same intensity traversing the city as he did while walking. It altered his perception of space at a mental and physical level. On his morning walks, he felt tiredness in his muscles, the full topographical awareness of how he was oriented on a gradient, a connectedness not possible at the same level of consciousness on the bus. He wondered what he was missing along the way. The bus depot was across the road. A few double-deckers were parked there. The sea lay in the distance, grey and still. A sailboat sailed towards the horizon. A feeling of internal dislocation swept over him, which way was South? Car dealerships and commercial spaces swept by. I have got to walk on my way home, he thought, even though he knew it was a long way. Unless he actually felt it in his limbs, he could not live it, make it a part of himself, a felt experience.

The bus took him deep into Restalrig, blanketed by the reek of the sewer works near the coast. The Magistrate clasped his hands together, his palms were sweaty. He went through Leith, past the Links, past the small QMUC campus and onto Great Junction Street. The streets were packed with young people going up town to the nightspots. He was close to his destination. Alfonso had given him an address on Ferry Road.

He got off after the BP garage and began to walk. Thank goodness it was Alfonso who told him how to get here. The natives gave directions using street names as if they were reading off maps, but how does one orient oneself without reference to a landmark in the environment? He checked his watch and saw there was only fifteen minutes before the start of his shift. He picked up pace, walking past a pub, checking the addresses. The pub was 183 and he needed to get to 205. His mobile rang.

"Where are you? Chenai told me you'd got a job. Why didn't you tell me?" Mai Chenai asked.

"You were asleep. I didn't want to wake you."

"Inga, makorokoto, what job is it?"

"I went to see Alfonso this afternoon and he arranged something straightaway." He hoped she wouldn't remind him that this is what she'd told him to do months ago.

"I'll have to thank him the next time I see him."

"I'm about to start my shift, how about we talk in the morning when we get home."

"Okay, but I don't like the idea of leaving Chenai at home alone. Perhaps it would be better if you did days and I continued with my nights."

"She's fifteen, she'll be fine. I've just arrived. We will talk later, okay." The building he'd arrived at was a double story Victorian house, built with the same grey masonry as most of the city. He pressed the buzzer and waited.

A woman buzzed him in. The stomach-churning odour of urine and faeces greeted him as the door opened. The smell was mixed with something else, something toxic and alien. Instinct told him it was the scent of human decay, death on the threshold, masked by talc. He took hesitant steps on the maroon carpet. A short woman wearing a plastic apron stepped into the corridor.

"Who are you?" she asked.

"The agency, Busy Bodies Recruitment and Employment Solutions, sent me."

"You're not Olu, we asked for Olu... She's a hard worker that one... Well, alright, don't just stand there, come on. I'll have to have a strong word with that Alfonso, sneaky wee cretin." She led him to the staff room that had seventies-style wallpaper and old sofas.

His tunic was tight across the waist and suffocating when he sat down on the sofa, which sunk as if it had no base. I need to trim a few pounds off the belly, he thought. Back home a pot belly was something to be admired, a sign of wealth and good living. It was the adverts mocking pot-bellied men that got to him. That was the power of the media. He recalled how when he'd first arrived they had saturation footage proclaiming Kylie Minogue had the best bum in the world. He'd scoffed at it, disagreed with their aesthetic judgement, but after months of the barrage in which prominent scientists had been wheeled out to postulate some mathematical formula on waist to hip ratio, proving that Kylie's body was biologically the epitome of fertility thus making her irresistibly attractive to men, the Magistrate submitted to the general consensus of science and reason, and agreed that she indeed had the best bum in the world.

"Oy, why on earth are you wearing steel toe caps?" the woman asked. "Never mind. It's time for handover. I'm Margo by the way." There were six other people in the room. One of them was a young man with a broad forehead and intelligent eyes. The young man listened to the nurse in charge attentively and took down notes. The rest were all women. The Magistrate couldn't make out what the nurse was saying; she spoke quickly, with an accent. He caught a few words, 'catheter', 'projectile vomiting', 'bowel movement'.

What have I got myself into? he thought.

"Right, any questions?" the nurse asked. She was in her forties, with a mole on her left cheek. An intimate look, unnoticed by most, passed between her and the young man. "Brian, darling, would you like to pair up with... erm." She turned to the Magistrate, "Sorry, I've forgotten your name, love. Brian, show him the ropes. You're used to the first-timers."

The Magistrate followed Brian through a brightly lit corridor lined with black and white portraits of old people. He struggled against an overwhelming urge to throw up. Now and again he held his breath. Brian walked casually through the putrid atmosphere, seemingly oblivious. They went into the sluice room.

"You haven't done this before, have you?" Brian asked.

"God help me," the Magistrate replied.

"Ah, I can tell from your accent kuti muri wekumusha. Makadini Baba." Brian clapped his hands. The Magistrate was surprised to find his countryman here of all places. Brian's accent was a hybrid with a Londoner's lilt mixed in with the odd Americanism. "Hang on, you're Chenai's father, aren't you? We came to your house a few months ago for a prayer meeting." The Magistrate didn't recognise him. His wife had taken up with a Pentecostal church and, while he tolerated her church guests, he left for walks once their prayer sessions started.

"Don't worry," said Brian, "I'll teach you everything you need to know. We have to settle all the residents in the east wing. Piece of cake, a few of them are bedbound anyway."

Brian packed a trolley with incontinence pads, urine bottles, wipes, catheter bags, sheets, pillowcases, tools of the trade alien to the Magistrate. They walked down the corridor to the first room with a brass number fixed to the door. The resident's name, Joan Dowler, was written on a piece of paper glued below the number.

"Hello Joan." Brian's voice had a higher pitch now, almost effeminate. "Joan's one of our oldest, she's been here forever. She's a lovely old thing."

The Magistrate cringed at the rotten odour coming from her bed. Joan made gurgling noises. She was lying on a bed with cot sides raised. She was a bony creature, propped up on either side by pillows, her hair a wild, curly mess. The Magistrate felt a mixture of pity and revulsion.

"God, is it worth living in such a state?" The words came out involuntarily.

"It's not for us to judge. All I know is that we're only here for the blink of an eye, and so every experience, good and bad, pain and pleasure, must be worth it. My job is to make sure they are comfortable in their last days," Brian said, stroking Joan's hair. The old woman cooed. There was a little radio in the room and Brian played a Jim Reeves CD. Joan lay still, looking as though she was lost in some sweet reminiscence. "She likes the music. It helps her sleep. We better hurry up, we have to get them all settled before Linda comes through on her drug round."

Outside the window was a pine tree. The sun had gone down and that side of the building was in darkness. Brian emptied the catheter and asked the Magistrate to roll her on her side. She had tubes running through her nose, feeding her yellowy syrup from a machine beside the bed. He cringed involuntarily as Brian pulled the covers off. He was not convinced that a life tied to one's bed was a life worth living. Putrid pus ran down her side from the bedsores on her back. He heaved but managed to stop himself.

"I have to tell Linda the dressings have come off again," Brian said, oblivious to the Magistrate's discomfort. "We need to turn her from side to side every two hours, all through the night."

They finished with Joan and moved to the next room. There was an old man within, sitting on a chair, talking to himself. "I killed Hitler, I killed Hitler. Oh, God save me, I killed him."

"Fred," said Brian, "it's time for bed."

"I killed Hitler."

"I know, and you got a medal for it, remember?" Brian winked at the Magistrate. "Fred fought in the war. He likes to remind us of that from time to time."

"There've been a great many wars in these parts," the Magistrate said. "It's funny how they almost turned it into sport."

"You'd all be speaking German if it wasn't for me," said Fred.

"I know, Fred, you tell me that every night. But here I am speaking English instead. Ain't that something?"

They propped him up on either side, Fred fighting them every step of the way. The Magistrate felt the full weight of the man against him. Fred wobbled with every step. "Come on, one foot at a time," Brian encouraged him.

"You bloody Nazis, the lot of you, let me go,' said Fred. "Is this how you treat a prisoner of war?" They reached the bed and gently helped him down. Fred kicked the Magistrate on the shin. He wasn't going down without a fight. There was a photo of him on the wall, a young man in military dress staring straight into the camera. On his bedside cabinet was another photo of Fred in a suit, holding his bride who wore a flowing wedding dress. A little of the young man was left in the old Fred, especially in the eyes, which had not lost their mischievous shine.

"I need to spend a penny," said Fred.

"You won't buy much with a penny these days," replied the Magistrate.

"He means he needs to do number one, to micturate, kuita weti… You'll get used to the lingo," Brian laughed. He gave Fred a bottle and they turned aside while he did his business. "Stay alert or Fred might baptise you by throwing the bottle at you. Trust me, he's got me a couple of times. Biological warfare is illegal under the Geneva Conventions, but he doesn't seem to care."

After they finished with Fred, they went round the wing, settling the other residents. There was another section upstairs where they had to drain catheters, give water, put people to bed and collect human waste at an industrial pace. They met Irene, who had a habit of howling all night, Tom, who was zombified, Susan, who could manage reasonably well with her zimmer frame, Kathleen, the grouch, who wanted to be left alone to die, and Eric, who liked walking around naked, flashing his willy, saying, "Not bad for ninety-five, hey." There were too many faces, too many people in these small catacombs. The Magistrate wondered how Brian knew all of them so well when they could only spend a few minutes with each one.

Brian handed him the wipes. "You have to learn how to do this eventually."

The Magistrate had heard about these places before and the reality was worse than the stories. It was incomprehensible to him that these people, who, after all, were fathers, mothers, brothers, sisters, could be rounded up in this Gulag, waiting to die. Was this the fate that awaited him should he stay in this country for too long? Would Chenai allow that? She was already too modern, too westernised.

They had a full yellow bag when they walked back to the sluice. He'd never once changed Chenai's nappies, there was always the maid for that sort of thing – how he missed her. His feet ached. The safety shoes pinched his small toes. Brian showed him how to use the sluicemaster into which they poured the waste.

"How can anyone send their parents to die in such a place?" he asked.

"You haven't been here that long, have you? They say people out here are cash rich and time poor. Haven't you felt how time speeds up as soon as you leave the airport terminal? Sometimes you have the odd long day, but the weeks and months rush by, like that." Brian clicked his fingers to emphasize his point. A buzzer rang. "I'll go and get the first one, you go over to the staff room and have a bit of a breather. Brace yourself, they'll be going off all night."

The Magistrate took a seat in the staff room, shell-shocked and dazed. He felt as though he was in a dream, drifting through a heavy fog, an alternative reality. The clock said it was after midnight. His back ached from hauling bodies up beds, bending over, picking things up. He was no stranger to the backbreaking hoe work in his grandfather's fields, yet he was convinced this was a different kind of pain. In the fields with the soft earth beneath your feet and the open sky above, you hardly felt the strain. It was massaged by the soothing voices of family, banter, the gossip about the neighbours, and the satisfaction that your labour was meaningful. There was nothing like watching your seedlings grow, tending them until they matured. It was different from this, this cultivating the field of death, the living dead groaning in their cots.

"You look lost in thought, pal," the woman in the plastic apron said to him. "Brian says this is your first time and you're doing alright. Fancy a cuppa?"

"Pardon?"

"Cup of tea." He nodded. "So what did you do before this?"

"I was unemployed," he replied.

"Before that. You couldnae 'ave been on the dole all your life now."

The Magistrate hesitated. It wouldn't make any sense, here of all places, to explain what his past life had been. "I had an office job. You know, pushing papers."

"I guessed it. No offence, but you dinnae look too cut oot for this line of work."

She gave him a cup of tea. He took a sip. It was too milky. The woman picked up a magazine. Another buzzer went off. An orange light on the board near the clock blinked on and off.

"That's one of yours. You've got the east wing, rooms twenty-nine to fifty-five. We've got the west."

As the night wore on, he could hardly keep his eyes open as they went about their patrols. Brian was cheerful and chatty all the time. The Magistrate wondered what a smart young man like him could be doing in one of these places. It was a travesty, he thought, and said it bluntly to Brian in the way one countryman can to another.

"No experience in life is ever wasted, that's my philosophy." Brian shrugged. The Magistrate didn't pursue the issue. He was far too tired for that.

In the morning he walked down the front stairs of the building and inhaled deeply, filling his lungs with sweet morning air. He'd survived the night. Cars crawled in both directions on Ferry Road. He'd forgotten his idea of walking home. It came back to him when he saw Arthur's Seat in the distance, but he was too exhausted. Every fibre of his being ached. Brian came running after him.

"You look terrible, Baba Chenai."

"It's called PTSD."

"Well, they liked your style in there, though Margo says you're too quiet, almost like you're used to hearing other people speak instead of talking yourself. You need to open up, let yourself go a bit. Not bad for a first night, though. There's a couple of shifts opening up and they'll have you back if you like." Brian's enthusiasm depressed the Magistrate.

"Let me go home first and recover." They laughed.

He caught the 21 marked for the Royal Infirmary, which took him home. The smell of the care home was snagged onto his clothes. He undressed and threw his clothes in the washing machine, lumbered up the stairs and ran himself a hot bath. He scrubbed himself raw, using copious amounts of gel all over his body. He even washed inside his nostrils to try and get rid of the smell that seemed lodged inside. When he was done, he lay in the water, soaking, feeling the warmth.

After bathing, he found Amai Chenai in bed, asleep. He kissed her on the cheek. Now he understood something about her world. He could forgive her irritability. One night shift was enough to make him see. She muttered something in her sleep. A slight smile was on her face. He embraced her and fell into a deep, dreamless sleep.

A knock on the door woke him. He rubbed his eyes and looked at the clock, it was only one o'clock. He stretched, grabbed his robe and went down the stairs, half asleep. When he opened the door he saw Alfonso holding a paper bag.

"I have so much to tell you," Alfonso said, dashing in.

"Can't it wait, we're still sleeping. Inga, you know I was on nightshift."

"Have some of this, it will perk you up." Alfonso thrust a quart of whisky at him.

"It's one o'clock in the afternoon."

"Then you need it even more," Alfonso said, grinning like a Cheshire cat. "Come sit with me. Look, I'm having a beer, just for you, but I have to dash back to the office in a little while." Alfonso switched on the TV. It went straight to one of Chenai's music channels. A rapper was bragging about how he'd been shot and survived.

"Before I forget, you have to listen to this one." Alfonso brought out a pirate TDK cassette and gave it to the Magistrate. "I told you I would find you a good job, didn't I? No one can say Alfonso doesn't keep his promises. They loved you at the care home. They are absolutely raving about you. They said you were magnificent, a stunning debut. Now listen to this, one of their care assistants is going on maternity leave and they want you to cover."

The Magistrate could tell the praise was exaggerated. There is only so much one could expect for shovelling Augean bucket loads of faeces. Still, any extra work would be welcome, given the circumstances. Alfonso sipped his Stella, his eyes darting about the place. He changed the channel to the news. An earthquake had hit some place and grim survivors loitered about in shock.

"Signs and wonders. The world is coming to an end," said Alfonso.

"They say that every year."

"I've heard of a man in America who has made the right calculations using secret codes in the Bible that only the righteous can know."

"I think Newton had it down for 2060, some say the Mayans have it for 2012. There was a guy who said it would happen in 1998, and guess what – we're still here."

Alfonso frowned. "My guy has it down for 2010. And now you've given me two other dates." He counted on his fingers. "So which is it?"

The Magistrate sighed, just keeping his eyes open was hard enough. Alfonso raised his can and proposed a toast to the end of the world. The Magistrate was glad to drink to it. Chenai walked in carrying her satchel.

"Hi, Dad. Hi, Uncle Alfonso." She sounded chirpy. "Dad, I have a surprise for you. Close your eyes."

The Magistrate closed them and felt like he would never open them again.

"Open them." He did so and Chenai was holding out a Sony Walkman with orange headphones.

"I haven't seen one of these in years."

"I know. It's so retro isn't it? I got it off Liam; he had it years ago but everyone's into iPods and MP3 players now. It still works. I figured you could listen to your gwash music."

"Who's Liam?"

"Just a mate from school."

The Magistrate reminded himself that things were different here. Girls could be friends with boys, something unheard of in his time. But still, he'd remember this name, Liam. Alfonso wouldn't leave it at that. "Is this Liam from a good family?"

"His father's a councillor." Chenai gave him a fierce look.

"Tell this Liam, I said, 'Thank you for such a kind gift.'" The Magistrate smiled and Chenai bounded upstairs. He took a sip of his whisky straight from the bottle and felt the inebriating warmth radiate through him, along with the beginnings of a new future.

Deco passes the ball to Ronaldinho who dribbles, nutmegs a defender and lays a sitter through to Eto'o who drives it over the top bar, kneels down and buries his head in shame.

'Eto'o, *uri kuda bhora rakaita sei*?' Farai shouts at the screen.

Brian breathes a sigh of relief, his Man Red defense is proving to be leaky against Farai's Barcelona, but the game is still 1-0 in his favor after a cheeky Rooney dink in the 25th. He's got to hold it together against wave after wave of Barcelona attacks. Farai pauses **I I**, goes to the settings, and substitutes Giuly for Saviola.

Eto'o
Ronaldinho   Saviola

Deco   Xavi

Edmilson
Van Bronckhorst   Oleguer

Puyol   Márquez

V. Valdés

'I'd have substituted Eto'o, he ain't doing nothing,' says Brian.

'Worry about your own team, dude.'

Play▶. The game continues, 90 minutes compressed into 10 minutes of uberhyperreality. The commentary follows every tackle, every through pass on the 42-inch plasma screen. Farai's thumbs ache, he keeps bashing the buttons. He's 2 games behind in the best of 5. He needs to get this one back or it's all over.

The Xbox 360 purrs away, 60GB of raw computing power. It could have sent the Beagle to Mars. Farai's first gaming experience was Pong on his Atari, a gift from Uncle Douglas in America. He played that thing to death. He remembers hanging with his mates, connecting it to their cathode ray tube TV on afternoons after school and waiting for the game to warm up. ZBC didn't start broadcasting till 4 pm, so there wasn't anything to watch anyway, except the multicolored round thing with the time on it. There was nothing more exciting than seeing that little square ball bounce back and forth on the screen. Back then it wasn't thumbs that hurt but wrists from turning the nob on the console.

In the 90s, progress happened. Big Bite opened at the Parkade just off Samora Machel. At the weekends, he'd go with his mates, pockets full of change, to the new arcade. They were all into Street Fighter and Mortal Kombat, which was cool, but Farai was retro, he was a Pacman guy, and sometimes Rally-X too. The lights in Big Bite were always dim. Around the walls were the blinking screens promising electropleasure for the malleable pubescent males who crowded round the games. You had to be savvy and have your wits about you, because the colored kids patrolled the den, crowding players and picking pockets. Farai fought epic battles in those mazes, and when he went home to bed, he'd dream of 👾, always 👾, chasing him around the house. He'd wake up in a sweat, horrified at the prospect of the GAME OVER screen and that soul-destroying electronic sound effect.

Rooney blasts 1 well wide of the net. That's half time, 5 minutes of play in real time.

'You guys fancy a beer?' Scott asks from the sidelines.

'I've never said no to a beer in my entire life,' Farai replies.

He watches Brian agonize over his substitutions, checking the energy meters to see which players are sagging, and the defense is, because Farai's attack has been relentless, and the back 4 always pay the price. He's sure he can sneak 2 in, and hopes that Puyol keeps things tight at the back. There's no need to play real football, the experience is packaged for him in the comfort of his living room. He doesn't even need to break a sweat for it.

'Come on, let's play already,' he says.

'Patience,' Brian replies. 'Mr Miyagi say, "Wax on, wax off."'

'That doesn't make any sense whatsoever.'

Brian finishes setting up his team. The `commentators` drone on about how it was an exciting first half and they are hoping for more of the same in the second. Scott comes back with the beers and hands them 1 each. There's a knock on the door.

'It's Stacey. Can you get it, Scott?' asks Farai, eyes glued to the screen.

Scott goes to the door and comes back with Stacey. She's wearing a pair of incredibly large hoop earrings. She kisses Farai on the crown of his head.

'I thought you said you'd be done with your ProEvo by the time I got here.'

'I know, babes, but it's the best of 5.'

'So, you expect me to just sit here while you and your boys drink beer and play video games?' She covers his eyes.

Farai wriggles out. 'Babes, don't. I'm waging a comeback here.'

'You haven't even looked at me, it's like you're psychoaddicted to this game. Come on, switch over to the TV, so we can all watch something.'

'That's what I've been saying to them all night,' says Scott.

'Only coz you got knocked out,' Brian replies.

Stacey pinches Farai's beer, sits down on the couch and twirls her long red hair round her index finger. They've been going out for a year now. Stacey did a short stint as a porno actress when she was 19. There's a brief clip of her on a free2view site in which she is pummelled from behind by a Neanderthal with a post-apocalyptic nuclear radiation penis, pulling her hair with 1 hand and slapping her ass with the other. In it she looks young, a little nymph. She gives an amateurish performance, moaning mechanically and not looking into the camera often enough – a crucial technique for enticing the viewer, who presumably would be getting off. The clip ends when the man pulls out of her abruptly, runs round to the front, jerks her head back forcefully and blows an incredible load of spunk all over her face, all the while crying, 'Raaaaaah'. All in all, it was a half-decent performance and Stacey clearly had potential in the field.

She'd told Farai about her short history in the industry and he'd encouraged her to pursue her career, but she was out of it for good. The golden age of the porno industry was all but over. In the 80s VHS brought porn into every home with a VCR. Tapes were sold under the counter, traded between aficionados. In the 90s, as in any industry, a new cohort of stars came through, primed and positioned for the DVD market. The films they made had production value; they had directors and something resembling a script, a storyline, pure entertainment value, no expense spared. But then the internet happened – a black hole of immeasurable gravitational power. It screwed up the market big time. Supply and Demand, simple economics. The free2view websites that popped up virtually killed off the commercial end of the market. Who would buy a DVD when there was this unlimited supply online, available discreetly, catering for every taste, mature, gonzo, anal, fisting, girlongirl, hentai, animalporn, bukaki? And so, future potential starlets like Stacey never got the chance to blossom.

'Goooooooaaal,' Brian cries out, as Saha runs to the terraces to celebrate.

'I get more attention from Mr Majeika,' says Stacey.

Farai throws his controller down and groans in agony. 2-0 in injury time. The ref allows him to kick-off and blows the final whistle after a couple of passes. The commentators drone on their rote lines about what a wonderful, action packed match it was.

'We wuz robbed,' says Farai, getting up.

'Loser,' Brian replies, disconnecting the console and switching from AV to TV.

Farai sits next to Stacey. She turns away when he tries to kiss her.

'Oh, so now you want me after you've lost.' She feigns annoyance.

'Babes, you know I have to do this. It's my life. I could get signed to the Premier League and our lives would be sorted for life.'

'We'll see if you're still singing that same tune later on tonight,' she says, giving him a peck on the cheek.

Farai takes the beer from her and drinks. There's a weird spasm in his left thumb, as if the vibration of the controller is still going through him. Mr Majeika is hopping about in his hutch. A rerun of *Dirty Dancing* plays on TV. Farai reaches for the remote to change the channel.

'Hey, I'm watching that,' says Stacey. She snatches it from him.

'You've got to be kidding me.'

'You boys had *your* football. I'm gonna have *my* Patrick Swayze.'

'Look at those pants, we can't watch this.' Brian enters the fray.

'Give me the remote,' Farai says. 'It's too powerful a device to be entrusted to a woman.'

Stacey resists and holds on to it. The boys endure the cheesy songs and the cheesy dancing. Farai considers getting a small TV for his bedroom. Stacey sings along to the Drifters, lingering over the word *tenderness*, her fist curled around an invisible mic.

'I wish I'd be born in the 50s or 60s, everything was just so glamorous back then. The music was real, it had feeling, you know what I mean?' she asks.

'I know,' Brian replies, sipping on his beer. 'Back in those days people were polite, they were more honest, everyone knew their neighbors. There wasn't all this type of stress that we have to deal with these days. It was just so much better. I wish I'd been born back then too.'

'Nigga please, are you kidding me?' asks Farai. 'You, Stacey, would have been in some tenement block with no central heating, sharing an outside toilet with a dozen other families. You'd have had your tits felt up by your fat, stinky boss at work, that is, if you were lucky enough to be something respectable, like a secretary, you know, women's jobs. But you'd have been doing alright. You, on the other hand, Brian, where do I even start? Dude, niggas ain't had it this good in 300 years and you wanna time travel back to the 50s? *Shiiit*, you'd have wound up in some township being tear gassed and having dogs set on you by those motherfucking Rhodies. You wanna go back to the 50s? Nah, bro, fuck the 50s!'

'You know what, we were just having a nice conversation, and you have to go and ruin it,' says Stacey.

'I'm just injecting a dose of realism into your fantasy.'

'Well, no one asked you to,' she says.

'Stacey, I love you, babes, but when the revolution starts, I'm gonna kill you first, just to show them I'm serious.'

'You're *sooo* full of shit, Farai.' Stacey leans over and kisses him.

Patrick Swayze is wriggling his bum on TV, offending Brian with his tight pants.

***

Friday morning. Farai heads to the library where he's booked a carrel. A steady trickle of people going to work walk along the paths. A man in a suit holds his partner's hand. She laughs at something he has said. It's cute, proper `Act1: They Meet`. Farai wonders how long before `The Chase`.

He walks up the steps, into the library, going through the EM detectors. Through the windows he catches a view of the park. Elms line the network of footpaths through broad, open grounds of green grass. A bunch of hippy-looking types catch the early morning rays. 1 of them, a guy with long, blonde dreadlocks, chats away, gesturing wildly. Runners in bright outfits do circuits around the park.

There are a handful of people in the library. The youngish looking kids are getting ready for resits, Farai reckons, even though he can't comprehend how on earth anyone could flunk the first year of uni. It takes him back to his time at Wits, doing his maths undergrad. He spent his first year prowling Joburg's nightlife, hitting the top class clubs in the city and the shebeens in Soweto, listening to kwaito, digong, and house. Farai is 1 of those charmed people for whom academic life never presented any real challenges. He breezed through school way too easily, without ever being stretched. Back then, going over Wiles' proof of Fermat's Last Theorem, he thought he would solve 1 of the Millennium Prize Problems. He was 19, with 24 points for his A-Levels, so he had had every right to be cocky and to expect that he would set the world alight. But, as he went through uni, he realized that he was 1 of those unfortunate souls who have an aptitude for comprehending complex mathematical theories, but lacked the extra genius to see behind the wall and discover new mathematics. That is, for all his processing power, he was merely a human calculator: `INPUT` $\rightarrow$ `OUTPUT` – the type of virtuoso who can play an instrument beautifully, but cannot compose to save his life. He was intelligent enough to understand that mathematics is a young man's game and by 30 the genius is gone. Though he occasionally picks up the odd unsolved problem, at 24 he's at peace with the idea that his 'contribution' to humanity would have to be in something else.

Farai picks up a few textbooks and goes to his carrel. He boots up his Vaio and listens to the voices from the park pierce through the double-glazed windows. Despite his discipline, the unregimented life of a doctoral student bothers him. He misses the odd caning, just to get himself into gear. He thinks about his mates from high school, scattered across the globe. It's like they all left: Australia, New Zealand, South

Africa, Botswana, Namibia, America, Canada, the UK, places in the Anglosphere where the natives spoke in strange accents. In pre-colonial times, when land was plentiful, bad chiefs were not deposed. Instead, people would break away to settle under a different chief or form their own arrangement. A chief without people to rule soon found himself powerless.

History seeps into the present. His laptop beeps, the Windows logo comes up; he types ************ and presses ↵ . He waits for the programs to load and wishes he'd brought coffee in a flask. He can't stand the ready-made stuff from the machine, which tastes like pig's pee.

He connects on to the wifi and checks his uni emails. He has to wade through rafts of announcements before he gets to 1 from Prof Marlow, asking him to come in for a meeting on Monday. He doesn't want the meeting just now. He's still got loads of work to do on his thesis, 'to make a small but *significant* contribution to human knowledge.' *Why do we bother with this stuff? It's like most theses go down a pit latrine anyway*, he thinks. It's a small consolation that Einstein bollocksed up his PhD on Avogadro's number, getting the calculation wrong by a factor of 3. It's on days like this he reckons he should have stopped after his Master's and taken that job with Alexander Forbes in SA.

Farai's doctorate is on The Economic Incentives for Sustaining Temporary Hyperinflationary Environments. He wishes he could add an extra 'S' word at the end so the acronym kinda sounds like testes; that way, when people ask what he does, he can say he's in the adult industry. Prof Marlow initially wanted him to consider doing something on game theory, because the department is full of game theorists.

'This is a PhD, not Freakonomics,' the Prof had said.

Farai argued that it was a subject worth exploring. He had, anecdotally at least, seen people at the very top benefiting from hyperinflation, acquiring prime real estate at a pittance and converting worthless paper into hard currency. Since hyperinflation in economies is always a temporary state, a study of how people in power and in business took advantage of this temporary state would be of academic interest.

It is easier for him to approach the problem from afar, as a detached academic, than to have to deal with the day-to-day effects of it. He remembers that he has to book a flight home for the holidays. The choice is between BA and Air Zim. The patriot in him chooses Air Zim. He figures if he got his mum to buy the ticket for him in Z$ he'd save about 30%; the trade-off is that he might find himself stranded at the airport if the president or his wife happened to commandeer that particular flight. On balance he has to decide if his time is worth £300.

He reads Sònia Muñoz's IMF working paper, *Suppressed Inflation and Money Demand in Zimbabwe*. The title seems a little ironic since Gono has the printing presses working full steam at the RBZ. It makes for dry reading on a Friday. *Financially repressed regimes are characterized by suppressed prices, which lower the rate of real economic growth and retard the development process. Suppressed inflation describes a situation in which, at existing wages and prices, the aggregate demand for current output and labor services exceed the corresponding aggregate supply* (Barro and Grossman, 1974). Try keeping your eyes open while reading that.

There are shouts from people playing footie in the park, taking advantage of a rare spell of sunshine. He doesn't think they should even call it summer here. Winter – Winter-lite would be more appropriate terms for this climate.

I should have gone to Charles Sturt or Queensland, he thinks, lingering on the Fisher Equation on the footnotes on page 5 of the report.

He logs back into his email, nothing new there. He flips to hi5, Greg has sent him a hi5 gift, a virtual `beer mug`. Everything's online, ethereal, bits of data floating through cyberspace, untouchable, unknowable. He sends Greg a `Warrior` gift. No need to even message each other. His mobile vibrates ✉:

Stacey
finkin abt u bb xx

He replies:

finkin abt u2 huni
will cme round 2
urs 18r xxx

She writes back:

Stacey
♥ xxxx

He scans the online news sites, newzimbabwe.com, zimdaily.com, herald.co.zw, the *Fingaz* link is down again. He reads a piece about a man in Muzarabani who caught his third wife cheating with his eldest son. As he is scanning through this, he comes across a story about a *n'anga* who's convinced some government ministers that she can get diesel from a rock. The cabinet seems convinced that this is a gift from the ancestors to help the country weather economic sanctions by the West. *That's gonna put BP out of business.*

No new emails, he refreshes his inbox. While studying Angola from 1991 to 1995, he came across the work of the little known economist, Chilala dos Santos Lima Climente, referenced in an IMF paper on Angolan fiscal policy. Farai could not find the paper online, written when Climente was an associate professor at the Universidade Agostinho Neto. He emailed the university in Luanda 4 times, but received no reply. He phoned several times, each time failing to get through because the receptionist didn't speak English. A sign of his anglicization is that he gets annoyed when he speaks with people who don't understand English.

He finally managed to get Nika, a Mozambican postgrad in the chemistry department, to make the call on his behalf. She deciphered that the receptionist had been trying all along to tell Farai that Climente had been shot dead in November 1999. A researcher in the *Department de Economia* readily agreed to send a copy of the work.

The paper came through, a month and a half later, in a brown envelope with tattered corners. There were 31 loose sheets, photocopied and bound together by a piece of green string that ran through a hole in the top left corner. The paper was simply entitled *Hiperinsuflação*, published in 1998. There were lines running across the pages because of the poor quality copier but the text was, in the main, legible.

Nika translated the paper for Farai, who, in return, helped her with the statistical analysis of the results of her own research. The part of Climente's *Hiperinsuflação* that inspired Farai was only 2 paragraphs long, covering just over half a page in which Climente outlined that there had been winners during Angola's hyperinflationary period. Climente argued that conscientious investment in hyperinflationary economies may prove to be a risky but highly rewarding investment strategy for people in positions of power, thereby creating a positive feedback loop rewarding negative governance, prolonging crises. There was some indication that Climente wanted to pursue this area further, but when Nika contacted the University she was told that he had not published anything else before he died.

Farai wanted access to other material by Climente. He found something irresistible about the dead economist's work as though, intuitively, he'd stumbled on something that was so commonsensical that someone else should have arrived at that position a long time ago. Did the world really have to wait for Newton to discover gravity when everyone else felt it and saw its effects? Those were the best discoveries, the ones that seemed so obvious that they were right there for the taking. He knew he risked forming an idea of a man whom he did not know, a fantasy in his mind that could prove fallacious but the idea was too tempting.

By the time his thesis is done, he'll have read over 100 papers. The thought depresses him. He logs off and shuts his Vaio. It's clear to him now that he won't get any work done today. It's difficult to concentrate with his mind hopscotching about the place. He packs his gear, dumps the books on a vacant table and walks out of the library. He goes to the Mosque car park, picks up his car and drives to Restalrig.

Stacey and her mum live in a 4-in-a-block on Lochend Avenue. It's a neat little place with a short hedge round the front and back garden. So many houses in such a small space. He reckons his parents' place in Highlands would have taken up half the street. He knocks on the first door to his right, number 1. Jane, Stacey's mum, lets him in.

'Hi. Not seen you in a wee while, Farai,' she says, pronouncing his name Fry. She kisses him on the cheek.

'I've been busy with uni stuff... J-jane.' He always hesitates with her name. It's like, he's never gotten the hang of calling grown-ups by their first name, let alone his girlfriend's mum. He still doesn't feel like an adult himself. Jane doesn't like being called Mrs Gordon – or should that be Ms? He hasn't a clue. What he does know is that mum's a MILF, 7/10, especially in her butt hugging bottoms. Jane's only in her late 30s, and swears the fags keep her slim. She's blonde, peroxide blonde – maybe – only her hairdresser knows.

'Stacey's just out getting some fags, she'll be back in a bit,' she says. 'Kirsty wants to see you. She's got stuff she wants to ask you for her maths.'

'Isn't she on a break?'

'Yeah, but she disnae want to end up like her poor mum or her sister, so she's on the books every day, ken what I mean?'

'Don't worry, I'll get her sorted. I should bill her for all the tutoring I've been doing.'

Stacey walks in with a shopping bag. She kisses Farai and gives the bag to her mum. Kirsty calls out 'hi' to Farai from somewhere in the bedrooms. Jane leaves to make a cuppa, and Farai and Stacey hang out in her bedroom.

The Magistrate struggled to adjust to the rhythm of the night. Busy Bodies had him on a four nights a week rota, occasionally calling him in on his nights off when they had extra shifts elsewhere. He found it hard to sleep on some days, instead, spending hours in the living room watching the repetitive news with its daily dose of terror. The TV showed bearded Arabs in caves pronouncing death threats to the West. It induced a civilized anxiety in him.

He left early while Mai Chenai was still readying herself for her shift, walked past the dentists' and waited for the 14. A woman with a buggy turned to him. She had no front teeth and her hair was tied back à la Croydon facelift.

"Wath thime is ith?" she asked, and he told her. "Ith's bloomin lath agin."

He didn't know how to reply. As far as he was concerned, the bus being a few minutes late was no big deal. The mere fact that one had some indication of when the bus might come was amazing in and of itself, and the cast iron guarantee that the bus would come was even more astounding. He'd have loved to tell her about kombis, though he'd owned a car for most of his working life.

"It's a windy day today," he said, finally.

"Aye."

He got on the bus, switched on his Walkman and caught a song halfway through. He laughed at the irony of Chimombe singing, 'Zvikaramba zvakadaro, ndinotsika mafuta, ndiende Bindura, handina zvinoera.' Now this song would fix his memory to the 14 going past the Craigmillar high rises, which stood at the edge of the estate, a stone's throw from Peffermill. They went past the playing fields and the commercial blocks opposite. He'd always associated James Chimombe with John Chibadura. The two singers, with their perms, had distinctly

71

different styles, yet, when it came to local artists, he always thought of them in pairs. His mind linked Mtukudzi with Mapfumo, Hosiah Chipanga to Mechanic Manyeruke, Zhakata and Makioni, Munhumumwe and Mashakada, as if to find a ying and a yang. Chipanga and Manyeruke both had a worldly, electric style of gospel music but with the rest it was more a fusion of convenience. He could never imagine Leonard Dembo without thinking of System Tazvida. That was just the way he thought of them.

The bus drove past the Commonwealth Pool. The Magistrate wondered why Sungura had so few female artists. He could not think of one off the top of his head, except maybe for Katarina, who was Safirio Madzikatire's backing vocalist and dancer, visible in her own right in the eighties, though her solo success had been limited. Male artists sometimes took female parts in the music, forming a sub-genre of the art form. The Marxist Brothers sang *Murume Wangu* in the voice of a battered woman telling her husband how his actions hurt her, asking if he no longer loved her so she could be free to return to her parents. This feminisation of the male artist was socially acceptable and an example of the range of social issues the Sungura artists covered. John Chibadura's song, also entitled *Murume Wangu*, had an abused wife asking her husband to return her to her parents' home. Then there was Simon Chimbetu's popular *Samanyika* that went, 'Samanyika murume wangu', yet again the same theme, the only variation being the inclusion of the eastern totem in the title. Was it right for these men to sing on behalf of women, to appropriate their voice, so to speak? The women in the songs were always begging for relief and the power to release them lay firmly in the husbands' hands. This was the unpalatable truth about society, and, perhaps, therein lay the reason there were no female Sungura artists of note. A song without a message could not be true Sungura. The voice behind the music had to carry authority and that authority lay in the male voice. This was not to say there were no female musicians. Mbuya Stella Chiweshe and Chiwoniso found international fame with their traditional mbira music. Ivy Kombo, Fungisai and others dominated the gospel scene, yet there seemed to be no space for these voices in Sungura, this dominant form of music.

He went through Newington, down Clerk Street, past Tesco and the little cluster of ethnic shops on Nicolson Street, down on to the Bridges. There were walkers, Thursday late night shoppers, going to and fro on the pavements. The road was alive with buses, black cabs and private cars. From his seat on the top deck he had a view of the castle caught in the fading light. Below were the transparent roofing sheets of Waverley Station. The Balmoral stood grand ahead of him.

He turned to the other side of North Bridge where he could see his beloved hill. The sea lay calm in the distance. The sky was full of grey clouds that he could not read. For much of the year they shrouded the heavens. Unlike the clouds back home which came rain-laden, where you could taste the moisture in the air and know rain was coming, here it caught him unawares every time. The temperature on the bus was set too high and the heavy winter coat he wore made him sweat.

The music on his Walkman provided his soundtrack to the city. The right song at the right moment could fix an image, an emotion, a memory in his mind for the rest of his days. He felt a flutter in his heart, a familiar feeling from long ago. He was falling in love again, falling in love with the city.

This was not the first time he had fallen in love with music as the backdrop. He could not tell whether it was music that made him fall in love or whether it had just been there at the time. Mai Chenai was a young student nurse then and he had just become a prosecutor. He was young and ambitious, with a full head of hair. His peers at the UZ were men like Mutambara, a radical student leader then, and he'd even brushed shoulders with the eccentric Warlord Chakaredza, who later styled himself Munhumutapa II, thus usurping every other Munhumutapa who came after Mutota. In those days they were anti everything and smoked a lot of pot, though he still left the UZ with a first in law.

The Magistrate hadn't wanted to be posted to Bindura, a backwater town. He'd hoped to make a name for himself in Harare. That was the hand of fate because Mai Chenai was in Bindura. He met her when she came to have photocopies of her school certificates certified at the courts. She had a Maya Angelou afro and wore a polka dot dress with shoulder pads. How could he forget that look? He had her name, which was all you needed in a little town where everyone knew everyone else. He asked around, found out she was at the Bindura School of Nursing and pursued her for a year. A year, not bad at all. Women weren't easy back then, and his opening line didn't help him when next he bumped into her:

"Girl, you must be tired, because you've been running through my mind all day."

He'd heard it in some American film where it had actually worked. But she gave him a disgusted look and walked away.

What he did then would have been called stalking in later years. He wrote poems, poems with lots of stars, fields and meadows in them. He sent flowers, an extravagance on a junior prosecutor's salary. In time, he wore her out, pulled down her defences, brick by brick.

"I gave up because I was tired," Mai Chenai liked to say when they exchanged stories with their friends at braais on weekends at their first home together on Tomazos.

The bus wound its way down Leith Walk. He got off after Pilrig St Pauls and backtracked onto Pilrig Street. He ran his hand along the sandstone walls of the church, darkened by pollution, as he walked by the arched windows. He was one of those peculiar people who felt the need to touch things, to feel them and connect with them physically. The wall felt rough against the palm of his hand. It had weathered rain, wind and snow for centuries; time had leeched and calcified within. It was solid, fixed in this point of space, and the act of touching it fixed him to it too. They shared roots for a brief moment in time. The spire rose high in the sky and he made a mental note to try to find it the next time he was on Arthur's Seat. Everything ahead of him was a mixture of stone, mortar and glass, with hedges and the green foliage of trees poking out in what spaces they could find in this conurbation. He did not get the same feeling of space or expansiveness here as he felt when he was back home. The sky did not feel as large. One could not look at the sky outside of its relationship with the land. The absence of space he felt was because everything here was owned, subdivided, surveyed, for sale, catalogued for use. On the other hand, the illusion of a large African sky was the product of the feeling that land was communal and shared, the absence of boundaries.

The tar was a mosaic of patches where the utilities people had ripped it open and patched it up again. New tar was a shiny black against the faded old tar. Cars parked on either side of the road since the houses in this area had no space for garages. He walked past the park, which was empty save for a tramp on a bench drinking Strongbow from a two-litre bottle.

The Magistrate felt the chill of the evening air. Friday was payday; he was happy for that. On £6.40 an hour (Alfonso assured him this was generous), he looked forward to each weekly pay. It was gone so quickly, swallowed up by rent, the gas and electric, the bus pass, Chenai's bottomless pit of demands. Sound as a pound, my foot. The 11 running towards Leith Walk stopped at the bus stop ahead and dropped off a young couple that walked hand in hand. The Magistrate remembered walking along Mt Darwin Road on long strolls with Mai Chenai. That was before they built the flats, when it had been virgin bush teeming with wildlife. The thing about Bindura was that he could understand its boundaries. He had a mental map of the town. He knew in which direction the sun rose and where it set. In Edinburgh, he was hemmed in by buildings on all sides. The parks felt like nature contrived, too well trimmed, too managed. His experience of the city was a series of micro-environments, no different to that of a tribesman in the Amazon with a limited range.

He stopped to change the batteries in his Walkman. It felt warm. He carried a couple of spares in his jacket pocket because they never seemed to last long. He opened the panel at the back, removed the two dead batteries and replaced them with new Duracells. He closed the panel, spun the Walkman round, ejected Chimombe and replaced him with Matavire.

No sound came; the headphones had fallen out of the jack. He plugged them back in and listened to the thumping drums and the trademark keyboard harmonies for which the Jairos Jiri Band were known. When he was younger, the Magistrate had paid no attention to this type of music. At the UZ he fell in with the jazz crowd. He'd wooed Mai Chenai with his Miles Davis records. But, one could not ignore Matavire. He was on heavy rotation on the radio and played on Mvenge-mvenge on ZBC every Thursday night, which the maid never missed. The music was in the Magistrate's subconscious, stored somewhere at the back of his mind.

Paul Matavire was a blind musician who wore dark sunglasses on stage. He was the court jester of popular music and his legacy was ensured by his wit and linguistic trickery. More than any other contemporary artist, Matavire's work found itself in the general lexicon, becoming established as part of the Shona language. He had that profound, near Shakespearean, ability to coin new phrases, new idioms, to find new ways of expressing the Zimbabwean condition. 'Nhamo yefodya yemudzanga, ukuyakarumwa, uku inotsva', 'Usafe nenyota makumbo ari mumvura', 'Kunyepera kutya dzvinyu,

75

akasungira nyoka muchiuno', 'NedzaAdam'. All these were his gifts to the language.

Listening to *Tanga Wandida*, the Magistrate realised that Matavire's best work came in the form of perfect vignettes parodying daily life. No one could argue that Matavire was vocally gifted, his range was limited. The composition of his background music performed by the Jairos Jiri Band was, at best, mediocre and, at its worst, downright diabolical, like the keyboard beats on *Diabhorosi Nyoka*, which sounded like fairground music from a broken organ grinder. Perhaps the joke lay in the music too, that is, the music was an expression of the lyrical absurdity within the vignettes. *Tanga Wandida* was Matavire at his best, an exquisite play in which the artist took on multiple roles, supported by a female backing singer, caricaturing patriarchy and the abuse women faced in the male dominated social sphere. And, like a true jester, the laughs elicited by the parody masked the serious indictment of society in the songs. Doctor Love, as Matavire was also known, was a singular genius, approximated later in the form of Leonard Dembo and System Tazvida, but never matched.

Despite his newfound love of the music, the Magistrate felt uncomfortable with Matavire's legacy. In the twilight of his career in the nineties, Matavire had been convicted of rape and served time in prison. The Magistrate wondered if Matavire's eloquence had deserted him on trial. Now Matavire was dead, he died during the great wave of the Pandemic that took so many other Sungura legends, was it possible to separate the artist from the art, the singer from the song, the dancer from the dance? To reconcile Matavire, the artist, singing about women's issues and Matavire, the rapist? The Magistrate walked up the steps, pressed the buzzer and was admitted to the familiar miasma of the care home.

They sit in the shade of Edinburgh's Shame. The giant pillars of the monument cast long shadows on the grass. They drink cans of Tennent's, killing the newborn day. Puffy clouds hang in the sky, floating lazily to nowhere. Stacey leans against Farai's shoulder, her long hair flowing against his sweater. Brian's gaze traces the horizon, somewhere in Fife. On Calton Hill, the city's delusion of being the Athens of the North lingers in hard stone. Farai thinks the monument a thing of beauty. There is something in the unfinished acropolis, a ruin before it became a ruin, eaten by moss on the lower fringes, which he finds compelling. Stacey is indifferent. He thinks her perspective is tainted by history, while he, the outsider, can see things with a little more clarity. The city's near universal rejection of the monument perhaps lies in the embarrassing fact that it was modeled on the Parthenon, with grand ambitions. Almost the same embarrassment the Scots feel about the '78 Argentina World Cup debacle. Both share the same aetiology, a small nation with overinflated ambitions.

Farai thinks about America, strong, proud and unabashed in its replication of old world architecture, with Las Vegas the Venice of the new age. The Greek influence on Edinburgh's architecture is evident everywhere Farai turns, even more so down in the New Town below. The city is an undulating surface of hills and dips, buckling and uneven.

'My butt's getting wet,' Stacey says.

'Anyone fancy a second?' Brian asks, cracking a can open.

'No thanks, I'm driving,' says Farai. Stacey takes 1.

'Did you get your flights sorted?' Brian asks.

'Yep, I'll be going in a few weeks,' he replies. 'The thing is, every time I go back, I feel more and more like a stranger. The lingo's changed, the bearer notes have more zeros, the whole vibe, the way people do things is completely different.'

'The last time I was home, my sister's kids didn't even remember me.'

'That's the thing, I've got no real mates left, you dig? I made friends at Wits and left SA. I've got mates here, but back home there's no one that I can hang with. Everything's so different, like how did that happen?'

'I can't imagine leaving this place,' Stacey says wistfully. 'Don't get me wrong, I mean, if I got a job, say, in Glasgow or Dundee, I might go there, but that's still pretty close, so it doesn't count.'

'You wait until your economy tanks and then we'll see how far you're willing to go.'

'No more boom and bust,' says Farai, with a chuckle, raising his empty can.

A pair of tourists approach them. The man wearing Aviators speaks to them in an American accent.

'How do we get down from here?'

'Just take that path, the stairs will lead you down to Regent Road and you can take it from there.' Stacey points the way.

'Thanks.'

Farai watches them walk down the hill, stopping to read the plaque beside the Portuguese cannon, which looks as though it's pointed at the castle, way over the buildings in the valley between Calton Hill and the Mound. The Americans take a photo of the cannon. Farai wonders if it ever killed anyone. There is something both terrible and fascinating about instruments of death.

'You should have told them to go back down the same way they came up,' he says.

'Eejits,' Stacey replies.

Farai stands and helps her up. Brian finishes his beer, crushes the can and rises. Stacey yawns, arches her back and stretches her lanky limbs as far as they go. They walk down the slope, with the Observatory to their right and Nelson's Monument to the left. The hard, grey stonework of the buildings below is tapered by the green foliage of trees that breaks the rows of roofs only visible from this vantage point, which captures a panoramic view of the city.

They descend, following the Americans down the stone steps. The side of the hill is awash with yellow flowers of gorse. Fallen leaves from trees, dry and brown, pile up in the corners of the steps.

'What do we do now?' Brian asks.

'I say Spoonies, for breakfast,' Farai replies.

'You're so cheap.'

'The word you're looking for is thrifty.'

'Are we taking the car?'

'Nah, we'll come back for it.'

It's a short walk down to Princes Street. A beggar sits outside Burger King. He's a 30-something white guy. They all are. Brian stops and drops £2.00 in his hat.

'Cheers, pal,' says the beggar, breaking into a brown-toothed grin.

'Nae bother,' says Brian as they push on.

'What the fuck was that about?' asks Farai. 'You leave the Third World, go out and bust your ass wiping old people's bumholes in a nursing home, and you give this bum your hard earned money so he can park his backside on the pavement tripping decent folk over as they go about their lawful business?'

'It's my money, dude.'

'You wanna give your money to someone who deserves it, then save a tenner and get a blowjob from 1 of the hookers on the Links, at least she'd have earned it.'

'Farai, what the–' Stacey cuts in.

'It's a point of principle; a man must earn his keep. Brian, go back and tell that bum to suck your cock.'

'I'm not having this conversation.' Brian looks at Stacey, bewildered.

They walk on to George Street, which runs parallel to Princes Street. Cars park in bays in the middle of the road. Shoppers and tourists walk on the sidewalks, popping in and out of the pricey designer clothes stores and jewelers.

They enter the pub and find a table. Farai goes to the bar with their orders. He returns because he's forgotten the table number. He notes it, goes back to the bar and orders 3 Scottish breakfasts, making a point of telling the barman he is feeling patriotic. He doesn't find a way of explaining the pints of Guinness he orders with them. His phone vibrates as the barman pours. ✉:

Stacey

♥ ya bbs xx

He replies:

mwah xx

'I wish Scott had come out with us,' says Stacey.

'I don't know about you guys, but that dude's got some serious issues going on. I've never seen anyone so depressed all the fucking time,' says Brian.

'It's just his time of the month – a long period, I admit.' Farai rejoins them, giving them the beers and keeping the half pint for himself.

'You guys are his mates, you've got to talk to him.' Stacey takes a sip. 'We should have taken Mr Majeika to the hill with us, he'd love it there.'

'He'd rather keep Scott company.'

'Try explaining that to the landlord with the whole no pets allowed rules.'

'Mr Majeika's different. He's no ordinary rabbit, he's got skillz, my nizzle.'

The waitron comes with their order, gives them some cutlery and shows them where to get the condiments. Farai goes to the wooden cabinet with salt and pepper sachets, ketchup, mayonnaise, mint sauce, vinegar... He takes what he needs and pockets a few extra sachets. He always pinches condiments whenever he eats out. His most extravagant trophy was a saltshaker from The Witchery. He reasons it's a victimless crime.

'Did you steal ketchup again, Farai?' asks Stacey.

'I'm insulted by that accusation,' Farai replies with an air of wounded dignity.

'You've got tons at home. Why do you feel the need to pinch some every time we go somewhere? If you really wanted it, you could just ask.'

'Iz it becoz I iz black?' he mimics Ali G. 'Stacey, I'm liberating the ketchup, not stealing it. I'm right up there with the Gnome Liberation Front.'

'There's a difference between stealing ketchup and stealing garden gnomes.'

'I said, "Liberating," didn't you hear me? This is a political act, a heroic act, a strike against the bloodsucking heart of modern Western capitalism, something Che Guevara would have done.' Farai waves his butter knife about in a grand gesture worthy of a revolutionary.

'Sometimes I doubt your sanity.'

He trades his potato bread for a strip of Brian's bacon. There are only a few other diners in the pub. Its carpet and oak panel walls lend the place the gravitas of a classier establishment, which the cheap stainless steel cutlery immediately dispels.

'So what's the plan for today?' asks Brian.

'Neither a planner nor a plannee be. That's my motto, and look how far it's got me.'

'How about we go to a ceilidh?" suggests Stacey.

'Babe, I respect your culture, heritage and all that, but the idea of hopping about like a fucking kangaroo doesn't appeal to me.'

'Clubbing it is then. We'll have to see if I can convince Kirsty to come out with us. I think she fancies you, Brian,' says Stacey, raising an eyebrow.

'She's a child!' Brian replies.

'She's 17, and you're what, turning 21?'

'Barely legal, dude. There's guys stalking chatrooms looking for that kinda action,' Farai says.

'I think she's a lovely girl, but she should concentrate on her school work.'

'Always the sensible one, Brian. I wish Farai could be a bit more like you – *mature.*'

'Hey, I'm a role model to all the single parent family black kids looking for a father figure out there.' Farai can't resist adding, 'Anyway, Brian's doing this old nurse at his work. She's *ancient*, like 40 or something.'

'Eat a dick,' Brian retorts.

'So you like them older, Brian? Nothing wrong with a bit of mutton every now and again as part of a balanced diet,' Stacey mocks him. 'The older the berry the sweeter the juice.'

Brian stares at his plate, embarrassed. He gives Farai the finger and refuses to speak for the rest of the meal, arguing he is too grown up for their nonsense. They finish their meal, down their beers and go back out onto the street. The sidewalks are busier with more people walking about. The weather is nice and mild, a good day to be out and about. They retrace their steps to the Royal Terrace, where the car is parked. A red plastic envelope sits on the windscreen of Farai's PT Cruiser.

'*Oh, for the love of fuck,*' he cries out. 'You cannot be serious!'

Stacey checks the ticket. 'We're only a couple of minutes late. Surely there's got to be some sort of grace period.'

'Did I do something completely and utterly unforgivable in a former life to deserve this? This, right here, my brothers, is an example of everything that's wrong with Western capitalist societies today.' Farai takes the ticket from her. 'It's completely ruined my lovely morning.'

Stacey hugs him, stopping him from talking, especially since some random guy a few yards away is recording his melodramatic rant on his mobile. Farai breaks away from her embrace and unlocks the car. He pouts, lower lip over the upper, the little boy within coming out.

***

The scent of their love rises from underneath the sheets. It merges with the salt air from the Forth that blows through the open window, creating something sweet and sour, a chemical signature only their union can create. He plays with her hair, braiding it in triple tresses. He watches her breathing, content, the feeling of her skin against his. Her free hand strokes his leg. She has red and purple striations on her forearm. There are angry pink lines where scars have formed. She once told him it gave her relief from the immutable pain of living.

'I've been thinking,' she says.

'Thinking is 1 of those things best left to experts,' Farai replies.

'It's like, won't it be awkward for you going places with me, when you're Doctor Farai PhD, and I'm just the girl who works in a shoe shop?'

'Is it supposed to be?'

'I'm thinking of going on a course at Telford or Stevenson. Maybe access to social work or something like that. I'm good with people, maybe I should get into a field where I work with people.'

'I'm all for it, but only if you're doing it for yourself. The last thing I want is you doing stuff that important because you think it will please me. I'm happy with you just the way you are.' He kisses her eyebrow.

'I always thought I was gonna be an actress, Hollywood, bright lights, cameras.'

'The only thing that can stop you is yourself. Go to LA, find a job as a waitron, work for tips, pay your way through acting school. It's been done before.'

He hates it when she doubts herself, trying to measure her life by that of other people. He strokes her flat stomach, tracing his finger round the soft horizon of her belly button, going down to the faint red patch that grows thicker and thicker. She arches her back, her body responding to his touch.

'I find it weird that, when I talk about the future, it's like you're happy for me to go wherever and do whatever. That means you're not thinking about a future with me.'

He stops. 'It's not like that at all. It's just, you're young, and I don't want to be the 1 stopping you doing the things you want to do.'

'So if I said I wanted to get back into porn, you'd be cool with that.'

'Hell yeah, it would be awesome being a pornstar's BF. Total fantasy.'

'I don't know too many blokes like that, you know. It's weird.'

'Do possessiveness and jealousy have to be part of a relationship? I certainly don't think so.'

'Well, I wouldn't let you act porn. I want this all to myself,' she says.

She turns over, lies on her belly with her knees bent so her feet dangle in the air. He looks into her eyes, holding her gaze. Scott shouts from the living room:

'*BOYZ HUYAI CHOP-CHOP*, WE'RE ON THE NEWS.'

Farai leaps off the bed and dashes out of the bedroom, naked. He bumps into Brian who's running along the corridor as well. There is a video of a crowd running away from baton stick wielding Black Boots. The footage is shaky and they can hear the cameraman's heavy breathing as he runs with the crowd, away from the police. The script below refers to something about the 'MUGABE REGIME' and mentions the President's advanced age. Farai knows the key words in these reports by heart, DESPOT, BASKET CASE, DICTATORSHIP, ONCE PROMISING, WHITE FARMERS, OPPOSITION, VOTE RIGGING, HYPERINFLATION, BRITAIN, DEMOCRACY, HUMAN RIGHTS, THABO MBEKI, SADC, UN, SANCTIONS, LAND REFORM, WAR VETERANS, MATABELELAND...

Stacey joins them, clothing herself in Farai's rainbow-colored dressing gown. They watch eagerly as the feed turns to a reporter on a rooftop in Johannesburg. The connection has a lot of static but the reporter is just audible, giving the impression he is speaking from the heart of darkness. He speaks in a hushed, conspiratorial voice, as though afraid of danger in close proximity. He points into the distance, somewhere north, across the Joburg night sky. He is the image of a man right in the heart of the action as he reminds the audience that the BBC is banned from reporting in Zimbabwe.

The feed cuts back to the studio where the leader of the Opposition is speaking via video uplink from Washington DC. He is a toadyish man with a pockmarked face whose tie seems like it is choking him. He uses the key words, REGIME, DICTATORSHIP, DEMOCRACY, HUMAN RIGHTS, CHANGE, and appeals to the INTERNATIONAL COMMUNITY to help. He urges more SANCTIONS and points out that if South Africa withdraws its support then the situation in Zimbabwe is likely to get better. He appeals to Pretoria to cut off its electricity exports.

'Dude, this guy is the *wrong* man at the right time,' Farai says.

'What do you know about it?' Scott demands in a harsh voice.

'Who on earth asks for sanctions against their own country? I'm sorry, but I just don't get it.'

'These are targeted SANCTIONS he's talking about, things like the REGIME's Swiss bank accounts.'

'How exactly is South Africa supposed to target power cuts? Even more absurd when we're their biggest trading partner on the continent.'

'Look, President Tsvangirai won the election, he should be in power, right now…'

'Will you guys shut up, I'm trying to watch the report,' says Stacey.

The feed has switched back to the studio in London. 2 experts, a professor from the School of Oriental and African Studies and another man from Oxfam, comment on THE SITUATION. Manufacturing consent. They use the key words, BASKET CASE, HUMAN RIGHTS, WHITE FARMERS, REGIME. There is no historical context to the issues upon which they air their expert opinions, broadcast to millions of viewers across the globe. The picture of a nameless, starving African child next to a skinny dog is superimposed onto the screen behind them. They have followed THE SITUATION closely from London.

The discussion ends and the anchor switches to a piece about an airline which has caused outrage by proposing that fat people pay double the fare if their fatty flesh crosses the divider between the seats. 2 aviation experts are at hand via video link to offer their expert opinion.

'This is some serious shit,' says Brian.

'The MDC is having a meeting at St John's in a couple of weeks and I want you guys to come with me so we can do something,' Scott says.

'You wanna do something from 10000Ks away?' Farai stifles a laugh.

'At least we're trying. What about you, Farai? You're so quick to sneer and dismiss people who're doing their best. What have you done for your country, motherfucker?'

'Language please, dude. The difference between you and me is, I'm going home after my PhD to run a business. *You*, on the other hand, are stuck here working your dead-end job in a call center, so forgive me if I don't agree with you on sanctions and bullshit that might harm my ability to run a business, employ people, and make a *real* difference on the ground.'

'Cheap shot,' says Brian.

Scott leaps up from the sofa, points to the screen, veins strained on his neck and temples. His eyes look like they're going to pop out. Spittle flies out of his mouth when he speaks.

'You're full of shit, man. Just because you come from money doesn't mean you have to look down on the rest of us trying to make a difference–'

'The only difference you fuckers make is how you start acting all brave when you get here. If you wanna make a real difference, I'll buy you a 1 way ticket home.'

'Boys, is this really necessary? Can't we all just take a deep breath, count to 10 and talk about something else?' Stacey rests her chin on both hands.

'People are dying out *there*, and I don't need your pompous arse acting all high and mighty, looking down on people who are trying to create change. *Uri mhata, mface!*' Scott pokes Farai in the chest.

'You don't wanna be jowling bumpers like that, exsir.' Farai's voice drops in pitch.

'Scott, chillax man,' Brian says.

Farai looks down at Scott who stands at his chest height, eyeballing him. Scott's skinny little figure quivering with rage makes him laugh and he turns to walk away.

'Don't you turn away from me!' Scott grabs his arm to try and stop him, but Farai brushes him away, easily, like a fly.

'Yo, Scotty, chillax, you're messing up everyone's chi,' says Brian, touching Scott on the shoulder. Scott pulls away and walks off in a huff to his bedroom. Mr Majeika watches all this from his hutch, twitching his whiskers.

'That right there is the reason democracy doesn't work where we're from,' says Farai.

Stacey leans against the wall and looks exasperated.

'You know exactly what he's like and you pushed him, Farai. You pushed him to get a reaction. You're like a child, tearing legs off a spider. No, don't smile, you wound him up. You can be such a prick sometimes.' She sighs.

'I was trying to have a civilized debate with the man.'

Brian switches the Xbox on and the TV goes to AV. Electronic music plays in the background to a digifootballer juggling the ball on the screen.

'Farai, go and apologize,' says Stacey.

'I'm about to play a game here.'

'Right now! And put some clothes on while you're at it.'

He reluctantly goes to Scott's room and knocks on the door. There's no answer. He pushes it open anyway. Scott's lying on his bed, staring at the ceiling.

'Dude, Stacey sent me to apologize.'

Silence.

'I cranked you up and I'm sorry, alright.' He crosses the threshold, grabs Scott and puts him in a headlock, ruffling his hair. Scott tries to pull out and they tumble from the bed to the floor wrestling. 'I ain't letting you out until you say, *hebo*.' They roll around the floor for a couple of minutes until Scott, exhausted, accepts the apology.

'I knew we were gonna have to do this the army way,' says Farai, releasing Scott from the headlock. 'And, if it's so important to you, we'll come to your MDC gig.'

'You don't have to if you don't wanna.'

'Nah, we'll come and check out what's going on. Who knows, there might be some hot chicks there. I'm telling you, bro, black pussy is at a premium in this city.'

Scott laughs. They get up from the floor and head back to the living room, but not before Farai grabs a towel from the bathroom and wraps it round his waist. Brian is knelt on the floor, setting his team up on the controller. Stacey smiles when she sees them emerge from the corridor.

'Did you kids kiss and make up?'

'With tongues, baby, with tongues.'

Farai picks up his controller. He chooses London FC to go head to head with Brian's Man Red.

'Scott, would you like to come and help me in the kitchen, since these 2 are going to play their childish game?' asks Stacey.

Farai goes to the kitchen 10 minutes later, jubilant after winning his first match. He walks up to Stacey and kisses her. She is chopping onions and has a thin film of moisture in her eyes. Scott stands at the sink, washing last night's dishes.

'So, what are you making tonight?'

'I shouldn't even be in the kitchen. I'm a guest in this house,'she says.

'Babes, you lost your guest status a long, long time ago. Now I'm gonna teach you to be a real Zimbabwean wife, hey, a good dutiful wife who knows how to look after her husband.'

'Don't you need to give my mum goats or something first?'

'It's your dad we'll need to find, actually. Your mum is a *mutorwa*,'

'*Mut-wa*,' Stacey mouths.

'*Mu-to-rwa*,' Farai corrects her, knowing full well she'll have forgotten in a few minutes.

'I want to learn to cook Zimbabwean. What type of food do people eat out there?'

'Usually nothing… Didn't you watch the news?'

The Magistrate's backyard was a small, rectangular space overgrown with grass, a few shrubs and a young fernspray in one corner. It hadn't been tended in a while and was reverting to a state of semi-wilderness. He went round the lawn, picking up small stones, a rake hidden in the grass, litter and other bits of debris. It was a mild day, ideal for gardening.

He was mowing the lawn when John, from number seventeen, popped his head over the fence.

"Alright pal," John called out above the roar of mower.

"Morning." The Magistrate turned the mower off.

"Great day for a barbeque."

"The sun isn't even out."

"Don't jinx it now. This might be the only decent day we have this summer."

The Magistrate nodded, then shook his head. He didn't have a suitable reply. He had yet to fully master that most subtle of British arts, talking about the weather in great detail. The nuance and dull observation required completely escaped him.

"Perhaps you can come and cut my grass when you're done then. I'll pay you in Zimbabwean dollars."

"I'll take toilet paper instead," said the Magistrate, laughing.

John waved and went back inside. The Magistrate kicked up the mower and went back to work. When he was done, he put the mower back in the shed and took out a hoe. All through the winter he'd thought of growing vegetables. The idea that a garden could lay fallow without anything edible growing in it riled him. He dug out the lawn at the far end, which he'd not bothered to mow. It was heavy work and soon his T-shirt was soaked with sweat. He liked the feel of soft earth giving in to his hoe. The sound of roots tearing out of the ground was music to his ears. It took him back to his childhood, the mornings before school, toiling in the fields. Then it had been a matter of life and death. Life kumusha revolved around the seasons, around agriculture. They had an intimate relationship with the soil. Even now, the thought of watching young delicate stalks growing, watered by the sweat of his brow gave him pleasure. Chenai came out of the house.

"Dad, what are you doing to the lawn?"

"The soil here is rich, I can smell it. I'm going to grow some veggies. Come and join me." He straightened up and beckoned her.

"You can get veg from Lidl or Sainsbury's," she replied as a matter of fact.

"It's not the same as growing them yourself, Chenai. Come, feel the softness of this soil."

"Eew, Dad, there's beasties in it."

The Magistrate laughed heartily. How quickly generations change. She could not have survived his childhood. He told her about how the worms and the bugs work the soil, making it richer for the plants that grow in it. I need to take her back home for a holiday when I have enough money, he thought. She had left as a child and had been away for too long. He wondered what her memories of home were, or were they already faded and this was her home? He explained how he would build the beds for the vegetables, raising them so the plants could get air, light and water.

"Perhaps you can start your own small patch next to mine," he said.

"I dinnae ken nothing about growing stuff."

God forbid his daughter should speak with this rough, guttural accent. What were they teaching these kids at school? Maybe I'll spend that money on elocution lessons instead.

"It's in your blood, mwanangu. All you have to do is give them plenty of love and a little bit of water and see how they grow."

She considered this for a minute. "It sounds like hard work."

"Your grandmother always used to say, 'A bit of hard work never killed anyone.'"

"Alright, I'll give it a go." She sounded cautious.

He took another hoe from the shed and told her to remove her shoes. That is how they did it back in the day, the soil underneath their feet. She tried to avoid the 'beasties' as she clumsily wielded the hoe. He was happy to have her by his side, occasionally stopping to show her

something or correct her technique. What felt natural for him, she'd
have to learn like ABC.

"This is so like going to the gym."

"You won't find any fat people kumusha."

He did most of the work, yet her presence brought a certain joy to
his heart. He thought that when he retired, a dreadful prospect now that
his pension had been wiped out by inflation, he would like to work the
earth. In his mind the two highest professions were in agriculture and in
teaching. The rest of the world with its technology and sophistication
was built on the backs of the farmer and the teacher. He'd stopped
asking Chenai what she wanted to do after school. Her answers varied
wildly from beauty therapist, to make-up artist, occasionally nursing, to
a number of sinister sounding prospects that filled his heart with dread.
He wanted her to go to university, do law, or any useful degree outside
of the humanities and build a safe stable career for herself. He thought
about his own mortality; she would need something solid once he and
her mother were gone.

The Magistrate saw Mai Chenai watching from the bedroom
window on the first floor. He waved and beckoned her to join them.
She shook her head and drew the curtains, leaving him to imagine her
walking over to the bed and crawling under the sheets. Chenai stood up.

"How come there's this distance between the two of you?"

A bold question, one she would never have asked if they had raised
her back home. "It's difficult when both of us are working so hard all
the time."

"It was the same before you were working, Dad."

Has she grown so much I can't tell her a grown-up lie? he
wondered.

"It's okay, you don't need to tell me. I was just prying."

"Sometimes things are difficult between couples. A marriage is just
like these plants we are growing. You have to water it and tend to it all
the time for it to survive."

"Then water it, Dad."

"I'm trying," he said with a sad smile. Chenai walked up to him and
hugged him. It was like she was trying to draw poison out of a wound.
He almost cried, but men don't cry, real men never cry. He felt the
weight of his age pressing down on every joint as he released her. His
little girl giving him relationship advice, the wheel of life turning. He
wiped his eyes with the back of his hand.

"Come, I think we've done enough for today. We'll continue another time," he said. "Can you print the news for me from the computer?"

"From the internet."

"Yes, find anything you can about Chikafumanheru for me."

"You're obsessed with that guy."

They washed their feet under the tap. The beds they'd made were heaps of fresh brown earth. Chenai's bed had wobbly lines, while his were neat and straight. There was a pile of grass and some shrubs that they'd uprooted. Chenai had wanted to put them in the brown bin but he told her not to. He would create a small compost heap with them in the corner of the garden. Nothing would go to waste.

He sat on the sofa and watched Chenai working on the computer, marvelling at how fast her fingers danced around the keyboard. He could barely use the thing, that had been the secretary's job at the courts. He wondered how they were getting on without him, whether they missed him. Part of him felt that he was long forgotten, a useless relic from the past. He did not like to think about this and was relieved when Chenai handed him some papers, telling him Chikafumanheru had not made the news. There was news about a Party cadre who'd died and been declared a national hero. Every couple of months a new national hero was declared. Zimbabwe must have been the most heroic nation on earth.

Just as he settled down to read, there was a familiar knock on the door. Chenai got up to answer it.

"Just like clockwork, every Saturday and Sunday, Uncle A's here," she said dryly.

She opened the door and Alfonso fell in, huffing and puffing, making a great show of carrying his alcohol laden plastic bags. The Magistrate rose and shook his hand. Alfonso held on and wouldn't let go. The little man had a firm grip.

"I'm always happy to be here with you and your family. This is like a second home to me," he said. He reached into his pocket with his left hand, took out a handkerchief and blew his nose, all the while holding on to the Magistrate like a leech.

"Is everything okay?" the Magistrate asked.

"Why wouldn't it be? I am here with you aren't I?" Alfonso took out a bar of Kit Kat and tossed it to Chenai.

"Thanks, Uncle A, maybe next time you'll bring some Bacardi for me too," she said. The Magistrate shot her a look. "Just kidding, geez."

Alfonso took himself to the kitchen. He poured drinks for them both, returned and handed the Magistrate whisky while he stuck to his beloved Stella.

"It'll be a big game today," Alfonso said.

"And who are you supporting now?"

"I'm a neutral. I'll watch it for the love of the sport."

"Whom did you bet on?"

"Well, that's a different question altogether. Man U of course. I have a friend who swears to me that Man U fans are never disappointed. It has to be true." Alfonso changed the channel to Sky Sports.

"How's your building going?"

"Ah, my mansion in Kambuzuma is coming along nicely. I get photos emailed to me every week, just to see what the builders are up to."

"I thought you said it was in Kuwadzana," the Magistrate said with a frown.

"I heard the story of Chipamba in London who sent money to his brother back home to build a house in Marlborough. The brother sent photos showing progress weekly, right from the foundation to the roof. Chipamba worked like a donkey, hurrying from one shift to the other. He and his wife did lates and nights, slaving away to finish their dream house. When it was done, they flew to Zimbabwe to see the fruits of their labour. Chipamba bought two suits from Primark with which to thank his brother, not to mention a little bonus payment for managing his affairs so well. They flew BA, not Chawasarira, they wanted to get home for sure. The brother wasn't there at the airport when they arrived, so they took a taxi, all the way to Chitungwiza and stayed with the in-laws. Chipamba tried to phone his brother, but each time he rung out to voicemail. The next day, or was it the day after, anyway, they couldn't wait." Alfonso's voice rose in pitch, he looked now to the Magistrate and now to Chenai, desperate they wouldn't get bored with him. "So they went to Marlborough in the father-in-law's 626. When they got to the stand they saw it was overgrown with weeds and only a little shed stood amidst the tall elephant grass. Chipamba was sure they had gone to the wrong plot but the sign was there, number twenty-seven. He took out the deeds, which confirmed this was the right spot, yet there he was, no house. Then the wife took the photographs from her handbag and when they looked at the photos they saw the house on the photos was the one on number twenty-three!"

"His brother had built the house on the wrong plot?" asked Chenai.

"This being Zimbabwe there was the possibility the signage was wrong, or maybe there was indeed a mistake in the deeds. They went over to number twenty-three and knocked on the door. A big man with a rock-like face came out. So the UK man said, 'Excuse me, how long have you been lodging here?' The Zim man said, 'You're disturbing my sadza.' The UK man said, 'This is my house, I am Chipamba. Is my brother renting out this house to you?' The Zim man was puzzled, he called his wife, 'Sweetie, this man is claiming our house is his.'"

"So, his brother had sold the house? " asked Chenai.

"The wife came out and said, 'You people are coming from abroad, aren't you? I can smell the scent of your foreign lotions coming off you.' Chipamba replied, 'Yes, we worked to build this house. We are your landlords.' The woman laughed, 'I see now from the resemblance. Can you see it too? It's in the nose.' She turned to her husband, who started laughing. 'We knew your brother. He used to come here every week to photograph our house while we were building it.' 'Every week,' her husband echoed. 'So your brother had been sending you photos of our house, telling you it was yours.' They began to laugh, but not for long because Chipamba collapsed on the spot. He had a heart attack."

"What a terrible story," said the Magistrate.

"It's all true, I assure you."

"How could he do that to his own brother?" Chenai asked.

"It's dog eat dog out there. Maybe the same thing's happening to me right now." Alfonso took a swig of beer. He increased the volume on the TV for the prematch commentary. Chenai excused herself and went upstairs.

The Magistrate thought about how people had become so callous, so corrupt. It seemed the disease was spreading its tentacles deeper into the heart of society. A society of crooks and tricksters could never hope to thrive. Trust was the very foundation upon which societies were built. Without it there was nothing but chaos. Were the country's leaders a reflection of the society from which they had emerged or was the society a reflection of the sickness inherent in its corrupt leaders? The chicken or the egg? He recalled his first meeting with

Chikafumanheru when he was still a junior prosecutor. It was at a function in Harare. They discussed the American system with its openly conservative and liberal justices.

"It shows that the law is a fluid thing, open to interpretation. The law is what the judges say it is, that's all," Chikafumanheru had said to him. "We are the last resort."

"What about truth?" he had asked.

"You must not get bogged down with abstract philosophies. Epistemology is a dead end," Chikafumanheru had said offhandedly. The thing that had struck him that night about the judge was his lack of shame. It was as though he was completely immune to what anyone else thought about his unethical approach to law. Maybe ethics too was a 'dead end'.

"You educated people are always reading the news," Alfonso said, snapping him out of his reverie. "I can never make it out, the *Herald* says one thing and the other papers say another. At least over here the papers all say the same thing."

"I try to keep abreast of the latest developments back home," he replied.

The referee blew his whistle and Manchester United kicked off. The ball ping-ponged between several players and then went to Beckham whose cross-field pass flew wide, going out for a throw in. The Magistrate poured himself another double and drank it straight. He watched Arsenal press on, only to lose the ball in the opposition's half.

"I have more shifts for you if you would like them," Alfonso said.

"I could always use more work. The money goes so quickly. You walk into a shop, everything is on sale, discounted, but each week you come out with less and less. The bills keep going up."

"Petrol keeps going up too, even after they bombed Iraq. You'd think they'd be pumping the stuff out to us free of charge. Whatever happened to the spoils of victory?" Alfonso was always a little naïve when it came to world affairs. The Magistrate felt a little sorry for him, the type of reflexive sympathy one feels for dumb people.

"The shifts I've got for you will not be at the same place though. I've won new contracts across the city, starting next month, so they'll be here, there and everywhere."

"I can do that, no problem." The Magistrate sighed. The money would never be enough, but he had to run faster just to stay still. He had to get used to the fact that his wife was earning far more than he was.

When they had first been together he considered her wage her own personal pocket money because he earned so much more. Funny how, as a carer in the UK, he now earned a lot more than his colleagues who remained on the bench at home. The world was turned upside down.

"There's another thing I wanted to talk to you about. You know how I'm the secretary of the MDC Edinburgh Branch, right? We have a meeting next Saturday and I would like you to come."

"That really isn't my scene," the Magistrate replied.

"Oh, come on now."

"Members of the jud–" The Magistrate checked himself. "I'm not into politics."

"I'm not asking you to join up. I just want you to come and meet some of the people in our community, that's all. Mavis is cooking mabhonzo. It'll be fun, I promise. Just come and see what we are doing, chete, chete." Alfonso looked at him with his little eyes, almost begging.

"I'll think about it," the Magistrate said.

The next Saturday he coaxed Chenai back to the garden. She planted a bed of carrots, while he sowed lettuce, tomatoes and spinach. He wanted to try some beetroot but Chenai threatened to pull out of the project if he did.

The meeting was at 8pm and he'd finally agreed to attend, worn down by Alfonso's badgering. They were holding it at St John's. He had been past the church many times in the past and wanted to arrive early to look at the building before the others got there. He'd decided that he would like to make a map of the city using music to pin it to his memory. St John's was a suitable landmark to start the experiment, though, in truth, he'd begun the day he acquired the Walkman.

He took the 2 and dropped off in the Grassmarket from where he walked to the church. It was still light. The long days of the northern summer still surprised him, as did the long winter nights. He walked down King's Stables in the shadow of the bare rock on which the castle stood. It sat impregnable, high on the hill, and was the navel around which the city turned. He walked past the multi-storey car park, studying the castle's formidable walls, the crenellations and ramparts above. When he found himself on Lothian Road, he only had to walk a little further, up towards Princes Street and he'd arrived.

Buses made their way through the West End. This was the main artery through which most buses travelled as they went on their routes across the city. Clumps of young people in various stages of intoxication walked along the pavements. A girl in a stripy leotard walked by, barefooted, holding her high heels in her hands. If he needed to contemplate the city in order to be part of it, the young were immersed in its spirit, going about their business without a thought.

The Magistrate walked through the black iron gates and lingered by the western doors. St Cuthbert's stood below, amidst the old graves and crypts of the city's luminaries. It was almost hidden by the great trees in the yard. Moss grew on the old gravestones. A crypt below had tall weeds growing on the roof. If the dead had sought immortality in stone, then nature was stealing it back amidst the lively bustle of the city.

He took out his Walkman and inserted a cassette Alfonso had given him, which was a compilation of music from three groups, Vabati VaJehova, Vabvuwi and Chiedza Chevatendi. His favourite was Vabati VaJehova comprising the Magayas – Wiseman, Timothy, Mamelodi and Kumbulani, plus Samson Tawengwa who completed the quintet. They came from the Mapositori faith, the first truly authentic African expression of Christianity in Zimbabwe. He preferred the traditional roots of the music, usually acapella, or in some instances accompanied with ngoma nehosho and the clapping of hands. The tape started with a bit of static, and then voices, male voices, came through.

He walked around the building looking up to see the high bell tower and the intricate carvings. He studied the stained glass windows and ran his hand along the masonry. The other buildings faded from his consciousness, as did the traffic and the walkers on pavements. The music shielded him from the outside world so he was focused solely on the church.

It was with some irony that the Mapositori – whose music blended so well with the old building – shunned houses of worship. They believed that the outdoors, under the vault of heaven, exposed to the elements, was the best location in which to glorify God. The Magistrate did not intend to step within the church, for he did not want their voices confined within a building. Outside was where their music best worked its magic. Powerful voices spinning through his entire being, connecting him with a higher plane. The Mapositori used unpretentious lyrics. Their voices sounded ancient as if they were drawn from an earlier epoch, before the time of the Shona, when there were only the Karanga, Zezuru, Manyika, Korekore and Ndau.

"Kana manzwa izwi rashe, musazo womesa moyo yenyu…" He was sure these lyrics were taken from a Catholic song he'd heard before. It didn't matter, they sounded better in the Vabati version. And the Magistrate opened his heart and leant against the stone walls, transfixed, so far from home as he listened to the voices. He felt at peace in a way he had not for a long time. Stood there with the solid wall supporting him, he felt the type of relief a marathon runner experiences when he finally stops to catch his breath after the finish line. He soaked up the last rays of sunlight as the streetlights came on, bathing everything in their unnatural yellow glow.

A hand touched him on the shoulder and he jumped, surprised.

"I'm sorry to startle you," said a man with a comb-over and flaming red nose. "Are you here with the NMC?"

"The who?"

"Aww, I might have got it wrong, let me see." The man fumbled about and found a letter in his breast pocket. "Here it is. The MDC."

"You're here for the meeting?"

"It says conference in the letter and I did wonder why they'd have that in a church of all places." The Magistrate shrugged and the man went on, "To tell you the truth, the city only sent me here because no one else would come. For a start, their letter was addressed to the 'Mayor's Office', secondly they wrote, 'Dear Sir'. You can imagine how well that went down with the provost who happens to be a woman."

"I don't know anything about it," the Magistrate said. He checked his watch, it was almost time.

"Where is everyone else?" the man said, looking around. "It says eight o'clock in the letter."

"We have another ten minutes." The Magistrate was a little annoyed at having been disturbed from his meditation. He'd captured a feeling and wanted to ride it for a while, alone with the ghosts and spirits. He stopped the cassette and hung his headphones around his neck. He yawned, causing the man to yawn as well. The man paced back and forth, in stark contrast to the Magistrate who was used to waiting and watching for long periods of time.

"It's eight o'clock," he said. "Where is everyone?"

"Probably on Zimbabwean time," and as the Magistrate said this, the tiny figure of Alfonso popped up, hobbling in the distance. "We'll soon find out from the secretary."

Alfonso arrived, wearing an oversized brown suit and a cowboy hat that overwhelmed his little head. He smiled as he came up the steps and gave the Magistrate a firm handshake.

"Is he with you?" Alfonso asked, pointing to the other man.

"The name's Peter McKenzie. I'm with the council."

"Alfonso Pfukuto, first secretary of the MDC in Edinburgh, Scotland, UK, European Union." He held out his hand.

"Where is everyone?" Peter asked. "I was told to be here for eight."

Alfonso looked around, as if this alone could mysteriously conjure the missing people. He opened his arms like the crucified Christ. He looked from Peter to the Magistrate as if waiting for an explanation.

"Well, what's going on?" asked Peter.

Alfonso whipped out his mobile, an old 5110 held together by bits of elastic band. He dialled, exchanged a few quick words with someone, swore in Shona, and hung up. A group of four young men arrived, asking about the meeting. Alfonso assured them that it would start soon.

"There was a mix-up with the guy who has the keys. Don't worry, someone will be here soon. Can I take a photo of you two?" Before they could answer, Alfonso whipped out a camera and snapped two quick shots.

"So what's your party's philosophy?" Peter asked.

"Change, that's all we want, that's all we stand for," Alfonso replied, fiddling with his camera.

"What do you mean? What sort of change?"

"Well, erm, democratic change. We are a movement, you see. What we want to do first and foremost is to change the names of the roads. At the moment a lot of the roads are named after their people and we have to change that."

"I don't think I quite follow."

"It's the same with the Heroes' Acre, at the moment they put their people in it, but we want to put our own people in there as well. You wait and see, a lot of things are going to change."

Peter looked uncomfortable, as Alfonso had latched on to him as though ready to physically restrain him from leaving. "You are our VIP," Alfonso said. The Magistrate could tell that Alfonso, as he hobbled back and forth, had fortified himself before the event. The young men passed round a bottle of Viceroy on the church grounds. The Magistrate thought better of asking them to desist. He had no authority here.

A car stopped in the bus lane and two men in baggy jeans got out. They went to the boot and removed speakers, along with decks and bags of CDs.

"The DJs are here," Alfonso said. He rubbed his little paws with glee.

"I thought this was a political meeting," Peter said.

"Yes, one hundred per cent political. But remember, these Africans are a musical people. Without a bit of music they get confused." Peter frowned, and Alfonso continued quickly, "We hope you have your speech ready. You are the guest of honour."

"Well, I had prepared a few words, not a speech."

"Excellent, excellent, here comes the man with the keys. The ball is already rolling, all by itself. Better late than never, a stitch in time saves nine." Alfonso dashed to get the fellow with the keys and hurried him up the steps. They'd hired the small room on the right wing of the church. The DJs lumbered behind with their equipment while the young men looked on, passing their drink around with a casual air.

Once inside, Alfonso scurried about, dashing from one corner to the other, arranging this or that. He instructed the DJs to set up at the front. The Magistrate did not offer to help. He'd come to observe, helping would be getting involved. Baffled as he was, Peter was prepared to sit through the whole thing just so he could see how much worse it could get. Or maybe a bit of white liberal guilt increased his patience.

Mavis arrived with some women and parked in the bus lane. They brought huge pots filled with food. Soup spilt onto the ground as they carried it in. "Imi vapfanha, help us with these pots," she said to the drinking youths. They grumbled, but obeyed. Alfonso ran out of the church and fussed about the food, kissed Mavis on the cheek, and flew back inside.

Small groups of people trickled in. The place began to buzz. It was almost nine. Alfonso dashed back to Peter and grabbed him by the elbow. He gnawed at his moustache, excited that something was about to happen.

"The chairman is here," Alfonso said, pointing to a man with patched up jeans, an ice hockey top and a gold chain around his neck. "He will make his speech and then you will make yours."

"No one told me anything about making a speech. A few words of solidarity, that's all."

"Chairman, chairman," Alfonso called out, waving his hands furiously. "Come and meet the mayor."

"I'm just a councillor."

The chairman strode over, bumping into a table laden with food that the ladies were selling. He stopped halfway to shake someone's hand and exchanged an anecdote. Then he made it across the room to where Alfonso, Peter and the Magistrate stood.

"Thank you for coming, thank you for coming. We had the head office in London send the letter, specifically. Thanks for coming. This is a very important meeting. If we are going to get rid of the Mugabe Regime, then donors like you are very important. We need all the help we can get. Peoples are dying every day, even as we speak. Salvation is at hand, the next election is our finalest push." Chairman Dzivarasekwa shook Peter's hand.

"That explains the five signatures on the letter. Rather extravagant, don't you think?" Peter felt the firm grip crushing his metacarpals.

"We will begin now," Alfonso said and rushed to the stage.

The Magistrate noticed Brian in the centre of the room chatting with two friends. One of them was a tall fellow with a haughty look and the other had a pulsing vein on his temple as though he was liable to explode at any moment. He went over and greeted Brian, who smiled widely in his usual fashion. The Magistrate liked his open nature and it was nice to meet outside of work for a change.

"Let me introduce you to my friends. This is Farai." The Magistrate shook hands with the tall one. "And this is Scott. I've told you about them, haven't I?" The Magistrate noticed Scott did not look him in the eye, keeping his gaze on the floor instead.

"It is nice to meet you, vakomana," the Magistrate said. The DJ was playing loud urban grooves and some girls were shaking it on the free space at the front. It did not seem particularly appropriate in a gothic church of all places. The Magistrate wanted to say something but remembered he was only there to observe. The music stopped. Alfonso tapped the mic a few times. He played around with his tie and waited for the people to settle.

"Tipeiwo nzeve," Alfonso said above the hum. "Ehhh, I greet you all in the name of Christ Jesus, our Lord and Saviour, and welcome you all to this conference in support of the MDC. We have here tonight our chairman, Chairman Dzivarasekwa, and Mayor Peter Kenzie of the British Government. So, without further ado, please clap your hands for the chairman."

There was feeble clapping of hands and general confusion. "I thought this was a bashment," said a voice. Someone whistled as the chairman made his way to the front. The chairman took the mic, muttered a few words and began to sing the Zimbabwean national anthem. A handful of people took it up. Alfonso removed his cowboy hat and placed it on his chest, standing to attention. The effect was mildly patriotic but mainly comical. Everyone in the room seemed to sing different words and the anthem fizzled out in the middle of the second stanza because no one, the chairman included, knew the words. The chairman stood with the mic in hand and looked at the crowd. Alfonso crept away and switched to the role of cameraman, taking photos of the gathering.

"Pamberi nemusangano," Dzivarasekwa bellowed, chest puffed out.

"Pamberi!"

"Pamberi ne MDC."

"Pamberi!"

"Pamberi naPresident Tsvangirai."

"Pamberi!"

"Pasi nemadzakutsaku."

"Pasi navo!"

"The party secretary Alfonso Pfukuto, chairwoman of the Women's League Mavis Pfukuto, the chairperson for the Youth League, the donor from the British Government, members of the diplomatic co, ladies and gentlemen, boys and girls," began his speech.

"Today is a historic occasion. We are here tonight because this is the finalest push. Robert Mugabe and Zanu PF are destroying our beloved Zimbabwe. We in the MDC have shed blood, sweat and tears for you. The Mugabe Regime is killing peoples every day. If you go on the BBC right now you will see they are killing peoples. There is no food in the shops. The peoples have no money. The peoples have no jobs. Mugabe has destroyed the country. He has destroyed the farms. I am sending out a message to Robert Mugabe. MUGABE MUST GO. Mugabe must go now. Not tomorrow, not next week, he must go now." He paused. A woman at the back, probably Mavis, ululated. There was a conviction in his voice as though his message would be transmitted across the gulf and land on the President's desk in Harare. "I am not afraid, I am prepared to die, right here, right now, for the freedom of Zimbabwe. Mugabe must go. We are going to put him on trial for what he did in Gukurahundi. He will be punished for our supporters that he killed. We are going to have justice. I am your chairman and I am not going to rest until that man gets his just deserts…"

By now Peter understood a few things, though he couldn't understand why the chairman kept looking at him whenever he uttered the word 'Mugabe', as if he was looking for approval.

1) There was a man called Robert Mugabe.
2) Mugabe was a bad man.
3) Mugabe must go (although it was unclear exactly where to).
4) Mugabe was 'killing peoples'.
5) The BBC had something to do with it.
6) The chairman was prepared to die for his beliefs.
7) Mugabe must go now (see 3).
8) Mugabe must stand trial and be found guilty.

The chairman continued with his speech. "Mugabe and Zanu PF stole the last election. Everyone knows the peoples voted for the MDC. The peoples voted for President Morgan Tsvangirai. The peoples voted for change. Mugabe stole the election from the peoples using fear and intimidation. Once Robert Mugabe goes we can rebuild our country. But not before he goes. For now we need the international community to give us more sanctions. We want plenty sanctions. They must ban Mugabe and his cronies from flying around the globe. They must give us guns to fight against Robert Mugabe. We are not afraid. I can die right now. I am not afraid. We want a democratic society. A free Zimbabwe today…"

The speech carried on in this vein, going on and on and on and on. The chairman demonstrated the staunch heroism of a man far removed from the situation. The people began to get restless; a drunk in the back row struggled to stay awake, his head nodding. The chairman in his animated state did not realise he'd gone on for too long. It was, after all, his first speech and there was a 'donor' to impress. He went round in circles, outlining his vision. The general idea was once Mugabe was gone, everything would be alright.

The speech droned on until someone from the back shouted, "Who the hell elected you?" It was Scott.

The chairman pretended not to hear and pushed on with his speech.

"I said who the hell elected you guys?" Scott shouted even louder.

"Hey, mfana, respect the chairman," someone in the crowd said.

Scott grew more agitated. "Since this MDC thing started, you guys have been stealing money, selling party cards, letters for papers, running a racket. You talk about corruption back home when you're doing it right here. It's true, everyone knows it!"

"Iwe, mfana, shut up, there's a donor here," a voice shouted.

The chairman called for order. Somebody threw a punch at Scott. Peter was horrified. Scott retaliated. A gang fell upon him. The women began to scream, leaping off their chairs trying to get away from the havoc. Farai and Brian flew in fists flying. Farai caught a guy on the nose and blood splattered. Fists were democratically flying everywhere. Peter felt a hand grab his arm. It was Alfonso ushering him away from the jambanja. He pushed people aside and kept a firm grip even as bottles and chairs began to fly. The sound of glass breaking, a hundred year old stained glass window. A plate smashed on the wall right next to Peter's head just as they made it out into the open air. He ducked but the danger was already past. Alfonso made a great show of dusting him and checking to see he was unhurt.

"Sometimes they are like that," said Alfonso, who dived back into the church.

Peter called the police and lingered outside. A minute or two later, Alfonso emerged from the fray, with the Magistrate and the takings from the food on sale tucked safely under his arm. They left the chaos at St John's and went home, flashing blue lights now spilling on the old church.

The first shreds of dawn, little shafts of light, appeared on the horizon. The Maestro felt groggy. He looked in the mirror and saw his reflection, bags under the eyes, branches of red veins in the whites. He peed, aiming straight into the bowl, the sound of his piss magnified in the small bathroom. The stubble on his chin felt rough against his palms as he washed his face. He drank some water and rolled a joint, his first of the day. The Maestro shared some of his water with the little spider plant on the windowsill, before opening the window to let the smoke out. It had been another sleepless night. A long night with books, TV, the internet, and his own thoughts and solitude. If only he had an off switch, the ability to unplug, to escape consciousness for a few moments. Something deeper than sleep. The night that had passed was like the distant echo of noise and, when he tried to remember it, all that came to him were faint images, light recollections, a phrase from a book, flashes of colour from the TV, nothing substantial, nothing he could pin down and form into solid memory. A slight ache in the head, fatigue in his muscles, a little back pain were the only tangible remnants from the night. He had pills from the doctor, but they didn't seem to do anything. What could he expect from a geezer who'd seen him for five minutes and written a prescription before the Maestro had even finished describing his complaint? Something was wrong with his mind and ingesting these chemicals was supposed to artificially restore balance. Everything was a dreamy haze. On the square below he could see the chemist's where addicts queued up for their meth. The shutters were down, it was still too early. There was the Chinese takeaway and a chippy called Mario's with a large sign with white and red lettering. The red and green sign on the sub post-office, next to Mario's, was broken in half. Furthest away was Calder Supermarket. All the shops were on the same row. There were mounds fenced off around the

109

square, on which wild grasses grew. In summer they were an explosion of yellows, purples and reds from the poppies and other wild flowers that grew there. The middle of the square had a climbing frame for kids. It was about twenty feet tall and rope was woven round, making a spider's web. He finished his joint, stubbed it out on the windowsill and flicked it out the window. He thought about what would happen if there were a fire. He remembered watching images of a tower block in London a few years ago that was engulfed in thick smoke. People had died in that blaze. Maybe he'd get rope, just in case, so that if there were a fire, he could rappel down to safety. He closed the window, went to the bedroom, put on a pair of jogging bottoms, and left his flat. In the cold air he walked past the primary school and had to hopscotch over turds on the pavement. No one bothered to scoop after their dogs here. The smaller blocks of flats that made up the rest of the estate looked like geometric shapes, trapeziums planted in the earth with slanted roofs. Their pebble-dash walls looked rough and grey and cheap in the dim light. Best described as dwellings, rather than homes. But that's why he lived here, because of the low rents. The trade off was the litter-strewn streets, the quotidian smell of piss in the stairwells, blasts of loud music from partying neighbours and the unsightly locale. Daisies and buttercups grew on the lawn. Walking parallel to Wester Hailes Road, the concrete bulk of the Westside Plaza stood in the distance, beyond that the outline of the Pentlands, which in his imagination formed a sort of defensive arc round the city. Though the Maestro was grateful for the comforts and protection of the city, he wasn't ready to give in to its seduction and charms, and to love it. So he sought to observe closely the dark underbelly, the grotesque sector that never made it to postcards in tourist shops. He stopped at the canal, bent down and touched his toes, feeling the stretch run all the way from his Achilles tendon, through the hamstrings, to his buttocks and lower back. He stretched his quads, then moved to his arms and upper body. When he was done he faced west and began to run, just a slow jog, pacing himself. The water in the canal was a murky brown, filled with sediment and plant matter that had fallen in and sunk to the bottom. He read enough crime fiction to know canals were notoriously full of dead bodies. There were ripples on the surface of the water, from the wind maybe, since the water was stagnant. He ran on the tarmac, cushioned by his soft Nikes. Reeds from the far bank threatened to choke the canal at the bend where it turned north briefly. The trees that stood beyond dipped their lower branches into the water and were reflected on its surface, so it looked as though there was an identical underworld running along the canal that he could enter if only he'd dive in and break the barrier. The rotting sediment created a musty smell. Snapping at his heels was the familiar longing for self-obliteration. He remembered the last scene from the second Terminator where the cyborg handed Sarah Connor the button saying, I cannot self-terminate. It was the first film that made him cry. He was ten when he watched the Terminator being lowered into a vat of molten metal, offering a final thumbs up as he was submerged in the smouldering, yellow pool and then his CPU shut down. Better than crying over Bambi, he thought. But Bambi had made him cry too, lots of films had made him cry when he was younger, so had novels and songs. It seemed that then he could access finer emotions that were locked to him now. As he passed under a bridge he tried to remember the last time he'd cried, but the memory wouldn't come. His breathing rate increased, he was taking deeper breaths, filling his lungs with air, taking more oxygen to fuel his muscles. He passed under a second, older bridge and then a third, newer one, all within fifty yards of one another. Near the National Trust offices, he could take a right, going into the industrial estate, or follow the canal as it veered west. He chose the canal. His reflection on the windows of the office block matched him stride for stride. The cool air brushed against his face, he felt like bursting into a sprint, but if he wanted to get to where he was going, he'd have to pace himself, making sure that his reserves lasted until he got to the finish. The canal went over the four lanes of the bypass, cars passed beneath, headed for Glasgow or the airport. The first beads of sweat trickled down his back. He could see into the distance, another bridge and the straight track ahead. On either side of the canal were green fields with what he thought was rape, but he couldn't tell. This was a familiar route, but he'd not once seen the farmer who worked these fields. There were times he'd seen the earth upturned, brown, where a plough had been, or, after harvest, the yellow flowers vanished, but never a sign of the farmer as though the fields tended themselves. He heard the ringing of a bell, turned round and made way for two cyclists riding single file. The one behind said, Cheers, and off they went, pulling away from him. Cycling seemed so much easier than putting one leg in front of the other with no mechanical aid to lighten the load. He'd done these runs for as long as he could remember. At school, the Maestro played rugby in the winter and cricket in the summer. He was a fair shot at the javelin too. That had all fallen by the wayside once the day-to-day business of life took over with age. Time itself seemed to speed up. He remembered how, in school, days were long, so long, and moving from one grade to the next seemed to take an eternity. Now the days and the weeks went by in a blur. He'd read somewhere, and it was difficult to say exactly where because he read so much, that the illusion of time speeding up with age may be due to the fact that, in youth, each day is a new experience filled with learning and novelty and, later on in life, memories have formed and routine replaces the novel creating this distortion. Or is it that time is perceived as a fraction of one's lifetime, so for a child of five a year would be a fifth, a significant chunk, while for a man of fifty, it is only a fiftieth? Across the fields was the Park and Ride, and Heriot Watt beyond it hidden behind tall pines. The day grew brighter; the sky was a light blue, promising decent weather for a change. He passed a melancholy thistle with its purple crown growing in the brush at the side of the track. He felt burning in his lungs as they took cold air in. His legs felt heavier. They were lifting of their own accord, setting a rhythm to his breathing. He took off his track top and tied it around his waist. The Maestro listened to the sound of his own breathing, everything else was a whoosh, the wind rushing past his ears and the traffic on the M8 somewhere beyond the fields, the mix of sounds was a sonic boom, signalling his breaking of the fragile barrier between town and country. He carried on, one foot after the other, just running, leaving everything behind, edging closer to the zone, his eyes no longer making out distinct shapes or objects, light scattering on his retina, the green of the plants, the black of the track, the brown canal, the blue sky, not objects but colours running in parallel lanes as the world was pushed back behind him to the past, and he was running west, away from the sunrise, fleeing the new day, outside of himself, reaching a state of grace where the only thing that mattered was movement, pushing his body to its physiological limits, and then a thud, and another, and another, the beating of an ancient drum going faster and faster, a loud percussion that pierced through the whooshing and the swirling of the atmosphere, louder and louder, this primitive drum that never broke rhythm only getting louder and stronger, hypnotic in its intonation of sounds from the savannah, the song of the hunter and the hunted, the powerful melody of life and death that plays on and on until he was no longer there, broken free from the shackles of reality into a running induced nirvana, becoming not himself but pure movement, becoming steps within the haze and the blur of the world around, until it was not he that moved but the earth itself under him like a treadmill. He did not make an effort, no more than to raise his foot and be propelled at the speed where time collapses and all that is left is pure energy beaming through the cosmos, conscious and unconscious, a probability wave in all places at the same time, the feeling of invincibility, going under bridges, along fields, lost in the zone, mind on autopilot until, suddenly, he came to, in Ratho where he slowed to a halt, panting, covered in sweat that soaked his entire body from head to toe. Now at his destination, the Maestro bent down, hands on knees, and rested. In that position, the distance, the fatigue, the pain he'd left behind caught up with him, piling on by degrees. The Maestro shuffled up to the main street and took the 12 headed for the city. He sat at the back, hoping his sweat would not offend the other passengers. He felt lighter, and was gagging for a fag. As soon as he got home he made himself a bowl of porridge. His mobile rang. It was Tatyana. Why you don't answer my calls, I am trying to call you for very long time, she said. He replied, I was out running. He put a spoonful of honey in his porridge, stirred and added a drop of cold milk. You are still coming to see me? she asked. He explained that he was busy reading, only just starting on Keyes' Flowers for Algernon. Look, you are always promising me you are going to come and see me for weeks now. Each time I ask, you say you are starting on another book. I can understand it if you say you are writing or something, but reading, really? She sounded pissed off. Are we friends or not? It sounded more like a desperate plea from Tatyana. The Maestro knew not to hesitate on this one and said, Yes, of course we are. Was he really anyone's friend? He lived his life on a knife-edge and anytime he might slip off. So, I see you at three then. She hung up before he could counter with an excuse. He didn't like the feeling of being committed against his will, but he had promised. He ate his porridge, watching two young girls in their pyjamas going into the supermarket. A Rottweiler was tied to the railings outside the shop. The dog looked at the girls disinterestedly. When he finished eating, he picked up Algernon and began to read through Charlie's disjointed notes, going through the bad grammar and horrendous spellings, the footprints of a retard. Sunlight streamed into his lounge, drawing a picture of the window frame against the wall. The temptation to switch the TV on or surf the net came upon him. It was so

113

much easier just to sit and click and watch, because reading demanded that he join Keyes in creating the landscape through which Charlie navigated. He felt tired, his eyes jumped around the page and so he stopped, lay on the sofa and stared at the ceiling. There was nothing else to look at; the walls of his flat were bare, with no decorations apart from the little bulges where the old wallpaper underneath the paint was coming apart. He closed his eyes, willing Hypnos to come, but the god had deserted him. After a while he got up and retrieved the brown envelope from the mantelpiece. He inspected it, as if worried that someone had tampered with it. He left the flat and went down to the sub-post office in the square. There were three people in the queue. A short Asian man was working alone behind a reinforced glass partition on which a number of advertisements were stuck. The Maestro's turn came, he walked up with his envelope and had it weighed. Where is it going? Are there any valuables in it? Do you want to send it first class, second class, or recorded? the postmaster asked from behind the glass. I've changed my mind, I won't send it after all, said the Maestro, hastily grabbing the envelope and leaving the post office. He went back to the flat and returned it to the mantelpiece, in the exact same position. At two o'clock he left again, taking the 21, terminating at the Leith Links, and dropped off in Pilton. He phoned Tatyana, who told him he was early so he'd have to meet her at the beach, down Granton way. The streets in this neighbourhood were litter-strewn. Seagulls raided wheelie bins, tipping them over, tearing black bags and scattering rubbish. They filled the air, squawking and circling the skies in their hundreds. A woman in front of him strolled along eating ice cream. She had long brunette hair. Suddenly she let out a piercing scream as one side of her was caked in slimy, white poo. He resisted the urge to laugh; that bit of schadenfreude latent in us all. You fecking, fecking, horrible arsehole, the woman shouted, and for a minute he thought this was aimed at him until he realised she was talking to the birds, their squawks now sounding more like laughter. She threw her ice cream away and took off her top, which she used to wipe away the poo in her hair. He remembered the Washington Sniper who'd hit the news before the war started. People were getting shot at random in America, and the best advice so-called experts could give was that people weave and duck as they walked through the city, going about their day to day lives. The Maestro kept on the pavement, walking in a straight line, now fully conscious that at any moment, without warning, he might randomly get shat on. A group of teenagers was hanging out by the door of a corner shop. Down the slope was the steel lattice of the gasworks and the sea beyond. He walked past builders on scaffolding, working on new blocks of flats. A few of them had been completed, square things with large windows and, thankfully, just a plain coat of paint where the old ones had pebble-dash. He wondered if these buildings would age well. They did not compare with the old Victorian and Edwardian buildings in the city, but now he thought about it, it seemed the city was a garden, and had to have this variety for its beauty to be realised. Did he think of that himself, or was it a thought plagiarised from a book? It was becoming more difficult to distinguish his own thoughts from what he'd read. Was it even possible in this age to have a single original thought? The question itself seemed highly unoriginal. There was a loud clang, as one of the builders threw some steel rods down on the pavement. Someone swore poetically. He wanted to stop and watch them work. They had to feel some sense of fulfilment, knowing that their work would outlast them. His own contribution to society, stacking shelves in a supermarket, paled in comparison to the builders' in their dirty jeans and high-vis jackets. The Maestro's was a dead end job, unless he aspired to be a corporate prick and, even then, he had no qualifications. Tatyana saw him and waved. He waved back and headed towards her. I was just about to call you, I thought you might go to wrong side, she said. You look different, Maestro. You're eating well? He shrugged. Tatyana was small, blonde, and traces of her Polish accent came out in her Ss and Zs. She wore a light green fleece and black track bottoms. They walked along the beach, ignoring the cans of super strength lager, the chippy wrappers and the plastic bags strewn across it. They bumped into each other, separated and touched each other again as they walked, doing a little dance, a ballroom step of which neither of them was conscious. Large mansions on the beachfront were hidden by trees. From Granton he could see Cramond Island in the distance. He hadn't been there yet, but he wished to go, if only to see the Roman road. Isn't it so much better to walk on the beach, than to read about it? asked Tatyana. She poked him in the ribs and he moved away. You know for someone who smile a lot at work, you're always so serious outside. Barry have a party, everyone go there, except for you, she said. I don't like parties, he replied. Okay, Grandpa, she said. She was right; it was nicer being out with her than sitting at home, alone. He stopped himself, bottling up whatever sentiment might have begun to form inside of him. Tatyana pointed at two kites, a red one and a blue one flying in the sky. They were too far away to see the strings, but he saw two boys leaning back, playing with their spools so that the kites danced in the wind. That looks like fun, he said. Maybe I'll go off and read The Kite Runner. Tatyana frowned, taking him literally. She was fluent in English but still tripped over the odd pronunciation or missed a joke. And she had that Polish characteristic of inhabiting a continuous present tense. In spite of that she was proficient enough to have even worked as a translator for an agency, only joining Tesco when that work dried up. She was the one person who hounded him to meet up for a drink, or chat about poetry, trying to form a bond at a time when he was drifting, cutting himself off from people. Her tenacity was written on the hard angles of her face, which didn't make her any the less pretty, but gave her a mature edge like she was wise beyond her years. I like coming here to the beach, she said. It reminds me of Kołobrzeg. I grow up there, on the Baltic Sea. He raised his eyebrows. I tell you this before, yes? He nodded. Then you moved to Gdansk when you were ten, I remember. Your father was a policeman and your mother is a teacher. Tatyana smiled and complimented him on his memory. When she was younger, Tatyana thought she was going to be an artist, but it never happened. The Maestro knew what it was to see your dreams vanish in a puff of smoke. The manifest unfairness in which the herd watched the precious few that had fulfilled their ambitions rise up the ladder, while they languished in the pit of bitterness, envy and regret. He pointed to a bench on the lawns ahead and they went to sit down. A large tanker sailed up the Forth. A man threw a stick for his Jack Russell to chase. After they were rested, they got up and strolled to Somerfield in the little arcade on Pennywell Road. The Maestro carried the basket, while she went ahead and did the shopping, guiding him from aisle to aisle. Red or white? she asked at the drinks section. He picked a bottle of Merlot. They paid and walked back to the estate, to her place. Tatyana lived in West Pilton, in a block of flats near a small park. Her flat was shaped in an L; the corridor from the door went past two bedrooms and a bathroom, turning into the lounge, which led to the kitchen. She had photographs of her family and her former life arranged in a collage, the centre of which was a black and white portrait of her father in his police uniform, staring into the camera. He looked only a little older than Tatyana was now, a young man trying to disguise his youth behind a moustache. What drew the Maestro to the picture was the focussed look, as if her father knew his purpose in life. It always seemed the older generation, the ones who believed in nation, queen, God, freedom or some other ideology, were more sure of themselves and their place in the universe. She turned the radio on and went into the kitchen to cook. It was always tuned to Radio 6 with its eclectic selection of music, playing subaltern bands the Maestro never even knew existed. There was a little fourteen-inch television in one corner that was never switched on. In fact, Tatyana had drawn a smiley face with large round eyes on the screen, giving it an Orwellian, Big-Brother-is-watching look. A miniature red and white Polish flag stood on it. The walls had photographs of various cities and resorts in Poland. There were books in Polish and Russian on a shelf. Even her cigarettes were a Polish brand. It was as though she had brought a little piece of the old country with her. Her flat was sovereign territory, an embassy of sorts. It was more than that, a sanctuary, a mausoleum of home. She called him through to the kitchen to open a can of tomatoes and ordered him out again, but not before giving him a glass of wine. He savoured the aroma from the kitchen, mouth-watering in the Pavlovian sense. Tatyana never rushed, for her the cooking process was as important as the dining. They had golumpki served with sour sauce. The Maestro told her he loved cabbage and was delightfully surprised by the texture on his palate from the minced meat mixed within. When they were finished, they stood side by side in the kitchen. He washed the dishes while she dried and stored them. This domesticity came naturally to them as though they had always been part of the same unit, almost like being a couple. They shared his glass of wine. Tatyana had left hers in the living room. The window by the sink looked out onto an open space with washing lines. I hang my clothes out there to dry when I first move here and when I go out to get them; they are gone, Tatyana said, with a laugh of disbelief. It's a rough neighbourhood this, said the Maestro. He wasn't too surprised. It almost felt right that something that low should happen here. They even take my thongs. I can't believe it. Maybe today we walk past somebody wearing my underwear, who knows? The half-moon hung low in the sky. The Maestro imagined it pulling him and Tatyana like the tide. They moved to the living room and sat together on the sofa. She lay her head on his lap and asked him to tell her a story. He thought for a moment, tried to reach into the depths of memory and pull something from his brain, but there was a screen, a paper-thin barrier that he could not breach. I don't know any stories, he finally said. Out of all those books he read, he couldn't find a single tale of his own. She looked him in the eye from where she lay and he averted his eyes. He had nothing to say, no story to tell. The radio was playing funk. The Maestro's hand moved close to her head to stroke her hair, but he stopped himself, mid-flight, and rested it back on the armrest of the sofa. Without the music playing there would have been silence, a vacuum to fill. It was nearly eight. If he went home now, he could have a few more hours to read. Tatyana said, Well, if you don't have story to tell me, why don't you tell me about your parents, where you are born, that sort of stuff. I want you to tell me about your childhood, your past. He sighed and replied, I have nothing to say. She sat up. Come on, Maestro, I tell you everything about myself, my family, school, you need to open up. Let's just start with where you are born, how hard can that be? He took a deep breath. His heart was pounding as if his chest was going to burst; he got up from the sofa abruptly, mumbled an apology of sorts and hurried outside.

Alfonso called at the Magistrate's, uninvited in his usual fashion. They'd not seen each other for days, not since the debacle at St John's, as if Alfonso was hiding his head in the sand, which was unusual for the shameless man. At work, the Magistrate had had to deal with Spiwe and, when he'd enquired after Alfonso, she gave excuses that he wasn't available, always at one meeting or another. And now, here he was with Scott at his door. Scott had bruises on his face and looked just as angry as he remembered him at that disastrous meeting.

"May we come in? We have something of the utmost importance to discuss with you," Alfonso said, his voice full of dignity.

Alfonso had a plastic bag with bottles in it and soon they were drinking. The Magistrate lowered the volume on the TV. He kept a wary eye on Scott who was crushing his can of lager by degrees, which made a clicking noise.

"What's this important business you want to talk about?"

"The incident at the church," Alfonso said.

"Shameful stuff," the Magistrate replied. "It was in the local papers. What a disgrace."

"You see, our community wants to come together. United we can achieve big things, great things. What happened last month was because of poor leadership." Alfonso nodded solemnly. "With the right leadership, the party can steer the people in a meaningful way and bring about the change we need back home."

"You'll need a miracle with that rabble."

"Who are you to call them rabble, Mr High and Mighty?" Scott's voice was shrill. "I told you, Alfonso, he isn't the right man. He looks down on the people. I knew he was one of those petit bourgeois types when I first met him. We're wasting our time here. We can find someone else."

"Hang on, hang on… I am sorry. My friend here has a sharp tongue. He means well, he doesn't mean to offend." Alfonso giggled nervously. "Scott cares for the people. He is one of those rare young men who are genuinely concerned about the fate of our country."

"Twenty-one is not young!" Scott interjected.

"You'd do well to listen to your elders from time to time," said the Magistrate.

"That kind of mentality is exactly why we are in this situation. It's not our generation that's created this mess. I've told you again and again, Alfonso, it's time for these old madharas to make way for us."

"I will not be insulted in my own house." The Magistrate stood up.

Alfonso leapt off his seat, waving his arms about. "This is just a misunderstanding. We're all on the same side here. We all want the same thing. We mustn't fight among ourselves. Scott, we discussed this. We need a mature, experienced, credible face that people can turn to. Please sit down. Let's talk like countrymen. We don't mean to cause any offence." He pulled the Magistrate back down on the sofa.

Scott drank his beer with an insolent air, staring into space. The Magistrate wondered why there was so much rage in him. He'd seen young men like this in his courtroom, the ones with their trigger finger on the self-destruct button. Only this time it felt as though he was the one on trial. He remembered a time when the young were more respectful. He remembered a time when people were decent and upright, or was it all just a trick of the memory, selective reminiscences filtered through the periscope of time. He'd been at Rufaro in 1980, amidst the crowd that danced to Marley, and watched the Union Jack come down. He sighed, feeling tired and exasperated as he did whenever he thought of home.

"We need to find a solution and we want you to be part of that solution," Alfonso said.

"I'm afraid I don't follow."

"Me and Scott have contacted the head office in London. We told them about our concerns over the way Chairman Dzivarasekwa is running the branch. They have agreed that the only way forward is by holding an election and rejuvenating our grass-root structures."

"Dzivarasekwa was never elected to that position in the first place," said Scott. "We just woke up one day and he was calling himself the founding chairman."

"I've even heard him call himself 'life-chairman.'"

"I wish you all the best with it," said the Magistrate.

"We need a credible candidate to stand against him."

"If what I saw of him is any true indication of his character then you won't have too much difficulty with that."

"We need a man like you. A man respected in the community. A lot of people have heard the story about how you were pushed from the bench because you didn't do what the government wanted. I have friends everywhere and they say, in Mash Central, you were known for being incorruptible. People talk, people have heard of these things. With a man like you leading us we could do a lot of good." Alfonso stopped and looked expectantly at the Magistrate.

"Hang on; you want me to join your party?"

"To lead it!" said Alfonso.

"I am flattered you think so highly of me, but I have no interest in politics."

Scott banged his can on the coffee table and stood up. He stared at the Magistrate for a good while, turned and walked over to the door before firing a parting shot, "I told you. He's not interested in the people. Come on, Alfonso, we're wasting our time here."

Alfonso stood up. He held out his arms in supplication. "At least you could give it more thought. We need a man like you." He ran out behind Scott, mumbling, huffing and puffing.

The Magistrate watched them leave, relieved the visit was over so soon. Through the lace curtains he could see Scott arguing with Alfonso as they walked down the road. He felt sorry for whomever it fell to lead this bunch. It would be like herding cats.

The Magistrate discovered Joan Dowler's dead body. It was a bright day in August. She lay on her bed, peaceful at last, having escaped from the medicine that had imprisoned her shell in the world of the living for far longer than it should have. Her passing so disturbed the Magistrate that he withdrew to the staff room. He could not understand why the death of this woman with whom he had no relationship would affect him so deeply. Was it her suffering that caused this pain he felt? Perhaps it was the fact that in a house with many people, she had lived completely alone and died alone.

The Magistrate had seen death before. Plenty of it. His brother, Ronald, had died of the Plague in the nineties. But he had been loved, with his family around him until the end. He listened to Linda on the phone, calling for a doctor. He watched as she ruffled through the notes to try to find the next of kin.

"Great, I have to call her solicitor," Linda said.

"She had no family?" the Magistrate asked.

"Nope."

"No one at all?"

"Look, pal, you look awful. Is this your first one?"

"I'm fine."

"Right, I think you should go home and relax for a bit, okay. You're no good to us in this state. Sort out your timesheet and I'll sign it. We've got most of the residents settled and I reckon we can manage until the morning staff get here."

The Magistrate left, relieved to be leaving this catacomb, this place where they piled people up to die. The night was warm. He took the 21 and sat in silence watching people get on and off. He was blank, unable to comprehend this emotion. His entire life had been dedicated to the ideal of being a rational being for whom reason held sway over emotion. That's what it meant, being on the bench, listening to proceedings, being impassive.

Now he was removed from that theatre, he was immersed in real life. Ordinary life had no choreography. The city rolled by but he was numb to it. It depressed him to think that one day he might find himself in that position: old, vulnerable, isolated, without the care and comfort of those he loved. And what would happen to him then? What was the point of life, if it was to end in pain and degradation?

He got off the bus and slowly walked home. The road was quiet, save for the occasional car passing through. He looked for his keys in his jacket pockets and only found them in his shirt pocket after a bit of effort. I don't remember putting them in there, he thought, opening the door. Thumping hip-hop beats came from the living room. He went inside, thinking he'd tell Chenai to turn the volume down before he went up to bed.

There was a kid reclined on his favourite sofa. The Magistrate paused. He had that odd feeling you get when you walk into the wrong bar. The young man was naked, his pale skin a contrast to the black material of the sofa. Chenai was knelt between the kid's legs sucking and slurping. Jay-Z on the TV sang something about 'niggers', thumping beats matched by the bopping up and down of Chenai's head. Something elemental froze the Magistrate right where he stood, invisible cords tying him to the floor. He turned ashen grey, then Michael Jackson white.

"OMG," said the kid.

"I'm fucking awesome," Chenai whispered in a hoarse voice.

"OMG."

"Yeah baby." Slurp, slurp, slurp.

"Stop!"

"You cumming already?" She sounded like one of the girls from the hip-hop videos.

HIS DAUGHTER HAD A PENIS IN HER MOUTH. Chenai stopped, looked up, saw her father and cried, "OMG!" The kid's penis was glowing scarlet, veins bulging, vibrating with the unfathomable power of teenage virility. He grabbed a cushion and tried to cover it.

"What the hell is going on in my house?" the Magistrate shouted, his power of speech restored. He took giant strides and tried to grab at the boy who cried, "Jesus Christ," and jumped away, just in time. The boy was nimble, like a gazelle, he leapt from the sofa and into the kitchen. He banged into a cupboard and knocked some plates over. In the blink of an eye, he'd unlocked the door and bounded into the garden. The Magistrate was hot on his heels the entire time, no more than half a step away, his hands open like talons ready to grab his quarry.

The kid ran across the lawn, trampled on the vegetables over which the Magistrate had laboured, and vaulted over the fence in a feat of superhuman agility. The fence was the limit for the Magistrate's middle-aged body. All he could do was shake it to let out his rage as he watched the pale, naked figure accelerating into the night.

He followed the boy with his eyes, then remembered Chenai. He walked back, shaking with rage, fists clenching and unclenching.

"Chenai!"

She'd hastily dressed by the time he got back inside. The button on her jeans was undone and her hair dishevelled. She had the boy's clothes and trainers in her hands. He grabbed her by the shoulders and shook her. She let out a sob and shut her eyes.

"I'm holding you now, Chenai. I'm holding you now," the Magistrate shouted. "Who is that boy? Tell me, tell me who he is."

She trembled under his grip but would not answer. He raised his right hand, the one that used to hold the gavel, high in the air, ready to bring natural justice down upon her.

"He's my boyfriend, Liam. Dad, you're hurting me."

He pushed her away. It took every ounce of will to muster himself again and order her to go to her room. She dropped the clothes on the floor and fled upstairs. The Magistrate took the Walkman from his pocket and threw it against the wall. It broke, cracking with the characteristic sound of plastic. The cassette flew out and spilt ribbon and screws. He collapsed onto the footstool by the door, his eyes fixed on the pile of clothes. One of the muddy trainers was turned up, exposing a worn out sole. The weight of the entire universe pressed down on him.

He sat on the stool that entire night, unable to sleep, the image etched in his mind was of his little girl with a penis in her mouth. Above the mantelpiece was a family portrait. Chenai was a baby sandwiched between him and her mother.

The Maestro woke up around three in the morning. He'd had one of those heavy, black sleeps that taste of death, which insomniacs have once in a while. He went to the kitchen and drank a glass of water. There was a mild throbbing in his head, a sort of proto-headache. In the bathroom he took two paracetamol, downing them dry. He yawned, scratched his balls, walked back to the lounge, drew the curtains and looked out into the night. The pine trees by the nursery stood shadowless under the relentless streetlights. The Maestro brought out his tin that contained Rizlas, baccy and grass. Part of the joy of smoking lay in the preparatory ritual, the slight delay of satisfaction. He crumbled the herb, picked out the seeds, mixed it with his baccy and rolled a joint. It made him feel calmer, eased the tension in his skull. He felt a warm glow, the burden of the world falling off his shoulders, and a certain mellowness as the smoke cloaked him in blue and grey. As it got light early, he was able to go out for a run, first taking a walk through the deserted estate to the canal. He decided not to follow the water, instead climbing up the steps that lead on to Wester Hailes Road. A mini-cab drove past. He ran past the traffic lights, along the back of the Odeon, over the deserted parking lot, under the railway line, into Wester Hailes. The flats here were three, sometimes four storeys high, long dreary-coloured blocks that created a sense of foreboding. He kept on Harvesters Way, running parallel to the main road. An empty N30 crawled past so slowly that, for a few seconds, he kept alongside it. He paced himself, going on and off pavements as he crossed the little streets that fed into the estate. A flat on the third floor had a balcony full of pot plants. That little touch of beauty made him feel better about the area, knowing that some people made this home. He only saw his flat as a base, a place to rest outside of work. Suddenly, a flash of lights, loud hooting, the screech of brakes. He got off the road, back onto the pavement, his heart pounding. A black cab appeared out of nowhere, just a few feet from him, the driver looked at him angrily. The Maestro apologised, embarrassed, and waited for the cab to drive past. The urban run was different from the countryside run. You had to stay alert; you couldn't let your mind drift and zone off. Look right, look left, then look right again, he reminded himself, as he went on to Clovenstone, past the vets. He caught up with the N30 again, idling on Clovenstone Drive, which looped around the estate. The driver stood outside, having a fag and said, Mornin'. Half the plaster on the next block of flats had fallen off, leaving raw brickwork exposed. The golf course was to his right and he followed it all the way round, until he left the estate again. This time he was watchful, looking out for cars. A little part of him was fearful that someone might jump out of the bushes and jack him. He wouldn't have much strength with which to protect himself; he was now just pounding the streets, feeling the build up of lactic acid in his calves. It. Was. All. About. Keeping. Rhythm. Maintaining. His. Pace. Moving. One. Foot. After. The. Other. Propelling. Himself. Forward. Under. His. Own. Will. A. Test. Of. Endurance. And. Fortitude. He ran, creating the mental map of the route ahead. Already he could see himself back at the bridge, his starting point. He met the canal again on Hailesland and ran along the path beside it, feeling good, knowing that, in a few more minutes, he'd be done with his circuit. There were times he thought about taking part in the Edinburgh Marathon, doing the 26.2 miles, but he knew he was lying to himself. His running was a solitary thing; he did not want to be part of the herd. It was a way of tapping into himself, which meant the discovery of his own limits at a time when he was beginning to accept the idea of his own mortality. He no longer had that invincible feeling of his teens and early twenties. He did not time himself when he ran, he never bothered to measure the distance either, it was a form of free styling, and though he had familiar routes he liked to follow, he needed the freedom of knowing he could go anywhere so long as his legs could carry him. It wasn't a test or a challenge, rather an essential act for him. He crossed the road, and ran to the Shell station, its bright yellow and red logo standing out like a beacon. The Maestro knocked on the window, waking the cashier who was half dozing in his kiosk. He ordered some baccy, threw the money under the serving hatch and received his pouch the same way. He put the baccy in his pocket and zipped it up. Only a few more feet, across Wester Hailes Road, and he was back at the bridge. A flock of mallards floated on the water. In order to warm down, he walked the rest of the way home. After he'd rested, he picked up The Grass is Singing. He lay on his sofa and read. Soon he was lost in this world of which he recognised glimpses, the characteristic of any good novel. But was it a good novel? How had he come to that conclusion? He liked Lessing, though now, thinking about it, he felt as though his decision to like Lessing had been made for him, not by him. He thought about how he bought his books, how he made the decision to spend money on this one rather than that one, and found that most of his choices were made for him by the Guardian, or a short reference in the introduction of some seminal text. These critics told him that a book was good, that it somehow captured the human spirit, and so off he went to buy it. This was a different relationship to the one he had with television, in which he was more likely to stumble on things, films about which he didn't care who the director or the actors were since he was no film buff. With film he was more ready to cast a negative judgement, to say that something was boring or mediocre. His relationship with the medium was a short promiscuous bonk. With books, on the other hand, it was a different experience. Most of his collection was of authors he'd heard of beforehand. There were few impulse buys, for each book represented not only a monetary investment but also an investment of his time. There was the awe that any mind that could produce a long text that passed through the gatekeepers of the industry, the publishers, must be a genius of sorts, and so the work itself must be worth reading. He was more likely to fear that he didn't get it, rather than to say that a book was bad. He envied the brave souls on Amazon, the dissenters hiding behind anonymous avatars, who gave War and Peace one star and told Tolstoy to go stuff it – too long, too slow, too many characters, what's with all the digressions, just get on with the story, Nikolayevich. One Casey Jones had asked if Tolstoy was taking the Mickey. Ms Jones wrote: I could not believe how many words there are in this book! It is just full of them. She felt it could have been a tenth of the size, and went on to say she had read The Count of Monte Cristo, which was a lot more readable. On a forum like that, Ms Jones was assailed by Tolstoyans, one of whom suggested she read Bridget Jones's Diary instead. But the fact remained that she was a brave nonconformist, one of the precious few. He'd drifted off the page in this reverie and went back to reread a few paragraphs that he'd skimmed. The phone rang, his landline. He picked it up. It was Sue, from HR, calling to find out why he hadn't turned up for work three days in a row. He said he was sick. Sue, from HR, advised him to get a note from his GP. He thanked her and hung up. This was the first time he'd missed work in four years. Come rain, hail or snow, he'd always made it. He did not feel bad about it at all. There was something liberating about pulling a sickie, snatching a few hours back from the man. He yelled a feeble, Woohoo, and raised his arms victoriously, touching the low ceiling of his flat. He put the book aside and switched on the TV. Jeremy Kyle was talking to a woman with a Geordie accent. Four men sat in a semi-circle around her. Jeremy was preaching, the woman was crying; Jeremy paused and called for a commercial break. The Maestro took some yoghurt from the fridge and ate, watching the commercials: some guy in a suit offering debt advice about PPIs, just call 0800 33... washing machines live longer with Calgon, an ambulance chaser asking if he'd had a fall or injury at work. No Win, No Fee. Daytime adverts were full of parasites. Cue music – Jeremy came back to the applause of his audience. A man in black handed him an envelope. He preached to the woman and her four men that they had to get their lives sorted. Then he read the results of the DNA test. The father turned out to be the skinhead on the extreme right with tattoos all over his arms. He stood up, victorious, and walked to embrace the sobbing woman. One of the other men, her current boyfriend, stormed off and the other two sat forlorn, losers in an evolutionary battle. The audience applauded. Was the applause for Jeremy, the woman, the skinhead, the losers? He couldn't tell. The phone rang and he groaned, thinking it was Sue, from HR, again. He picked it up and said, Hello. A voice, neither human nor mechanical, came on. It sounded ethereal. Hello, good morning, my name is Scott, and I'm calling from Ipsos MORI, we are doing a survey about... The Maestro stopped him right there, said he was not interested in doing surveys and hung up. He switched on his laptop, watched it booting up, the bleeping and the noise of the fan coming on. He entered his password, then logged on to the internet and checked his emails. No new messages, save for some spam about penile enhancement. He went on to Amazon. Jeremy was moving on to a lie detector story about a woman who suspected her partner of cheating, and now she wanted to know the truth on national TV. The Maestro checked his recommendations, mostly literary novels. He wanted something light, fast-paced, John Grisham or Dean Koontz. He settled on Grisham's The

Chamber, clicked and ordered it. He liked bookshops, there was something romantic about them as cultural hubs, but everything was cheaper on Amazon, and on his wage that sealed his defection. Yet each time he made a purchase he felt the niggling guilt that he was being responsible for the slow death of an institution he so adored, an awareness that using the website was not without consequences. But he did it anyway. The next day he did not go to work again, nor the next or the one after that. He ignored the ringing phone and the natural urge to go back into the routine he knew. It occurred to him that he could create a new routine for himself and he wanted it to centre on his books. If he devoted himself wholeheartedly to literature and gave up his soul to it, then he hoped that at the end of his inquiry he would have glimpsed the secret to life itself. The Maestro was not well educated; he'd left school after his O Levels and drifted from job to job, staying with family friends, never quite finding the direction in which to point his life. The idea of giving everything up to be a reader appealed to him. But how could he make people at work understand that he was taking a sabbatical to read? They would want to know what he was reading, what qualifications he hoped to gain. Why not go to college? they might say. He knew stories about people who'd given up their jobs to see the world, but he didn't have the money to do that. Yet, he would be a little like them, he decided, circling the globe through the page. He'd heard of people who'd given up everything to become writers and he admired them. He carried the image of the starving author, huddled in a cold garret, gripped by the muse, dipping the quill into his own soul and marking the page in blood. But the writer carried a hint of vanity, the desire to see his name immortalised in print. The Maestro had never imagined himself a writer. The true reader had to be stripped bare of such narcissism. The reader was a vessel, a stage on which words and stories played out. In a world where video games, pop culture, the internet, television and a million other distractions were calling, being a reader was now something of a vocation, keeping the flame of an old art form alive. He imagined himself a hermit in his flat, a medieval monk chained to his desk. He dreamt of absorbing every book ever written, including the traces of truth hidden in Mystery, Romance, Sci-fi and Fantasy. He would start from Cervantes and work his way through literature. The truth waiting at the other end was a sort of grand unified theory, if only he could make it across the chasm of text. The idea was as intoxicating as his pot. As the Maestro followed this plan through, he began to lose track of time. The arbitrary division of time into seconds, hours, weeks, months and seasons became meaningless. Only day and night mattered. In the mornings he went running, varying his route at whim so he covered Baberton, Broomhouse, Longstone, even pushing as far out as Colinton and Oxgangs in one direction and Craiglockhart in the other. In the evenings he went down to the chippy for his meals. One particular evening, there was a man there, skinny, with sunken cheeks. The man had a bulldog, a stocky black dog that ran around weaving its way between people's legs. When the man was served, the Maestro stepped forward and ordered a portion of chips, which he drowned in mayonnaise. He paid one pound and twenty pence to the Turkish man at the counter and left. Outside of his running range, he now seldom ventured far from his flat. Everything he needed was on this little square. He went back upstairs and ate his supper, sitting on the sofa, watching television. The chips were not well cooked in the centre, but the taste was bearable. This was a good batch by Mario's usual standards, compliments to the chef. He listened to the low roar of traffic on the bypass. It sounded like a river and, if he closed his eyes, he could see it, a wide river, powerful like the Zambezi. He could only hold this picture in his mind a short while, then it vanished. Images from his past tried to stream into the present. They were a soft knock from the hidden caves in his mind. He blocked them out, finished his supper, picked up a book and began to read. He read until his eyes were sore, lay on the sofa and slept. There he had a dream in which there was a snake, a little green snake coming towards him, and try as he might to run away, he could not. He was frozen in space, straining to move against a short circuit in his nervous system, somewhere between the thought of running and the actual act itself. In this dream, he was not so much trapped in his body, as he was a disembodied spirit, outside of himself, watching things happening to himself, making him both the subject and the observer. The snake, which turned into a cobra, kept coming at him, hissing, full of menace, but never actually reached him. They were trapped in an act in which nothing quite happened, a wave of potential energy. He could feel the fear course through his being... His mobile rang and woke him up. It was Tatyana. Hello, you sound sleepy. Did I wake you? He lied that he had been awake, even though his voice told a different story. He half-listened to her speak, recalling his dream, the helplessness he'd felt. This had been his first dream in a long time. I heard you don't come to work anymore, are you okay? she asked, the concern evident in her voice. I'm fine, he said. She pressed on. You sound horrible. He just wanted to get back to sleep. The light from outside was coming in through a gap between the curtains; it made a reflection against the ceiling that looked like the blade of a dagger. I'm fine, he said. She replied, I'm coming to see you tomorrow. He tried to put her off, saying he was doing something important, but he kept tripping up and failed to come up with a plausible excuse. After she hung up, he closed his eyes and tried to get back to sleep. He watched the back of his eyelids, a swarm of colours imprinted in the dark. His back ached. He went to the bathroom and took a couple of sleeping tablets. If only Tatyana hadn't fucking called. He felt like the living dead, body and mind caught up in different realms. It was hard to keep his eyes open and even harder to sleep. He drank a glass of milk and lit a fag. When he was a child, his mother used to sit with him in the dark, singing lullabies. Hush-a-ba, babby, lie still, lie still; your mammie's away to the mill, the mill... He couldn't remember the rest of the words. And yet in the not so distant past, people did remember these things. They remembered birthdays and phone numbers. He'd been on safari with a man who knew the names of every tree, every shrub, every flower, every animal, every bird and every insect they came across. Some Muslims memorised the whole of the Quran so they could recite it. He'd heard of a man who could recite all of Shakespeare's sonnets by rote. The Maestro, for his part, only remembered the names of cans on shelves and aisle numbers in the supermarket. That was all his mind seemed to contain, that and books. These random, fleeting thoughts made it impossible to sleep. Light rain fell against his window. He tried to find the right name for it, a drizzle, or was it better described as a smirr? He'd read somewhere on the internet that the Inuit had many words for snow and this meant that they perceived it differently to outsiders. The specialised vocabulary meant that they could tell different types of snow, subtle variations where the outsider only saw a uniform blanket of white. It denoted a type of intimacy with the land, though the types of modern Inuit he saw on TV nowadays tended to go about on snowmobiles and hunt with rifles. In any case, he'd also read this was a modern myth, as though every truth was balanced by an equal and opposite untruth. He decided to go out and run in the rain. It made no sense to try and understand it from the warmth behind his double-glazed windows. Smirr-Drizzle,

135

words were shadows in Plato's cave. So he went out and ran around the square until he was soaked. After a warm shower, he settled and read the City of Glass. He came to the part where the old man, Stillman's father, was pondering the inadequacy of language in describing the world. The old man was wandering New York, picking up broken things and he happened across an old umbrella with no cloth across the spokes, and pondered if it was still an umbrella when it could no longer perform its function. His buzzer rang. Navigating the house by instinct, reading as he walked, the Maestro moved to the door and buzzed Tatyana up. He waited, listening to the cranking of the lift as it came up the shaft. Tatyana emerged, her wet hair plastered to her cheeks and forehead. She stepped over a stack of letters on the floor of the threshold. Each day more letters came, along with flyers and advertisements, adding to the pile. She removed her jacket and hung it on the hook in the corridor. He took her to the living room where he unmuted the TV. It would be a filler to the lulls he anticipated in the conversation. Tatyana excused herself to go to the bathroom to dry her hair. Would you like a cup of tea? he called. He didn't hear her reply from the other room. It was short, sharp and could have been a yes or no, so he went ahead and boiled the water. She came back and said, Do you mind if I open the window? It smells of chips in here. He apologised and let her open it. You look so skinny. My God, you're turning yellow. That explained the feeling he sometimes had when he looked in the mirror and saw a reflection that was not quite himself, a close replica, but definitely not the original. This junk food is bad for you, said Tatyana. Look how your bin is full of wrappers. Oh, and all these books on the floor... I'm sorry. She stopped. The look on her face said she had more to say. Tatyana was right, the flat was a mess. He made a mental note to do some housework once she'd left. He gave her tea with a dash of masala. She took a sip. This is really nice, you should teach me how to make it. There's no limit to what you can do with a good cup of tea, he replied. She sat opposite, looking at him, more watching than looking, as though she was trying to probe what was going on in his soul. The Maestro looked away and said nothing. How come you are not going to work for long time now? He replied that she sounded like his mom. Tatyana threw her hands up in despair. I can't get through to you, can I? I'm only trying to help. It's like you're not even here. You can't even look at me when I talk to you. He got up and stood at the window, watching figures walking in and out of the

136

supermarket in the rain. Maestro, sit down, I'm talking to you, she said, exasperated. It's these books! You're filling your head with this nonsense. Books can't replace real life, this Paul Auster talks shit. I prefer his wife. Your beloved Dostoevsky is an anti-Semite, he has sneaky, money grabbing Jews and little Poles in his novels. Oh and there's Lovecraft, I won't even go into him. Why don't you talk to me? I'm here, I'm alive. He watched the flashing lights of a plane on approach at the airport in the distance. How nice it would be just to fly away from everything, to be stranded on an island with nothing but his books. What do you want from me? he asked. He was beginning to feel the temper stir in him, but she kept pecking away like a piranha in his face. I want your friendship, I want your love, she said, ever so simply. He did not turn to her, but said, Get out and leave me the fuck alone. Tatyana stood up. Her face was red from the blow, the humiliation of bearing her soul and being rebuffed like this. Why? she said, and she gathered her things. She lingered in the corridor for a good few minutes, taking her time to put on her coat, hoping that he would come out to her. Instead, he stayed rooted to the spot, watching the rain until he heard the door open and shut. He let out a long breath. A few minutes later he turned round and saw her cup on the table. He touched it. It was still warm. There were wet patches on the sofa where she had sat. The ghost of her presence lingered in these small traces. He took the cup to the kitchen and washed it. He spent the rest of the day in bed, reading his novel. Tatyana's face kept popping up in his head. It was not a clear image, rather something imprinted on the pages of the novel, a daemon hidden in the text. He threw the book down. He had to get rid of the distractions in his life for the sake of the journey upon which he had embarked. Reading was to be a religious vocation, a retreat, and he had to push the world out so he could focus. It came to him that the world was clawing at him and he needed to block it out. It came through the letterbox, on TV, on his phone, his computer. The world was in the furniture on which he sat, woven into the clothes he wore, branded on the toothpaste he used. There was only one thing for it. He got up, went to the lounge, unplugged the TV, the DVD player and the digibox. He took them downstairs, one by one, and left them outside in the rain. He unplugged his landline and the wireless router, and took them outside along with his laptop. A bloke in a shell suit approached. What you doing with these, pal? the man asked. Throwing them away. Yous dinnae mind if I takes them, do ya? asked the man, rather gleefully. The Maestro shrugged. Right, can you watch them for me? I need to get the missus to give us a hand. The Maestro waited, he saw no reason why he should deny the man these things for which he no longer had any use. The bloke came back with a pregnant woman. The Maestro helped them take his stuff to their flat on the fifth floor. Their flat had flowery wallpaper, a radio, a small television and some old furniture. I have some sofas and a bed to go, he said. Yous moving out or summat? He shook his head. Getting new stuff? The Maestro shrugged. He took his neighbour with him and helped him carry more stuff from the flat. They dismantled the bed, which would not fit through the door, and took it away in pieces. He gave the man his microwave, his excess plates and cutlery, leaving only one plate, one spoon, one fork and a knife, together with a pot and a frying pan. He got rid of everything he thought superfluous to life. Alright pal, ya not gonna ask for any of this back, are ya? asked the man with an anxious laugh. I really appreciate it. Here, have some of this. The man tried to hand him a small packet of white crystals. The Maestro shook his head. Suit yaself, said the man, and shut the door. Back in his flat, the Maestro studied the new, free space that he had. He piled up all his clothes and branded trainers, put them in some black bags and resolved to drop them off at a charity shop. Now that he no longer had a sofa, he sat down on the floor and looked out the window, the view being the top bit of Dunsyre and the starless sky. He was going to learn to immerse his body in this more natural rhythm. He felt like Kirillov, an idea incarnate. The air felt freer without the unnecessary things that he'd rid himself of. He picked up his book and read.

It was light around four in the morning. This was unnatural. The Magistrate was trapped in a restlessness intertwined with helplessness. It felt as though his life was rushing along on its own course and, where once he'd been in control, he now just drifted along, swept up by events. The girl sleeping upstairs could not be his daughter. She wasn't the little girl he'd bought pink ribbons for just a few moments ago. Some supernatural agent full of mischief must have swapped his little girl for this... this succubus. The boy must have forced her. But, no, he had seen it with his own eyes. She was undeniably a willing participant. There was real skill, craft, in the rhythmic motion of her head. He shook his head trying to remove that image from his memory. It was seared in there now, and the fear that he was doomed to replay it over and over crept into his soul.

He went to the bathroom, washed his face and took his meds.

Mai Chenai walked in later that morning carrying an orange plastic bag from Sainsbury's. She came into the room and was startled to see him sat behind the door, his head between his knees as though he was about to retch.

"Mangwanani. Is everything alright here?" she asked tentatively.

The Magistrate laughed as if that was the most absurd question he'd ever heard.

"I came home early from work last night because I was feeling sick." That was all he could say. She put her hand on his forehead, checking his temperature.

"I'll make a cup of tea," she said.

Without thinking, she stepped over Liam's clothes on her way to the kitchen. She boiled the water, took out two cups and put the tea bags in them. It had been a busy night on her ward and she was tired. She added milk and sugar to both cups and stirred. The music of the spoon whirling around the cup like a Tibetan singing bowl soothed her.

She went back and gave the Magistrate his cup.

"Are you going to tell me what the matter is, Baba Chenai?"

He pointed at the pile of clothes on the carpet.

She noticed them now. The torn jeans. The T-shirt. Underwear turned inside out. Muddy Reeboks. She did not recognise them. The significance of them was dawning on her, but she did not yet fully comprehend what they were doing there. Her husband had to tell her in no uncertain terms that the thought forming in her mind, hidden behind doubt and confusion, was true.

"Whose clothes are these?"

"Your daughter–" said the Magistrate. His voice abandoned him as it had during the night when he saw the act. Could he name it? It seemed impossible to say the word fellatio. How could he describe the horror he'd witnessed, changing it from images to words. It would be like passing on a deadly virus. He let out a long sigh and leant back.

"We should have left her in Zimbabwe. This is not the sort of country in which to raise a little girl." Chenai walked in. She wore her formal work experience clothes, with a handbag slung over her shoulder. She looked like a woman and a child at the same time, as though by some trick of digital photography there was juxtaposition of what had been and what was to be. It was impossible to tell if this was her or someone completely different.

"Morning, Mum, Dad." Her voice broke a little, but there was nothing else to give away anything about the night before. "I'm off to my placement."

Kahure, thought the Magistrate.

"Yes, you better go before I do something I'll regret," her mother said. "Come back straight after work. We need to have a serious talk."

Mai Chenai helped the Magistrate up and led him to the bedroom. She went back downstairs and threw the abandoned clothes in the bin. She tied up the black bag, took it outside and put it in the wheelie bin. It would not do for her husband to have to face them again in the afternoon. She washed her hands and walked back up the stairs where she found him lying in bed, staring at the ceiling.

Something in her was moved, seeing him like this. It was a wave of pity merged with love for the man she had once known. The man who accosted her at the gates of the nursing college. She saw in him the man who had taken her to the altar joking that, for all the lobola he'd been charged, they should have at least given him a spare wheel. Looking at his face in pain brought back a flood of memories. He was a good man. She knew that. He was trying, trying so hard and she was giving little back.

She got into bed and snuggled up next to him. She took his head and rested it on her bosom where she could feel his breath against her naked flesh. That warm air caressed her. It was a reminder of what had once been, of things that had passed between them, special things that only they knew. A secret garden with a forbidden tree. It was their place, theirs alone, a refuge from the world. She held him closer and allowed him to swim in her chisipite, battling the currents that swelled up and gushed along the shore. He was drowning. She pulled him to life, deeper under the currents in the darkness that was itself being and nothingness. There was a familiarity in their struggle, a battle that contained the memory of love, the feeling of something lost and something rediscovered.

Farai lounges on the sofa with his Vaio on his lap, surfing the net. Brian walks in, announces he's off for his nightshift and leaves. Farai flicks from YouTube, logs on to his uni email account and scrolls down his inbox until something catches his eye.

Dear Colleague,
I do not come to you by chance. A mutual associate of ours, Nika da Graca, was in Lisbon for a seminar and informed me, in passing, of your interest in the late Angolan economist Chilala dos Santos Lima Climente. I am sorry for the short notice, but I will be in Edinburgh for a conference on Thursday and Friday. Can we meet before my departure on Saturday?
Regards,
Dr. José de Alenquer

Farai checks the email address @ics.ul.pt and discovers it is that of the University of Lisbon. He picks up his mobile, scrolls to Nika's number and dials. It goes to voice mail. As he listens to her recording with its mild Portuguese inflection, he remembers that she's gone home to Mozambique for the summer holidays. He does not recall her mentioning de Alenquer in any of their conversations. Curious, he emails back and agrees to the meeting, proposing that they meet at a pub on George Street.

Farai is restless over the next few days as he waits for the meeting. He occupies his time visiting the library, playing Pro Evo, hanging out with Stacey and the boys. On Saturday he wakes up at his usual 6am. He showers and dresses in blue Levis and a black polo shirt (Ralph Lauren). He drives to George Street, finds parking in the center street bays, and goes into the pub.

He picks a table near the front door where he can see people walking along the street through the glass front. A man catches his eye, tall, olive-skinned, with thick glasses. He assumes this must be de Alenquer, but the man walks past. He sees other potential candidates – none of them his man. An old couple enter the pub, the man holds the door for his lady. Farai thinks about how OAPs are a rare species in Zimbabwe. Sure it had its advantages; the sidewalks were not clogged by slow, tottering, cane-wielding biddies, and one wasn't liable to get his foot run over by a mobility scooter, but something about the elderly altered the character of a place, civilized it, creating a bridge between past and present, a sense of continuity across generations.

A traffic warden wearing a high-vis jacket is on the beat. Farai keeps a close eye as he walks past his PT Cruiser. A refuse truck is held up by the traffic lights at the west end of the street, opposite Charlotte Square.

At 8:30 prompt, a skinny man with his hair parted, 80s style, walks in. He drags a small brown suitcase behind him, the sort frequent fliers on low budget airlines are wont to have.

'José de Alenquer,' says the man, extending his hand. 'I was expecting you to be a little bit older for some reason.'

Farai rises from his seat. 'Dr de Alenquer, it's a pleasure to meet you.'

'Please, call me José. Have you been waiting long?' He checks his wristwatch, an old piece with scratch marks on the glass.

José says he's famished and picks up the menu. He warns Farai about the dull routine of academic conferences, urging him to rethink his position if he is considering a life in academia.

'It's no fun without the hard core Marxians. Since the Soviet Union collapsed, it's all become very boring. There simply is no real alternative to the current system, just variations to the same. We have lost our radical edge.' He taps the menu. Goes through it a second time, scratches his head and throws it on the table. 'I can't decide. My wife always chooses for me when we go to restaurants.'

'Just have a regular fry up.'

'The cholesterol will kill me.'

'Take the vegan option.'

'Give me a few minutes.' José holds out his hand. He goes through the menu again, stopping to point at a particular choice, before moving on. He mumbles, alternating between English and Portuguese, translating each selection between the two languages.

'You've heard of the paradox of choice?'

'Schwartz?' Farai replies.

'It really should be called the paralysis of choice.'

Farai laughs politely. He is used to lame jokes by folks in academia.

'I surrender, I wave my white flag, my battleship is sunk.' José throws the menu down. 'I shall have to go hungry after all.'

'How about coffee?'

'That might be an option.'

'Do you want a filter, an Americano – black or white, latte, chai latte, cappuccino, espresso, mocha, you can have it caffeinated or decaf? There's tea as well if you're a tea drinker, you can have...'

'Alright, alright, I get it.' José laughs. 'Just get me anything you think I can stomach.'

Farai goes to the bar and waits for 2 other people to be served first. The server is a man in his early 40s, wearing the black uniform of the establishment. His badge says he is the manager. Farai used to get vexed at the differences in the roles between Zimbabwe and the UK. In Zimbabwe, the manager was the guy who gave orders, did paperwork and never lifted a finger. The sight of a manager behind the till feels a little bizarre.

He orders his quadruple espresso and a latte and traditional brekkie for José.

'What's your table number?'

'D'oh! It's that one by the door. I always forget to get that.'

'Don't worry about it, sir. I'll just make your coffees and your meal will be about 5-10 minutes.'

Farai pays, takes the coffee and goes back to the table. José is gazing out on to the street, watching the cars drive by, commerce starting up by degrees.

'So, how long have you been an economist?'

'I am actually a political scientist. I have a special interest in Portugal's African colonies, *ex colonies*. As you know, we were not as successful as the English or the French in Africa, but more successful than the Germans and the Belgians, and equally as barbaric as the rest.

We only had a handful of colonies. Now the Mozambicans are leaving us, they want to join the Commonwealth. We have nothing to offer them. Even the Brazilians tower over us,' he says with a dry laugh. 'Nika's father is a political scientist in Maputo, a good friend of mine, and that's what he thinks anyway. The old world must give way to the new.'

'You worked with Climente?'

'Oh, him, I'd forgotten why we were here. We were doctoral students at the same time. We shared a room. He looked a lot like you but with sharper features. He was intense, you know, like an eagle. When he walked into a room everyone noticed him instantly, he had this sort of magnetism. That's how we got the girls. He would lead and I would happen to get the friend. Sometimes I got the beautiful one too. We were very close. There is a certain intimacy that happens when 2 men make love in the same room.'

This sounds like my kind of guy, Farai thinks.

'He had a way of seeing the world that was so incisive it drew you in. He saw the layers underneath the obvious. That's why we got on so well. We would be cruising Eduardo Park at night, checking out prostitutes, and he'd say something like – *this right here is economics at play. I want to conduct a study to understand the economic imperative driving these women. What determines the going rate for pussy, a blow job or anal.* These were trivial matters to me. That is where he and I differed. He wanted to go deeper and explore the various relationships going on, the power dynamics, and all sorts of crazy shit.'

'Sort of what your Levitts and Harfords are doing these days.'

'Those are clowns. The point is that Climente wanted to make economics relevant to Africa. The discipline to him was about people and power. That is why he became interested in corruption because he saw it not as the cause of Africa's problems, but merely the symptom of a more fundamental illness. He published a paper, I think in '89, on the dynamics of bribery in wartime Luanda. It was well received but fizzled out. Academia was more interested in traditional avenues. And African economics didn't exactly interest a lot of people back then, well, not the people that mattered anyway.'

'Do you have a copy of this paper?' Farai remembers Prof Marlow warning him on the dangers of being sidetracked.

José points to his case. The waitron arrives with the breakfast, which Farai had ordered for José. Farai thinks she's cute, but a little on the heavy side for him. He scores her 6.5/10, just on the cusp of doable if you round up to 7. José adds salt before tasting the food. 'The wife won't let me have salt at home.' He eats, focusing on his meal, clearly famished. A few minutes later José looks up from his plate and appears startled as if he wasn't expecting Farai to be there.

'There are still a few of us out there interested in Climente, in getting him the recognition he deserves. By a few I mean me and 1 other person. It certainly won't happen in his own country. Some of the people he wrote about are still alive. There are reputations to protect and money to be made. I even attempted to write a biography at 1 point, but I decided against publication. It simply wasn't worth the risk – not to me, but to others close to him. Slowly but surely he is being buried in that academic junkyard to which we must all go 1 day. I wouldn't have known it when I was doing my first degree at Cambridge, back then we thought we were going to set the world alight. A few of us did, most didn't.'

Farai watches José eat hunched over his food, 1 hand on the plate as though afraid someone might snatch it away.

'I eat too slowly, or so I am told.' José reaches down to his bag, opens it and brings out some documents. 'These are the most important papers I have from him. The only ones that we managed to rescue. I believe they hold his central ideas.'

The wad of papers is about the thickness of several telephone directories. Farai thanks him and thumbs through them. They are all in Portuguese. He feels the slight anglophonic annoyance at text in a foreign language.

'Did he have a wife and children?'

'She lives with me.' José looks him in the eye and stops eating. 'I married her soon after he died and brought her to Portugal. She was pregnant at the time. We named our daughter Clementine, but she carries my last name.'

'Just out of curiosity, why haven't you published these papers yourself?' Farai tries to change the subject.

'I take a man's wife and daughter, and publish his work too?'

Farai really wants to change the subject. He's not interested in this wife swapping business.

149

'Angola was not the place for her, not with all the enemies Climente had made. He was an economist playing the role of investigative journalist. I told him to stick to macroeconomics, churn out papers about nothing like the rest of us and secure his tenure, but he didn't listen to me. But that's a rather long story for another time. I have a plane to catch.' He stands up, only half his meal finished. 'If I could resurrect Climente from the dead, I would. He was convinced that his discipline is the key to solving Africa's problems. It is his wife, *my* wife, who wanted you to have these papers, so they don't remind her of why he was killed. I hope in your own way and in your own work you carry his ideas forward. Look after them well, they are the only copies we have.'

Farai stands up, shakes José's hand, and watches him leave. He sees him on George Street, flagging a taxi. And then he is gone. The papers are mostly bundles of old typewritten pages, smudged ink, paper turning yellow from sun and humidity. Some of the papers are bound together by a simple hole in 1 corner and green string. They might as well be in hieroglyphics. But it's the mathematics that intrigues him. The bits that he can read. He lingers on a formula he hasn't encountered before. To most eyes it would just look like a squiggle of indecipherable lines and numbers. This is a language he understands and he tries to piece what he can together. He goes to the counter, orders another espresso and returns to his table. He flicks through the papers page by page. He recognises people's names, names of places, currency signs, tiny bits of information filling in the whole. Cars drive past outside. People walk by. The sun goes across the sky on its charted course. He is absorbed in his work, flicking a dried brown flake off the page he is reading to reveal the letters below. He cannot fully understand it, until he gets to a section on the Congo with names alongside US$. His mobile rings. The coffee gets cold. The pub fills up with people. There is the hum of chatter, conversations spoken. The air is thick with the aromas from the lunch menu. He takes a sip of his cold coffee. Some of the names are familiar to him. The US$ keeps gaining extra 0s on paper. He stops. He will need to call Nika, or find a translator. When he thinks about what José said about carrying Climente's work forward, he wishes he'd told him to go fuck himself. It's a heavy burden to be asked to do something like that, by and for a stranger. It's nearly midday by the time he finally leaves for home. There are 3 parking tickets waiting for him on his windscreen.

***

The TV's on Fox News, which Farai loves because it's entertaining. He respects how Fox dispenses with any pretense of objectivity and just spews its right wing agenda. Fox is honest in this regard. And it's an added bonus the female anchors are hot. Farai trusts Fox in the same way he trusts the ZBC. His awareness of the subtle distortions, the bending of facts to fit certain angles, means he feels safer watching it than he does with the so-called objective news channels. This is important because, like the average person, he consumes news about situations and places he knows nothing about, relying on media corporations to tell him their version of the truth. On the table are pages of Climente's work.

He skims though the part that he knows is about the DRC conflict. The mention of Angola, Zimbabwe, Namibia, Chad on 1 side and Rwanda and Burundi on the other makes it obvious. This is a good starting point, because if he is to describe the dynamics of the origins of the economic catastrophe then he must be able to outline how the DRC conflict bled the treasury and combine this with War Veterans' gratuities in the late 90s. He has to limit the scope of his paper, so (at least for now) he chooses to ignore the IMF prescribed ESAP.

There's a knock on the door. A strange knock, tat-a-tat-rat.

'I'll get it,' he calls out, and goes to the door.

He opens it and sees a little man wearing an oversized brown suit. The little man smiles and clears his throat. Farai remembers this face from the past. He says, 'Wonderboy,' grabs the little man by the collar, slams him against the wall, studies his face for a minute, and then pulls him inside the apartment.

'Oooh, oooh, what are you doing, *mai weeee*, Jehovah God,' the little man cries, waving his arms about, trying to break free.

Farai keeps a firm grip. 'Come here, you little bastard.'

'Oooh, oooh, Jehovah God,' he cries out in a squeaky voice. 'Please, *ndapota.*'

Farai throws him on the sofa and the little man lands head over heels. He wriggles like a worm, cushions fall to the floor and, as he tries to right himself, he falls off the couch. Stacey comes running from the bedroom. Farai grabs the little man and pulls him back up, lifting him by the collar so his feet dangle in the air.

'Farai, what the hell are you doing, put him down,' she says.

'I know this little bastard. I thought I recognized him when I saw him at the MDC gig, but I wasn't sure. Now I've seen him at my front door, I know exactly who he is,' says Farai. He hovers between anger and bemusement.

'Oooh, oooh, Jehovah God.'

'Put him down, Farai,' Stacey repeats.

Farai drops him to the ground. The little man bolts and hides behind Stacey, peeking out from behind her shoulders, crying, 'Oooh, oooh.' He gets on his knees and kisses Stacey's feet, thanking her for saving him. 'You are my hero,' he says.

'Do you mind explaining what's going on here?' she asks.

The little man squeals from his place on the floor, until Farai silences him.

'This guy used to be our security guard, back home. I remember when I first saw him in his blue Fawcett overalls, with a *mahobo's* cap and a baton stick and handcuffs dangling off his waist. You could see straight away from his shifty eyes that this guy was up to no good. Just look at him. Back then he used to call himself Wonderboy Magenje.'

Farai's parents had a 7 bedroomed house in Highlands. It was set on a few acres surrounded by a bougainvillea hedge that turned purple when the flowers were in season. As with most rich folk, they had the habit of paying poor folk to guard their wealth. Farai's father was a hotshot lawyer who had other investments on the side, but found a niche in human rights law when the situation started. He used to tell Farai that the crisis was the best thing that ever happened to his business, his firm doubled in size. They had stacks of cases logged with the High Court and Supreme Court, getting paid in forex by the NGOs. His clients included the MDC, NCA, CFU, ZCTU, WOZA and virtually every other acronym reeling under the state's iron fist. This was the golden age for law firms in Harare; any hack who passed the bar was guaranteed good business, though major players with complex cases sought established firms. The city was awash with donor US$ in those days. His mum was a trauma specialist with her own practice in the city centre, and business was good there too, especially as she moonlighted for Avenues, though she was not as boisterous about it as his father was. There was a boom in business from people with injuries, and checks signed in blood came in from organizations with battered memberships. There'd never been a better time to be a doctor or a lawyer in Zimbabwe.

'This guy strutted about our yard, trying to look officious; he saluted visitors at the gate, looking ridiculous. Mum had misgivings about him, but Dad said some bollocks about judging people by the content of their character. And it was true for a while, because we never once caught him sleeping on the job or anything like that. Still, there were signs, the way he skulked about at night, poking his nose here and there. He chatted up the house girl Matilda, unsuccessfully, and leered at her lustfully whenever she was bent over scrubbing the floor. He shared his cigarettes with the garden boy and, on their days off, they took to drinking Scuds together.

'When we had guests at the house, he tended to hang about the house a little too close for comfort. He stared at them for far longer than was necessary. He was a creep, but none of these things alone was reason enough to ask Fawcett for a replacement.

'Then 1 weekend, we went for a holiday to Chimanimani. When we came back, we found the garden boy and the maid tied up, half dead from starvation and thirst. Everything was gone, furniture, jewelry, clothes, files, electronics, a total wipe out. Wonderboy was nowhere to be found. We called the cops. Dad knew the OIC at Highlands Police Station, so they came chop-chop, took fingerprints and statements from the house staff. The maid said that 2 trucks had pulled up by the house the Friday night we left. A bunch of men jumped out, beat up the garden boy and tied him up. She tried to call the police but the line was cut. The men felt her tits up and tied her up next to the garden boy. Then they stole everything, going back and forth over a number of trips...'

'What about the neighbors?' Stacey asks.

'They didn't see or hear anything, the houses are too big, too far apart and we're surrounded by a tall hedge. It's obvious that this cat was behind it all, because he'd gone missing after the heist. The guys even pulled my dad's safe from the wall. There was no sign that Wonderboy here even tried to stop the robbery. He was in on the whole thing. It was an inside job.'

The little man on the floor gnaws at his moustache nervously; his eyes wide open, looking back and forth from Farai to Stacey.

'This little prick stole my PS1,' says Farai.

'And used the money to come to Scotland?'

153

'But it isn't the money or the property that really matters, babes. We have plenty of that. What really gets to me is that, a few weeks after the robbery, some of Dad's clients started to go missing. I'm telling you, activists, campaigners, opposition supporters, tons of people who were in Dad's files were taken. Some of them popped up, beaten and tortured, and the others just disappeared like that, never to be seen again.'

The little man begins to sob. Large blobs of tears streak down from his eyes. He takes a crumpled handkerchief from his breast pocket and blows his nose.

'Oooh, oooh, it's so true, it's all true,' the little man says.

'You see he admits it!'

'I will never forget that night,' the little man speaks from behind a veil of tears. 'I was in the guardhouse when the trucks arrived. I went to talk to the men, but they hit me on the head with something hard.' He parts his hair to show a scar on his scalp. 'I passed out. When I came to, I was in some sort of base. I was tied up and I could hear the men debating whether to douse me with petrol or not. 1 of them said petrol was too rare to waste these days, and that's how I survived. Instead, they beat me to within an inch of my life–'

'Bullshit, can you believe this guy?'

'Let him finish,' says Stacey.

'He's lying through his fucking teeth.'

The little man turns round and lifts his shirt to expose his back. There are rough, bumpy welts all across it, dark lines and deep troughs. He turns round and bares his chest. It has ugly scars all over it. Black patches where new skin had grown. He looks like 1 of those slaves from *Roots*.

'Oh my God,' says Stacey. 'You poor, poor thing.'

Farai is silent. The sight of these signs of torture makes him feel sick. The little man covers himself up. He slowly adjusts his suit, trying to regain some dignity. Stacey helps him up and leads him to the sofa.

'Would you like something to drink?' she asks.

'Give him a beer,' says Farai. As Stacey goes to the kitchen, he asks, 'Why didn't you come back and tell us?'

'I woke up in a hospital in Chitungwiza, not really sure of who I was or anything. They'd stripped me of my uniform and my wallet. By the time my memory came back to me, the police were looking for me.

You know how they do their interrogations, Mukoma Farai. I couldn't take it. That's when I fled to Botswana and became Alfonso.'

'Bummer, that's a total bummer, man. I'm so sorry. I didn't know this shit, man. All along we thought you were a thieving wanker and now, here we are.' Farai sighs.

Stacey brings them both a beer.

'So what brings you here, anyway?' Farai asks.

'I came to see Scott, on party business.' Alfonso puffs his chest up, trying to seem important.

Farai goes to the bedrooms. He finds Scott at his computer, typing an article. Scott writes articles and manifestos, which he shoots off to online newspapers that never publish them. Sometimes he makes Farai read them and, though he knows what he wants to say, he lacks the skill to express his ideas in coherent form.

'Won-eh, Alfonso is here to see you,' Farai says.

'I'll be with you in a minute. I just have to finish typing this,' Scott replies, not taking his eyes from the computer.

Farai returns to the living room. Stacey is sat with her chin in her hands. She's close to tears, fighting to hold them back, eyeing Alfonso, unable to say anything. Alfonso is thumbing through the papers on the coffee table with a puzzled expression. He looks up to Farai and smiles.

'Mukoma Farai, I always knew you were so smart, look at this Greek with all these numbers and these signs. Jehovah God, how do you understand all this?'

'It's for my thesis. I'm going to have it translated at some point and see if I can make use of any of it. Next week I fly home. I want to see some people at the UZ for more material. Hell, I even have a meeting set up with Eric Bloch.'

'Who's that?' Alfonso asks.

'Never mind.'

Farai gathers the papers and organizes them. Scott walks into the room. Farai takes Stacey by the hand and leads her out of the room. In their bedroom his suitcase is wide open. A few clothes are already packed for his trip. *Mom and Dad will never believe me when I tell them about Wonderboy.*

The death rattle of the Pfukutos' VW shattered the morning's peace. Birds rose from the branches of trees, flying high into the air for safety. The Magistrate spilt tea on his lap and an involuntary groan escaped him. His nerves were shattered. The weeks spent thinking about Chenai had taken their toll. This was the job of the tete; a father should never have to deal with this sort of thing.

He met Alfonso at the door. The little man was dressed in a Nigerian outfit, a deep blue buba and sokoto with a fila that sat on his head a few sizes too big so that it kept dropping onto his eyes. He held a well-worn Bible in his left hand, clutched close to his heart.

"My broda, today is Sunday, praiz da Lord," Alfonso said. "Ant you komin to chech wit os?"

"When have I ever come to church with you?" The Magistrate struggled not to show the contempt within.

"How kan you sey dis. Don't you no da world is komin to an end?"

"Will you stop with that silly accent!" The Magistrate rubbed his temples. The doctor had told him to avoid overexcitement because of his hypertension. That was easier said than done when you had to deal with people like Alfonso. And, it was not like he could cut him off entirely either; the man was his employer after all.

"Baba Chenai, hamusi kuuya nesu kereke here?" Mavis called from the driver's seat. A double assault from husband and wife. "You should come with us. It's a very welcoming church. Look at your brother Alfonso. They made him treasurer. A man like you could become an elder in a matter of months."

The Magistrate smiled at her, clapped his hands and evaded the question, launching into a long greeting instead. He even managed a few lines about the weather. Mai Chenai and her daughter emerged wearing identical floral dresses. They looked like sisters. He stepped

157

aside to let them through. The strangest thing for him had been their abandonment of the Anglican faith for this West African evangelical cult whose name he could never remember. All he knew was that there was a Jerusalem, a River and a Kingdom somewhere in the title.

Just then, Alfonso began to tremble like a leaf caught in heavy wind. The Magistrate feared he was having an epileptic fit. Alfonso wiggled his bum, his feet shuffled quickly as if he was a boxer, he leant back, feet criss-crossed. He stopped, turned, and marched back and forth like a Kremlin guard, feet going high in the air, body as stiff as a board. He stopped, began to tremble again, head bobbing like a rag doll. His eyes rolled until only the whites remained visible.

"Uyo Alfonso, Holy Spirit Dance," Mavis called out.

"Praise Jesus," Chenai cried out, her voice quivering with fervour.

Mai Chenai began to incant some things in a strange, unintelligible language. It took the Magistrate a while to realise she was speaking in tongues. Alfonso hopped about, going round and round like a deranged kangaroo. It seemed in part to be a grotesque variation on the Borrowdale. There were two key innovations in Sungura, the talking guitar and the Borrowdale. The dance involved fancy footwork, blindingly rapid, vigorous and energetic, a rhythmic matching of the dance and the beat. It was named Borrowdale after the famous racecourse, invoking the speed and grace of the horse. The Magistrate prayed the neighbours wouldn't see this madness. Alfonso was the discoverer of the Holy Spirit Dance. He'd fallen into a trance one day at church and done his little routine. Before long, all the children in the church were doing it and it spread like wildfire. The pastor declared that while the other churches had the gifts of prophesy, healing and speaking in tongues, the Holy Spirit Dance was the sign that his was the true Church of God. It was not long before Alfonso had risen up in the ranks to the trusted position of church treasurer. The Magistrate imagined an entire congregation hopping about like kangaroos. The world was truly coming to an end.

When Alfonso stopped, his face was covered in sweat. His fila had dropped off his head and lay on the ground. He blinked his eyes and looked about, confused, dazed.

"What happened?" he asked.

"The Holy Spirit took over," said Mavis.

"I don't remember anything," said Alfonso in a quivering voice.

"Ndizvo zvinoita Mweya Mutsvene."

Alfonso walked to the car and sat in the passenger seat, silent, in deep reflection. Mai Chenai and their daughter sat in the back. The Magistrate watched, perplexed, as they pulled away and rolled down the street, on their way to Gorgie. John stepped out from next door. He was in his pyjamas, holding a cup of tea.

"What on earth was that about?"

"I'll be damned if I know."

"No offence, but that mate of yours is a bit queer-like, you ken what I mean?"

"All too well." The Magistrate waved and went back indoors.

He watched the news for a bit and grew restless. He put on a pair of trainers and went out for a walk. At least Mai Chenai and her mad church still believe in something, he thought.

Minutes later, he'd arrived at Duddingston Kirk. The stained glass, the masonry and the ancient gravestones gave it an immovable, eternal aura. Nine centuries of history lay within those walls. The Kirk looked as though it had always been there and, by extension, would always be. It had been a while since he'd last been in church. The Kirk opened up the prospect of a fresh start; perhaps he too could find the spiritual anchor he so badly needed within. He knelt and crossed himself and sat in one of the middle pews. Light scattered through the images of the saints on the windows. The pulpit had a large cross emblazoned on it.

He bowed his head in prayer but found nothing to say. He searched for something, anything, but found he ended at God, Jesus or Lord at each attempt. A thought crept into his head about the ridiculousness of his entrance. Walking in with his head bowed, genuflecting, crossing himself. Would not Mwari who created him prefer that he crouch and clap his hands instead? Mwari would want him out in the open like the Mapositori, a tiny human being under the canvas of the vastness of his creation which no work of human hands could ever hope to imitate. He saw now the absurdity of his presence in this building and stood up. Chipanga's song *Makomborero* came to mind. As he left, a friendly elderly woman smiled and asked if he was not staying for the service. He mumbled some excuse about work and fled against the stream of parishioners trickling in.

In the afternoon his family came back home. Chenai went dutifully to her bedroom. She was grounded with no prospect of parole until she turned fifty. In a bizarre way, the sight of their underage progeny

159

engaged in fellatio had spiced up their own love life. The Magistrate and Mai Chenai made love every day, making up for lost time. They'd begun waking one another in the middle of the day to satisfy their lawful, lustful longing. It had been years since they had been this passionate and had felt this longing for intimacy. Then they had been young; now those same intense feelings returned as if by magic.

The Magistrate went with Mai Chenai to explore the city. They took the 2 and dropped off at the Commonwealth Pool. They walked down the road onto St Leonard's, through the Pleasance and found themselves in the Cowgate in the Old Town.

"This is the first time I've walked down here," Mai Chenai said. "It's easy to get lost in work and forget you're entitled to a life in this country."

They strolled hand in hand, the Magistrate guiding his wife along as though they were on First Street in Bindura. But, they were anonymous here. There was no one to stop them every few steps, to greet or petition the Magistrate. They walked unimpeded, sharing the pavement with strollers and tourists, and passed under the South Bridge.

"It used to be a road for cows," explained a tourist with a Texan accent who was reading something from a brochure. "Says here they had a fire a while back. Couldn't control it cause there's vaults and all sorts of underground tunnels everywhere."

"This used to be a road for–" the Magistrate started.

"I heard it too," Mai Chenai laughed. "You're turning into Alfonso."

He grunted, a little embarrassed, like in the old days when they had been courting and she teased him mercilessly. A suitor had to be made of sterner stuff in their day. They passed Faith, a church that had been converted into a nightclub. Mai Chenai was outraged at what she felt was sacrilege.

"These people don't know God like we do," she said. "When I was in London, some Nigerians used to stand on the street corners near the Underground, preaching the gospel. It's funny how we are bringing religion back to them."

"If we are then I don't think it's working," said the Magistrate looking around. "What need do they have for God and old superstitions when science has answered all their questions? The sick turn to doctors, not faith. The poorest people on welfare get free housing and more money than most people in the world. They've won the lottery of life."

The street was narrow and the few cars that passed by did so slowly. There were posters in windows and on walls advertising acts for the Festival. A pink glossy one for the Lady Boys of Bangkok, another advertised the Soweto Gospel Choir, one with acrobats proclaimed that the Chinese State Circus was a show not to be missed. They emerged on the western side and went over the roundabout onto the Grassmarket. The restaurants and pubs there had tables on the pavement where tourists sat and enjoyed pints of cool draught.

"I know where we are now. There's Lothian Road." Mai Chenai was excited getting her bearings. "Let's find Jimmy Chung's."

"Who's that?"

"You'll see."

They walked on, taking streets they had never walked before, passing some old government buildings. In no time they arrived at Jimmy Chung's, a Chinese restaurant near the Citrus Nightclub. The waiter, who could have been from anywhere in the Far East, but whom they assumed was Chinese, found them a table. The aroma from the buffet filled the air. The restaurant was noisy, many voices speaking at once. Several tables were joined together for a colourful group celebrating a birthday.

"It's quite pleasant in here," the Magistrate said.

"I love Chinese."

"There are so many of them in Harare now. They'll probably have a Chinatown by the time we go back." He said it so casually, as though they could step out the door, out of this life and emerge in Harare. The waiter returned and placed their drinks on the table.

"Help yourselves at the buffet," he said and retreated.

They took their time, the day was theirs. They had starters; she had aromatic lamb while he took the soup. An old couple next to them, sharing ice cream, offered a possible glimpse of the future.

"Is that nice?" Mai Chenai asked.

He took a spoonful, reached across the table with a steady hand and fed her.

"Yummy, what is it?"

"Dog soup or something like that."

They watched diners come and go, waiters sailing between the tables. Their waiter returned and offered them more drinks but they asked for water instead.

"We should go for a movie after this," he said.

"And get naughty in the cinema." She winked suggestively.

They both took an incomprehensible mix for their main course. A little bit of this and a little of that. Some mushrooms here, prawns there, fried chicken, virtually everything the buffet had to offer piled onto their plates. By the time they were done eating they realised their blunder. There was no room for dessert. He settled their bill and they went out onto the street.

They headed for Lothian Road, but the Magistrate noticed a large poster for *The Man of La Mancha* on the display in the Lyceum. "Why don't we try the theatre instead?"

"We can do anything you like," she said. Their wills were bound into one. It was impossible to disagree that day. They were happy together and it didn't matter what they were doing, so long as they were with each other.

The chap at the box office told them the show was starting in ten minutes. He said the best seats were already taken, but they would get a good view in the upper circle.

"Enjoy the show," he said, handing over their tickets.

They took their seats from which they saw over the crowns of the heads of people sitting in the stalls. Here, a bald head, there, blond locks, long hair, short hair and everything in between. The naked woman singing at the start of the show caught them off guard. The Magistrate fought to suppress a grin. Mai Chenai playfully slapped him on the arm, knowing in truth that her body was the only one he desired. It made her feel good.

Enter Cervantes and his manservant. They had been arrested by the Inquisition and were due to stand trial. The Magistrate noted the obvious error that they were allowed to enter prison with their possessions, then concluded that the law in Spain then must have been different, like the period costumes the actors wore on stage. Suspend disbelief. The prisoners wanted to burn Cervantes' manuscript but he convinced them to allow him to act out his story on stage. Dipping into his chest, he emerged as Alonso Quijana and his manservant transformed right there on stage into Sancho. The actors all played instruments it seemed. The incident with the windmills played out. Mai Chenai squeezed his hand when Don Quixote began to sing Dulcinea, the sincerity in the voice and the look of devotion on Quixote's face reminded her of their courtship. The actress on stage for those few minutes was transformed into the most beautiful woman in the world.

In each act they were hooked, going deeper into fantasy. The entire audience was drawn into the experience that seemed truer than life itself. Everything propelled them to the point where Don Quixote sang *The Impossible Dream*. The audience, unable to restrain itself, burst into spontaneous applause.

When the musical finally came to an end, after many misadventures, with Cervante's manuscript, *Don Quixote de la Mancha*, returned to him, and he was taken to trial by the Inquisition, the audience gave a rapturous standing ovation. The Magistrate forgot himself and whistled.

The actors took to the stage all smiles and bowed, soaking up every iota of adulation, which was rightfully theirs. They returned backstage, but were called out again by an audience eager to show its appreciation. This beautiful moment could never have been captured in the cinema. The theatre was alive and full of living, magical possibilities that camera tricks and CGI could never match even with 3D and terabytes of computing power.

The audience poured onto the street into the artificial light. Voices round them were talking about what a wonderful performance it had been. Baba naMai Chenai did not need to say it. Their own love life played and interwove with performance. He thought of the days when they had not been getting on, did he not look like the Knight of the Woeful Countenance then? Leaving his position in Zimbabwe, where he was someone, and coming here to a new reality was surely a quixotic act of love and devotion. They hailed a taxi and kissed in the backseat. The taxi took them onto Earl Grey and through the Meadows. A bunch of neo-hippies sat on the lawns drinking. The driver sensing romance was in the air took them round Arthur's Seat and past the Loch, the more scenic route. He stole little glances of them in his rear view mirror, perhaps thinking of his own wife at home in bed. The romance of mature people chipped rough at the edges and stripped of the thoughtless idealism of youth was in itself a thing of beauty.

When they got home they lingered at the door, not wanting the night to end.

"You are my Dulcinea," the Magistrate said, imitating the accent of the actor on stage.

"Then sing to me," she said, and laughed under the night sky. He embraced her and they went inside.

Chenai was sitting in the living room, watching MTV. They joined her and sat next to each other. Chenai was lost in the entertainment, rappers and half naked buxom women gyrating for dollar bills. It was a good night. They were back home with their daughter, together as a family. All the troubles of the past seemed to wash away, swept away by love and warmth on that one beautiful night.

"Mom, Dad, there's somefing I need to tell ya," Chenai said, without turning away from the screen. "I'm preggoz."

The Maestro gritted his teeth, listening to the sound of the wind as it whistled through the grooves of the zinc metal plating on the walls outside his flat. It was insistent, never once letting up, like a bad tune from an inexhaustible pair of lungs. This was the soundtrack of the high rises, an architectural quirk, nature's punishment for the low-cost, post-war housing abomination. His mind drifted to Tatyana. No doubt she would be leaving voicemail after voicemail, sending texts to the mobile he no longer had. Maybe she wasn't, but part of him wished this were true. It felt as though having her in his life was not a choice he could make, rather a connection fate had chosen for him. Still he would not allow himself to bond with her; he wanted to be alone with his books, to live his life on his own terms. Was such a thing even possible? He recalled a short story he'd read, The Autonomy Directive, by the mediocre Soviet Sci-fi writer Grigor Grigorovich Bogomolov. In this story, the decadent westerners – read Americans – had dreamt of a plan in which each individual would have unfettered freedom. To this end they built a giant computer and, after years of working on the problem, the computer decided that each person be hooked up to a life-support machine, a device that contained an entire world within itself. The story ended with high-tech megacities of gleaming aluminium coffins, each lined with a claustrophobic velvet interior, in which the individual was fed and nourished, but could never have contact with anyone else in the world. The Maestro reached to his side and grabbed a half-full, two-litre bottle of cider and took a swig. The drink burnt its way down his oesophagus and stayed lodged someplace high up in his chest. He was bloated from his bad diet and his mouth had a bitter taste. The rent was two months overdue and the Maestro had taken to ignoring the stream of brown envelopes with red tags that poured through his letter box every day. He had stopped running, preferring to do calisthenics indoors instead. For a brief moment he wondered how much longer he could keep at it. The temptation to give his hermitage up and go back to work was ever-present in his mind. He shrugged it off. Reflecting on his twenty-eight years of life, he wondered if they had been worth anything at all. But what measure could be used to value a human life? Did the value lie in the wealth a man accumulated? Wealth that would be eaten by moths once he was gone. Perhaps it was in fame, the adulation of others, but this in itself seemed hollow. Maybe it lay in passing on genes, in a man's role as a carrier of genetic material that had to be transmitted down generations, mixing and diluting with others, propagating in a mindless way that was no different to that of beasts and bacteria. And thoughts were just that, thoughts, nothing more. He chugged the cider down till he finished the bottle, then lay down and passed out. When the Maestro came to, the sky outside was cobalt blue, vast, and it seemed like the most beautiful thing he had ever seen. He wanted to reach out and touch it. The feeling passed quickly and the Maestro became bored once more. It came to him that the reason we die is captured in the cliché: bored to death. After a while, life with its soul-deadening routine grinds us down, the groundhog that keeps popping back up from its lair day after day. It is this feeling, the great dark, cancerous cloud, that stops the heart beating. He reached for the cider and was horrified to find the bottle empty. He got up, waddled to the bathroom, stood at the sink and jerked off, blowing a load of spunk into the basin. He opened the cold water tap and washed the creamy effluent down the drain. Next, he took a shower, brushed his teeth, got dressed in a pair of jeans and a blue T-shirt and left the house. It took five or so minutes to get to the bus stop where he boarded the 25 to Restalrig. It was packed but he found a seat on the upper deck. Most of the passengers were young people, late teens/early twenties. He reckoned they were students from Heriot-Watt where the bus terminated. A woman seated on the opposite side was reading a novel, her lips half curved in pleasure. Almost everyone else on board was reading the Metro or had created a wall of sound around themselves with headphones. That was the pretence of the Edinburgh bus, that everyone was an island unto themselves and the enforced proximity was a minor inconvenience to be tactfully ignored by way of averted eyes and silence, except for the odd, Excuse me, I need to get off. The Maestro had heard rumours that in a far off place called Glasgow human beings on the bus actually initiated conversation, a bit of craic and banter. He tried to see what the woman was reading, but the cover was hidden. He was caught up with a sudden, violent urge to find out what the book was. He absolutely had to know! It did not occur to him that he could simply lean over, tap her on the shoulder and ask. The bus crept past Saughton and into Gorgie, which was bunged up by cars going into the city. There was a yeasty smell in the air from the old breweries. He'd applied for a job there once and been turned down – we regret to inform you... A lot of jobs were closed to him, not enough experience, no qualifications. The limitless potential of his youth had finally made a home for itself in retail: shelves and checkouts, the thought made him even more melancholic. Shops in Gorgie were situated below the old tenements. Tynecastle Stadium appeared between the capillaries that fed off the main road, but on a weekday there were no Hearts supporters marching in, the street ablaze with their maroon tartan scarfs. The woman got off at the stop in Haymarket and the Maestro followed her. A hearse passed; behind it were two black limos. The woman made for an easy mark through the packed streets with her silver hair comb tucked above the bun in her hair. She turned into Starbucks on Palmerston Place. The Maestro stood behind her in the queue and heard her order a macchiato and a blueberry muffin. The barista was a mid-thirtyish blonde and he felt something resembling pity at her predicament, certain that behind her solicitous smile was the existential angst common to bottom-feeder workers in the capitalist hierarchy, something to which he could relate all too well. He asked for an Americano, black, unadulterated, and paid with his credit card. He sat at the table opposite the woman with the book and waited. The coffee hit his empty stomach hard and he took small sips, certain he would puke if he drank any faster. He needed something to eat, but not here, not with these prices. The woman tore tiny bits off her muffin and placed them in her mouth, sucking like she was eating sweets. Her red lipstick accentuated her thin lips. She picked up her paperback and opened it. The Maestro saw it was a Nora Roberts romance and he smiled. There was something about the status of the Romance genre that infuriated him. It was pulp, no different to Sci-fi and Crime, but it had followed a different trajectory in the bullshit hierarchy of literary works. At some point thinkers and readers had agreed that Sci-fi and Crime were worthy works of art that, from time to time, should be taken seriously and given the same consideration as that due to literary fiction. People said Sci-fi was a vehicle for analysing society and predicting technological trends – 1984, Brave New World – even contemporary works were accorded a certain respect. The same could be said of Crime Fic, especially Noir and the Hardboiled detective novel. Chandler, Hammett, James M. Cain and their peers from the pulps in the 40s and 50s were all writers whose works had been elevated above the mockery of the literati of the time. Their work found itself under serious review in modern universities and intellectual spaces. But the same couldn't be said of Romance novels; no one ever picked something up from the Mills and Boon catalogue and held it up as a work worthy of thoughtful interrogation. To the Maestro, this bias was not based on any true literary merit, but more a reflection of gender-based discrimination. To say that works with men killing each other or zooming around in space, powered by faster-than-light warp drives, were more worthy of study than intricate stories revolving around the most important human activity, that of finding a mate, was, if not insulting, then downright bizarre. The Maestro finished his coffee, wiped a stain off the table with a napkin and left. He headed up the street, past St George's, through the West End and crossed over onto Princes Street. The pavements were heaving with tourists brought in by the spectacle of the festival. The streets were full of colour and the sombre grey of the city seemed like something from a distant epoch. He weaved his way through the chaos, slowed down by the mass of bodies around him, finding a channel in this omnidirectional river that moved in his direction. On Frederick Street, he crossed the road and walked down to the gardens where he sat on the lawn with a few other people, soaking up the insipid rays of the sun. The gardens were alive with the bright reds, oranges, yellows and blues of the flowers in bloom. The Maestro knew the popular history of the gardens, familiar to everyone who had been in the city for any length of time. How the whole area had been a loch until the putrid smell of sewage dumped from the Old Town had so offended the gentry that they took action and had it drained. It was said that they found human skeletons lying at the bottom, because the old loch had been used for witch dunking in the middle ages. The trial by water was simple, the witch was bound by rope and thrown into the water, if she – it was almost always a woman – floated, then she was deemed to be in league with the devil and would be executed by hanging or burning. However, if she drowned then she was innocent and her soul would ascend to heaven. Sitting on the manicured lawns, the Maestro did not feel any palpable residue of that savage history. It had been sanitised until all that were left were legends with which to entertain tourists. But the monument of the Great War below bore a reminder of the sporadic violence common in Europe, a history filled with blood in these genteel gardens. From the distance came the sound of marimbas playing. The Maestro got up, wiped the grass off his bottom and began walking towards the sound, as if drawn by the Piper himself. He walked past the galleries and the market stalls nearby, pushing through the crowds. A lot of heads were turned towards the break dancing Koreans who performed next to the silver human statue in front of M&S. The marimba players set up at the corner of Waverly Bridge and Princes Street were a group of Africans in feathered headbands, orange T-shirts, jeans and New Balance trainers. They had attracted a fair few spectators and one of the performers, a tall man with tribal markings on his face, was handing out flyers to their show. The group was called Siyaya and they were from Bulawayo. The Maestro pushed his way to the front and stood watching the performance. He swayed to the rhythm of the marimbas and clapped along to the beat. It was some time before he noticed something strange. A small space had opened up between him and the other spectators. While the rest of the crowd was tightly packed, it was as though there was something repulsive about him that kept everyone away. The Maestro worried briefly about body odour, then told himself it was impossible because he had groomed himself before leaving the flat. It had to be something else about him. He peeled away from the performance and walked down the road, onto Market Street and from there up the Mound. He came to the Royal Mile, which was littered with tourists and locals, glossy fliers from numerous shows strewn on the cobblestone street, open air acts jostling for audiences and diners sat outside the pubs and cafés that had their tables out on the pavements. The Maestro stopped by many acts and, each time, he felt the same thing happening to him, the crowds disconnected from him as though he was undesirable, like a beast that had a strange, alien disease. He could not blend in. When he had had enough, he went on to North Bridge, took the 33 and went back home. He lay on the floor of his flat and immediately picked up Ghostwritten, a book that he was reading for the third time. Since he began his quest the Maestro had taken to having several books on the go. Where once he had read them in series, now he preferred them in parallel, hoping that this way of reading would make it easier for him to see the cross connections he sought between each universe. As he went on the journey from Okinawa, around the globe and back to Tokyo, via the intersecting narratives, he saw how Mitchell had provided the template for his quest, how within it lay the Maestro's desire that every author be linked to the others, so that in effect they were faces of Uluru, changing perspectives of the same rock. But even as he was spellbound by the book's brilliance – the structure and style, the exquisite prose, the breadth of imagination – he was no closer to finding what he was looking for. The sky was yellowy-black outside; darkness had descended without him noticing. The rumbling of his tummy was a reminder that he had not eaten all day. He threw the book down and his hand instinctively searched for the remote control. He lifted the sleeping bag, shook it, checked on the windowsill, in the kitchen and the empty bedroom, but of course it wasn't to be found. Back in the living room, the Maestro picked up another book, flicked through the pages, prrra, and threw it back on the pile. Then he kicked out with his foot and knocked the stack of books onto the floor. He looked up at the ceiling and winced. A hundred different thoughts ran through his mind as he stood in that spot, thinking. His head throbbed as if his brain had swollen, pressing against the walls of his skull. The pain came in pulses, hot and hotter. He stood still, defeated, flashes of red and white dancing in the periphery of his vision, Athena, fully armed, trying to cut her way out. Shouldn't have thrown away his meds. Perhaps he'd taken the wrong turn in his enquiry, maybe it would be better to give his life over to religion, to a single book – the Bible/Quran/Torah – that carried the word of the Divine and which held the answers to all the mysteries of life. Hadn't the Grand Inquisitor said: Man is tormented by no greater anxiety than to find someone quickly to whom he can hand over that great gift of freedom with which the ill-fated creature is born. But even within the mystery of religion lay so much doubt and division; these texts split the faithful into a multitude of denominations and sects until even the unity of the sacred word could not be divined. Or maybe he could join Dawkins and co., those for whom every question would eventually be answered by the brute force of science and reason. But the Maestro could not begin to see the world as a mechanical clock in which reversing the movement of the cogs would only lead to the Blind Watchmaker. In fear he lay down on his sleeping bag and passed the night in random thought that led nowhere. In the morning he made himself a cuppa and rolled his first joint of the day. His reflection in the double-glazed window scared him. The puffy red eyes with dark rings and wild hair made him look like a caveman. As the weed took effect and mellowed him a bit, he remembered that his journey was not a sprint but a marathon. It would not do to give in to despair and leave the path to return to what he knew. The Maestro vowed he would continue for as long as it took. The THC and caffeine went a long way in helping his mind come to this decision. In the days that followed, the Maestro renewed his focus, reading for twelve or more hours a day. He watched the seasons change, trees near the canal burst out in technicolour, except for the arrogant evergreens that cared not for autumn or winter. The Maestro lived in a blur of time and reality in which the physical world melded with the world of books. The two became one thing, a symbiosis, the imagined world lending texture to the real and the real world, by its very being, standing in as the scaffolding through which the tumour of fiction attached itself to his mind. The blurring was only magnified by the Maestro's consumption of narcotics and alcohol, but it was a safe bubble that he could inhabit away from the rest of the world. This did not stop the envelopes pouring through his letterbox. He ignored everything. The days shortened and the sky grew dark both day and night under a perdurable shroud of heavy grey clouds. In all this time, the Maestro felt like he was walking underwater, so that every move he made entailed great effort and each thought was conceived with great difficulty. As he finished reading a book he found he couldn't remember anything in it. He flicked to the start and, yes, the words were familiar, but they meant nothing to him. It was as though his mind were made of Teflon. Fuck, fuck, fuck, he thought. He picked another book from the pile and found it was just a jumble of words with which he had no connection. His entire body trembled. He went to the wall, leant against it and banged the back of his head again and again. Trying to think, trying to clear his mind, everything was all jumbled up, an incoherent mass of letters and graphemes. Banging his head, putting himself into a trance, took him to a bleak, empty space outside of colour and sound. And when he came back, he knew what he had to do. It was now all so clear. The Maestro walked to the window and calmly opened it. He bent down, picked up an armful of books and threw them out of the window. Then he did it again and again. The sound of paper rustling in flight, the breaking spines, the slap of the covers as they hit the ground did not stay him. It felt good, this cleansing frenzy. It only took minutes to discard the collection that had taken years to build. The living room was now a blank canvas – white walls, blue carpet, limitless potential. The Maestro took a White Lightning from the fridge and drank. It was like a Shake Shake without anyone to pass it to; he poured a drop out the window to the spirits in the ether. The Maestro left the flat and walked down the stairs, his face hidden inside a hoodie. He passed through the security doors into the open. He picked up the books, torn pages and all, and threw them over the fence onto the grassy mound, working quickly until he had built up a pyramid. Not a soul stirred from the high rises to ask what he was doing. The few windows with drawn curtains had the tell-tale blue light of the television screens flickering through. The wild flowers that had blossomed in the summer were now green stalks indistinguishable from the grass. Martin was devouring Tolkien in the pile, Bessie Head sat in one corner, buttressing the pyramid, and, on top, at the very apex, was a book with two men on the cover, falling from the sky. The Maestro lit a fag, the light illuminating the right side of his face, took a drag and contemplated his work. After a few puffs, he threw the stub onto the pile and waited, feeling calm and detached. At first nothing happened, the stillness of night, then, a tiny wisp of smoke rose, curling round and round as it did, dancing in the air, a hypnotic spiral, curling round on itself as it rose ever higher. Then one of the books caught alight, at first the flame as small as a candle. It grew, slowly, almost reluctantly, licking the pages of that one book. The fire began to move, lazily at first, from book to book, creeping like a predator sneaking up on its prey. Then, suddenly, it burst forth. The fire came up to the Maestro's chest; orange flame danced in his eyes, crackled and roared, devouring paper and ink. He could not take his eyes off the hypnotic blaze, the blues and yellows and greens, the way the flames swayed, rising and falling, dancing, deadly and beautiful in equal measure. Is it because the fire is prettier by night, more of a spectacle, a better show? a raspy voice whispered from behind his shoulder. The Maestro turned around but there was no one there, just the smoke-scented air, but he'd heard it, clear as night. It came again from behind him, around him, from within the fire itself, as if it expected an answer, even as the glow of the fire lightened everything around. Is it because the fire is prettier by night? It grew taller than him, licking the green grass around the books, a ravenous beast, hungry for more, growing, growing ever larger, trying to touch the sky itself. He shielded his eyes from the blasts of hot air and heard something like the scream of a thousand voices in hell. It was terrifying, anguished, primordial, the sound of a thousand chariots on the battlefield, the roar of a mighty torrent; it was all these things, and none of them, a shapeless mass of noise and flame. The Maestro became filled with fear and ran inside, scrambling up the stairs back to the safety of his flat, where he stood by the window and watched the blaze, ferocious and brilliant, as it lit up the phone booth in the square, reflecting off the glass. The light came as far as the eighth floor, piercing through the window and casting dark shadows that climbed the walls of his flat. The voices within were quieter now, as though they finally understood that there was no hope, the fire would win, fire always won. It burned with a final flourish then dimmed until all he could see were bright orange ambers glowing from beneath the thick dark smoke that rose, filling the night air like a deathly smog. He could smell the burning pages, the chemical of the ink, as the wind carried the ashes and raised them up. They floated away like dark snowflakes; the larger ones rolled along the grass before breaking up into tiny pieces, which rose up into the night, away from the ambers smouldering on the grass. When it was finished, the Maestro curled up on the carpet and cried himself to sleep.

"We should take you to the doctor, you look grey," said Mai Chenai.

"I have my own night nurse," the Magistrate replied, buttoning up his suit. Mai Chenai wore a sombre black outfit that matched his mood. Their last few weeks had been busy with visits to the midwife, meetings with the school and the social worker.

Autumn crept in regardless. The remaining vegetables in the garden were dying. The trees were crowned with orange leaves that they shed with each passing day. The wind blew the leaves along the street where they gathered in piles in the gutters and blocked drains.

"We have to face this together. That boy's father is coming soon. We must look respectable."

"What kind of man lets his son run around like a wild buck sticking his..." The Magistrate straightened himself. He could not finish his train of thought.

"They are both children and they've made a big, big mistake. We have to deal with the consequences now. There's no changing the situation."

But they had tried. Mai Chenai had taken Chenai to the GP, to see if there was still a chance. It was too late. The Magistrate had been relieved. He'd sent away a few women in his day for terminations. Even here, where it was permitted by law, he still had been unable to face the idea, preferring instead to let Mai Chenai deal with it. He was ashamed of his cowardice, like Pilate washing his hands.

He held Mai Chenai's hand and kissed her cheek. She laid her head on his shoulder and wiped a tear with a handkerchief. The air was suffocating, a heavy silence settled on the house.

There was a knock on the door. The Magistrate opened it and Alfonso burst in. He grabbed the Magistrate's arms and looked at him.

"Are you okay?" asked Alfonso.

"This is not a good time."

Alfonso pushed his way through and sat on the free chair opposite them.

"Amai Chenai, I was so worried about this man." His speech was a little slurred. They could smell the whisky on his breath from across the room. "He's like a brother to me. I've been getting shifts, doing my best to make sure he gets the best jobs and all of a sudden he disappears. I tried phoning, more than a dozen times, I had to come to make sure that everything was okay."

"You are working yourself up into a state. Would you like a cup of tea?" asked Mai Chenai.

"I have my strong stuff." Alfonso waved a quart in the air.

"I'll get you some tea anyway," she said, and went to the kitchen.

Alfonso took a sip straight from the bottle. He offered some to the Magistrate, holding the bottle out, almost a gesture of supplication. The Magistrate refused. He looked at Alfonso gnawing at his moustache, trying to figure out how to get rid of him as soon as possible.

Before he could think of an excuse, the doorbell rang. The Magistrate felt a wave of panic. He wiped his palms on his trousers.

"Perhaps you should go upstairs and lie down for a bit," he suggested.

Alfonso shook his head. The Magistrate went to the door and opened it. He was taken aback by the familiar face that appeared in front of him.

"Well, this is a surprise," he said.

"You're telling me." It was Peter McKenzie.

The Magistrate led him in; he would have preferred to have this whole thing settled in camera. Peter shook hands with Alfonso. The three of them recounted the incident at the church, the crockery that had almost caught Peter on the head. Alfonso was all too keen on recounting his heroic rescue, getting them out of danger as the old church was violated.

"I must say, things would be a lot more exciting if that's how we handled our politics here," said Peter.

Mai Chenai came out and greeted him. She'd brought everyone a cup of tea. Alfonso alone insisted on having alcohol. They talked about the weather, the football, Zimbabwe, anything at all they could find to avoid the real subject at hand. There was an awkward silence, the calm before the talk. Alfonso crossed his legs and uncrossed them, fighting a full bladder.

"So, we have this situation," Peter finally said.

Mai Chenai sighed. There were lines on her face the Magistrate had not seen before. Little crow's feet around her eyes. He pulled her close, rubbing her back.

"Your son accepts his responsibility?" the Magistrate asked.

"Liam," Peter emphasized his name as though to say, he is an individual, it's not my fault, "loves Che very much. They are both young and have made a mistake, but now we have to find out how best we can deal with it."

"What mistake?" Alfonso blurted out. He became animated, leaning forward from his armchair, looking from the Magistrate to Peter as if watching a tennis match.

"The most important thing," the Magistrate continued, ignoring Alfonso, "is that the child must not be allowed to suffer in any way."

"It will be loved, no doubt about that. I suppose the first step is to find out from both Liam and Che what their intentions are. If they intend to stay together, how the baby will impact on their education, their careers and so forth. This whole thing is a right old mess. I'm sorry, since the wife died I don't feel I've been able to get through to Liam like she could. I'm telling you if she was still around, she'd have known what they were up to."

"Women can't always know these things." Mai Chenai sounded defensive.

"Sorry, I didn't mean to be old fashioned. I was just trying to say that maybe we could have done something in time."

"It's too late for that now."

Alfonso cut in excitedly, "Chenai is pregnant and your son is responsible. Jehovah God, she is so young. A minor. Under age. Statutory. This is a catastrophe. It must be handled the traditional way. There can be no other solution. Your son is responsible. Statutory. He impregnated her. He has a lot to answer for. It's a sin, it's a sin before God and before man."

Peter frowned. The Magistrate coughed loudly but Alfonso would not stop. He jumped up from his chair, knocking the cup of tea Mai Chenai had brought him to the carpet.

"That's right, we have to solve this the traditional way. You come in here walking about like you own the place, talking about the weather.

You have no right, no right at all. You are a mukwasha to my brother and you must show some respect. Your son didn't show any respect. Look now. She's under age. No sir, there is only one way to resolve this. You must pay damage."

"Damage?" asked Peter, startled.

"Yes, you must pay damage," Alfonso said, oblivious to the Magistrate whose hand was clenched, holding an imaginary gavel ready to call order, to have him locked up for contempt.

"What are you on about, man? She's pregnant not damaged."

"We knew you'd try to get away without paying. Didn't I say it? They'll try to rip us off. She's an only child, zai regondo. You have to accept responsibility. You must pay damage and lobola. We will accept nothing less than five thousand pounds."

"I've had enough of this. You would try to sell your own child?" Peter stood up. Alfonso rushed towards him and grabbed the leg of his trousers.

"No sir, you can't leave without paying five thousand pounds!"

"Alfonso, Alfonso!" the Magistrate shouted, which unfortunately sounded to Peter like he was egging him on.

Peter shoved Alfonso away, but no sooner had he recovered did Alfonso jump back and tackle him, wrapping both arms around his right leg. He huffed and puffed, clinging on with all his might while Peter tried to kick him off.

"Get off me, man," Peter cried out.

"You must pay for our daughter. There is nothing for it. You've used her and now you want to cheat us. Statutory. She is underage. Five thousand pounds you owe. It's our culture. It's the law."

Peter struggled to get rid of the little man. The Magistrate got up and came towards him. Perceiving a threat, Peter shoved the Magistrate hard and he fell on his wife's lap. He kicked Alfonso off and grabbed a half full cup of tea from the table, which he brandished as a weapon.

"You bloody scoundrels, trying to sell a little girl like this," he said, waving the cup about while retreating to the door. Alfonso got up after him but tripped himself up on the corner of the coffee table and fell flat on his face. Peter opened the door and called back to them, "I am going to report this to the police, you blooming eejits."

Farai drives down to the Links. He slows down as he turns onto a cobblestone road. A hooker with a junkie face approaches the car from the shadow of the brick wall on which she was leaning. She braves the cold in her miniskirt. Farai shakes his head with a bemused grin.

'MONKEY,' the hooker shouts at him.

Farai stops and rolls down his window.

'It's ape, actually. Or, better still, hominoid. Do you want me to spell that for you?'

'Fuck you,' says the hooker, staggering back to her perch.

Farai shrugs and continues on his way. He worries about the education system that's producing *these* people. *Perhaps I should write a letter to Holyrood.* He turns into a car park and stops, leaves the car, walks into a 4-storey building and goes up to the first floor marked Ipsos MORI.

He goes through a set of double doors, across a carpeted corridor and through a second set of doors. The room he walks into hums with the sound of voices. It has several pods, each with 8 people wearing headphones and staring at computer screens.

'Hey, Farai,' Angus calls out. 'What brings you back here?'

'Just here to pick Scotty up.'

'I thought you wanted to come back and work for us again.'

'Never.'

Angus laughs and leads him to his desk. 'It'll be a few more minutes before they finish. Do ya fancy listening in to Scott?'

'Yeah, why not, should be fun.'

Angus clicks on a few icons and the screen changes. Farai sees Scott on the next pod, eyes glued to the screen. Angus hands him a pair of headphones. He hears Scott's voice, the screen changes as Scott interacts with the CATI. The line goes quiet, the screen goes black with only a hypnotic cursor blinking to show something is happening under the surface. After a few seconds there is a beep and Scott springs to life. The recording from an answer machine plays in his headphones and he hangs up. The screen has a list of 15 options.

```
1) proceed with interview
2) engaged
3) no reply
4) hard appointment
5) soft appointment
6) switch/other/refused...
```

He presses option 3 on his keyboard. The screen goes blank, with the letters Y/N at the bottom. Scott presses Y and it goes back to the blinking cursor. Scott has been doing this since 9 in the morning, his mind and the machine Vulcan-melded into 1. Wooden partitions separate his space from the other drones beside him. A choir of male and female voices, the sound occasionally broken by beeps and the screech of the dialer. Scott is perfectly attuned to the will of the machine, filtering out the background noise, focused on the cursor. There is a note attached to his screen that reminds him to smile when he speaks, to make his voice sound *friendlier*. The same sheet commands NEVER 2 OR 3 A DEFFO.

Scott takes a sip of water from the plastic cup on the table. The phone bleeps again. A woman's voice comes on.

'Hello, hello,' she says.

The screen commands him to reply:

```
hello, my name is scott and i'm calling from ipsos
mori the independent research organisation. we're
carrying out a survey about a variety of topical
issues and i was wondering if you could spare a few
minutes to answer some questions?
```

He does not deviate from the script. It has to be read out word for word and somehow still sound natural, human even. The woman says that she is not interested. He politely thanks her for her time and codes 7. The interplay of voices, fax machines and answer machines carries on for 5 minutes. Each exchange is dispassionately coded. There are of course variations – some people ask him to *fuck off*. Farai and Angus find this amusing. Others hang up on him as soon as he speaks. Some ask how he got their number since they are ex-directory. Being told to go *fuck* himself is all part of the job. He replies this is technically impossible. 1 man asks if he is calling from India. At all times Scott exhibits a detached professionalism.

After what seems an eternity a woman on the other end agrees to take part in the survey.

He codes 1 and the screen tells him to say: this call may be monitored for training and quality control purposes.

He asks her age. She falls in the right quota aged 35–44.

how likely are you to vote in a general election?
1)very likely
2)fairly likely
3)neither likely nor unlikely
4)fairly unlikely
5)very unlikely

'I believe it's a civic duty and everyone must participate. It should be like Australia where if you don't vote you can go to prison. You see all these scroungers on benefits moaning and complaining about the National Health, immigration, but they don't blooming vote. How are you going to change things if you don't vote?' she replies.

He asks her whether this means:
1)very likely
2)fairly likely
3)neither likely nor unlikely
4)fairly unlikely
5)very unlikely

'I always vote, every time,' she replies.

He asks whether in that case he should code:
1)very likely
or 2)fairly likely

'The first one, of course,' she says.
1)very likely

It goes on like this until she understands that her verbatim responses are of little consequence and she has to use the scales provided by the computer. The poll asks questions about whom she voted for in the last elections and whom she intends to vote for if there were a general election. He asks her opinions on her local authority, the education system, the economy, her optimism about the direction the country is taking. When these are done, he asks for her ethnicity, her postcode, the

185

occupation of the chief income earner in the household and whether she would be willing to take part in any future Ipsos MORI telephone surveys. She tells him she would and that she likes giving her opinion on things.

Scott thanks her for her time and offers her the head office number and the number for the Market Research Society in case she has any queries about the survey. She declines, thanks him and wishes him a goodnight.

Farai removes the headphones and laughs.

'How on earth do you guys do it?'

'Best job in the world,' says Angus.

A supervisor at the other end of the building calls time. The interviewers log off their terminals. They look relieved to be done with it. Scott sees Farai and waves.

'What are you doing here?' asks Scott.

'I've come to pick you up. We're going to Brian's graduation thingy and I didn't want you to be late... More like to forget in your case.'

'Brain's fried after a suicide shift.'

They leave, amidst the stream of shellacked call center workers who march silently as if they have used up their day's allocation of voice. Farai and Scott drive back home, where they have a couple of drinks with Stacey and call for a cab.

The cab arrives and they ask to be taken to the Scout Hall in Granton. The cabbie thinks for a moment, mapping the route out in his head, says, 'aye,' and off they go. The drive takes them onto Commercial Road, which has rows of tiny businesses, the Woollen Mill, some restaurants, and a Jobcentre. Ocean Terminal and the sea are to their right, as are the new flats under construction all along the sea front. Stacey's perfume fills the cab, sweet and fruity.

'So what are yous doing tonight?' asks the cabbie.

'We're just going to this party, see what it's like and take it from there,' Farai replies.

They go through Newhaven and Trinity. Fife lights up the coast at the other end of the straits. Farai has a buzz that happens every Friday. It starts in the morning, a need for stimulation, an addiction in its own right. He can't imagine spending a weekend indoors, like when he was on holiday, going round Harare visiting 1 set of relatives then the next, having to endure long prayer sessions and to listen to biddies crowing advice about how he should live his life, simply because that was the done thing. He needs bright lights, loud music, laughter and dance.

'Have you ever wondered how come we don't have any white friends?' Brian asks out of the blue.

'What the fuck are you talking about?' Farai responds.

'White friends,' says Brian.

'Hellooo, white person here. I am friend.' Stacey waves an arm to get their attention.

'Yeah, we've got Stacey.'

'Stacey is your chick, dude,' says Brian. 'I'm talking about niggas we can hang with.'

'White guys?'

'Like, we're not doing enough to mix with the indigenous population.'

'Wear kilts and eat haggis with the natives?'

'The aborigines.'

'Does that make us racists? Segregationists?' Farai asks.

'White person here!' Stacey calls out, waving her arm madly about.

Waves splash over the wall that provides the coastal defense on Lower Granton Road. The water sprays some walkers on the track by the wall. The sky above is cloaked in grey clouds, which glow from the illumination of the city lights. They get to the Scout Hall and Farai pays their fare.

Loud music pours from the building. *Ndizvo chete, zvandinoda, kukutaurira asi ndashaya mazwi.* Stacey holds on to Farai's arm. They go down some concrete steps and into the building. The music is louder inside, the bass makes the floor vibrate, traveling right through their bones. Farai goes to say hi to DJ Smoothspinner. He knows it's going to be a good night. The way he sees it, there are two types of DJs, the entertainer and the artist. Smoothspinner falls into the latter category. While the entertainer lays hit after hit, relying on the familiarity of the music to move the crowd, the artist paints different layers of music, remixing, splicing, scratching, crafting a collage of sound, gauging the mood on the floor and responding to it, so that his work for the night has to be appreciated in its entirety as a piece of art in its own right. The DJ nods and winks at him. An acne-ridden, dreadlocked guy rushes over to Farai and thrusts his hand out. He seems overly excited to see Farai.

'Hi, I'm Tendai, Smooth's flatmate, we live together.' Farai fights the urge to back off from the reek of booze.

'Pleased to meet you, I'm Farai, and this is my girlfriend, Stacey.'

Tendai shakes her hand and tries to kiss her cheek, but she backs away.

'I know you, Farai. I see you in clubs and stuff. You've seen me before, haven't you?'

'No, I haven't. Listen, Tinashe, I have to go round and meet some people. We'll chat later.'

'But–'

They walk away and find Scott chatting with Brian and a group of people in the corner.

'That guy once grabbed my ass in the club. Look at the way he's staring at that girl's boobs, he's a total sleaze ball,' says Stacey, from a safe distance.

'He could do with some serious Clearasil too.'

Brian introduces them to Melody, Sekai and Makanaka, who is wearing her gown and cap. These are the girls on his course who have graduated with him. *It's like every fucking Zimbo's a nurse now.* Farai puts his arm around Brian's shoulder and announces in a loud voice that his mate has a first. Brian pretends to be embarrassed. Alfonso hobbles over and takes a photo, before going to another part of the room to photograph more people.

'I wouldn't have finished the course if Brian hadn't helped me so much,' says Melody with a smile.

'Are you sure there wasn't an ulterior motive?' asks Farai.

He is called away by an older man. Farai claps his hands and says, '*Makadini baba.*' The man, whose name he can't remember, asks him questions about his holiday in Zimbabwe. Where did he go, what did he see, how is the situation, any news on the president's health, is there any sign things are changing?

'As soon as things are alright, I'm out of here. UK *inoda imi muchiri kutemwa dzinobva ropa.*' The man has the pretense of all first generation migrants, that they are just passing through and, as soon as the timing is right, they'll return to the motherland. The pregnant bellies on some of the young women and the little kids running about prove those intentions may turn out somewhat complicated by time and life.

'It's just a phase we're going through. Very minor from a grand historical perspective. Every nation goes through these cycles. Nothing special there,' says Farai. 'Look at Mozambique and Angola, they're on the up already and these guys had long civil wars. Wars damage infrastructure, ours is mostly intact.'

'But the movement of people, so many young people, professionals have left the country.'

'All surplus to requirements. Look, we were churning out graduates we couldn't employ anyway. Already investors are snapping up assets at rock bottom prices and just riding it out, waiting for the thaw. You've got to look at the silver lining – as soon as we get back on track, we'll still have the most educated workforce in the region and at least there won't be as many unemployed people as there otherwise would have been. Labour will be cheap for investors...'

The man listens to him respectfully, as if the virtue of youth comes with an improved perspective on national affairs. The aroma of the buffet catches Farai's attention halfway through his analysis. He excuses himself and goes to the table laden with food and settles for some *bhuruvhosi*. The room is filled with music and the sound of chatter and loud laughter, African laughter. An invisible line runs through the center of the room separating the men from the women. Tuku's *Dande* plays and a cheer goes up in the room. Farai grabs a drink to wash down his food.

He scans the room, looking for Stacey and doesn't see her. He goes outside, weaving his way through the crowd, and finds her near the door, having a fag.

'Those girls were giving me dirty looks.' She clenches her jaw.

'That's because of the stunning dress you're wearing. They must be thinking, damn she's the hottest chick in the building.'

'You know exactly what I'm talking about. It happens every time we go somewhere together.'

'Oh, come on, you're making a mountain–'

'Can't you see it? You know it's because I'm white and I'm with you, like, *what's he doing with her*. It's so fucking obvious.'

'There are some known knowns, some known unknowns, and some unknown unknowns and you know that is an unknown unknown.'

'I'm not kidding, Farai. It's fucking crap.' She throws her fag down and crushes it with her stiletto. Farai pulls her close, embraces her, and gives her a kiss. He's about to say something soothing when he feels someone tugging at his elbow.

'I heard you were doing a PhD.' It's Tendai, who leers at Stacey's cleavage. 'I'm a writer you know.'

'Great, what have you published?'

'Nothing yet, because my stuff's brilliant, but publishers don't get my flow, because it's intense, thermonuclear intense, twenty-first century existentialism with a twist. I ain't gonna sell out to the system and go commercial because that's what they want you to do. I think I'm going to be published posthumously. My readers ain't even born yet, that's how deep my prose is. Maybe I can show you my stuff some time. No one knows I'm a writer, it's not like I go about telling people. It's a personal thing, private.'

'Thanks for sharing, I'm touched, but I'm too busy to read your stuff. Best of luck.' Farai can't mask the dry sarcasm in his voice.

'Can I bum a fag, I'm all out?' Tendai asks Stacey. 'That's a nice necklace you're wearing. Is it real gold?'

She rolls her eyes and ignores his question, neither does she share her cigarettes with him. Farai places his left hand on Stacey's lower back and drinks with his right. He shares the bottle with her. After she takes a swig, Tendai reaches out for the bottle and the back of his hand 'accidentally' brushes against her tits.

'This is not a Scud! Tawanda, Tatenda, whatever your name is, go and get your own, geez,' says Farai, frowning. Tendai laughs, holds his hand out for a handshake and when that is not reciprocated, slinks away, back into the party.

'Can you believe that guy?' asks Stacey.

'Cocksucking loser.'

They watch cars coming in, more people for the party. Farai feels happy here, among his own, these rare moments when they can be together, reminiscing about the old country. The feeling of community in a foreign land. They hear the sound of a woman screaming inside. The music stops. Commotion. Raised voices.

'Oh, shit.' Farai runs back inside. His instincts are correct. Scott is on the floor, taking a beating from a big *blazo* in black. Farai runs over and pushes the *blazo* away. Scott gets up and tries to push his way past Farai to re-enter the fray, but Farai holds him back. Brian negotiates with the *blazo*.

'*Haubati chimoko changu, shasha*,' the *blazo* shouts.

'Steady, *mudhara, bhora pasi,*' says Farai.

'I think we should leave,' says Stacey.

'I agree.'

'That kid needs to be taught a lesson. *Kujairira madhara* so!'

Brian takes Scott outside. Farai negotiates with the *blazo* in black who seems a little less inclined to violence now that he's there. When the negotiations and apologies on Scott's behalf are finished, Farai and Stacey follow their friends outside. They hop into a cab that's just dropped more people off. Brian's furious, taking deep breaths. Stacey rubs his shoulder to try and calm him.

'Scott, why the *fuck* do you always have to fucking start *jambanja* whenever we go somewhere? Please answer me. We're tired of having to save your skinny ass all the fucking time. We should have left you to get kicked, then maybe you'd learn,' Brian says.

'Fuck you.'

'Fuck me? Fuck me, when I saved your ass? This is my graduation party you've just fucked up, you fucking fuck. Thanks a lot, Scott. I really mean it, thank fucking you.'

Farai raises his hand and tells Brian to stop. It ain't worth it. Scott's too wasted anyways. The taxi passes bright lights, flashing lights. The bright moon breaks through the clouds. Farai tells Scott he's drinking water for the rest of the night. The night is still young. Fuck it, they head into town, to Mambos.

***

Farai and Stacey walk back from Ocean Terminal. They have just watched *Transformers*, which reminds Farai of *Voltron*, *Saber Rider* and *Challenge of the GoBots* from his childhood. They take a short cut past the Scottish Executive, the symmetrical 3-storey building built on the old docks. It's a clear day, the building is reflected in the water. Stacey is wrapped up warm in a jacket. Farai, contemptuous of the cold, braves it in a Lanvin shirt. It's a short walk, going by the restaurants and pubs, to get back to Sandport.

Farai opens the door and they are greeted by a wonderful aroma from the kitchen.

'Something smells nice,' says Stacey.

'Must be Brian on the hob.'

They get to the kitchen and are surprised to find Scott cooking.

'Do my eyes deceive me?' Stacey gasps.

'A spectre is haunting Europe!' says Farai.

'Hey guys, you were out when I got up. Brian's just woken up and showered, I reckon he's got a night today. I just wanted to say sorry about my behavior last night. I know I can be a pain sometimes and I was a dick. Go sit at the table, dinner will be served soon.'

'I'll get Brian.' Stacey smiles.

Farai, Brian and Stacey sit at the table, which Scott has already set. There are 2 candles burning and a bottle of red wine. It's South African, the closest thing to home.

'He's really going all out with this apology,' Stacey says.

'I forgive the wee cunt already,' says Brian.

Scott emerges from the kitchen with a platter of roast potatoes in 1 hand and another of roast vegetables, parsnips, onions, swede and carrots. He goes back and returns with a pot of stew.

'I'm sorry there's no starters guys, but I had to be quick because of Brian's shift,' says Scott.

'This smells lovely.' Stacey squeezes Farai's hand.

Scott dishes out a portion onto everyone's plate. The stew has sprinklings of mint, other herbs and carrots that give it a rich color. Farai dips a potato in the stew and eats, he closes his eyes, savoring the taste and the texture.

'This is some Michelin star gourmet skill you've displayed here, dude. Seriously, you might wanna ring Kitchin up for a job in his kitchen.'

'Just a little something from my grandma's secret recipe book.'

'Bollocks, everyone claims to have one from their grandma. Take credit for yourself, dude.'

'What kind of chicken is this, it's just so delicious,' says Stacey, taking a second bite. She imitates Farai, closes her eyes and enjoys the taste.

She stops, suddenly, opens her eyes, stares at her plate and wears a puzzled look.

Farai smiles and nods. 'Yep, Scotty's outdone himself today, I can tell you that.'

Stacey frowns, she looks about the room, a little confused. She puts her fork down and scratches her head. It takes a few more seconds for her to ask,'Where's Mr Majeika?'

They all turn to the empty hutch. The door's shut, a few leaves of lettuce are in it, but Mr Majeika is nowhere to be found. It's like he's vanished into thin air.

'*Murderer,*' Stacey cries out and throws her fork at Scott. It catches him on the chest. She heaves and throws up in Farai's lap.

'You *sick* bastard,' Farai says to Scott.

'Dude, Mr Majeika was 1 of us!' says Brian.

'I know, and I thought he'd want to do something special to celebrate your graduation. He wanted this.' There's a sanctimonious air of conviction in Scott's voice that irritates Stacey even more.

Farai gets up and takes Stacey to the bathroom. She kneels and heaves into the toilet bowl, while he pulls her hair back. 'Oh my God, oh my God,' she cries, retching her guts out. Farai rubs her back. When she is through, she spits and flushes the toilet. Farai removes his soiled trousers and dumps them in the bin. She rinses her mouth at the sink.

'What a fucking bastard. I'm going to call the SPCA.'

'No, babes, don't do that. Let me talk to him and find out what's really going on.' Farai leads her to the bedroom and lays her down on the bed. 'Have a bit of a lie down for a few minutes, okay. I'll handle this.'

He goes back to the living room.

'Please tell me this is some sick stunt and that Mr Majeika is hidden somewhere.'

Scott shakes his head. There are stains on his shirt where Stacey's fork hit him.

Farai fishes around the stew, inspecting bits of floating limbs, trying to reconcile them with their furry friend who was running about in the hutch a few hours ago.

'How did you do it?'

'A blow to the back of the head, like that, blam.' Scott motions with his fist. 'Quick and painless, humane.'

Farai picks up a piece of Mr Majeika's hindquarters, sniffs and takes a bite.

'He was a tasty bastard,' he says. They laugh. Brian digs in and finishes off his dinner. Scott joins in as well. 'I'm still pissed off. Stacey ain't going to stand for these kinds of shenanigans. But, there's no use in wasting him now.' Farai watches the corridor, fearful that Stacey might come out of the bedroom. He dreads to think what she would do if she saw him eating Mr Majeika.

'We at least have to give him a decent burial,' Farai says, when they are finished. 'Scott, since you did this, you collect the bones, the pelt, the offals, anything left of Mr Majeika, and put it in a black bin bag. We'll bury him tonight.'

'You guys can do whatever the fuck you want. I've disposed of our friend as best I can. Later alligators.' Brian gets up to go.

'Crocodile.'

***

Farai and Scott leave with the remains, walking up the Water of Leith whose brown waters bear witness to their infamy. They find a quiet park, just after the bridge on Great Junction Street. Farai gives Scott a tablespoon and tells him to dig.

'I can't use this.'

'This was murder most foul, dude. You'd better dispose of the body before Stacey calls the SPCA.'

'Can't we just stuff some rocks in there and throw it in the river?'

'We're not Mafioso, Mr Majeika deserves better than that. Dig.'

Scott kneels down and digs. Farai sits on a bench and watches him. It's hard work with a spoon, but the ground is soft and moist and Scott has no choice but to graft, digging a hole a foot or so deep. They deposit Mr Majeika into the hole and cover it. Farai makes a little cross out of some twigs and places it on the grave.

'Do you know what denomination he was?' asks Scott.

'Probably C of E.'

Farai crosses himself and turns to his friend.

'Tamuka, *shamwari*, this is some crazy shit you just pulled here. Seriously, you're cracking up and you need to pull yourself together otherwise fuck knows what you're going to do next.'

'What did you call me?'

'I called you by your real name, Tamuka, so let's forget this "Scott" bullshit for just a second.'

Scott/Tamuka looks at him like he just said, *Lazarus come forth*. He goes to sit on the bench. A couple with 3 greyhounds walk towards the Shore.

'No one's called me that for a long, long time, Farai.' Scott stares out to the bank across the river. 'You know what I did when you were in Zim? I went all the way to St Andrews where Scott Murray's parents live.'

'The dead kid whose birth certificate you used to get your passport?'

'Yep. I just had to know who they were. Getting their address wasn't that hard, everything's online. They live in a neat little neighborhood, a double storey house with ivy on the walls. They had a red Civic and black Land Rover parked out front. I could see through their window, a shelf of books, some photographs on the wall. A woman, I think she was Mrs Murray, was watching TV, so I went and knocked on the door.'

'Oh, dude, that's some serious psychostalker shit.'

'Mr Murray came to the door. He's about my height, grey hair, maybe in his late 50s.'

'What did he say?'

'He said, "Can I help you?" And I said, "I'm lost, can you tell me how to get to town?" So he gave me the directions and I left.'

'That was it?'

'Yep, that was it.'

'Why did you do it?'

'I don't know. I just thought... since I'm walking around masquerading as their kid...'

'Dude, that's some fucked up shit right there. *Jesus.*'

'Everything's fucked,' says Scott/Tamuka. 'I wouldn't be like this if C hadn't left me, man. I saw her today in Word of Mouth with some *blazo*. She didn't even notice me as I walked past. She looked happy with him and it was like I didn't even exist. How am I supposed to live if I'm not with her? Everything's just fallen apart since she left me. I can't go on like this.'

Farai stands, picks up a rock and throws it into the river. He hears his friend sobbing in the background and searches for the right words to say.

'She was always going to leave you, buddy. This is how I see it. C was a smart girl, loving, caring, kind, everything a man could ever want. *Wekukanda pakitchen chaiye.* But she fell in love with the ghost of Tamuka that remained in you as you morphed into Scott. I remember her saying to me 1 day, how she didn't really feel like she knew you. Like you were Jekyll and Hyde. She met you when you'd just done the deed and you were in transition between Tamuka and Scott, neither 1 nor the other. I don't wanna go all Freud on you or anything like that, but names are important, man. They define who we are, where we come from, where we're going, yo. A person's name is important. You have it from birth. As you form and develop your own personality, that becomes inextricably linked with the name you have. That's why rappers change names to boost themselves for the game. Cassius Clay becomes Muhammad Ali, a superhuman, Malcolm Little becomes Malcolm X to fight oppression, Solomon Mujuru becomes Rex Nhongo and kicks serious Rhodie ass in the war. Go to churches, man, they baptize people and change their names, slaves lose their original names so they're broken. You see this throughout history, people change names and they achieve greatness or they fall down a deep, dark pit. That's what went wrong between you and C. She didn't know who you were. She couldn't know who you were. Sometimes even I don't know who you are. No one knows who you are right now, least of all yourself.'

'You think so?'

Farai faces him. 'That, and you're an asshole, a big, gaping asshole!'

Scott trembles, full of pent up emotion. Farai puts a hand on his shoulder. They sit there for a few minutes. Traffic goes by on the bridge above them. A man on a bicycle rides past, towards the shore.

'I don't know what to do.'

'You either need to go back to being Tamuka, or fucking move on totally, erase your past and become Scott Murray for shizzle. Otherwise you're always going to be fighting these demons, not going forward or backward. Whatever you choose to do, you're going to have to live with it. That's the way of the world, my nigga.'

Farai turns away so he won't see the tears in his friend's eyes. *This is so undude.* He overcomes himself and gives Scott a hug, a man-hug, no touchy feely. Scott breaks away after a few seconds.

'I say we go through Tesco, grab some bread and milk, and go back home. Just apologize to Stacey about Mr Majeika, and let's move on.'

***

They leave the park and go up on to Great Junction Street. Farai pops into Tesco and buys their supplies, slipping in a sneaky 6-pack of Bud. A voice calls his name from across the road as he comes out. He waves. It's Nika. She crosses over to their side.

196

'I haven't seen you in a while,' he says, giving her a hug.

'I was away again, but now I'm back.' She taps her backpack to show it's full of books. 'This thesis is driving me insane. I just want to get it over and done with.'

'You've met Scott before, haven't you?' asks Farai, introducing them. 'Listen, Scott, why don't you go home, smooth things over with Stacey. I'll be back around 12. Nika and I have some catching up to do.'

'That's a bit presumptuous of you. Maybe I'm on my way to a hot date,' says Nika.

'Darling, you're going to die old and lonely, surrounded by your cats and your chemistry set.' He laughs and hands the shopping over to Scott. It's just after 8 and they have time to kill. He takes Nika to Sofi's on Henderson Street. It's a chic little pub sandwiched between a physio's and a newsagent's. They find a sofa to sit on with loads of cushions. It's a slow night, a lone performer plays the piano in the far corner of the room. Farai orders drinks.

'I need you to do more translation work for me,' he says.

'It's gonna take a lot more than a piña colada for that, Farai. I'm really busy with my own stuff at the moment.' She raises her glass.

'But it's these papers your guy José gave me. Seriously, they look pretty interesting and I know you'll wanna do this. I'll split the cash with you when I get my Nobel.'

'Cocky, arrogant, overconfident, immature.'

'You forgot to add good-looking too.'

'Don't even try. I'm not like those airheads on campus who go weak in the knees when you walk by, Mr Macheke.'

'Okay, how about I help you with your figures again? Fair deal?'

She mulls it over, swirling the drink around the glass. 'Let's see the papers first.'

'Right now?'

'No time like the present.'

'But I said I'd be home after 12.' *Stall her, she'll say no once she sees how thick that stack is. Get her to say yes first, and then show her.*

'So what?'

'You want to go right now?'

'After we finish our drinks.'

Farai sips his drink slowly and ups his charm to DEFCON 2. He compliments Nika's hair, the way her skin tone has darkened under the

Mozambican sun, the loveliness of her smile, the color of her eyes. She's a living goddess, he tells her.

'Instead of your stupid talk, maybe if you set me up on a date with your mate, I might seriously consider it.'

'You mean Scott?'

'Who else?'

'Erm, he's not really your type.'

'That's for me to decide. He's got this intense aura about him.'

Sell Scott and seal the deal – make it so, Mr Sulu. Farai agrees. They leave the bar. It's a short walk across the river, over Commercial Road. Nika tells him all about her trip to Mozambique. Boats are moored on the docks head. She says she wouldn't have come back if it weren't for her damn course. It's been years since Farai has been to Mozambique and he suggests that maybe they can go together sometime.

They reach the flat. Farai opens the door. Music is playing, moaning and gasping coming from within, above the soulful melody.

'I see this is the *house of love*,' Nika says, with a coy wink.

Farai walks in, she follows him. He opens the door of his bedroom, his hand gripping the sock on the handle. Right there, in plain sight, Stacey is riding Scott. She moves rhythmically, like a belly dancer, eyes closed. *Funny, I remember her doing that to me.* Farai is almost bemused. He smiles and turns to Nika.

'You still want that date with Scott?'

Stacey leaps off and pulls the duvet round herself, leaving Scott exposed.

'*Oh fuck*, oh fuck, oh fuck, Farai…'

'I suppose this is awkward, babes.' A wry smile passes Farai's lips.

'I can explain. I'm so sorry. Scott came to apologize and, and…'

'You slipped and fell on his dick?'

'Oh fuck, I don't know what happened.' There's desperation in her voice.

'We only need Joey Greco and this scene will be complete.'

'I think I'll come back another time,' says Nika, backtracking to the door, a bewildered grin frozen on her face.

'No, stay, you still have to see the papers even though my end of the bargain seems to have fallen through.'

Scott stands next to the bed, pulling his jeans on.

'At least he doesn't have a bigger dick than I do.' Farai laughs. An awesome wave of relief washes over him. This actually makes him feel better about the situation.

'I don't know what happened.' Stacey's agonized. She holds her hair in clenched hands, tears begin rolling down her face. Her face is red, but it's unclear whether this is from shame or the exertion of the night.

'I know what's happening. The 2 of you can finish off your session; let no one ever say Farai Macheke was a cockblocker. When you're done, get your stuff and leave, the both of you.'

'Farai–'

'I'm doing my best to be civilized here. You have 8 minutes, the established average length of a bonk in Great Britain, plus 5 minutes to get your stuff. That gives you a grand total of 13 minutes. Chop-chop, kids.' His voice drops to a low, menacing tone.

He closes the door and takes Nika to the living room. Nika sits down and places her backpack on the desk. Farai goes to the fridge, peers down amidst the vegetables and perishables. No beer there. He goes to the cupboard under the sink, which is their BWS section, and retrieves a pack of Asahi. He puts some in the freezer and takes 2 cans with him to the living room.

'I'm sorry they are warm, but you Mozambicans must be used to that, what with no electricity and all.'

'Funny, I thought that was Zimbabwe. Why don't you put them in the fridge?' Nika asks.

'I have. It's just right now I need a drink.' He raises his can and they clink them. They can hear the noises from the bedroom of Scott and Stacey getting their things.

'You play ProEvo?' he asks.

'Are you okay?' she responds.

'Lugubrious.'

'Wanna talk about it?'

'This ain't a biggy. I know a guy who was told after 30 years that the kids weren't his. Now that's serious. This, this right here, nah Nika, this is a breeze. Check out the papers, tell me what you think.' *Sympathy card – at least she can't say no now.*

Stacey comes from the corridor with her big handbag stuffed full of things. She has a black bag full of stuff as well. *How did she get all this*

199

gear into my house? She stands by the door, looking sad, hair disheveled.

'Can we talk?' she says in a quiet voice. 'I made a mistake.'

Farai doesn't turn from Nika.

'Can you at least translate this section for me? I think it covers the DRC conflict.'

'Sure, but don't you want to talk to her right now,' Nika replies.

'I think she knows her way out.'

They hear the sound of the main door open and close, Scott leaving. Stacey hovers, hugging herself as though she is cold, looking at Farai with his back to her. He tells Nika about Climente and his meeting with de Alenquer. Stacey lingers for a few moments longer, whispers 'Farai,' then turns and heads out. As she reaches the main door, she shouts, 'You snore!' and slams it shut.

Mavis Pfukuto arrived at the Magistrate's looking a right mess, her hair dishevelled, eyes puffy as though she had not slept in a long while. She sat in the living room, drinking Mai Chenai's tea-hobvu. She kept her eyes downcast, embarrassed to be there after what had happened. The TV was on God TV, with an American preacher bellowing away something about how God did not like poverty and how, if Jesus came back today, he would be a rich entrepreneur employing twelve people. His voice was occasionally drowned out by the affirmation of his mega congregation.

"This man is a powerful preacher," Mai Chenai said.

"Hallelujah! Last week he was preaching about forgiveness," Mavis said, spotting an opening. "That's why I'm here. Alfonso told me everything."

"You have no idea of the trouble he caused us," said Mai Chenai, turning to her husband.

"He only remembers bits and pieces. He was drunk," said Mavis.

"Do you know VaMcKenzie was going to call the police to tell them that we were some sort of child traffickers trying to sell our daughter and her unborn child. Even worse, he has a son who is a police officer. Baba Chenai had to talk to him to smooth things over. Easier said than done, murungu anga achivava iyeye. Can you imagine what would have happened if the issue had been taken further?"

The Magistrate rose to leave the room. Lately, he'd felt under the weather. The doctor said it was because of stress. The stress was here in his own home, hounding him at every turn. He felt it every morning when he saw Chenai before she went to school, a tiny bump showing beneath her cardigan. Somehow, he had to create a future for a fifteen year old and a baby in a country where he was fit for nothing but menial work.

"Can we please talk about it?" asked Mavis.

"I will have nothing more to do with that man," the Magistrate said in the severe voice he'd once reserved for sentencing.

He was walking away when Mavis knelt down, clapping her hands right over left. To walk away from this most humble gesture of supplication by a woman would be a grave insult. He stopped. He had no choice. Mai Chenai asked him to sit down.

"At least listen to what she has to say," Mai Chenai said.

"I have nothing against you, Mavis. I think you are a fine person who probably deserves to be with someone a lot better than Alfonso. The thing is, I feel it's best we part ways after what he put us through."

"I can't blame you, but Alfonso is sick. His heart is killing him. He refuses to eat, or drink, or leave his bed." Mavis stayed kneeling. "You should know how highly he thinks of you. There hasn't been a day since you moved here that he hasn't spoken of you. He says you are like a brother to him. Alfonso is not an educated man and we all know he's not the smartest of men either. You are the type of man he would never have had a chance to brush shoulders with back home. Chokwadi, after the incident I spoke with him, tried to encourage him to come and see you himself but the shame was too great. Now he's talking crazy, saying that it is better for him to die than to be without your friendship."

"Is this true?" asked Mai Chenai.

"He hoped to improve himself, so he could be a gentleman like you. Now he imagines himself returning to the gutter. Murume wangu is not a bad person. He has no family. He's spent his whole life all alone in this world with no one to guide him. He considers you the big brother he never had, the closest thing to family. Please do not leave him like this."

The defendant is guilty, his lawyer pleads in mitigation. The feral underclass, men he locked up by the busload during his time on the bench. Then he had no doubt that they would only reoffend, but here, here in this country where there were many possibilities, even a man like Alfonso might have a chance to improve his character. The Magistrate was silent, weighing things like he had done in the past. Mavis looked at him, her every hope pinned on his inscrutable face.

"Baba Chenai, no lasting harm was done. You sorted things out with VaMcKenzie. If not for Alfonso then for mainini vedu ava," Mai Chenai pleaded.

Trapped between the two women like this, the Magistrate had no real choice. He was the old fashioned sort who felt that, despite modern ideas on equality, a man must lay his coat over a puddle on a rainy day. He bowed his head, showing scatterings of silver hair.

"Tell him it's okay. We are very disappointed, but he is forgiven."

"Praise Jesus," Mavis cried out. "Please come with me and tell him. He won't believe me if I go by myself."

She insisted on taking him to Alfonso straight away. He thought how fortunate Alfonso was in having a woman who could not only tolerate his vile eccentricities, but was also willing to humble herself if it meant his happiness. Reflecting now, in a calm frame of mind, he saw that Alfonso had been a fool, yes, and had butted in to matters that did not concern him, but he had done so, pathetically, to try to prove himself in the Magistrate's eyes. He understood it better now, the poor man who steals a loaf of bread.

Everything Mavis said confirmed this hypothesis in his mind. From now on I must treat Alfonso like a pup, so he heels when I say and walks when I command. It will be for his own good. I may raise him up to be a better man yet, he thought, as he put on his jacket.

They drove to Niddrie in Mavis's banger. It took less than five minutes to get there. She was anxious the Magistrate might change his mind. Mai Chenai came with them, just in case.

"He's upstairs. Follow me," Mavis said, her voice a stage whisper.

They went up a flight of stairs to the main bedroom. The curtains were drawn and it was dim inside. Alfonso lay on the bed with his eyes shut, a bag of frozen peas on his forehead. He groaned and raised one paw in the air. Mavis went in and shook him. He rose slowly and turned to the door where the Magistrate stood.

"Do my eyes deceive me? I see an angel in the doorway. My time is at an end," he said to Mavis with the melodrama of a bad thespian.

The light shining in through the doorway did give the Magistrate a semi-divine aura.

"It's him," said Mavis.

"That is better than an angel. I can't believe it." Alfonso groaned and coughed a few times. "He has come to see me at the very end, even though I sinned against him. You told me, Mavis, that man is higher than any of us."

She took a wet towel from the bedside table and wiped his forehead. Then she went to the window and opened the curtains, letting light into the room. Alfonso sat up, his back propped against the headboard, squinting, dazed by the light. He coughed and cleared his throat.

"I have to apologise. How do I find the right words?"

"You don't need to. We've forgiven you already," Mai Chenai said.

"It's the drink that made me do it," Alfonso began to ramble. "Mavis always tells me, 'Alfonso,' she says, 'you can't handle your drink. You must stop this drinking.' And it's all so true, so true. I can't handle it. I see the Magistrate drinking and I think maybe I can handle that strong stuff too, but I'm weak, after a drink or two I lose all control. The Rhodesians knew it, that's why they said – 'You kaffirs mustn't drink clear spirits, stick to your Chibuku.' They knew it. They saw we couldn't handle it. I couldn't stop myself. Once the alcohol is in me, it's like Legion himself has fallen upon me. I can hear my own tongue running about in my mouth. I can't stop myself. I am so sorry, Magistrate. The Devil's brew made me do it. I will never drink another drop as long as I shall live. I swear it on my mother's grave."

He covered his face with a pillow to hide his shame, peeping out with one eye then hiding again. The Magistrate thought this whole performance pitiful, even as he was overwhelmed with sympathy. The devotion Alfonso showed him, coupled with remorse, went a long way in shaping these finer feelings.

"Make him something hot to eat. I'll take him out for some fresh air," said the Magistrate. His former authority had returned to his voice. There was a confidence about him that had been missing for a long time, as though he was slowly regaining the strength that had been sapped by the cold Scottish air.

Alfonso was led down the stairs in his striped pyjamas. They found Scott in the lounge, watching rugby. He'd fallen out with his flatmates and Alfonso was kind enough to offer him the spare room until he could sort himself out. The Magistrate was pleasantly surprised by Alfonso's generosity, another indication that Alfonso could be a better man.

"I called London and they said we'll have our election within the month," said Scott, without acknowledging anyone.

"Good, now we just have to hurry and find a candidate," Alfonso replied.

"Aiwa, no talk of politics until you are well," said Mavis.

Scott was cutting some cheese on a wooden chopping board with a carving knife, which the Magistrate though was too big for the task.

"Wouldn't you be better off with a cheese knife?" the Magistrate asked. "That's a…"

"A big man uses a big knife," Scott replied nonchalantly.

"He is the only one who uses that knife. It's too dangerous," said Alfonso, following the women into the kitchen.

Mavis and Mai Chenai made a fry up. Alfonso gobbled his portion down, stealing little glances at the Magistrate to make sure he wasn't going anywhere. The conversation turned to Alfonso's health and he said that he was fully recovered now that the Magistrate had returned to raise him from the dead like Lazarus. Mavis piled bacon onto the Magistrate's plate until he protested the cholesterol would kill him.

When they were finished, Alfonso got dressed and went out with the Magistrate. He wore his favourite oversized brown suit, hobbling a step or two behind the Magistrate with his hands behind his back. Alfonso asked if they could take the bus, there was something he wanted to show the Magistrate.

They took the 30, got off on the South Bridge and backtracked to Chambers. The Magistrate was impressed by the solid, grey architecture of the buildings on the row. But the old masonry held no memories for him and, in his despair, he failed to see that, even without music, he could and was in fact creating new ones one brick at a time. They passed the Jazz Bar and walked towards the museum end of the street. Alfonso stopped at the black wrought iron gates that stood at the entrance to the courts.

"I've always wanted to bring you here. I thought you'd like it, being a lawman and all that," he said.

They went through the gates, across the courtyard and through the revolving doors.

"We can just go in, you see," said Alfonso. "Very transparent. Very democratic."

The metal detectors beeped when the Magistrate went through. He emptied his pockets and went back in again. The security guards frisked him, then allowed him to proceed. The Magistrate was impressed by its size, the ceramic floor reflecting the lights above. They went into Court 5 at the bottom of the stairs. Alfonso went straight for a seat, but the Magistrate bowed to the Sheriff before taking his.

Alfonso fidgeted, unable to stay still, while the Magistrate's entire focus had transferred to the proceedings below. This was one of the few times he had watched from the gallery. His early work as a prosecutor saw him working in the pit. The lawyers in gowns sparred over the fate of a young man in a tracksuit with drink driving charges levelled against him. It was routine since the defendant had entered a guilty plea, but the defence appealed for a lighter sentence that wouldn't affect his work. Alfonso tried to speak to the Magistrate but was silenced by the clerk of court. Not that the Magistrate noticed, because he'd now turned to the man on the bench, sitting elevated above everyone else. The coat of arms was nailed to the wall above the Sheriff. His face was stern as he listened to the defence lawyer mechanically plead for leniency in a voice void of passion.

The Magistrate's mind drifted back to his old courtroom in Bindura. It had been hot and stuffy with a fan on the ceiling that broke down more often than not. Even now, with the slight difference in traditions, he could relate to the performance taking place in front of him. The Sheriff seemed to be weighing an appropriate sentence, riffling through discounts for an early plea.

They sat for hours listening to arguments going back and forth, traffic violations, violent offences, petty theft. The thrill of the theatre of court coursed through him. The cast was laid out with part of the script written for them, and the rest, impromptu performances. The audience in the gallery, only half understanding events, was kept engrossed all the same. Many of them were a captive audience. The Magistrate, from his vantage point at the back of the room, began to see things from a different perspective. He noticed the stiff way the defendants carried themselves, how they tripped up under pressure from the barrage the procurators fired at them. It was funny, he thought, how with a little twist of fate, he could be in that chair being tried as a child trafficker. It was as though he had received an electric shock. He nudged Alfonso and they left the court. He took care to bow one last time before they left.

"Well, what did you think?" Alfonso asked once they were outside.

"There are slight differences, but the essence is the same," he replied." Let's go to Arthur's Seat. I hope you are up for the walk."

They went up the hill, with Alfonso always a step or two behind, huffing and puffing away. From the crest, they could see spires all around the city, pricking the sky. The sun was high above them, filtering through a wispy layer of clouds. The air was humid and the temperature mild. Alfonso stood in the Magistrate's shadow. "I am not a clever man, Magistrate. In fact, I am a fool, and everyone knows it." Alfonso sounded lucid and composed. "But, if there is one thing I've learnt in the last few years, it's that everyone needs a story. That's all our lives amount to, nothing but stories that we hope will live on after we are gone. We have hope that our names will be remembered. Mere men like me are soon forgotten, but great men like you, if they have a story, then their names will be remembered for all time. I know a woman from Mvurwi who was standing outside her gate one day, when a Swedish journalist in a bakkie happened to stop by to ask for directions to a farm during the invasions. He noticed several emaciated dogs running about in her yard and asked the woman why they were so skinny. Her English was not very good, neither was the journalist's, so she answered, 'From the farms,' referring to the fact she had bought them as pups from a farm. He assumed she meant she'd rescued them after the owners had fled. He took a photograph of her and the dogs and drove off. An article was published in his paper about this remarkable woman who, despite her meagre resources, was looking after pet victims of the jambanja. It was noticed by some animal lovers, who contacted the journalist to ask for the woman's details. The journalist managed to get her address from a local contact and, before she knew it, she was getting letters of support from all across Scandinavia. The Swedish Ambassador asked to visit her, by which point she was savvy enough to borrow more dogs from her neighbours. They took photos and statements about how she was virtually sharing her children's food with the dogs. Soon cheques were flying in. A month or so later they flew her to Stockholm and gave her a medal for services to dogs. By this time she was genuinely going to the farms and rescuing dogs that had been left behind. That's now her business, saving animals. What came first was the story, then the deed. It's happening all around us, journalists are writing articles, authors spinning money off novels and memoirs, the charities, NGOs, asylum seekers, all making hay of the Zimbabwean situation. That's why men like you must step up to the mark. Genuine men of honour and courage are needed right now, because, when all is said and done, all anyone will ever care about is your story."

The Maestro lay still on the carpet, eyes looking up into the void, frozen like a corpse. Being alive, he felt the acute pangs of hunger digging into his ribs, his stomach growling, empty. He reanimated, taking a sip from the bottle of cider next to him. It was flat, the backwash at the bottom of the bottle. Thank goodness it was still medicine. It was the silence he couldn't stand, a talking silence full of accusation. Every day, he felt it as a crushing pressure on his chest, as though he were lying under a pile of bodies in a mass grave after a massacre. Yet each man kills the thing he loves. The coward does it with a kiss. He'd done it with a lighter. What are books if not vessels containing minds? Conscious thought comes in words, and, if a book contains an idea, then it contains something of the writer's soul. The Maestro saw that, for all his time in the flat, he'd not once been alone. He had been at the centre, playing the role of moderator for conversations between a thousand other minds. At the fore were those who had written the works he'd read, but, in the shadows, lay other thinkers, other minds that had influenced them. A slew of minds linked through time and space had resided in the flat with him, challenging one another, contesting, arguing, seeking a higher truth. But, these minds had not done it alone. It had happened through him, with him, in him. They had spoken to him and each idea was only as good as his interpretation of it. It was he who brought them to life. And they had lived within him, had breakfast with him, went to work with him, watched TV with him, jerked off with him, thought of Tatyana with him. They had become him, and he had become them. The gravity of what he had done dawned on him. It took a while for it to be formed into thoughts that he could fully understand. Initially it was just raw emotion, heartburn, a constriction in the throat, a weakness deep down in the bowels. The burning of the books had not been an assault on something external to him. It was violence against the self, against his own mind. It was self-immolation, the renouncing of life itself. He waited to hear voices in his head, but, there was nothing. Stillness, loneliness, emptiness. He saw a glimpse across the ages of why the burning of books had been such a powerful force. Why states and religions so loved to burn treason and heresy. It was an assault, not only on the author, but on every single mind that had been touched by their work. He threw up yellow bile onto the carpet. Mustering superhuman strength from a reserve he never knew he had, he got up, grabbed a few belongings, his wallet, a rucksack, a few clothes and a pair of shoes. A hole had been blown through his universe. His flat was no longer fit for human habitation. The Maestro left the brown envelope on the mantelpiece, stepped outside and began to walk, to walk alone. It was not so much walking as staggering, dragging himself step by step away from Medwin South. The pavement had black streaks, lines of ash that had painted themselves there. He stumbled, falling to his knees. He pushed himself back up with his hands and saw they had black marks, the stigmata. There were people on the square looking at him. People with no faces. They parted to make way for him as he stumbled through. He felt their eyes boring through him. It's a disgrace being pished like that this time of the morning, and in front of the bairns too, a woman's voice said, as he went past the school. The sound of children's voices filled the air. He hurried along, holding on to the railing to support himself. Absolutely disgusting, someone else said. His eyes were half open, everything was a blur. Cars hooted. Drivers shouted. He crossed streets. Walked through hedges. So much noise. He bent over and threw up again on Sighthill Park. When he was done, he hid himself in the woodland near the football grounds and rested against a birch. From there he watched people walking on the pavement, hidden from them by the trees and the long grass. In the undergrowth was a decade's worth of litter. Aluminium cans and plastic mostly. He reached into his pocket for a fag and put it to his mouth. He tried the lighter five times before it caught light. His hands trembled. Why did I do it? What does it matter? Why am I here? His mind was that of a seven year old, asking questions for which there was no prospect of reply. The questions came from a part of it that he hitherto did not know. He smelled burning in his nostrils, or was it just the cigarette? He licked his dry, cracked lips. After he finished smoking, he fell asleep right there, in the bushes. The sky was ablaze in rich shades of orange when the Maestro came to. Baby seagulls in their brown plumage tested their wings. He wiped the trickle of drool that ran down his beard, which grew red, a stark contrast to his sandy-coloured hair. The cold was tiny paper cuts all over his body. He took out a Rhodesian camouflage jacket and wore it over his hoodie. He stood up, a dark silhouette in the fading light. It took a second to get his bearings. There was a bitter, foul taste in his mouth, like a pill mixed with decaying entrails. He spat and began to walk down the road toward Corstorphine. After fifteen minutes he arrived at Tesco where he covered his head with the hoodie and stood by the petrol station, scanning the car park until he was sure it was clear and no one who knew him would see him. The Christmas decorations were already up. They went up earlier and earlier each year, trying to push Christmas right into summer. He made his move, keeping an even pace, staring down so the cameras could not capture his face. He got to the back, at the delivery bays, and hopped into a rubbish skip. It was a gold mine. Loaves of bread, bagels, milk, eggs, pepperoni, salad, avocados, yoghurt, lettuce. Throwing away perfectly good food used to be his job. He ate a mouthful of pepperoni, aware of the irony that what he was doing was illegal. Taking food from the bin destined for landfill was against the law and, so, he was now a criminal. He stuffed whatever he could in his rucksack, which hardly made a dent on the waste. He took off, going up Drumbrae, and pushed on to Clermiston, weighed down by his backpack, drinking milk from the container. It was all uphill walking this part of town and he felt the strain. It was dark by the time he got to Corstorphine Hill. This late in the year, dusk did not linger. The walk warmed him up a little. The memory of the last few months came back in pictures, images to which he could not fix his self. Even as he walked, he felt like it was someone else's journey, some predestined event that must play out whether he willed it or not. His mind was slowly mending into a single, coherent entity again. It brought to him the theological argument on omnipotence and free will, which tried to reconcile how free will could truly exist if God already knew everything that was going to happen. How could a human being do anything other than what God already knew he was going to do? And if God did not know the future then God was not omnipotent. The arguments laid out to try and reconcile the two rang hollow to him, relying on clever wordplay and circuitous reasoning, the type of angelsonapinhead nonsense. From the hill, he had a sweeping view of the west and the south-west of the city. He could make out the Calders from the high rises, and from there past the fields to the Pentlands. The city looked beautiful under the glow of the lights. He found a spot under a chestnut tree. Cars went by, and he was utterly alone, the king of his hill. He gathered some twigs on the ground and lit a fire. The warmth of the flames cheered him up. He remembered camping when he was a little boy and his father teaching him to make a fire. The past came through tiny cracks in the present. He used his sleeping bag to shield one side so the fire couldn't be seen by people on the paths below. The Maestro did not know where he was going. There were no stars in the sky to guide him home. He was a migratory bird, blinded by the lights, not knowing up from down. He felt freer on the hill, less constrained by the suffocating air of civilisation. He imagined himself out somewhere on the savannah, on a vast, limitless plain on which roamed herds of buffalo, antelope and zebra. He smiled to himself and felt happy, letting his mind travel across the night. The cold woke him up early in the morning. By then his fire had completely died out, so he retrieved the sleeping bag and got in, using his rucksack as a pillow. The ground under him was like ice, he could feel it through the sleeping bag. After a while, unable to rest any longer, he rose, shook the dirt off his sleeping bag, rolled it up, collected his gear and descended the hill. The volume of traffic on Queensferry Road suggested that it was some time before eight. Mist formed with each breath he exhaled. He put his hands in his pockets. The Maestro went down to Davidson's Mains and found the shops there closed. He kept moving to stay warm. The houses were larger here, with well-kept gardens, a far cry from the squalor of the Calders. The streets were clean too, save for autumn leaves that blocked the drains. The sea was a large grey mirror in the distance. He headed for it, going past the golf course, down to Cramond. There was a café by the seaside where the Maestro stopped and ordered a black coffee. He did not know how, when, or why the humble filter has been replaced by the Americano, though, in a time when French fries were being renamed freedom fries, anything could happen. He sat near the window, looking out onto the boats on the quay gently rocking on the waves. The café smelt of roasted coffee beans and the heat made him feel sleepy. He stayed in the café as long as was politely possible, and then left, going along the quay. There was a public convenience nearby where he performed his ablutions, washing bits of leaves and grass out of his hair, and changed his underwear. He went down to the seafront with a view of the concrete balustrades that led to Cramond Island. And then he waited for a minor miracle. Dog walkers and tourists strolled along the beach. They crammed up by the noticeboard that displayed the tide timetable and a history of the area. A stoic braved the cold in a pair of shorts. Sailboats headed towards Forth Bridge. And, while he waited, the tide pulled back. A Mosaic miracle, revealing the causeway, a narrow black road that ran between the island and the mainland. For much of the day it was submerged beneath the sea, but at low tide it revealed itself. A group of tourists began to make the crossing, walking where just minutes before there had only been water. In a few hours the tide would return covering everything once more. He thought briefly about making the crossing, but he decided against it, instead going back up to the road, past the whitewashed houses, to the main road where he caught the 41. It was warm on the bus. He sat at the back, with his rucksack on his knees. A little man in an ill-fitting brown suit was talking loudly on his phone in a foreign tongue. He listened to the way the words rolled off the man's tongue, and found himself staring, mesmerised by how he moved his free arm about like a conductor, punctuating his sentences. Hameno kamurungu kari kungonditarisa nemaziso egreen, hakanyari. The Maestro turned away, embarrassed. He got off at the West End, went into Boots, and bought a toothbrush and toothpaste, before he headed down to Dalry to the cemetery sandwiched between Dalry Road and the Western Approach. Even with the traffic rumbling along these busy streets, the cemetery was a peaceful space. Some of the tombstones had fallen and lay prone in the grass. This was an old cemetery and no one laid flowers for the dead here. Long grass grew wild on the graves so that the ones in the middle were inaccessible. The dead man's flourish also grew in abundance. Great trees dug their roots into the graves, their branches touching one another in a deathly embrace. The wind blew. Leaves rustled. A wire mesh bin overflowed with uncollected rubbish, plastic bags, wine and cider bottles and cheap beer cans, as though someone had thrown a party on these houses with no windows. He read the inscriptions on the headstones as he passed by the graves. Some of the older gravestones were so worn that the names were no longer legible. Time had erased them from history. He sat down and lit a fag, resting among the dead. From here he went to North Merchiston Cemetery, just up the way on Slateford Road. There he found the same, fallen headstones and lost memories. The grass grew unchecked. The only hope a man might have for immortality was to be recycled back in the carbon chain, he thought. Everything else was temporal. That winter, as it grew colder, the Maestro visited many cemeteries, old and new, across the city. He went to Greyfriars to see the ancient vaults and tombs, some of which were protected by iron railings to deter the resurrection men who'd made their living selling fresh corpses to the medical school. He went to the Canongate, Old Calton, New Calton and St Cuthbert's graveyards, and newer sites further out in the city. At night he slept in parks, enduring the cold, never sleeping in the same place twice. Edinburgh being full of parks, he never wanted for choice. When it was too cold, he slept under the hot air vents on the Royal Mile and Rose Street. A dense haar descended upon the city. From a distance, the people walking on her pavements seemed like ghosts. The buildings became ethereal shadows. They could have been from the past or the future, for time itself blurred in the thickness of the fog. The reality around him seemed fragile, as though the city would vanish with the haar when it lifted. Bright fog lights on cars pierced the mist. Among these dark figures, the Maestro trudged along, trying to keep warm. His step was a slow shuffle, a kind of drunken walk, accentuated by purposelessness. He traversed the city, appearing in Portobello, Restalrig, Seafield, Trinity. There was a day he wound up in Dalkeith, with no idea how he got there. It was as though his mind cleared and his feet simply willed themselves where they would. He no longer bathed regularly. He ate infrequently. His red beard grew to the size of a fist. There was a glazed look in his eyes that gave him a prophetic mien, or, maybe, he just looked like a bum. He stopped in a narrow doorway on Thistle Street and tried to light a cigarette. The first light fizzled away because his numb fingers couldn't hold the lighter properly. He tried again and managed. The warm flame lit up his face for a few seconds and died out. He coughed and spat out a blob of thick, yellowy phlegm. The cough became an ever-present companion. Each drag he took warmed up his lungs. He'd picked up a trick or two in his time on the streets. Instead of wasting money in coffee houses, he could get breakfast at the Ark. The kindly staff there tried to strike up conversations with him, but he kept to himself, always polite to a fault, but never indulging. When the itch got unbearable or he could no longer stand his own body odour, he took showers at the Contact Point and, sometimes, at the Salvation Army. There was nothing like the feeling of hot water washing the dirt away after a hard day's tramping. The board on the M&S window declaring six days till

Christmas was his only way of knowing where he was in time. How it moved so fast. Where did it all go? He sat in the gardens on Princes Street, watching children on the rides with flashing lights, listening to the fairground music. Couples shared mugs of glühwein at the stands near the galleries. This time of the year, this part of the gardens was given over to amusements. He'd spent last Christmas alone in his flat, reading. This was always a lonely time for him, and the sight of families didn't make him feel any better. There was a Ferris wheel and, below, people skated on the ice rink, bathed in the Christmas lights. He could see North Bridge, on which buses passed. A dark force there attracted suicides who jumped and splattered on the roof of Waverley Station. He returned daily, people-watching in the freezing cold. When the board announced there were three days till Christmas, it began to snow. Small flakes falling out of the sky. It was the snow in March, a few years earlier, which had earned him his nickname. A heavy snowfall, which had caught everyone underprepared. The council blamed the weathermen. They, in turn, said it was unprecedented, just short of calling it an act of God. Grit ran out, snowploughs broke down. There was chaos on the motorways and disruptions on the trains. The Maestro had made it to work, but half the staff failed to turn up, claiming to be snowed in, always a good excuse for a few days off. He was asked to stay on by his manager at the end of his shift. They were a twenty-four hour establishment, capitalism at its finest, come rain, hail, snow, or apocalypse. When he'd finished his second shift, a different manager asked him to stay on, and stay on he did. It was only on the fourth day that someone noticed he'd pulled seventy-two hours solid. He was sleepwalking on the shop floor. They put him in a taxi, sent him home, and gave him the rest of the week off. When he returned, his tale was legend. Tatyana called him The Tesco Maestro, in the staff canteen, and the name had stuck ever since. Lost in these memories, he walked away, down London Road. He fought his aching feet and chesty cough, making it all the way to Musselburgh, where he spent the night behind Brunton Theatre. A performance was taking place. The strings and bass of musical scores filtered out into the night. The Maestro rubbed his weary legs. His mind was empty until he heard people walking away from the theatre talking excitedly about the performance. He wondered briefly what it had been before drifting off to sleep. Seagulls screeching woke him at dawn. The sun came up over the horizon. He walked toward the sea and found himself on the

217

promenade. There, he sat on a bench, wrapped himself in his sleeping bag and watched the waves dance in the light of the new day. Runners and walkers came up the promenade. There were boats out at sea in the distance. The crisp air cleansed his lungs, even as he reached for a fag. An old woman wearing thick spectacles sat beside him. You're wrapped up nice and warm, duck, she said. Her warm sounded like wor-rom. It's me arthritis in the morning, you see. If I dinnae get up first thing, I cannae get going for the rest of the day. She threw bits of bread to the pigeons. She told him she'd been married to a sailor in the merchant navy. When he was away she would stand by this shore to wish him a safe return every day he was out at sea. Sometimes the sailor was at sea for months at a time, but she knew he would always come back to her. He died last year of the flu, she said. I still come here and will him back, every day. She seemed to grow younger in the Maestro's eyes. There was beauty in her still, because she held on to that love for what was lost. The old woman defied logic, common sense, and all reason, perhaps finding something more fundamental in this small act of defiance against the coldness of existence. After wandering from Musselburgh to Portobello, he caught a bus to the city and found a skipper on Hillside Crescent, a little off London Road. From his skipper, he watched the snow pile up until it covered the window that let light into the basement. The Maestro brought out a bag of charcoal, which he lit. He was conservative, only throwing a few lumps on at a time. It blackened his hands. A draught came into the room, but it was better than being outside. He shivered and blew on the charcoal, which glowed fiery red. That illusion was necessary to tell his brain that everything was okay. He coughed and spat out a blob of phlegm. For a moment his lungs felt clear. Soon the gunk would accumulate again and he would find himself short of breath. It was okay so long as he kept the fire burning. He drifted off to sleep and dreamt for the first time in weeks. In this dream he saw Tatyana in a white dress, the wind blowing through her hair as she stood by Granton shore, willing him home. The waves broke at her feet, and her arms beckoned. He woke with a start. The dream had been so vivid, as though she could see him. It was Christmas Eve. He'd spent the last few Christmases alone, convincing himself that the holiday meant nothing. He gathered his belongings and peered out into the dark. Dawn was still a few hours away, Apollo's chariot on the other side of the world. And the Maestro would move at first light for he hoped she would be there. But then, she might have gone home to Poland to be with her family. His heart sank at this thought. She'd spoken of the big family Christmases they had in Poland. Then why was she calling to him in his dreams if she knew she would not be there if he came? His ears felt like ice blocks glued to his head. He stared into the darkness and waited, with only the mist from his breath to keep him company. He thought of Dickens. How could he not, it was Christmas, and it came to him that novels were messy because life itself was arbitrary, and they were but the palest of reflections of it, Petri dishes in a laboratory. Novels were never supposed to have contained an indivisible truth, instead, they only contained the minute, limitless possibilities life had to offer. He sighed. The first 44 went past on London Road. It was time to get moving again. He bought a bottle of water on Broughton Street and pushed on to Warriston, admiring the warm houses that he walked past, looking through windows with blinking lights, and wondered who the occupants were and what they were doing for the holiday. At the petrol station he bought a card with Dalmatians wearing red bows and proceeded. An old couple was walking a pug, which wore tartan on its back. A woman was jogging, listening to music on her MP3 player. The Maestro rubbed his hands together to keep warm. The walk depleted his remaining reserves. He felt like a drowning man. Each breath of cold air felt like sharp daggers piercing his chest. Still he walked on in hope. Ferry Road was now before him. He was familiar with its length, and trudged along, one foot after the other. A snowplough drove past, clearing sludge onto the side of the road. The college's grounds appeared to the left, but he took no notice as they looked pretty much like everything else in that sanitizing blanket of white. He pushed on, his chest bursting. Twice, he coughed out a copious amount of brown gunk that stained the snow, but he did not stop, for he knew that, if he stopped, he would not be able to start up again. The end was in sight as he went past Morrisons, with banners advertising seasonal bargains and overpriced turkeys. Onto Crewe Road, under the bridge, and onto the estate he went. His steps grew shorter to a shuffle. It took all his effort just to stay upright. His eyes were half shut, the road ahead a blur of white. He kept up this gruelling march, past children building a snowman. One of them lobbed a snowball that caught him on the neck. He was in a parallel dimension fixated on the fire in his lungs and the lead-like weight of his boots. He almost slipped on a patch of black ice, but steadied himself. This took the wind out of him. He coughed and spluttered, walking still, gasping for air as he went. The red door came in sight. He leant against the wall and pressed buzzer number one. The sound of the doorbell travelled out to him, and he waited. No reply. He buzzed once more, and, then again, and again. She was not home. The Maestro had no strength left in him. It had been a dream, nothing more. He crawled over to the hedge, lay in the snow curled up like a foetus, the Christmas card in his hand... He felt warm. And then, he was running, running through a long, dark tunnel, running in bare feet, feeling the ground beneath, a sludge of oil and mud that seeped between his toes, running in no particular direction, not knowing exactly where he was going, not caring, running away, running to, tearing through the fabric of the universe itself... He felt her shaking him. Maestro wake up, her voice came from afar, a long distance phone call. Wake up, damn you. What you are doing here? He opened his eyes and she was there, pulling him up, willing him back. He used what little strength he could to help her lift his body from the ground, someone else's body. On the snow was her shopping that she'd spilt in shock. She took him inside. The flat was an inferno, hot, tropical, welcoming. It's stupid, stupid, to sleep in the snow like that, she said. What the hell do you think you're doing? She left him to retrieve her shopping and came back inside. She ran the bath, stripped him naked like a child, and put him in it. He winced as his skin broke the water, the flesh thawing from the cold, blood rushing back to his extremities. Tatyana, he said. Shut up, stupid, stupid, little man, she said, and he saw she was crying. She left, and came back with a black bin bag in which she put his clothes and shoes, and told him, because they stank, she was throwing them in the bin. Then she washed him, scrubbing the dirt of the streets off his skin, telling him to raise his arms, washing his intimate parts with the detachment of a nurse. When she was done, the water was black with floating debris. A dark ring of filth ran round the bath. She unplugged the stopper, drained the bath and filled it with clean water. I want you to soak for few minutes, when the water gets cold, dry yourself with my towel and shave using my razor. She left with the black bag with his clothes. He soaked, feeling fresh, clean, reborn, rising from the ashes. The bathroom was filled with steam. He lay back, there was so much he wanted to say. He looked at his bony limbs, barely recognising them. When the water got cold, he followed her instructions, got out and shaved. The reflection in the mirror was of a gaunt old man with tired eyes. He left the bathroom and found Tatyana in the kitchen. She averted her eyes from his nakedness. I put some clothes out for you on my bed, she said. He went and dressed. She laughed for the first time that day when he came back wearing her track bottoms that only came halfway down his calves. But he didn't mind, the clothes were clean. She made some lentil soup, which they ate with bread. Then she took his hand and led him to the bedroom. They lay together, looking into one another's eyes. I look everywhere for you. I am so worried. I try calling, but your phone was switched off. I ask around at work, I go to your flat and ask your neighbours, but none of them knew who you were, let alone where you are, she said. The hard tone of her voice told of the anger and relief mixed up in her. I went on a journey of discovery, trying to find the meaning of life, he said. I discovered that it is many things to many people at many times, and that, for me, and for me only, because you can only discover the meaning of your own life and no one else's, that the meaning of life lies in giving a bit of yourself to someone else. It lies in love, Tatyana. She laughed so much that he had to join in, tears streaming from their eyes, genuine emotions from their core bubbling up to the surface. You're so silly, I could have told you that already. So, now are you going to tell me about yourself? And he lay there and told her everything: wide open spaces, blue skies, laughter and the sound of sweet rain falling on zinc metal sheets, the brown puddles the rain makes, splashing in the puddles under the moonlight, cups of tea in the sunshine, cricket pavilions, of time that is measured not by the tick-tock of a clock but by its nearness to eternity, how the crickets sing their song in the night and birdsong picks up the refrain at dawn, all these things and more, as their hands were clasped together, the warmth of their bodies the only protection from

The Magistrate spent the rest of the autumn at home. He cared for Chenai as she grew bigger, took her to appointments with the nurse, and looked after the house. When Mai Chenai had been pregnant, he'd not needed to do half the things he found himself doing now. She'd had her tetes and maigurus to help her out.

He spent his free time drafting a proposal to improve the MDC structures in the diaspora. This was after he'd been elected by a landslide 14 votes to 3 in the election Alfonso and Scott had orchestrated. The turnout was a reflection of how many people were actually interested in politics back home, as opposed to the day-to-day business of survival. Chairman Dzivarasekwa resigned from the party, alleging vote rigging and other unspecified procedural irregularities. This meant the party lost a member as soon as democracy prevailed. Dzivarasekwa declared he was forming a splinter faction called The Real MDC in Edinburgh.

The Magistrate identified Zimbabwean professionals in different fields, creating a database so that they could be called upon for their expertise in specific areas. To Alfonso's dismay, the Magistrate found an accountant willing to work on their books pro bono. A final year law student at Edinburgh University agreed to provide legal advice and network with groups specialising in immigration matters. He looked into starting a free childcare group that taught Shona and Ndebele. This was a promising start. The Magistrate, finding himself at the centre of things once more, became energized. His phone rang all hours and he was either dashing between appointments or sinking under paperwork. Mai Chenai saw her old husband return and felt happy too.

In December, the McKenzies invited them for Christmas. Though it was a short trek from Craigmillar to Duddingston, they took a black cab, for Chenai's term was near. She walked slowly, her back curved into an S. The Magistrate remembered when Mai Chenai was pregnant, not so long ago. It felt like yesterday. Mai Chenai paid their fare and left a small tip. 'Twas the season of goodwill and all that.

The McKenzies' was at the end of a cul-de-sac. Their feet crunched on the freshly fallen snow. The Magistrate saw his beloved hill capped white like an old man's head. Peter opened the door, looking comical in his paper crown.

"Come in, come in. Get out of the cold. Merry Christmas."

Peter helped Mai Chenai remove her coat. The house smelt of pine from the tree in the corner that had shed its needles generously on the carpet. The mantle over the fireplace was decorated with cards and stockings.

"The turkey is in the oven," Peter said. He poured some mulled wine into three glasses and offered Chenai some tea.

"You needn't have gone to all this trouble," said Mai Chenai.

"Nonsense, it's Christmas. Now where's Liam?" Peter excused himself and went to find his son.

The Magistrate tensed up. Mai Chenai noticed and struck up a conversation about the weather of all things. Chenai reclined on the sofa, her belly thrusting out. She seemed tiny behind it, her hands round it protectively. Liam came in, a skinny figure behind his father.

"Hiya," Liam mumbled and sat awkwardly next to Chenai.

"Merry Christmas, Liam," Mai Chenai said, handing him a present wrapped in blue paper with white ribbons.

The Magistrate fought against the memory of the scarlet penis, Christmassy bright, that forced its way back into his mind. A horrible memory, a terror no parent should ever endure, etched forever in his mind. Now, seeing the kid, he felt like giving him a good licking. He watched Liam whisper something for Chenai's ears only. They are so young, he thought.

"Can we go to my room and play on the Wii?" Liam asked.

"I thought you were helping with dinner," said Peter, resigned.

"Yeah, but it'll take a while," Liam said, and off they went.

The Magistrate could breathe again. The photos on the walls had the image of a tiny brunette woman. He knew she was Kat, Peter's wife. There she was on their wedding day. Another showed her in a family portrait beaming with joy. A third was a picture of her playing with a Labrador. Her absence burned through the photos.

"So, I heard you're with the NMC now," said Peter.

"I felt it was my duty to try and sort the MDC out. It was full of charlatans and people who didn't know what they were doing. I'll do my best to serve," the Magistrate replied.

"Good luck sorting that lot out, you'll need it. Never seen anything like it in my life," Peter laughed. "Though, I suppose the Tories..."

"Please, no talk of politics... Now my church, there's something for Christmas. Are you saved, Peter?" Mai Chenai asked.

"No, not really. Anyway, no politics, no religion, that's my motto," said Peter.

"That just leaves the weather."

"A very British subject. I know a bloke who can go on and on about it for hours at a time, analysing every little detail, comparing it with previous years that only he remembers."

"Napoleon was wrong. This is a nation of meteorologists."

Bo' Selecta came on TV and wished everyone a Merry Crimbo. The one constant on Christmas Day, all over the world, was bad television. They drank their wine, listening to carols, old hits mixed with the new. Everyone agreed the old stuff was better, especially when The Darkness came on. Who could compare that to Cliff Richards? Peter flicked through the channels trying to find something else. The phone rang and he gave the Magistrate the remote.

"Don't you dare switch that to news," Mai Chenai said. He grumbled and left the channel on the Queen's Christmas message just to wind her up.

Mai Chenai sniffed the air, turning her head, looking round the room for the source.

"Do you smell something burning?"

"No."

She dashed to the kitchen, guided by her nose. Peter got off the phone and rushed behind her. She opened the oven and a plume of smoke poured out, engulfing the kitchen. The fire alarm in the corridor went off. The Magistrate took a cushion and fanned it. Peter coughed, choking on the fumes until Mai Chenai opened the window. They assessed the damage. Peter declared they would have toasted fowl, a Scottish classic.

"I followed the instructions to the letter," he insisted.

"I think you used a little too much heat," said Mai Chenai. "Amateur's mistake."

225

"The guys on TV make this look easy," Peter said, wiping his brow. "Gets harder every year. I don't know how Kat did it."

"I think we can still rescue bits of it that aren't quite as burnt. I hope you don't mind if I take over."

"Thank God."

"See, now you are a believer. You should join our church."

The doorbell rang. Peter went to get it before she began proselytising. The Magistrate moved to the kitchen table, watching his wife working the turkey, carving the burnt portions out, rescuing the rest. Peter returned with two other guests, a man and a woman in their mid-twenties.

"Is this how it's done now, Dad? Getting your guests to do the cooking for you. Smart move," said the young man. He shook hands with the Magistrate.

"If you two had come earlier then you could have helped out," Peter replied.

"It's not my fault, seriously. I was patrolling in Pilton, just before the end of my shift, and this woman came running out saying her boyfriend was dying. Anyways, we had to call the ambulance and, because we were there, we tried to resuscitate the guy. Then we had to take a statement, go back to the office and write it all up. The paperwork's crazy for a stiff."

"Some Christmas that is," said Peter. "Let me introduce you all. This is my son Callum and his partner Susan – these are Che's parents."

They hung about in the kitchen, chatting away, getting in Mai Chenai's way. Peter was only useful insofar as he could point out which cupboards held the various ingredients and utensils. The Magistrate argued that Christmas was not complete without killing a goat. That's how he remembered it from his childhood, the warm blood draining from the animal, skinning it. The hide would be cured, the offals cooked, the waste composted, nothing was thrown away.

Susan and Callum set the table and, when it was ready, they all sat round it. Mai Chenai coaxed Peter to say grace, which he did, stumbling over his words. The tatties were overdone and the sprouts a little soggy, but the gravy was okayish and so were the scraps of turkey, and most of the sides. They spoke over one another and exchanged crude jokes about the baby to come.

"Looking at both granddads, I can bet it will come out bald as an egg," said Callum, whose shaved head only did so much to hide his own receding hairline.

Forks and knifes scraped on china. The Magistrate saw Peter looking at the photographs and guessed what was on his mind. The empty chair beside him made it all the more obvious. Yet, here they were now, the beginning of something new. The natural passage of time in which some things are lost and new ones gained. The food and the wine kept coming. It felt as though they had known each other for an eternity and this is how they'd always spent Christmas. Because that was the essence of the holiday, a familiarity rooted in old tradition.

In the middle of dinner Chenai let out a piercing scream. Liam turned pale, the blood drained from his face. Mai Chenai took one look at Che, saw the water on the floor and said, "We have to go to the hospital, right now."

"She needs CPR," said Liam.

"I'll drive... comes with the job," said Callum. "Liam, no ducking out of this one, pal. You come with us, the rest of you can follow with Dad."

"Make sure you get her bag when you pass by our place," Mai Chenai said to the Magistrate.

They left the table, the dirty plates with bones and gravy, the soiled linen waiting to be washed and put away until next year. The Magistrate's heart beat fast. He sat next to Peter and they drove through the slush.

"It's probably not a good time to say this, but I don't think I'm ready to be a granddad," said Peter.

"I feel old."

"This sort of makes me an aunt, right?" said Susan from the back.

Light snowflakes fell from the sky. They flitted round, tumbling to the earth. And when they got there, they became part of the indistinguishable white blanket, mere threads in a tapestry. If each flake was unique, that uniqueness only served to form something larger, something common.

"They'll want to get the ploughs out tonight at this rate. Then we'll run out of grit. Happens every year," said Peter.

"It's my first White Christmas," the Magistrate said.

"Well, it's one you won't forget any time soon."

They stopped by the Magistrate's, picked up Chenai's pregnancy bag, and left. They made their way past Craigmillar Castle, going down the treacherous little road that led to the Royal. It was a big modern hospital. They found a parking space and rushed into the hospital through the wide glass doors of the main entrance.

"My daughter is giving birth," the Magistrate said to a nurse walking along the corridor.

"A Christmas baby, how exciting. You'll be wanting maternity then." She gave them the directions and they ran, their shoes squeaking on the polished floor. They went along an endless series of corridors, up the lift and found Callum and Mai Chenai waiting for them by the nurses' station.

"Where's Che and Liam?" Peter asked.

"It's alright, they're in room five. Just thought we'd give them a bit of privacy. It may be a while."

"Has the doctor been round?"

"Soon, this isn't Holby. We'll be here for a good while," said Mai Chenai. She asked them to wait in the corridor outside the ward, because there was a limit to how many people could visit a patient at the same time.

A photographer was hanging about, his camera dangling round his neck. Christmas babies were big in the press, a sure sell every year. He lounged in a chair, eating a Mars bar, waiting for the next one. He checked his wristwatch and yawned.

The Magistrate waited with Peter, Callum and Susan, drinking cup after cup of coffee. He badly wanted a shot of whisky, something to numb the swirling anxiety surging through him. The clock on the wall barely moved. A nurse walked by. The Magistrate looked up, hoping she had some morsel of information to give, some indication that everything was going to be alright, but she went past them, then down in the lift.

"How long does this all take?" Callum asked.

"How long's a piece of string, son? You kept us waiting a good thirty hours. Your mum was a wreck by the time they pulled you out of her," Peter replied.

"Don't gross us out, Dad."

"You were there, remember?"

The Magistrate knocked his knees together. In the old days, men were excluded from this business. He didn't have to endure Chenai's birth. Now he saw how that made sense. This whole thing was a nightmare. Men were made for battle, war and a million other horrible things, not childbirth. He sat back, resting his head against the wall, watching the second hand on the clock make another circuit.

"You alright, pal?" said Peter.

"In articulo mortis."

"Afraid my Latin's a bit rusty, crammed it all in school and lost it again after the exams. It will be fine. These things always come out alright in the end. I wish Kat could have been here to see it though."

Mai Chenai came out to them. The Magistrate and Peter rose together as if joined at the hip. She looked weary. The Magistrate noticed the streaks of grey in her hair, which had not been there yesterday. She was already morphing into a grandmother.

"It's happening now," she said, rather simply.

"What about Liam?"

"He's staying with her."

"Good lad," said Peter. "He's got some growing to do, quickly too."

The Magistrate wondered what kind of inhumane society forced men to be in the same room as women giving birth. The boy will be scarred for life, he thought, but he bloody well deserves it. Susan and Callum went to the vending machine to get more coffee. The Magistrate, on his fifth cup, noticed for the first time how it tasted like stale cough syrup. It needed a drop of whisky in it, no doubt. Mai Chenai sat beside him, her head on his shoulder. Peter was sandwiched between the two couples looking lost. Susan held his hand and patted it. He smiled and exhaled. At the far end of the corridor was a window, dark and opaque, the world outside of no concern to them.

Hogmanay. Farai is alone in the living room, watching *Wallace and Gromit: The Curse of the Were-Rabbit*. It reminds him of Mr Majeika and doesn't make him laugh as it should. He loves it though. It's comforting to watch the plasticine figures running about on the screen.

The cartoons of his childhood, *BraveStarr, Dungeons and Dragons, the Moomins, the Smurfs, Captain Planet*, have vanished under the radar of cultural consciousness. He scoops a spoonful of vanilla ice cream from the half empty tub between his thighs.

The flat is quiet, too quiet. His treacherous mind keeps drifting back to Stacey. So many unanswered questions his sore ego won't let him ask. Deep down he knows it really doesn't matter anyway. *Shit happens*. He feels sorry for himself. The year's coming to an end and he has little to show for it.

His mobile rings, it's his dad.

'Comrade Fatso, *gore rapera*, we're in Gutu with the whole family. I had to climb up the hill so I could get a signal just to talk to you before the New Year.'

'*Makadini henyu*, Daddy?'

'*Aiwa tiripo, Mhofu, tototyira imi muri mhiri kwemakungwa.*'

'3 more years and I'll have served my sentence, Dad.'

'Your *sekuru's* rearing *kamhuru* especially for you for when you finish that doctorate of yours. You should have come home for Christmas.'

'I know, Dad, I've been tied up with work, so much to do, so little time.'

'Listen, comrade, I have to go back. They're *gocharing matumbu* and they'll be finished if I hang around talking to you.'

'Have a nice one and say hi to Mum for me.'

He hangs up, flips the phone round and round in his hand. He scrolls through his 200 odd contacts and finds no one he wants to call. There's a knock on the door. He opens it and lets Nika in. She holds a bottle of bubbly in 1 hand and a bag in the other.

'What's with the bag?'

'You think I'm going out in my jeans?'

Farai shrugs and sits on the sofa near the empty rabbit hutch. Nika goes to the kitchen, pops the bottle and pours it into 2 tumblers. She's been coming over more often lately, checking up on Farai. They had Christmas at hers and she made them traditional Mozambican fare. She's assumed the role of the third musketeer. Farai finds it a little odd to have a 'girl friend'. Most women fall into 1 of 3 categories for him: acquaintances, pussy, family – it keeps things simple, but here's Nika. She carries in her caramel skin traces of her Makua father and her mother, who carries the mixed-up DNA of her coastal people. Farai finds her attractive. *It's a worrying trait to find your mates attractive.* Then again, he's cutting it pretty fine on the 4 week rule. *Must be the testosterone.*

Brian comes in, sleepy-eyed, in his boxers.

'Oh, shit,' he says when he sees Nika and dashes back to the bedroom.

'Nothing I haven't seen before, Brian,' she calls after him.

Definitely 1 of the boys, Farai thinks. Nika changes the channel to 1Xtra. Grime replaces *Wallace and Gromit*. Farai feels a little of the old buzz listening to Lethal Bizzle. Takes him back to the night he met Stacey in the club and he shot her, pow, in the heart. The rest is history. He smiles at the memory, his fingers – the gun – were the equivalent of the fishing rod dance move. Smooth.

Brian returns in track bottoms and a vest.

'Hey Nika,' he says, and hugs her.

'Have you got a job yet?'

'I thought I'd take a break. If I'm gonna be stuck wiping bums for the rest of my life, then I might as well chillax before I really get into it.'

'There's worse things you could be doing, I'm sure.'

'No moaning today of all days, oh my brothers. The New Year cometh. Brian, go shower, dude. Big pimpin tonight, yo,' Farai says.

'You know I could have got a shift tonight and worked for double pay, right?' Brian replies.

'You achy breaky my heart, bro.' Farai strikes a revolutionary pose. 'People didn't die in the sexual revolution so you'd have to go to work on New Year's Eve!'

Brian salutes, makes an about-turn and quicksteps to the bathroom. Farai looks out the window. This time of the year, the cold air has its own color; the light shimmers as it cuts through it, giving the atmosphere a dreamlike quality. He can see the boats moored on the Water of Leith and revelers walking into the Granary across the river. Christmas lights hang off the lampposts casting their red, yellow and green colors onto the black water.

'What did you guys do for New Year's in Zim?' Nika asks.

'We used to go to my grandfather's place in Gutu. *Sekuru* has his kraal set up at the foot of a col. This time of year, the fields that run around it are green with maize, millet and rapoko, and *magaka* and pumpkins grow in the undergrowth. If you stand on the summit of the col, you have a view as far as the eye can see: trees, bare earth, huts and the fields of the villagers. There's no electricity and, at night, you just sit around the fire and tell stories with cows lowing in the distance. You could travel the whole world and never see anything as beautiful.'

'We're of the sea, but I know what you mean,' says Nika, as though trying to merge her narrative with his.

'And on New Year's, the kids go round the villages, getting treats from home to home. My *sekuru's* yard is full of cars. Relatives come in from the cities. People gather around, we have music, song, *ngoma nehosho*, and *sekuru's* an ace on the *mbira*, you should hear him sing 1 day. We drink 7-Days until we're as high as kites. And if you get tired, or you're just too fucked to carry on, you just find a warm spot among the bodies and plonk yourself to sleep right there on the floor.'

'You've taken me there already.'

Brian shouts out that he's done.

'Do you need to shower?'

'Do I smell?'

'I was just checking.' Farai stands up and goes to the bathroom.

He takes his clothes off and leaves them in a heap on the floor. The shower is just about bearable because Brian's used up most of the hot water. Farai lathers himself with a minty shower gel. It has a tingling sensation and smells good. When he's done, he stands under the nozzle, letting the water wash the year and the dirt away down the tiles, into the little plughole at his feet. He remains there, feeling the warmth run down him, turning round to let the water spray his back, and then his front. Droplets splash against the glass partition. The bathroom is steamy and the mirrors foggy.

'I need to pee.' Nika knocks on the door.

'The door's open,' he says.

He turns away, while she sits on the throne, looking at him. He knows she can see the silhouette of his nakedness through the frosty glass. The sound of her water hitting the bowl cuts above the drip of his shower. She goes on for a good while. *Jesus, I wish I had a bladder that big.* When he hears her flush, he turns back. She walks out.

'You could offer to wash my back, you know.'

'Ask Brian to do it.'

The joke was because of his coursing testosterone – his reactor's hit critical: meltdown imminent. Farai turns the shower off and grabs a towel off the rail. He wipes the condensation off the mirror and brushes his teeth. *Hello, good looking. Your mission tonight, should you choose to accept it, is to get laid. This message will self-destruct in your ball sack should you fail.* He deodorizes with a touch of Beckham's essence. *Don't fail me tonight, Becks.*

He leaves the bathroom and gets dressed, choosing a pair of Levi's and Steve Madden Boots. Nika looks him up and down when he finally emerges.

'You took your time like a bitch,' Brian says. Farai gives him the finger.

'How do I look?'

'Better than when I came in,' says Nika.

She gets up and goes to the vacant bedroom to change. Brian and Farai play a quick game of ProEvo. Farai wins. *Good omens.* Nika emerges, in a short black dress, with a single sleeve. It follows the contours of her body. *Friend or ho?*

'I can safely say you're the best looking among us,' says Brian.

'Gee, thanks, you're such a gentleman.'

They turn the TV off, leave the house and wait for a 22 on Commercial Street. It's virtually impossible to get a cab on Hogmanay.

They don't have to wait long. The bus arrives, packed, carrying people in various stages of inebriation. A group of lads at the back sings Hibs anthems. In no time they drop off on Leith Street. Nika sits in the bus shelter and changes from her pumps into stilettos, which were stashed in her handbag. When she stands up, she's taller than

Brian, a little shorter than Farai. A group of girls stumble down the slope. *The sea's full tonight.*

They walk up to Q Bar. The bouncer high fives Farai. The place is jam-packed. The DJ drops old skool beats, RnB from the 90s. Farai heads for the bar and squeezes in between 2 girls. The fat one to his left smiles and says, 'Hi.'

'Hey.'

'Yous havin a good time?'

'Yeah, you?'

'Aye, I'm just out with my geros and we're having a laugh. Yous with anyone?'

Jehovah God. 'Yeah, that's my girlfriend over there.' He points at Nika. *Deploy flares, evasive maneuvers.*

The fat girl backs off. *The first and, probably, only act of fealty required to be an Edinburgher is to thumb your nose at Glaswegians, especially fat ones.* The bar staff work as fast as they can, but there are so many people there. He waits patiently for his turn. When the barman finally does come round, he orders 6 shots of tequila, 2 bottles of Bud and a piña colada. He slips the beer bottles into his back pockets, somehow manages to carry the shots and cocktail, and works his way between bodies until he finds Nika and Brian in the corner.

They drink a shot each to Scottish independence and argue whether the second should go to Zimbabwe or Mozambique. They settle on adding a few extra nations and drink to Africa instead. The air's thick with smoke. Nika takes out a pack and offers them. *Why not?* A group of students from Uni recognize Farai and come over. They speak over each other. The drinks keep coming. A few Zimbos they met at the party join the group. Drifters pile in and, before long, they have become a posse of nearly 20. The drinks keep coming.

'I ain't seen you in ages,' an Indian chick says to Farai and kisses him on the cheek.

'I know, I've been underground, you know, hustling.' *Who the fuck is she?*

'You said you were gonna call me but you didn't.'

'Oh, lost my phone and had to get a new one. You know how it is.' He drags on his ciggie. She takes it from him and he notices henna on her hands. It turns him on.

'You don't remember me do you?'

'Of course I do.' *Who is she?* 'Superman never lies.'

235

'What's my name, Farai?'

'Erm, Shilpa.'

'You're not a very good liar. We've never actually met before, but I know you. I've seen you around.'

Farai laughs. 'You've got me.'

'Now you owe me a drink, penalty for lying.'

He blows smoke her way. He's been out of the game for a year, come out on the pull and now he's being chatted up. *Wicked.* Nika sees him in action and winks. He realizes he's been set up and he loves Nika for it. Farai talks to the chick, still doesn't have a name, doesn't even know what he's talking about. It doesn't matter 1 bit.

Brian signals it's almost time and nods to the exit. A group of them walk out. Across the road, near St James, a loner staggers up the road with a traffic cone on his head. Black cabs and minicabs are held up at the traffic lights. Traffic is sealed off from the bridge. Policemen in high vis jackets patrol the area. There are hundreds of people on the bridge, right from the Balmoral up to the Scotsman, looking toward the castle.

Fireworks shoot up in the sky. They explode, painting the sky with all the colors of the rainbow, an electric display, art in the sky, dazzling, loud, mesmerizing. The smoke from the explosions hangs in the cold air. The chick holds Farai's hand. *What's her name?* The crowd gasps and a cheer goes out when a particularly powerful one goes off, turning the sky green.

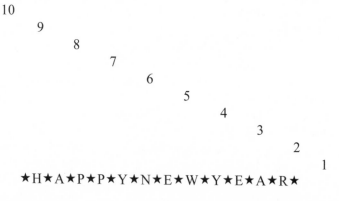

A cheer goes up in the crowd and strangers hug each other, everyone's smiling, everyone's happy to have made it. The earth has circled the sun 1 more time. They break out in a rendition of Auld Lang Syne.

'So what's your name?'

'Supriti.'

'It's pretty, like you.'

'Cheesy,' she says with a laugh.

A skinhead with tattoos all over his head breaks through the crowd and grabs Farai by the collar. He is a stocky man, muscular with a fearsome face. He opens his mouth revealing bad teeth.

'Where yous fae?' the skinhead demands.

Farai has 1 cocked, ready to launch a pre-emptive strike. A perfectly legitimate response, these are the Bush-Blair years.

'Zimbabwe.'

The skinhead holds Farai tighter and then hugs him.

'Nah, you alright, pal. It's those English bastards ah cannae stand. Happy New Year.' He lets go and walks away, a shiny egghead going through the crowd.

'What was that about?' asks Supriti.

'...'

The crowd begins to move, walking away from the bridge in the 2 possible directions. They walk to the Scotsman and descend a long flight of stone steps that leads them down to Market Street. His phone vibrates ✉:

> 07731008371
>
> hey bbs, jst wnt 2 say
> happy nw yr. maybe we can
> talk sometime. hope u not
> still mad @ me. i'm so
> sorry. oh god i'm drunk x

He clicks delete. Brian and Nika lead the way but as they join the long queue outside Massa Farai takes Supriti's hand, winks at the bouncer, who greets him, and jumps the queue.

The music is loud and the floor is packed. A drunken guy sees Farai, shouts 'hey,' and hugs him. Farai smiles, feeling the love in the air. A thick haze of cigarette smoke fills the room, mixing with the perfumes and deodorants of the clubbers.He elbows his way to the bar, keeping her close as he ploughs through.

'I THINK I OWE YOU A DRINK.'

'Bacardi and Coke.'

'WHAT?'

'I SAID, "BACARDI AND COKE."'

Farai gets her a double. He leaves her with the drinks and heads to the gents. He stands beside a kid with purple hair as he takes a piss. When he is done, he washes his hands. The toilet attendant stands nearby, handing out paper towels with which he dries his hands:

Wash the mingers off your fingers

No sanitation, no penetration

The toilet attendant, who speaks with a West African accent, is also something of a poet. Farai's been to many clubs up and down the country, and the toilet attendant is always an African immigrant. It seems to Farai, as he dries his hands, that African immigrants have cornered this aspect of the British night-time economy. He wonders when the backlash will come, just like the backlash against Jews in global finance, or did it already start with Cheryl Cole? He can see the *Daily Mail* headline in his head – **BRING BACK BRITISH BOGS**. He allows the attendant to spray him with cologne – *Smell nice for pussy tonight* – and tips him a pound.

He goes back to Supriti and they glide their way through 1 of the little paths that have a mysterious habit of opening up in crowds. Farai gives the DJ a thumbs up and gets a wink in reply, a subtle gesture under the flashing disco lights. They make it down the steps, on to the dance floor. It's hot and packed with gyrating bodies. Farai spots Nika and Brian at the bar. He doesn't bother with them, his attention is taken by the grace and litheness of Supriti as she moves her hips to the music. He moves closer, intoxicated by the smell of her perfume and the tiny beads of sweat on her neck. He feels the subtle rhythm of her movements as she dances with him, her head against his chest. His 1 free hand feels the skin under her open back dress, his other keeps the cold Bud away. She turns and begins a slow movement until she's facing the other way, her bum pressing against his crotch. She's so close in a dance that promises more. *Fuck me, I hope my stiffy doesn't scare her.* His mind has flashes of lucidity through the moments of ecstasy. Underneath the strobe lights she appears and disappears in front of him. He stops, allows her to grind on him, letting her take over. Just off the dance floor, he feels a pair of eyes looking at him. He's a quantum wave particlized by an observer in the dark mass of bodies swaying together like one large organism. He's felt it before, he knows exactly who it is. He disentangles from the looker, merges his wave with Supriti, in phase, and rides it, coasting along on the dance floor. Brian and Nika arrive. Nika's smiling at Farai. *This is better than a translation.* In the flashing lights he gets more and more intoxicated, feeling Supriti pull back. She turns, faces him, smiles and holds his hand. The track changes.

'This is how we do, *muthafuckers*,' the MC shouts into the mic.

Farai loses himself in her brown eyes, feeling 1 with her, feeling content. The idea of pimpin, the goal of getting laid, begins to recede in the background. *Systems failure.* He likes her, he doesn't know anything about her, but he likes her. He falls into those brown eyes with the confidence of a young heart; there is no reason or logic behind the feeling. It's the product of a random unfathomable universe. The music washes over them, swirls around them, and locks them together, an arrow from an invisible bow. Under the pulsating lights, through the thumping beats, within the mass of sweating bodies, they dance the night away.

The Magistrate held the baby in his arms, close to his heart, gently rocking, mesmerised by the sweet scent of newness rising through the blanket in which she was swaddled. The baby opened and closed her eyes, safe and secure in his arms, just as he was secure in the happiness she gave to him. A flash of light. His wife taking a photograph, making memories, preserving them as she listened to the lullaby he sang. Chenai lay on the sofa in her nightdress, hair messy, looking like the sole survivor of a long war in a faraway place.

"Ruvarashe is a quiet baby, she hardly ever cries. Her mother was a nightmare, kept me up on many a night," said his wife.

Ruvarashe, the flower of God, was the baby's name. Her very being had changed everything; Baba Chenai had been transformed into Sekuru VaRuvarashe, Mai Chenai into Mbuya VaRuvarashe, and Chenai into Mai Ruvarashe. An ancient custom, everyone was bound to kin and children formed the centre of this bond. Their very names changed, for a name had to mean something, and what more fundamental meaning could be bestowed on a person than their relationship to others in the family? They'd buried Ruvarashe's rukuvhute in the garden and planted a plum tree on top of it, binding Ruvarashe and, by extension, themselves to this place.

"It's time for the baby's bath, Sekuru."

"Five more minutes."

"You said that half an hour ago."

He reluctantly gave the baby to his wife, depositing her gently into the pair of waiting arms. Ruvarashe murmured a feeble protest at being passed around. He watched daughter, mother and grandmother go up the stairs to the bathroom. The fears, anxieties and disappointment he felt in Chenai, Mai Ruvarashe, fell away with each hour that passed when he saw the perfect result of her mistake.

His mind turned to the meeting he'd been invited to in London in February. Headquarters had received his plans and wished to meet him in person. He kept the letter on the coffee table for the whole family to read.

The Magistrate wore his long coat and wrapped a blue scarf around his neck. He also wore a woollen hat and gloves. Just as he was about to go out, the doorbell rang. It was the McKenzies. He let them in.

"It's freezing out there. I don't think we've had weather like this for years," said Peter.

"This global warming thing better hurry up," he replied.

"You look like you were on your way out. I hope we're not holding you back. It's just that we want to see the wee bairn."

"Don't be silly, I was just going for a stroll. It can wait."

"Getting a bit of exercise, hey?"

"More like escaping from the women," he said.

Liam said hi and went upstairs to see his baby. The Magistrate was pleased to see he had a few things in a plastic bag for her. There was something more serious, more mature about him, or was it just his imagination. He reminded himself that the kid was still only seventeen.

"Cup of tea, anyone?" he offered.

"No, no, we've just had some. Went out to do a bit of shopping for Ruva and Che. It was pretty confusing if you ask me. Kat would have known what to do, I can tell you that."

"You remember that story about the dead guy?" said Callum, who was in his police uniform.

"What dead guy?"

"The call out we got on Christmas day. Remember? That's why I was late for dinner. It turns out he's one of yours, technically, well, sort of on the fence. We got his details from his girlfriend, she's from Poland or Ukraine, or somewhere near there, but we can't find his next of kin. She didn't know much about his relatives. I mean, fancy that, being with someone and not knowing anything about them, their family, friends, the important stuff. Anyway, it turns out the guy was a bit of a loner, so we went to his flat and found it empty, except for one thing, a brown envelope on the mantelpiece – that's if you don't count the bills and letters that were piled up at the front door. It's one of those skanky council flats so no one noticed anything for a while. Anyway, in this brown envelope we found a form he'd filled in to get British citizenship, some sort of ancestry thing, completed five years ago, but looks like he never got round to sending it."

"That's rather odd," said the Magistrate.

"Thing is, technically, legally speaking, he's still one of yours."

"One of ours? I don't follow."

"Zimbabwean. He's a citizen, so anyways, we rung up your embassy, trying to see if they could help trace his family or repatriate the body."

"I was just about to suggest that."

"You're having a laugh."

"—?"

"For starters I had to ring ten times, got bounced around between so many different people my head was spinning. I finally spoke with some lady, and I said to her, 'Right, I've had enough of this, are you going to repatriate this body or not?' You know what she says to me? 'We're not a travel agency.' And hung up, just like that."

"Christ."

"I just thought I'd let you know since you're an elder, or chief, or… Dad, what did you say he was again?"

The Magistrate said, "Come with me, I know a man who knows everyone in the community. He'll be able to help."

"That'd be great because if he's left there he's getting a pauper's burial. They can't leave him in the freezer forever."

The Magistrate and Callum left and walked down the road. The sky was overcast, full of the indecipherable clouds that so puzzled the Magistrate. He felt the cold biting through his long johns and pulled his coat tighter around him.

When they arrived at Alfonso's office, he was with a woman in a blue tunic, filling in a form. He was so startled to see the policeman he nearly fell out of his chair. He gnawed at his moustache, looking from Callum to the Magistrate, trying to figure out what they had come for.

"Officer, officer, welcome to Busy Bodies Recruitment and Employment Solutions, your one stop shop for all your staffing, business and HR needs." He stood up and shook Callum's hand. "Please sit down, sit down."

"This is Alfonso Pfukuto, my secretary in the MDC," said the Magistrate. He turned to Alfonso. "We need your help."

"Do you know a David Mercer?" asked Callum.

243

"Am I under investigation? I can assure you that all our business practices are ISO 90012 compliant." Alfonso pointed to a faded certificate on the wall.

"Wow, no, not at all. I need your help to find if anyone knows this man."

"He's dead and we must find his family," the Magistrate added.

"David Mercer, never heard of him. Do you have a photo?"

"I can get one sent to you. He's about five-nine, sandy coloured hair, green eyes."

"He's white?"

Callum nodded.

"Zimbabwean?"

"Is that a problem?"

"No. I'll need his date of birth, whatever else you have on him. See if you can get his ID or passport number too. If I can't find someone who knows him here then I have a few contacts at the embassy who can run a check for me. Give me forty-eight hours," said Alfonso, his voice suddenly confident.

"I'll get you all the info we have."

Callum got up, shook Alfonso's hand and left. The Magistrate looked thoughtfully at Alfonso, pleased that he had a task for him that would be the beginning of his project to try and improve him. He saw it now, how in a few years he could transform him into something better. Alfonso fell back in his chair and slouched. He made sure Callum was well away before he spoke.

"This is how they get you. One day you're minding your own business, paying your taxes, and the next thing you know, they've thrown a dead white guy on your doorstep. It's a trap, can't you see? They are testing us, waiting for us to trip up. They want something. I can feel it in my bones. They want to dump this dead white guy on us, on us? They've been doing it to us since 1890." Alfonso wailed all of a sudden, burying his head in his hands. He turned to the woman in the blue tunic. "Olu, Olu, you Nigerians are so lucky, you know how when you people wanted your independence, the British just said, 'Okay, you can have your damn jungle country back, we didn't want it anyway.' Well, not us! We had to fight for twenty years in the jungle before they'd give up, and they've had their hands around our necks ever since."

"Hang on, are you saying you lied to him?" the Magistrate queried.

"Of course not! But I don't like cops coming around here. Once they start, you can never get rid of them."

"Just find out whatever you can and get back to me." The Magistrate stood up.

"And if I can't find anything?"

"I hope you do your best. If you find he really doesn't have family, then we'll have to bury him ourselves, as a community."

Alfonso sank back in his chair, gnawing at his moustache, and watched anxiously as the Magistrate walked out the door.

Winter is at her most ferocious, devouring the landscape. It is bitterly cold outside. Farai lies on his bed, reading through new material he's been advised to cover by his supervisor. Brian knocks on his door and walks in. He wears a blue tunic with a nurse's fob watch dangling from the breast pocket. His eyes are red after his night shift. The new job in orthopedics suits him or perhaps it's just the better pay.

'I need a car,' says Brian. 'The buses are killing me.'

'Aren't you supposed to get a license first?'

'So they tell me. I need you to get dressed.'

'I thought you liked looking at my sexy chest,' says Farai.

'Seriously, dude, we have a funeral to attend.'

'Who's dead? Scott? Stacey? That cheating cow.'

'Some random white guy. Alfonso rang me up a few weeks ago asking for donations to help bury this guy.'

'This white dude, is he some relation of yours?'

'I don't even know his fucking name, man. He's some random Zimbo who got caught up in the snow or something and *wafaed*.'

'I thought white people were designed for this climate.'

'Very scientific, Farai.'

'Well, it's not my problem, dude. I'd never get any work done if I went to every random white person's funeral.'

Brian sits at the foot of the bed.

'I promised Alfonso I would go.'

'That's between you and Alfonso then, innit.'

'Dude, you have to come with me.'

'This is getting boring. I'm young and immortal, I don't do funerals. Call Nika if you need some eye candy to go with you. The only person who can get me to do anything these days is Supriti.'

'You're pussy whipped.'

'If that's a crime then I'm guilty, lock me up and throw away the key.'

'Have you hit it yet?'

'Please stay out of my private life.' Farai pauses, then wilts under Brian's look. 'No, man, it's been 2 months and I'm still waiting. Don't laugh. It's called courtship, okay? That's what Romeo and Juliet did. That's what your mum and dad *should* have done.'

'You've fallen foul of the 4 week rule. You're now officially a danger to yourself and to society.'

Farai's phone vibrates ⊠:

Supriti

Morning handsome :) x

Farai replies:

I dreamt of u last night xx

Supriti

Liar pants on fire ;) x

Brian stands up and walks to the door.

'Dude, I'm dog-tired, you have to take me there and back. I can't do the buses.'

'I ain't your chauffeur.'

'If you don't come with me, I ain't jamming ProEvo for 3 months.'

Code red, terror attack imminent. Brian might as well wear a keffiyeh and record that last statement with an AK47 on his lap.

'Alright, dude, no need to go nuclear.' Farai pulls the covers off, stands up and stretches.

Brian winks and tells him he has to get ready in 30 minutes. Farai goes to the bathroom, taking his mobile, texting Supriti. He takes his phone everywhere; the minutes stretch and extend to infinity as he waits for her to text back. He showers, dresses, and has some cereal. Brian comes out in a black suit, white shirt, black tie, looking all *Reservoir Dogs*. They drive through the empty Sunday streets until they arrive at Mortonhall Crematorium.

'I watched *Final Destination*, you know the part where the girl gets toasted on the sunbed–'

'Farai, come on, dawg, you gotta be serious for this.'

'Sorry, death gets to me. A little levity relieves the tension.'

A small group of people dressed in black wait outside the chapel. A skinny blonde girl, wearing dark shades, stands away from the crowd, staring into the woods nearby, lost in her own thoughts. Alfonso hobbles over and shakes Farai's hand vigorously. He holds on with both his tiny paws, looking up at Farai deferentially.

'Mukoma Farai, I am *so, so* happy you could make it,' says Alfonso.

'Who is this dead guy anyways?'

'He's called David, David Mercer.'

'Never heard of him.'

'No one has. He's a nobody. I searched everywhere for his relatives and couldn't find them.' Alfonso lowers his voice to a whisper. 'You know *mavhet* don't look after each other like we do. I had people turn Zimbabwe inside out looking for this kid's relatives. He should have gotten a pauper's burial, free of charge, all provided by Tony Blair, but no, the boss' – he points to the Magistrate talking to Mai Chenai – 'wanted us to bury him good and proper. *Kunge mavhet anomuka ngozi, nhai veduwe.*'

'Hmm.'

'When I was in Zimbabwe, I used to hunt for funerals because there was always free beer there. Look at us here, dry throats. How can a man face death without a little Dutch courage?' he asked. "But don't worry, no horror show here, the body has already been cremated. We are just here for the service."

Alfonso snaps a photo of them and hobbles away. Farai and Brian follow. It's a small group and they barely make 10 people. There is a dry atmosphere, perhaps a little confusion, and definitely lots of boredom. Alfonso is prancing about, but it is clear no one quite knows how things are going to proceed.

'Baba Chenai,' Brian greets the man with a pot belly.

'Brian, I heard about your new job. Congratulations. I'm glad you came to the service. I had hoped more people would come, but never mind. We wanted to ship his body home, but it's too expensive. In any case, we couldn't find anyone to receive the body, so we have to do it ourselves,' Baba Chenai says, taking Brian's hand.

'I heard of a dead singer who was stuck here for a year because his family couldn't afford to ship his body home. *Inobva kupi* 5 grand *yekubhururutsa chitunha nendege?*'

'If I die here, make sure my body goes back home. You young ones can be transplanted, but my roots are very deep. It's too late for us oldies,' says Baba Chenai with a sad smile. The minister in a dark suit steps out and nods solemnly. 'Let's go inside, they are calling us.'

They go into the chapel. The skinny girl sits alone up front, her head bowed. Alfonso leans up to Brian and Farai, and whispers, 'That's his girlfriend. I don't think she speaks English. Before I came here I didn't know they were white people who couldn't speak English. It's disgraceful.'

The minister stands at the pulpit. He is an old man, a foot or 2 from the grave himself. He prays, speaks for a few minutes, some kind words about David, who he obviously didn't know, and commends his soul to the Lord. Alfonso bursts into tears, crying, 'Oooh, oooh, so young, so young.' Large drops of tears roll down his face. He reaches down for his handkerchief and blows his nose. It's a short, quick service. The minister thanks them all for coming. The music they play is Live's *All Over You*. The skinny girl sniffles as it plays.

They step back outside, into the cold. The trees in the woodland have lost their leaves. They stand there, looking dead, waiting for spring – resurrection. Farai is grateful the affair doesn't drag on, Zimstyle. He walks to the car, but Alfonso runs over and stops him.

'It's not over yet. End of part 1 only.' He gnaws at his moustache. 'We need you to drive the girl to Granton. We will follow you in my car.'

'No problemo,' says Farai. *So much for the great escape.*

He waits beside his car, watching the people milling about the church, that very Zimbabwean trait that stops them from getting things over and done with in time. Brian is among them, chatting with Baba Chenai. The skinny girl comes to him. She clutches a copper urn to her bosom. Farai opens the door for her, allows her to sit, and closes it. He walks round to the driver's side, and gets inside.

'I'm sorry for your loss,' he says.

'Thank you.' Her emotions are hidden behind dark shades.

'I'm Farai.' He offers her his hand.

'Tatyana.'

'How long had you guys been together?'

'A night.'

That silences him. He nods respectfully, not knowing what else to say to her. The small gathering begins to disperse. When Brian gets in, he confirms they are going to Granton. Farai starts up the car and drives on to the B701, which takes them through Oxgangs and Redford. Alfonso follows with Baba Chenai and his wife. The others that were with them for the service declined to come for this last part. Farai wonders how many people would come to his funeral if he died. Tatyana cranes her neck, looking out the window at the high rises in the estate they go past. She smiles wistfully, as if remembering something. He drives slowly, not hearse slow, but a respectful, measured speed.

'He used to live here, right there in that block with the yellow strip,' she says.

Farai sees it, a tall block, 1 of 3 that tower over the smaller flats. He imagines that maybe the dead guy used to travel on this same route, that they are crossing time streams, but he doesn't even know what the guy looked like. He could have been any one of a million white guys in the city. Because that's what cities do, they make people anonymous.

They are on Pennywell Road when Tatyana instructs him to drive all the way down to the beach. *The Dude abides.* It's a dual carriageway with a central reservation of grass and trees. He finds parking among the many free bays at the shore. He gets out and rushes to the other side to open Tatyana's door. A man and a woman walk a dog in the distance. Alfonso's car pulls in. Tatyana walks ahead, leading them across the grass, on to the wet sand, right to the edge of the water. She is lost to her own thoughts. They do not rush her, but stand around her, waiting, withdrawing into themselves, reminded of their own mortality, the fickleness of human life.

She hands the urn to Baba Chenai.

'You do it,' she says and hugs herself, tilting her head to the left.

The Magistrate clears his throat. Alfonso hides behind Farai, peeking out, as if afraid the wind might blow the wrong way. Baba Chenai pours the remains out slowly. Some of the ashes fall to the ground, some are carried to the sea, but the wind carries most high into the sky in a grey cloud that rises above the sea, growing larger and larger and larger until it is a fine mist, becoming invisible to the naked eye.

Tatyana keeps her eyes on the nothingness, for she imagines what is happening. The ashes are being lifted far above the clouds into the stratosphere where the cold air carries them above the jet liners, flying across the world, over the seas, over the great deserts and the mighty forests that lie on the equator, until, at some indefinite point, they begin to settle and drop lower and lower and lower until they find a cloud and in this cloud each single grain of ash settles into a raindrop, and this rain falls onto the fields, and homes, and mountains, and lakes, and cities, and forests, until, for 1 brief season, everything bursts forth in vivid green, because David is home at last.

'Are you okay?' says Farai, touching her shoulder.

She nods and begins to walk away from them. She takes a few steps, looks back, smiles sadly and waves. They watch her, a solitary figure, her black dress blowing in the wind, going further away from them.

'I have to go and pick Mavis up from Dunfermline,' Alfonso says to Farai. 'Can you please take Baba na Mai Chenai to Craigmillar?'

'Sure, no problem.'

'I know it's out of your way. Here's a little something for petrol.'

'Don't worry, it's Sunday,' says Farai. He waves away Alfonso's crumpled £5 note.

Alfonso gets into his car, reverses and drives away, full throttle as though fleeing something. Farai takes his passengers and starts up. The sea is left, the last witness to their ill attended funeral.

'Can you pull over?' Baba Chenai says. 'I think we'll take the bus instead. The 21 comes this way.'

'Don't worry, we'll take you all the way home.'

'No, no, I appreciate this, but I want to show the missus things I've seen on this route. We're in no rush.'

Farai is not in the mood to haggle. He stops the car at a bus stop to let them out.

'God bless you,' says Mai Chenai as they get out.

'Well, that saves us a few minutes,' says Farai to Brian. 'Did you see the dead guy's chick? I'd score her an 8, what'd you think?'

'I'd do her,' Brian replies.

'Have you no morals? She just lost her boyfriend.'

'You're telling me that if you had an open goal, you wouldn't tap that?'

'For shame!'

They carry on, straight along Ferry Road. A row of cars for sale is parked on the opposite side of the road. They make it to Great Junction Street where Brian asks Farai to turn right and go to Tesco. Farai stops outside the shop and Brian gets out of the car.

'Go ahead, Farai, I need to get a couple of things. I'll walk back home.'

'Are you sure? I can wait.'

'I wanna walk along the river for a bit. I need to get my head straight after this death business. It's got me thinking about my own life.'

'So long as you're not planning to throw yourself in the river, or do anything crazy like that.'

Brian laughs and slams the door shut. Farai drives down the bumpy cobblestone road. He likes the sound his tyres make as they bounce along. He gets caught behind a 22 going to Ocean Terminal and is trapped behind it at every stop. He gets home and parks. His mobile vibrates ⊠:

> Supriti
> wat u up 2?

He replies:

> just home from weird
> funeral xxx

> Supriti
> Come over

He replies:

> Right now? xxx

> Supriti
> Duh, wat do u fink
> I mean… Next week?

He replies:

> D'oh, let me go inside
> 4 a bit, will be there
> in 20 mins xxx

He gets out of the car ⊠:

> Supriti
> No, drop everything
> & come to me!!!

He replies:

> Your wish is my command xxx

The Mathematician

He gets in the car ✉:

Supriti
Just kidding. I'm not that
mean!!! Go get your
toothbrush ;) x

He replies:

Ok!!!!!

Oh my God, she asked me to bring my toothbrush. I'm sleeping over? Okay, be cool, play it smooth. Farai gets out, unable to contain his grin. He says 'hi' to a neighbor getting into her car. The door to the flat is already unlocked when he turns the key. *I'm sure I locked this. Supriti's asked me to bring my toothbrush.* He switches the light on and walks in. A figure emerges from the living room.

'You little shit, what the hell do you think you're doing here?' asks Farai.

The man freezes.

'I fucking warned you, mate, now you're gonna get it... Is that my stuff you're holding?'

Farai pulls out his cell and dials 99, the man rushes him, but Farai blocks the exit – maybe he sees it, maybe he doesn't – the flash of cold steel under the incandescent bulb, the beautiful flicker of silver. An unalterable sequence of events, a fixed point in time. He feels the fire, hot molten lead flowing through his chest. It's not like anything he knows, a supernova of pain, nerves screaming, impulses flooding his brain, 👾 the narrowing of the walls, crushing him. The collapse of the maze. He gasps for breath, looking into the man's eyes, the question, *why, why, why, why* swirling round his mind. He keels over and falls to the ground, clutching at the knife embedded in him.

'Would you like me to wait with you while you die?' the man asks. 'Death can be such a lonely business... No reply... Suit yourself. *Até logo, amigo.*'

From the floor, Farai watches him walk past casually. *I don't want to die, not like this, God, not like this.* His brain sucks up what oxygen remains from what blood remains in his arteries. His hands clutch his burning chest 👾. *She asked me to bring my toothbrush.* His mind

254

flashes white, thinking of his mother, family, hoping, holding on to life. *Dad*. The world grows dimmer around him. His ear on the floor picks up the sound of footsteps coming up the stairs... too slowly, too slow. *Dad*.

'Dude, I am going to whoop your ass. ProEvo, baby,' Brian shouts, opening the door.

Light travels through Brian's retina. His brain doesn't, can't register the image. *Help*. Blood everywhere. A fine spray on the wall, trickling to the floor.

'Oh my God, dude!' Brian calls out.

There's a flicker, no, a spark of light still shining in Farai's eyes. All those years in Uni, this is Brian's moment. The training kicks in. Call for help first. Then assist.

999 emergency services what is the nature of your call?

'My friend's been st-stabbed.'

do you want police, fire or ambulance services?

'My friend's been stabbed, goddamn it, I need an ambulance... call the police, bring everyone.'

what is your address?

'Flat 3... 20...'

please speak clearly into the microphone.

'Fuck's sake...'

Brian tells the woman on the other end the address. He tells them to hurry. His best friend is slipping away in front of his eyes. His hands, buy time, putting pressure on the wound. Blood everywhere. He tries his best to hold the life in. Farai groans. He's an astronaut drifting in outer space. *She asked me to bri*

LONDON

Early in the morning, darkness held at bay by the streetlights, the Magistrate and Alfonso caught the 35. Alfonso promptly fell asleep, complaining that it was too early. The Magistrate took out his Walkman. The front cover had broken off, the plastic casing was cracked and the whole thing was held together by bits of elastic band, but it still worked. Reliable Japanese workmanship. He put a cassette in. With the casing broken, he could see the mechanism going round, the progress of the music represented in motion.

The bus crept up Abbey Hill, over Regent Road, on its way to the Royal Mile. The Magistrate listened to the high-pitched strumming of the electric guitar that lent some colour to the drab morning. Hard thudding drums joined the piece, a long instrumental prelude before the vocals kicked in. This was the opening of *Simbaradzo,* the breakthrough third album by Alick Macheso that came after *Magariro* and *Vakiridzo.* Alfonso swore by Macheso, who was Nicholas Zakaria's protégé, and had been in a state of great excitement when he gave the cassette to the Magistrate. Macheso represented the ultimate synthesis of the Sungura genre, blending the three core elements, guitarmanship – message – Borrowdale, in perfect harmony. The child of immigrants, born in Bindura Hospital to a Mozambican mother and Malawian father, he took the country's most popular musical form and claimed it as his own, experimenting with guitar riffs from Jonah Moyo and Leonard Dembo, breaking tradition and fusing Sungura with the seductive rhythms of Congolese Rumba, creating a new sound that came to dominate the airwaves and influence the work of his peers. The link to Bindura flattered the Magistrate's ego, though Macheso didn't come from the middle-class suburbs, he came from the farms, far from the centre of contemporary Zimbabwean pop culture, and had had to make his way through wit, talent and a bit of luck.

The Magistrate

The bus drove past the old brewery in Slateford, headed towards Chesser. Alfonso jerked up and looked around, fearful he'd missed his stop, then went back to sleep again, slumped against the Magistrate. The talking guitar in the song *Amai VaRubhi* enthralled the Magistrate. The singer became a backing vocalist to his own instrument. It was an innovation that reminded him of the grainy ZBC footage of John White, the albino busker who plied his trade on the Harare-Bulawayo trains. But under Macheso, the sound was crisper; it had an electric sharpness that cleaved the listener in two. And listening to the music was to enjoy only half the performance, for his act was an audiovisual show. The musician was tall and skinny, with boyish good looks and a youthful athleticism, which he used in the Borrowdale. He created new variants of the dance with 'Razor wire' and 'Kangaroo', moves that fired up his fan base that hailed him the undisputed King of Sungura.

Sungura was the music of the time, focussing mainly on social issues in an age of hardship and despair. Macheso and his band Orchestra Mberikwazvo were a soothing balm to their fellow Zimbabweans, for who but a man who grew up on a farm, a man with little education, could speak in their voice, to their experience? And he could use his lyrical mastery, this gift of poetry, in Shona, Chichewa, Sena, Venda and Lingala, the languages of the working-class poor. The Magistrate felt a warm connection with the artist and his music and promised himself that he would take Mai Chenai to see a performance the next time he heard Macheso was on tour.

The Magistrate settled back, relaxed and saw parts of the city he had not seen before. The last time he had gone to the airport he took the 100, a more direct route. The 35 wound its way through the industrial estates in Sighthill, past the banks at the Gyle and the shopping mall, then out on the motorway to the airport.

He woke Alfonso, who grumbled incoherently and followed him out of the bus, the little man huffing and puffing with his hand luggage, which he insisted on lifting despite the wheels on the bag. Alfonso, a camera around his neck, looked very much the tourist. They checked in amidst the throng of the early morning business commuters. The Magistrate went to the far end of the terminal, the international arrivals section, to the shop filled with curios, saltire mugs, Edinburgh T-shirts, postcards and jimmy hats. He chose a map and paid for it.

The Magistrate sat behind the wing, listening to the roar of the engine and watched the wing flaps as the plane taxied the runway. Alfonso looked pale, holding a sick bag and mumbling a prayer. He turned to the Magistrate.

"I don't want to die but if I die on an aeroplane, please, let it not be easyJet. I want Qantas, or Emirates, or Lufthansa, something with class, Lord, not easyJet."

"Given the statistics, you should count yourself lucky if you die on an aeroplane," the Magistrate replied, dryly.

"I know it's the safest way to travel, but, but..." Alfonso's voice trailed off and he slumped back in his seat.

The plane took off, away from the city bathed in a bright orange glow. The lights looked like thousands of stars glued onto a canvas. The higher they flew the more the ground below began to resemble streams of lava from a volcanic eruption, Edinburgh's dormant volcanos come to life. The plane flew through the clouds, then above them, where it was bright and bathed in sunlight. Stewards walked along the isle peddling sandwiches and coffee.

The Magistrate took a piece of paper and drew on it what he remembered of the city so that he could have some perspective on what he had seen and where he had been. This way he hoped that, when his memories abandoned him, they would return if only he played his cassettes. When he was finished, the page was full of lines tracing bus routes that terminated at nursing homes. Along each line he wrote the bus number and the artist he had listened to en route. He compared his map to the one he'd bought from the gift shop. In it he saw the city in which he lived, a city that he dared not call home.

February was miserably cold in Edinburgh, so when the Magistrate and Alfonso emerged at Gatwick they were overdressed. The climate was milder down south. They walked around the arrivals hall with their hand luggage in tow. The Magistrate was surprised to see the Union Jack on so many advertisements, almost as though it was the marker of a separate sovereign nation. Alfonso led the way to the trains. The Magistrate had only very briefly passed through London on his way to Edinburgh when he'd first arrived in the UK. Then, the sights and scents had all been very alien to him. His thoughts turned to the rehabilitation he envisioned for Alfonso, how he would mentor him towards becoming a more useful member of the community.

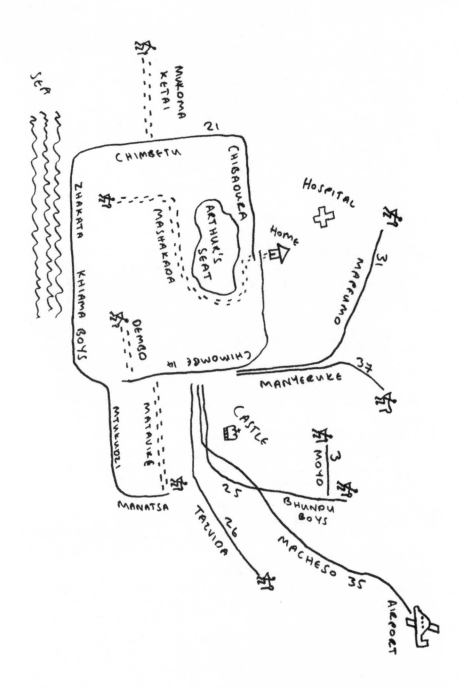

They sat side by side as the Express cut through the boroughs sprawled around London. In the preceding days, this meeting had been on the Magistrate's mind a great deal. He'd tormented his wife with questions on what to wear and the style in which he should approach matters at hand. The new pair of Clarks he wore was a little tight.

"I want Chenai and Liam to consider you for Ruvarashe's godfather," he said to Alfonso, thinking inwardly that the responsibility would do him some good.

"You are too generous," said Alfonso with a weary smile, and he returned to gazing out the window of the train. The blur of houses, bridges and nature outside whizzed by.

Nerves must be getting to him, the Magistrate thought. It felt good to be back at the centre of things, even if this was a small orbit. The dreadful slide to obscurity that he so feared was gradually receding into the background. A lot depended on the outcome of this meeting.

Alfonso guided him through the underground and the streets through which the morning commuters jostled. They reached the Strand Hotel and the Magistrate was suitably impressed. It took him back to nights spent at the Meikles on state business. They were booked into a twin suite and, after they checked in with the Asian girl at the front desk, they went to freshen up. He took his papers out and reviewed the details of the meeting.

"This could be the beginning of something big if we get this right," he told Alfonso, who replied with a nod.

Just before midday they went down to the conference rooms. The receptionist took them to the Trafalgar Room, which had a boardroom table with five seats on either side. The polished table gleamed. A jug of water was positioned at either end of the table with glasses set by each place. The room was pristine with natural light filtering in through the windows. They sat at one end of the table and waited. Alfonso brought out his own notebook and pen despite the fact the hotel had provided these. He checked his camera had memory for more photos.

"Could you print some of the photos from today for me for when we get home? I would like Mbuya VaRuva to see."

"Of course."

"Perhaps we can take a few of you as well. It never hurts to be seen in a picture with important people."

"Never mind me, today is all about you."

The Magistrate

The Magistrate was pleased with Alfonso's generosity. It seemed that the positive influence he was exerting was beginning to take effect. Now he just had to touch the lives of other people like Alfonso. He checked himself, warning himself against egotism, but the thought was hard to resist. He took out his notes and read them; the various proposals he'd penned and rewritten in his own hand lay sprawled in a little pile of papers.

A short-haired woman in a pinstripe suit arrived at the quarter of an hour mark. She greeted them and they clapped hands.

"I'm Marjory Nhete, we spoke over the phone. Are the others here yet?" she asked.

"No, you're the first one to arrive," the Magistrate replied.

"I'm already ten minutes late. There was a problem on the District, so I had to catch a bus."

"We're here all day, a great hotel room, lovely facilities. We're in no rush, are we, Alfonso?" Alfonso smiled and shook his head.

A few minutes later, a man wearing horn-rimmed spectacles and an older white man entered the room. They introduced themselves as Lloyd Makamure and Steve Barnes, and proceeded to talk about the weather; that is, how it was so much better back home. Alfonso took a photograph of them all. He promised to email it to Marjory.

Makamure sat with his colleagues at the opposite end of the table and said, "We have heard quite a bit about the wonderful work you are doing for us in Edinburgh." He flicked open a file. "It seems that when you got there things were rather messy."

"It was my associate, Alfonso here, who got the ball rolling by telling HQ of the leadership crisis we were having. This is only the beginning. There's a lot more work to be done," the Magistrate replied.

"Yes, Alfonso and his friend hounded us into action. It's good to see that level of involvement and commitment in these difficult times when most people are liable to hunker down and look out for themselves. Tell me, this idea of yours, how did it come about?"

"It was a simple observation of the conditions our people were living in. I asked myself, if I was a party member what would I want from the party here? I mean the embassy doesn't do anything for anyone, so there's a gap to fill right there. That's all there is to it really."

They asked him to go on and expand on this. He went through his proposals to make the party socially relevant, instead of merely focusing on fundraising activities around election time. They listened enthusiastically, stopped him to seek clarification on one point or another, but in the main they allowed him to freestyle through it. Then he gave them feedback on the progress made so far. The links created through the community, skills identified and so forth. The woman nodded along throughout his talk as though she understood him fully. He went on to outline his vision for the future. They were impressed that, already, the registered membership had risen from twenty-five to a little over a hundred since the initiative started.

"Looks like you have managed to shake off the apathy that we are suffering all over," Steve Barnes said.

"No doubt this is a good approach that will bridge the gap between our political role and our social responsibilities," Marjory added.

"Filling the space that the state is neglecting could have major electoral benefits down the line," said Barnes.

"If you could both leave us for a few minutes and wait in the lobby. We'll call you in when we're ready," said Makamure.

They sat on the chairs in the lobby. "What do you think this means?" Alfonso asked. The Magistrate shook his head and slouched back in the chair. All they could do was wait. They watched businessmen and women in dark suits go in and out of the other conference rooms. The Magistrate loosened his tie. It was warm in the hotel. This was the world he wanted to become a part of once more.

After half an hour they were called back in. Makamure grilled the Magistrate on a few other points they were not quite sure about, and then stopped, satisfied the Magistrate had thought of everything.

"Not only do you have good ideas, but you also have the zeal and ability to implement them. That's something we don't see too often in our other branches," Marjory said. "Prior to this meeting, we'd talked about creating the role of a development co-ordinator to spearhead ideas like this and implement them at grassroots level. We are all satisfied that you would be more than capable of taking this task in your stride. We have yet to fully define this role, but should you agree, your role would be to liaise with all our branches in the diaspora."

"Across the UK?" the Magistrate asked.

"And America, Canada, South Africa, Botswana, Australia, New Zealand and Namibia. You will find these are not the only countries to which our people have flown. There will be a lot of work to do. But we're convinced you're the right person for the job."

"It sounds like a big role," the Magistrate replied.

"One that can be expanded too. There'll be plenty of work to do, starting here, should you choose to accept," said Marjory, raising an eyebrow.

"I will need time to consider it."

"Of course, let's fiddle while Harare burns," Steve Barnes said. He rapped on the table impatiently. This did nothing to sway the Magistrate, a man used to taking his time to think things through.

They discussed the new role briefly, had a late lunch, and then the officials left. The meeting had gone better than expected and, as Alfonso repeatedly pointed out to him, this was a salaried job. It meant real work and stimulation and, beyond that, the ability to shake off the shackles of the menial jobs he so hated. He called Mai Chenai to tell her the news. It went to voicemail and he figured she was probably still fast asleep. They proceeded to the hotel bar and celebrated with a few stiff drinks, the Magistrate drinking three to Alfonso's one.

Alfonso then took him on a tour around the city. They started at Trafalgar Square, where they took photographs, and continued on to Chinatown and Camden. The Magistrate marvelled at the architecture that he'd previously only seen on television, on postcards and in books. This mix of history and modernity so intimately merged together made him feel giddy as they bumped through crowds of tourists and shoppers in Covent Garden. Alfonso dropped his memory card off in Jessops to get his photos developed. He would pick them up on his way back to the hotel.

Alfonso's mobile rang as they left the store.

"Hello...Yes, I can talk... What's wrong, you sound shaken up... Arrested? For what? Speak up, I can't hear you, it's noisy here... Murder? Over a girlfriend, I don't believe it... He is a good boy, that can't be true, that can't be true. Someone is lying, he would never do such a thing... Jehovah God... Are you okay? I'm coming back tomorrow, go and stay with Mai Chenai, you'll be safe there... I'll call you when we get back to the hotel." Alfonso hung up and stopped walking, trembling with emotion.

"What's the matter?" the Magistrate asked.

"That was Mavis. She says the police came to our house and arrested Scott on suspicion of murder."

"My God, that's serious."

"I don't know what to do. He's a good boy. I can't believe we could have lived with a murderer for months and not known it. They say he killed his friend, the tall one. It's not true."

"The boy has a temper."

"But he wouldn't go that far, not over a girl, surely."

"These young men need guidance. They are so far from home."

"Zvava mumaoko aMwari izvi. Isu tiri vanhu venyama."

"We'll see what sort of support we can give him when we get back home. There's nothing we can do from here," said the Magistrate. He remembered the two boys well. Farai, the tall one, intelligent, but with an air of arrogance, as though he didn't give a damn about the rest of the world, and Scott, so full of anger and malevolence. They were both so young, full of life and very foolish.

They went to a Mexican restaurant, ate and drank for some time, and then staggered back to their hotel, their joy dampened by the news of Scott's arrest.

The Magistrate woke up in the morning with a mild hangover. He was surprised to see Alfonso getting dressed and asked him the time. "It's before nine," said Alfonso. "Go back to bed." The Magistrate got up anyway. Something about Alfonso was different; he wore a black suit and a white shirt and was fumbling with a navy blue tie. The Magistrate came over and helped him with the knot like he was a child on his first day of school.

"Where are you rushing off to so early?"

"I have some relatives I must see in Whitechapel before we go," replied Alfonso.

"Our flight leaves at three."

"I'll catch up with you at Gatwick. Don't worry about me."

"Well, don't be late. I don't want us to miss the flight." He finished fixing Alfonso's tie. "Who would have thought you and I could achieve what we have? I'm sure I'll find an opening for you too once I establish myself in the party."

"That would be nice," said Alfonso in a melancholic voice.

The Magistrate noticed Alfonso had shaved his moustache and whiskers off and looked handsome for it. A light whiff of cologne wafted from him. He did not want to push things, so he went back to bed. "You've really grown in character over the last few months," he said, as Alfonso was leaving the room.

Alfonso went out of the hotel clutching his case and merged in with the morning crowd. He walked tall and straight, the limp was gone. He completely blended in, anonymous, cosmopolitan, a Londoner in an instant. The sad little ditty he whistled matched the sombre mood of the morning. With one hand in his pocket, he made his way past the offices and theatres that lined the street. He took in every face that passed by, noticed registration numbers on parked cars, and the security cameras looking down on him, his mind processing, cataloguing, remembering minute details.

It only took him five minutes to get to Zimbabwe House. The flag overhead fluttered in the winter wind. A receptionist led him through to the back, past the office of the ambassador and right round to the end of the building, to an office with a black door. She knocked, opened the door and gestured inside.

A man sporting a full beard with sprinklings of grey sat behind a heavy mahogany desk. The room had two Zimbabwean flags on stands behind him, and a miniature on his desk. A black and white portrait of the president hung above him. It was one from the eighties. In it, he was young, confident, his hair parted on one side, a studious Jesuit look about him. The man's desk was tidy with paperwork arranged in neat columns.

"Ah, Comrade A, in whom I am well pleased," he said, and pointed to a chair opposite him.

Alfonso stepped forward and opened his case. The man cleared a space on the desk. Alfonso pulled out two large brown envelopes and a laptop. The man nodded and opened the first envelope. It contained photographs. He studied them one by one, frowning whenever he recognized a face.

"Very good," he said, and opened the second envelope.

There were documents in Portuguese together with their translation. There was also a half complete English language thesis on hyperinflation. He took his time flicking through them. When he got to the list of names and figures, he looked up at Alfonso and back down to the page again. He went through the list as if committing each name to memory. He saw his own name on the long list, stopped and tapped his index finger on it for a moment. The man sighed.

"We have the password?" he asked, pointing to the laptop, his focus still on the documents in front of him.

Alfonso wrote 'LoVerMan1984' on a piece of paper and slid it over to him.

The man got up and went to a digital safe on the wall, behind the portrait of the president. He blocked Alfonso's view and punched in a code. The safe opened and he placed the documents and laptop inside before closing it.

"What is my code, Comrade A?"

Alfonso wrote down '6922149451#' and slid the paper across the desk.

"Impressive. Perhaps you would like to come for a walk with me. The cold weather does wonders for one's constitution." The man took a black trench coat from the hanger on the door and put it on. They walked out and headed down the road.

"My first assignment, when I got here on my first rotation in the eighties, was to debug the entire embassy from top to bottom. It took me two weeks, crawling on the floor, going through every nook and cranny. All that work, but I got them all, and guess what, after the weekend they were back, double the number. Flower had warned me it was pointless. They've been listening to us since UDI." The man took out a pipe, filled it with tobacco and lit it. "Forgive me, the smoke is coming your way. I know you don't indulge. It's a filthy habit. Sad to say, I picked it up in Moscow. In those days if you didn't smoke and drink vodka you'd freeze to death."

"Maybe it would be worse if they stopped listening," said Alfonso.

"That'd mean we didn't matter anymore," the man replied with a nod. "The traffic isn't as bad as you would remember it, thank goodness. Livingstone's congestion charge appears to be working."

"Perhaps I can brief you on the meeting we had yesterday?"

"There's no need for that. I already have a report on it." The man frowned. "What's the saying again, 'For where two or three of you come together in my name, there I am with them.'"

"Matthew 18 verse 20." Alfonso laughed.

They walked down the road through the arch with its Roman numerals. Trafalgar Square was behind them. The fourth plinth was still empty. The idea of the two Nelsons had been shot down. Every idea to fill the space only sparked more controversy. They strolled leisurely along the boulevard. Clarence House was to their right, a large sprawling complex.

"You did a good job with those Angolan documents."

"That was pure luck. I just stumbled upon them."

"Fortune favours the prepared. That stint you did for us in Mozambique is still paying off I see."

"I still have the scars on my body, courtesy of RENAMO," Alfonso replied with a slight grimace.

"I take it you left no loose ends?"

"The boy's flatmate, real name Tamuka Nhamoinesu, alias Scott Murray, was arrested for the murder yesterday. The police will match his fingerprints with the ones on the murder weapon, a kitchen knife."

"Nicely done. We have never been this powerful, Comrade A. Never been this close to the levers of power. Crisis is just a synonym for opportunity." They walked towards the lake. "Tell me about your adventures in the colonies. God, I'd have hated to wind up in that cold little shithole back in the day when I was still working in the field."

Alfonso told him everything about what he'd seen and done in Scotland, leaving nothing out, the disorganization of the opposition there, its structure and key members, useful information if they needed to apply pressure to families back home at some point. He narrated how he wooed the Magistrate and how, by chance, he had encountered the Angolan documents.

"That was very fortunate for us," the man said, as they stopped in front of the lake. "In the wrong hands such information could be embarassing. You continue to exceed all expectations. If only we had a few more like you." The man patted Alfonso's shoulder.

"What I don't understand is, why the Magistrate? Why help strengthen the opposition by giving them someone like that?"

"Sometimes the shepherd leaves ninety-nine in order to find one lost sheep. Are you a gambling man, Comrade A? You have encountered the term 'hedging' before, haven't you?" The man took a packet of grain from his pocket and sprinkled some on the water. "I like it here. I like the politics. They've spent this decade waging war on an abstract noun. I was here to see a million people march up and down the streets of London, protesting they did not want a war with Iraq. Guess what? It changed absolutely nothing at all. You see, democracy only truly works when there are no fundamental differences within the ruling class. Only when the vote doesn't matter can democracy function, otherwise all

270

you get is chaos. Look at what we do, beating up the opposition, destroying buildings and deploying marauding youths to rampage through the townships. It's primitive and grotesque. We live in an age of twenty-four hour news. PR is important; our way of doing things is old fashioned, unsustainable.

"We're creating necessary illusions. They did an experiment once, where dogs, or was it rats... rats, people, dogs – what's the difference? Anyway let's says dogs for argument's sake. So these dogs were given electric shocks from a steel floor of some sort. Now half the dogs were given a little button they could push when they got the shock, in order to stop it, the others did not. And though, over a period of time, all the dogs received the same amount of punishment, the same level of torture, the dogs with the little button were content with their situation, while those without sank into depression and suffered great anxiety and psychological problems, signified by high levels of stress hormones in their blood. The ballot is that little button, Comrade. What they've learnt here is that the illusion of choice is the key to stability. We are already filling up the opposition with our members. Alongside these we put men like the Magistrate, upright men willing to work selflessly for the greater good. We cannot continue haemorrhaging them at the rate we are. Remember, they are products of the system, honourable men who can be trusted with things. When he was on the bench, did he not, under POSA, convict and sentence men from the opposition that we brought before him? It was his job, and he followed the law to the letter. In time all we will have is two factions of the same party and the electorate can vote to their hearts' content. But, for now, we put the blocks in place, one by one. Only then will this so-called *democracy* come to our little corner of the planet, my friend. This is how the modern state is managed in the twenty-first century."

Ducks swarmed around them, feeding on the grain the man was sprinkling. He made a great effort to feed the smaller, weaker ones at the back of the scrum, scattering the grain far and wide. Buckingham Palace, in the distance, stood in the morning mist. Alfonso waited for the man to speak again for he did not want to seem overeager.

"Some people give them white bread. It's not good for them, too processed, they get obese," the man said, then turned to Alfonso. "Your talents are wasted here."

"Then you've thought about my transfer back home?" Alfonso's voice barely masked his excitement.

271

"You're far too useful for that. The country is full of informers tripping over one another, what good could you possibly be there?" The man reached into his breast pocket, pulled out a maroon passport and gave it to Alfonso. "We shed blood and spent a fortune in the Congo only to see our friends, the Chinese and South Africans, pinch it from right under our noses. Young Kabila has forgotten who his true friends are. His father would not have left us out in the cold like this. You are to wind up your business here, shift your assets to Comrade K and fly out within the week. Your work here is done. Is that understood?"

Alfonso's heart sank. He thought of Ebola, malaria, sewage on dusty streets. All he wanted was to go home. He was tired of the acting, the lying, the restlessness. These thoughts lasted a second, maybe two. He was a professional, a patriot; duty came above all else. Before he even knew it, he was thinking about Chaos and Coltan, War and Wolframite, Dirt and Diamonds, Blood and Bauxite. This was just another new opportunity, a new part in a different drama. The sun was rising over London and, as it did, Alfonso's star was rising with it.

Acknowledgements

Laura Tainsh, Mr Chauke, Cynthia Hungwe, Martin Gotora, Swabrina Salim, Gregory Maumbe, Tafadzwa Gidi, Cynthia Gentle, Tapiwa Muererwa, Munyaradzi Chirapa, Irene Staunton, Murray McCartney, Lindsey Regan, Ted Schlicke (Pacman Afficinado), Bernadeta Zyla, Kennedy Madhombiro, Enias Mugadza, Helen Mugadza, Maximillian Musavaya, Hildegard Musavaya, Haggai Huchu, Josephine Huchu, Rujeko Huchu, Rufaro Huchu, Roy Nyamufukudza, Mike Barnes, Mitchell Mnemo, Tinofireyi Mandaza, Ignatius Mabasa, Alan W. Robertson, Patrick Musavaya, Lucy Musavaya, Mr Machakata, Wilson Muvuti.

Special thanks to the Hawthorden Institute and Instituto Sacatar for their fellowships in 2013, which gave me much needed space and time to write. I'd also like to thank the Authors' Foundation and the Kate Blundell Trust for the generous award of a financial grant that aided me through the period I was writing this novel.